DEMONS
WALK AMONG US_ _

Praise for *The Dead of Mametz*

"A superb mystery as well as one of the most
moving war novels I've ever come across."
Betty Webb, *Mystery Scene Magazine*

"This satisfying historical debut partners abundant military
and battle details with breathtaking spy adventure
on both sides of the front."
Library Journal

"A pacey mystery... the writing is excellent, the characters
and dialogue very believable... a superb effort."
The Great War Magazine

"Hicks has taken the reader on more dead ends and twists
and turns than it would at first seem possible and then, just at
the end, when you think you have finally understood his
methods and solved the crime at the same time as him, there
is another astonishing twist that further hints at the
abilities of this very capable author."
Justin Glover

"... need-to-read tension and riveting detail... recommended to
all those interested in WWI or who love a great mystery... a great
mix of an intriguing storyline and superb historical detail."
South Wales Branch, Western Front Association

"The plot convincingly intertwines itself between the genres of a
detective novel and a soldier's-eye account of trench warfare to
create a compelling and intriguing hybrid."
Paul Simon, *Morning Star*

DEMONS
WALK AMONG US

Jonathan Hicks

To Wendy

*And in memory of my great uncle Ossie –
a victim of the Great War*

First impression: 2013

Cover design: Sion Ilar
Cover picture / illustration: Teresa Jenellen

The publisher acknowledges the
support of the Welsh Books Council

ISBN 978-1-84771-595-1

FSC

Published and printed in Wales
on paper from well maintained forests by
Y Lolfa Cyf., Talybont, Ceredigion SY24 5HE
e-mail ylolfa@ylolfa.com
website www.ylolfa.com
tel 01970 832 304
fax 832 782

It is easy to go down into Hell; night and day, the gates of dark
Death stand wide; but to climb back again, to retrace one's steps
to the upper air – there's the rub, the task.

Virgil

CHAPTER 1

The Dardanelles – Thursday, 4th March 1915

T HE MEDIEVAL FORT sat quiet and lifeless in the early morning sunshine, squat and solid on the hill that it crowned. Once a mighty fortress with crenulated battlements and square towers at each corner, shielded by a curtain wall to act as a first line of defence against attackers, it was an anachronism in the face of the armada now arrayed against it.

For what was approaching was no army of knights on horseback or foot soldiers armed with swords. The weaponry that was now to be unleashed would simply punch its way in like a giant, gnarled fist. The stronghold that had stood impervious and regal for centuries was about to be destroyed in minutes by the unrivalled power and cruelty of the machinery of modern warfare.

A ramshackle town lay scattered across the plain behind, cowering in the lee of the fort, defenceless against the threat that waited out at sea. The conglomeration of dwellings that had provided shelter from invaders in times past was now helpless, its citizens waiting in terror for the onslaught to begin.

Fishing boats bobbed up and down on the glistening tide, anxious in their movements, nervously twitching as they warily eyed the gathering force of destruction. Their way of life was coming to a temporary end but long experience had taught them it would return one day after this intrusion was over and had passed on to another theatre of war. When the combatants had finished with their locality the fishermen would return to carry out their daily lives as they always had and always would.

Private Osmond Burgess of the Plymouth Battalion of the

Royal Marine Light Infantry squinted into the blazing sunlight, looking for any sign of movement on the ancient battlements. There was none. The Turks were keeping their heads down; they knew what was coming. He grasped the ship's rail in front of him to steady himself, eyes searching the shore, the tension beginning to build in his body.

The concussion wave of the first gun blast from a nearby battleship hit the troopship he was on, causing him to clutch the rail even tighter; the second almost deafened him. The screech and roar as the heavy projectiles tore through the air left him quivering. Whether it was with fright, suspense or excitement, he was unsure. For a nineteen-year-old former office clerk from Cardiff, this was something quite outside his experience.

Seconds later the shells blasted into the fort and huge gouts of flame and debris were hurled into the air. The smoke rolled upwards like some great sacrificial pyre and the Marines on the deck of the *Braemar Castle* cheered the first dozen or so explosions, until the novelty faded and a stunned silence settled over the men. Some were more thoughtful now, contemplating what was to come. Burgess looked along the row of apprehensive faces, some bearded and weather-beaten. Many of them were robust ex-miners who had done what he did – answered his country's call that previous summer. The initial flush of excitement was gone, the laughter and cursing over. This was the first time they had seen such destructive power, and no doubt several of them were currently questioning the wisdom of enlisting so enthusiastically.

It had been a drawn-out business, standing with the hordes of other volunteers for hours outside the recruiting headquarters in Queen Street, Cardiff, before appearing in front of a desk staffed by a middle-aged, grim-looking army NCO. A batch of men for the Royal Marine Light Infantry was required and someone had seen enthusiasm, even potential, in his ingenuous blue eyes.

That was what he had liked to think at the time anyway. Later he had realised that he had simply been part of a random group of men who had been siphoned to one area of the vast recruiting room. He had waited in line again, eventually standing in front of another desk where a ruddy-faced Marine sergeant filled in endless papers that seemed to require the same information over and over again.

And here he was, a product of months of intensive training, part of the force about to land on the Dardanelles, one of a specially-assembled force that would cut a swathe through the Turkish defences. A seaplane buzzed overhead, observing for the guns of the battleships and he marvelled again at the power of it all. They were invincible, all-powerful and formidable. Good had come to batter the forces of evil. A just war, a quick war and then they could all go home. But he was a long way from home.

The invasion fleet was all around him – he gazed on the stirring sight of no fewer than thirty-four vessels: battleships, cruisers, destroyers and minesweepers. The Dardanelles now lay before them and the guns of the British ships were pounding Johnny Turk into submission.

The previous evening, perhaps aptly, ominous clouds had eventually burst forth a heavy thunderstorm, soaking the Marines who had lined the decks for final inspection. The rain had coursed off his pith helmet, dripped on the back of his neck and begun its slow, irritating trickle down his spine. The smell of damp uniforms had filled the air. He had resisted the temptation to shiver – fearful it would be taken as a sign of cowardice and open him up to the scorn of the NCOs and, more importantly, his pals. Burgess had stood there proud and still, months of training having prepared him thoroughly for what was about to come. At least, he very much hoped so.

Suddenly a terrific explosion rent the air and brought him back to the present. "Bleedin' 'ell! That's their magazine gone, I reckon," a voice exclaimed at his side. Burgess turned to see the profile of Bill Mercer staring out across the blue water. "If they carry on blasting 'em like this there'll be bugger all left for us to do when we land."

He had met Mercer during basic training at Stonehouse Barracks in Plymouth the previous autumn. Forty-one men in a hut designed to sleep eighteen meant you got to know your companions very quickly. Mercer was a railway worker from Newport, the same age as Burgess, and the two had hit it off from the start. Surrounded by ex-miners and ex-seamen, the two young men had formed a common bond. Their youthful faces soon sported beards in an attempt to make them appear older and more experienced. They had helped each other out, even polishing each other's kit when the other felt exhausted after the long route marches and endless drills.

Another deafening gun blast. Mercer turned towards him and grinned but each man saw that the other was anxious, nervous of their destiny – about to go into action against the enemy. *About to kill or be killed.*

At 7 a.m. the command came at last and Burgess's Number 3 Company boarded a torpedo boat before transferring to one of the whaler boats for their slow journey to the sandy, dusty shore of Kum Kale. The Marines looked anxiously up at the muted colours of the steep cliffs as they approached their landing area. They were to act as a screen for the demolition parties whose mission was to destroy artillery guns and ammunition dumps which had not been obliterated by the naval gunfire. If there were any survivors of the devastating bombardment on the fort they were to be killed or captured.

Nothing happened for some time and Burgess felt his spirits

rise and he began to relax a little. He nudged young Charlie Hinchley who was beside him and gave him a nod of reassurance. Hinchley had told him once that he was not afraid to die – death was, after all was said and done, inevitable. He gave Burgess a wary smile and continued to quietly recite the Lord's Prayer but then flinched and jerked backwards. His boyish face contorted in pain as he clutched at his arm, bright red blood seeping out between his fingers.

Immediately, Lieutenant Pearce's voice rang out. "Snipers! Keep your heads down, men. And pull harder on those oars!"

The rowers' eyes bulged and their faces reddened as they complied. They were not far away now, perhaps fifty yards, the beach tantalisingly within reach. The heavy whaler made its torpid way across the water, the beach appearing to come no closer as the seconds grew into minutes.

A hailstorm of bullets ripped through the air but the shooting was becoming wilder now, inaccurate, the Turks growing increasingly anxious as the boats drew nearer to the blood-red shoreline.

At last he heard a thud and felt the crunch of gravel as the whaler ran aground. Burgess did not need Lieutenant Pearce's command to vacate the boat. Within seconds he, Mercer and the others were running up the beach towards the cliffs. Only the dead and wounded remained behind.

He took cover behind a large rock and tried to ascertain from which direction the now desultory firing was coming. A shrill whistle sounded and he looked to his left. Mercer was pointing towards what looked like a ruined windmill some one hundred yards away. Burgess watched carefully and saw the faint puff of smoke come from a window on the first floor as the sniper fired again.

He turned to Mercer and gestured for him to move forwards. They both knew what to do after the thoroughness of their training. Burgess opened rapid fire on the window while Mercer stood up and ran towards the building.

By the time Burgess had emptied his rifle magazine Mercer was pressed up against the wall of the windmill. The Turk inside was evidently still alive as he resumed firing, the bullets whining past Burgess as he reloaded rapidly, two clips of five, and then opened fire again. Mercer made his way around the side until he found an entrance and disappeared inside.

Burgess waited for a short time and then murmured, "Where the hell is he?" To his relief, moments later Mercer appeared in the opening and waved. The Marines around Burgess cheered loudly and they began to advance.

The Turk lay lifeless on the wooden floor, a pool of fresh blood beneath him. Mercer was casually wiping his stained bayonet on a piece of cloth when Burgess entered the room.

"Bastard didn't even hear me coming," said Mercer, half grinning. "Ran him right through. Jabbered some bloody foreign rubbish for a while before he croaked."

They both stood there looking down at the dead man. As Burgess solemnly studied the Turk's face it brought home to him the kind of mission he was now on and the danger he was in. He had been under fire for the first time in his life but he had survived.

CHAPTER 2

Gallipoli – Sunday, 25th April 1915

S ECOND LIEUTENANT THOMAS Oscendale of the Military Foot Police was watching a fat fly crawl across the back of his hand. Bloated and black, the insect moved jerkily towards his wrist, stopped and rubbed its legs together. Slowly, Oscendale raised his other hand and brought a glowing cigarette end down onto the fly, which popped in an instant, spewing a viscous, dark red matter onto his hand.

"For God's sake, Tom!" complained a voice at his side. "Can't you find something better to do?"

Oscendale rolled onto his side. His fellow subaltern Jack Parry was frowning at him from below his tropical helmet.

"Sod this for a game of soldiers," uttered Oscendale with a sigh. "If something doesn't happen soon I'm taking my toys and I'm going home."

Parry and he had come ashore earlier that morning in the company of hundreds of British troops. Their landing had been unopposed from the moment they had plunged into the cold waters of the Aegean to the present time, where they lay at the foot of a gully, staring upwards at the skyline.

The Turks were up there somewhere, watching them.

As military policemen they were not regarded as frontline fighting troops, nevertheless he and Parry had been unable to resist the temptation to fight alongside the ranks of khaki-uniformed soldiers as they came ashore at Y Beach on the Gallipoli peninsula. They had expected swathes of machine gun fire, Turkish snipers picking them off with monotonous regularity and savage hand-to-hand fighting. It was what they had been told to expect, what they had trained for, but all they had was a sense of frustration and annoyance. There had been nothing, absolutely nothing, in the way of resistance.

"Why don't we just push on?" asked Oscendale, unable to hide his irritation any longer, his voice loud enough for others to hear. "There's no-one up there. If there were we'd be surrounded by dead bodies by now."

"Because his lordship says to stay here," replied Parry, gesturing at an officer who crouched some forty yards away from them. They both watched him as the man peered tentatively over a rock, Webley revolver in hand, trying to see if the gully really was as clear as it appeared to be.

Oscendale fidgeted again. It was not his first taste of action – the previous year he had been part of the long, demoralising retreat from Mons in Belgium, attempting to hold back the irresistible force of the German Army, but this was different, very different. The sun was shining, the sea was bright blue and the enemy seemed to have run away. His impatience began to grow.

"Look, Jack, we're not strictly under his control, you know that. What if you and I push on up the gully a bit? The lads will cover us. Imagine if there's nobody there. If the road from here to Krithia is clear this could all be over soon. It's got to be better than just sitting here waiting for Abdul to come back and start shooting at us."

Parry looked up the gully again and mulled over what Oscendale had just suggested. "Go on then. You bloody fool; you'll probably kill the pair of us." With that he began to clamber up the gully. "I'll go first – I'm quicker than you. Keep close and cover me."

Oscendale followed him immediately, ignoring the frantic shouts that came from the officer behind them. The sound rebounded off the cliffs and bounced between the sides of the gully. Oscendale was sweating, not just from the heat, but with the exhilaration of it all. His whole life seemed to be slipping past him, out of control. Like the sand oozing away beneath his feet as he followed Parry up the slope. Ahead of them nothing else moved. Any moment now the Turks up above them would open fire and he or Jack, or even both of them, would jerk backwards with the impact of Mauser bullets. He gripped his revolver tightly, clenched his teeth and tried to make himself as small as possible. *What the flaming hell was he doing?*

Parry shaded his eyes against the glare of the sun. Resolutely, he pressed on up the gully.

Was that a movement on the clifftop? Oscendale stopped and raised his pistol but whatever had caught his eye was gone. It had disappeared into the arid landscape, hidden among the rocks and dust of the cliffs.

The minutes passed and Oscendale entered a state of calm acceptance and felt the tension ease from his body. If this was to be the end, then so be it. There was nothing he could do about it so what was the point in worrying? If death came he might not know anything about it anyway. But Parry's confidence was infectious and Oscendale continued to follow him.

Parry raised a hand as he stopped abruptly. Oscendale halted too and searched for some sort of cover. Then Parry waved him on again. Moments later they emerged onto the clifftop. The breeze blew dust into their flushed faces and there was nobody to be seen. The plain stretched for miles where a white-walled village flickered in the heat, its walls buckling and twisting in the haze that radiated from the baked and parched ground.

He looked behind them and saw the clear turquoise waters of the Aegean rolling and rippling below them. *Was this really a battleground?*

"That's it then, Tom. Success! We have conquered the first

part of the Gallipoli peninsula." Parry grinned at him and waited for a response.

Oscendale slumped to the ground, worn out by the tension of the past few minutes and said with diminished humour, "Jack, if I ever suggest anything as bloody stupid as that again you have my permission to shoot me."

"What? And do the Turks a favour? No, dear boy. I'll let them have that pleasure," said Parry jovially and with that he began motioning to the expectant soldiers far below them to come forward.

Moments later the figures began sweeping up the gully, led by their reluctant officer who eventually arrived breathless, florid and furious at the top, his mouth set into a narrow dry cut in his face before shouting, "Lieutenant Parry! That was totally against my explicit orders! I told you to wait at the bottom until I was absolutely sure that the area was clear of Turks!"

"Yes, sir," replied Parry indifferently. "And just how were you going to tell that from down there?"

The officer wiped the sweat from his face and glared at Parry, struggling to control his temper. "None of your damn business, Parry. Listen, you MFPs might be a separate unit but for the moment you're under my command, do you understand? Your actions endangered not just your own lives but those of my men as well. It was downright…"

"Well, I don't understand that, Lieutenant…?" Oscendale suddenly realised that he didn't even know the officer's name.

"Lucas. Edmund Lucas," retorted the officer, his face still displaying the signs of his exertions.

"Well, Lieutenant Lucas, the only lives we really endangered were our own and I think your men are rather glad that we did because otherwise you and they would still be stuck down there, sitting targets for those Turks over there."

Lucas swung to his left and squinted to the east where a line of brown-green Turkish soldiers was indeed marching out of the collection of buildings behind which they had been forming up.

"Well spotted, Tom," said Parry. "I suggest we start digging ourselves in, sir. And the sooner the better. We're going to be a bit busy in about half-an-hour."

Lucas nodded reluctantly, knowing they were right and called his NCOs to him. The Marines soon began digging rapidly into the hard, stony soil. They cursed and strained as they worked and Oscendale and Parry joined them, each man knowing that his future depended on the effort he made over the next thirty minutes.

CHAPTER 3

Gallipoli – Sunday, 25th April 1915

PARRY AND OSCENDALE became separated as the violent fighting raged, intense and at close quarters. The fury of battle made their worlds immediate: the focus being on the square yards to their left and right. Oscendale fought for his own personal survival in the loneliness of hand-to-hand fighting. His mind focussed on the now, the present, on survival. *He wanted a future.*

Time after time the Turks came forward, screaming *Allah!* and yelling their battle cries, glistening bayonets fixed in defence of their homeland. The ones that survived the hundreds of rounds of British rifle bullets suddenly switched from shapeless forms to individual men as their features came into view. Not for the first time in his life Oscendale looked into the eyes of men who wanted to kill him and he thought he was going to die. Bayonets were jabbed at his face and body, and he parried the blows feverishly. After his rifle ran out of ammunition he drew his revolver and shot his assailants at point-blank range.

At last the attacks began to slacken and the time between them grew, until at last they ceased altogether. Oscendale jumped back into the hole he had dug and slumped down. He pulled off his cap, his legs splayed out in front of him. The dust lay caked on his face. He tried to swallow but his throat contracted on a vacuum which made him cough and retch. The beads of sweat were flowing freely and he wriggled inside his clothing as it lay like a second irritating skin between him and the rough woollen fabric. He wiped a bloodstained sleeve across his brow and reached down for his water bottle, taking a long draft of the tepid water in a futile attempt to slake his thirst.

Where was Parry? There was no sign of him. All he could see were the Marines sprawled across the ground on either side of him. Some were sitting as he was, exhausted after the fury of the fight, others lay stretched out on the dusty ground, eyes closed against the arid heat that had dried throats and lips. The unlucky ones who had been detailed to act as guards scanned the battleground in front of their position, the adrenalin still coursing through their veins.

When he recovered some of his strength, he set off along the lines. He dared not think the unthinkable. There was no other officer to be seen so he kept going, stepping over the outstretched legs of the prostrate Marines. At last he came across a captain who was staring out across the open ground through a pair of binoculars.

"Excuse me, sir," said Oscendale, saluting. "I'm looking for Lieutenant Lucas's platoon."

The officer put down his binoculars and turned to face Oscendale. He was evidently surprised to see a military policeman here in the front line but answered only, "Over there, I believe." He pointed further along the British line.

Oscendale found Lucas sitting on a box talking to a major who had a hand on his shoulder. He caught the end of the conversation as he came round the corner of a rocky outcrop. "… wonderful bravery. I shall put this in my report this evening," the major was saying.

Lucas raised his head jadedly as Oscendale approached. His cap was missing and a thin line of blood was trickling down the right side of his face, mixing with the sweat and the grime. His uniform was dusty and his right sleeve was torn.

"Lieutenant Lucas, where's Parry? Have you seen him?" asked Oscendale.

Lucas heaved a sigh, frowned for a moment then he shook his head. "He's dead, Oscendale. Out there. The Turks got him." He pointed wearily towards the Turkish line.

Oscendale was stunned. "What are you saying? How?"

The major replied, a little unnerved by Oscendale's frozen stare. "I sent Lucas and some of his men out to recce that collection of buildings over there. They ran into some Turks and Lucas led his men back to our lines. Most of them came in safely. I'm afraid it looks like your friend Parry was not so lucky. I'm sorry."

Oscendale looked out across no man's land and saw three ancient stone buildings, dilapidated but excellent cover for snipers. Without a second thought, he sprang up onto the parapet and leapt out onto the open ground.

He was dimly aware of Lucas bawling behind him but his attention was taken by the firing that was immediately unleashed from the Turkish lines. If Parry was out here Oscendale was determined to bring him in. *Lucas could have been mistaken. Perhaps Jack was just wounded after all.*

The bullets thudded into the ground, throwing up dust as he ran as fast as he could towards the buildings. Just a few seconds more and he would be there. If there were snipers hiding inside he would just have to deal with them. His friend was not going to be left out here alone, whatever state he was in.

Oscendale became aware of more shouting behind him and realised that the Turks were firing at other targets. He dared not look back and kept running until he reached the first building. Crouching down behind it, he dragged in lungfuls of warm air, gasping with the exertion of the past minute.

Turning back towards his own lines, Oscendale could see a group of men firing and moving towards him. In the middle of the line of men was the major, urging his men forward, his revolver in the air. About half a dozen or so Marines were alongside him, kneeling to fire their rifles, then standing and running.

It was working. The Turks had turned their attention to them and had forgotten about him. Or so he thought.

Something told him that he was not out of danger. Within seconds he was face to face with a Turkish soldier, eyes black and wild. Oscendale leapt to one side and with the barrel of his rifle knocked the bloodied bayonet out of the man's hand as he tried to plunge it towards his belly. The Turk was now off balance and fell face down on to the ground. Oscendale dropped his rifle, drew his revolver and shot the man in the back of the head with a feeling of deep satisfaction.

At such close range the impact of the bullet wrought terrible damage. The skull shattered and bits of brain flew in all directions. Oscendale discharged another round into the man's back in a senseless act.

The first Marine to arrive threw himself against the wall of the building, closely followed by several more and the major, who turned his wrath on Oscendale.

"That was a flaming stupid thing to do, Oscendale!" he barked and glared at him.

But Oscendale ignored him as he looked around furtively. Parry was around here somewhere and he had to find him.

"Over there, sir!" someone shouted. A party of about a dozen Turks had slipped away out of the rear of one of the buildings and were running across the open ground back to their own lines.

The Marines raised their rifles to their shoulders on the major's instructions and opened fire. The Turks began to tumble immediately and Oscendale felt a primeval force run through his body as he joined in with the killing. He was numb to all feeling except that of hate. Within seconds, all bar one had been wiped out. The lone Turk continued to race for the safety of his own lines. Oscendale aimed and squeezed the trigger gently. The rifle barked and the barrel leapt, reducing the man to a crumpled heap.

By now the Marines were entering the building, proceeding cautiously in case any Turkish soldiers remained behind in ambush. It took them just a few minutes to establish that the building was clear.

Clear of Turks that was.

Oscendale found Parry lying face down in a room on the ground floor. He was not alone; two enemy soldiers lay lifeless nearby. Oscendale walked slowly towards him and noticed Parry had been shot in the back. Turning him over gently, he saw the vacant look in his friend's eyes. He felt for a pulse under the jaw but there was none.

The madness disappeared in an instant and he felt ashamed. It had flown out of his body, leaving him feeling human again. He lifted Parry up onto his shoulders, surprised by how light he was, and rejoined the party of Marines outside the building, each one anxious to get back to the comparative safety of their own lines before the Turks counter-attacked. They watched him as he emerged and immediately understood the bond that had existed between the two men. One reached out and took Oscendale's rifle from him and he nodded in silent understanding. He shifted Parry's weight on his shoulders and began to make his way back to the British positions.

Numb, he was inured to every physical pain. Once again, he was consumed only by the emotion of sorrow. He felt like the last grieving soul on Earth, a man rising above the human condition. It was his loss yet it was apparent to all. He was detached from the men around him, imprisoned in his sadness. This was the end and yet a beginning. The beginning of something more than revenge. It would be his destiny. God had touched him with this pain and now he was rejecting God and everything he stood for.

His best friend had been taken from him. All that time together. Gone. All that kinship. Gone forever. Snatched away by this bloody war.

Oscendale came to a depression in the ground and laid the body down. He dropped into the hole and then reached back for his friend. A man stepped forward to help but he brushed him away irritably. This was his duty to his friend, his alone. The lifeless body was carefully lowered to the bottom of the dusty channel. Oscendale positioned Parry's arm over his face as if obscuring the sun. He did not want to see that look in his dead friend's eyes again. *Dust to dust.* He sat down alongside him and stared up at the sky, blinking away the tears from his own eyes.

Was God up there, omnipresent and omnipotent, among the all-too-few clouds that hung in the sky, looking down on his wretchedness? Oscendale shook his head at the absurdity of it all and looked again at the body of his dead friend, lying ignominiously in the dust. It was the end of their friendship but it was the start of something else: an urge for revenge. From now on he would kill every Turk he saw, without mercy and without feeling. They would pay for what they had done to his friend.

CHAPTER 4

Ypres Salient, Belgium – Monday, 16th April 1917

O SSIE BURGESS LOOKED at the tired faces of the infantry.
Now in their fourth year of fighting, the British soldiers
had given much and it was showing. The professional army of
1914 was gone, what remained now was an amalgam of men.
The old, the new, the borrowed and the blue. The old army was no
more, the number of regulars whittled away by the unforgiving
attrition of modern warfare, while the eager new army had
been blooded on the Somme, attacking over open ground with
discipline and vigour – but also with naivety. The borrowed
army of Territorials, the weekend soldiers, had done their bit,
and for longer than a weekend. Back in Britain were the blues
– the hospital blues: the maimed and the scarred.

Here were the remains of Kitchener's Army of 1916,
reinforced by a fresh intake of conscripted men, forcibly drawn
from the length and breadth of Britain, who had answered their
country's demand. Last bloody summer the volunteers had gone
into action on the Somme. They had hurled themselves against
the defences of the best army the world had seen, until they were
pushed back, battered and somewhat more than bruised. Ranks
emptied. Roll call was much quicker. And the mass graves were
everywhere.

All around him men had thrown themselves down in untidy
groups, rifles scattered, on the ground of the town square.
Nobody stood to salute him. Discipline was breaking down.
Chaos was in the air, bleak resignation too. He was glad the lorry
taking him to the Front was merely passing through.

The vehicle bumped and lurched its way out of the town,

along roads which then became lanes, then tracks, then a road again until he was deposited at a crossroads and told by the driver to head north-east. "It's not far, sir," he added optimistically and drove off in a cloud of grey-black fumes.

As there were no hedges along the sides of the fields he was able to look for miles across pastureland with only the occasional wood as a landmark. Dull, featureless and flat. *What a country this was! A country worth fighting for? A country worth dying for?* A wet country certainly, as he noticed from the increasing amount of mud clinging to his boots. *Not dry and dusty like Gallipoli.*

The ground was sodden and boded ill for the attack that was coming. He kept to the side of the road as endless columns of men snaked their way along. Burgess listened to their chatter as they marched. There was plenty of it, which he found surprising. He had thought that the men would be quiet, reflective, contemplating their journey towards oblivion, but instead they were vocal. Marching songs, hymns and jokes were interspersed with the usual grumblings.

"I couldn't 'arf do with a beer."

"My ruddy blistered feet are hurting."

"How much further, Corp?"

"Is it ever going to effing end?"

The tramp of feet and the rancid smell of sweat – an infantry battalion on the march.

He turned off the main road and continued along a much quieter lane. Even this seemed endless and he walked for about half-a-mile without seeing another soul. A murder of squawking crows broke the silence, startling him as they flew above, and he reflected that at times like this it was hard to believe the destruction that was happening just a few miles away to the north. He watched them disappear into a small copse of trees.

It was the calm before the storm. Leaving the column of men

made him feel isolated and gave him a rapidly growing sense of unease. Like a man plucked from the comfort of the crowd and placed on a stage, he felt he was the centre of someone else's attention, as though he were being watched and his every movement scrutinised.

He looked back and could see the battalion of soldiers growing ever more distant, the noise of their passing receding with every step he and they took. Their ways were separate for now but there would be one end in mind. Their paths would be directed to cross again.

The sun came out and shone down, comforting and yet uncomfortable. It made him feel dispirited. *A glorious spring day for the vainglory of war.*

He halted almost involuntarily and turned again towards the way he had come a few minutes before. It was an instinctive reaction and his mind wondered for a moment why his legs had stopped walking. A nagging extra sense told him there was someone or something there, behind him. He raised his hand to his sweating brow, squinting into the sunlight.

Nothing. The soldiers had marched away into the distance. There was no-one there. He was a solitary figure in this unfamiliar landscape.

He rubbed his eyes and turned away, satisfied for the time being. But still the sense of being watched persisted. He attempted to shrug it off as natural nervousness, his mind playing tricks. He was going back into the hell of war again after six months at Scapa Flow and eight months of officer training. It was entirely to be expected that he should feel anxious, he told himself. But why did he suddenly feel as if he were being hunted down?

Scapa Flow. Burgess had arrived, shivering, with a company of Marines in the depths of winter. The bitter wind was howling in from the North Sea which lay ice-cold, black and menacing in its vastness. They had been shown a pile of timber, half-covered with snow.

"There's your barracks!" bellowed a fractious sergeant. "I suggest you get busy before we all freeze our balls off!"

It was here that he had manned a shore battery for six long months, watching for German naval attacks that never came. Men who had once been close friends became irritable with each other, bickering grew and small disagreements became sullen feuds. He found some solace in writing regularly to his father and mother, wishing to be anywhere but here.

The British Grand Fleet had relocated to Scapa Flow just before the outbreak of the war. On the evening of 30th May 1916, Burgess had witnessed the impressive sight of the fleet setting off for the major naval engagement of the war so far – the Battle of Jutland. He watched the majestic warships, carrying enormous turrets holding guns of such power and magnitude that they seemed destined to carry all before them, steam out towards the bleak horizon, billowing black and grey smoke behind them in farewell.

The following month, the Secretary of State for War, Lord Kitchener, had arrived at Scapa Flow. Rumours abounded that he was on his way to Russia to meet the Czar. His ship, the *Hampshire*, was a powerful armoured cruiser and had just returned from action at Jutland. Burgess would have liked to have spoken with the sailors and quiz them about the battle, but no-one was permitted to leave or board the ship. This was evidently a top-secret mission of some importance and it appeared the rumours might be right for once.

There was a fierce gale blowing that evening, which beat against the sides of the wooden huts and ripped flags from poles, slamming shut any door that opened. It made communication out in the open air almost impossible, grasping the Marines like an invisible hand and pushing and shoving them this way and that as they watched the *Hampshire* slip her moorings and sail forth. There was talk among the men that the ship was to travel up the west coast of the Orkneys in order to be safe from submarine attack.

But later a huge explosion lit up the sky. A German mine had blown a hole in the ship and Burgess heard the blast that sent Kitchener and hundreds of others down into the dark, cold depths of the North Sea.

In the morning they had been detailed to search the beaches for the bodies. Pale, bloated corpses soon began to appear on each tide. They were told to collect together any personal effects and hand them over to the NCOs. Searching a cold corpse was undoubtedly the most gruesome thing he had ever done and he had to steel himself every time they discovered yet another one lying on the beaches or wedged between the rocks.

It had also made up his mind for him. He was not going to see out the remainder of the war here; he had his own ambition – to train as an officer. A disparaging sergeant had scoffed at the idea, but he had persisted, asking repeatedly for the application form until at last it had been reluctantly handed over. Burgess had filled it in carefully in a manner that took him back to his days as a railway clerk, a lifetime ago.

At last, in late August 1916 he found himself at Officers' School in Cambridge, crowded in with other young men, all intent on making the grade as an officer. His days had started at 6.30 a.m. with a drill or a lecture and had then continued through a variation of routine tasks: scrubbing floors, map work, studying *The Manual of Military Law*, and other preparation for the examinations in musketry, reconnaissance, as well as drill. For two hours each evening he had spent his time cleaning and polishing his kit and preparing for the next day.

Finally, he had joined the congregation of aspiring officers in the large hall, which became a church of examinations where he had taken his pew and had bowed his head in prayer while he scribbled the answers to the questions that were placed in front of him. Looking around him when he had finished, he saw other heads bent, as if praying for success, while an officer looked on, priest-like, in blessed reverence from the front.

He had made some acquaintances but had never really fitted in with the others, many of whom had not seen any front line action, as he had done, and he had been glad when the time came to pass out and head for France.

As he continued to walk, Burgess pondered the ebb and surge of his life and wondered if it would end soon or later. The memories pulled away with a jolt as he was shaken back to reality by an animal scuttling nervously across the road a dozen yards in front of him. A blur of ginger-red. *A fox. A creature of nature in a place like this!* Nature survived all things, even when it was frightened and alone. It barked once, a strange, unsettling cry that rang out across the fields.

He saw the rooftops of a château poking out above a clump of trees, giving stark contrast to the open land. Intact, not blasted by shellfire, it looked incongruous compared to the carnage he knew would lie beyond.

This was it then: the headquarters of the division. He halted in front of the impressive iron gates through which could be seen what remained of the once formal gardens. The fountain had long since dried up and the perfume of flowers had been replaced by the odour of soldiers, forlorn and unkempt, bedraggled and some so exhausted they had fallen asleep. Were they coming or going? It was hard to tell.

Burgess walked up the stone steps and approached a desk in the hallway, behind which sat a flustered clerk.

"Good morning. Second Lieutenant Burgess. Reporting to Major Scott."

"Yes. Good morning, sir." The clerk stood up and saluted, wincing as the telephone at his elbow rang shrilly. "Up the stairs and third door on your left."

Burgess left the man to his hubbub of noise and paperwork and made his way to Scott's office. He knocked timidly on the elaborately carved door and cursed himself once more. *If you want to be a proper officer, bloody well act like one.*

"Come in!" a voice called from the other side. *Authority, presence and gravitas.*

He opened the heavy panelled door and stepped inside. *A private library.* Scores of leather-bound books lined the walls, some encased behind glass. His boots tapped on the parquet floor, disturbing the calm, musty atmosphere. An oak desk was placed in front of the flamboyant rouge marble fireplace over which hung a large oil painting of the château.

A man he took to be Major Scott stood at the tall, leaded windows, staring into the blue sky. He sniffed and turned as Burgess entered. A sharp-featured face, devoid of humour, stared at him, deep in thought.

"Second Lieutenant Burgess, sir. Reporting for duty." He saluted, stood stiffly to attention and waited for a moment or two. *Was that a look of disdain in the man's eyes?*

At last he spoke. "Burgess, eh? Second Lieutenant Burgess. Fresh out of OTS are we?" The sneer was tangible, palpable. Another middle-class new boy joining the regulars of the army, full of hope and ideas and ill-formed notions of what consitituted courage. Scott, marooned behind his desk, had left all that behind some time ago. Too many dead friends and too little progress for three years of fighting. The attrition of this war was wearing him down too.

Burgess drew breath sharply. Officer Training School at

Pembroke College had been his first introduction to life as an officer. And he had not taken to it. He had assumed, wrongly, that his fighting experience at Gallipoli would have gained him some status among the fresh-faced, ex-public schoolboys who had been part of his cadre of officers. But the reverse had happened. He had been treated with suspicion and snobbery. And being one of the best at the various tasks that were set had only exacerbated the situation.

The coldness of the room tallied with the reception he was receiving and he shuddered a little but felt it was incumbent on him to reply so he stated, "Yes, sir. Number 2 Officer Training Battalion, Pembroke College, Cambridge. I passed out three weeks ago."

"Three weeks." Scott sighed heavily. "And you think you can lead men who have seen more in three days than you have in your lifetime?"

Burgess felt the anger growing within him. "I did serve at Gallipoli, sir. Royal Marine Light Infantry."

It made no difference. Scott merely replied, "So did I, lad. So did I. And what a balls-up that was. Look, Burgess, you're going to find it tough in the line. You're going to meet resentment from a lot of other officers who are… how shall we say? Not your type. We're seeing an awful lot of you Johnnies at the moment. Just hope you can do your bloody job properly or Lord help us all."

He moved to his desk and picked up a buff envelope.

"Here are your orders. You're to go up to the Ypres sector. They've had it pretty rough over the past few days. Plenty of officers killed so you're next in line. Sorry, didn't mean it like that, but you know… Anyway, do your bit and good luck," he added without enthusiasm and turned back to the window again.

Burgess took it as his cue to leave and ensured that the door closed noisily behind him. *Blast the man.*

CHAPTER 5

Ypres Salient – Thursday, 10th May 1917

THE CANDLE GUTTERED and died; the dugout was plunged into darkness.

"Damn!" exclaimed Clarke. He ceased humming the tune he had been murmuring for the past few minutes – 'Roses of Picardy'.

"Light another one, Burgess, will you? Can't see a bloody thing."

Burgess groped across the table until his fingers closed around the marble-like texture of a candle. A thought flashed across his mind. The candle became the lifeless, cold finger of the corpse on the beach at Scapa Flow. He had prised the hand open thus revealing a silver cross – a drowning man's last hope of salvation. Shuddering, he attempted to force the memory back into the depths. This was now, that was then. It was gone. He was gone. The person he had once been was dead and buried. *And there would be more to come – so get used to it.*

He lit the candle. Once more Clarke's face appeared across the box they used for a table and he felt relieved. Burgess felt the dark thoughts recede. *Because of the candlelight or the companionship? Both perhaps.* Francis Clarke had been friendly from the outset, another middle-class boy in unchartered waters. They had struck up a rapport, though it was too soon to call it a friendship. More an understanding of what the other felt, out here, like this.

The corrugated iron sheets curved over their heads, holding back the tons of soil that protected them against the constant thudding of the German shells. Burgess's steel Brodie helmet hung in the centre of the roof, gently oscillating with the tremor of the earth. Clarke removed the bag containing his gas mask from around his neck and unbuttoned his jacket.

"Hellish stuffy in here, Burgess. No wonder the candle can't breathe."

The candle flame whirled and spat as the gas curtain was pulled back and another officer entered. "Good evening, fellow troglodytes. Like Mercury I bring interesting news for you."

"Like Mercury, I wish you'd be gone in a flash," replied Clarke at once.

"Very droll, Clarke. Give me a drop of that Scotch and I'll enlighten your dreary world with news of a great event." The man removed his cap and tossed it onto one of the wooden bunks, exposing a mop of brown hair that he scratched for a moment or two.

Clarke grinned and poured a measure of amber liquid into a chipped tumbler. The newcomer downed the small measure in one swallow and gasped. "Ugh, that's awful stuff, Clarke. Has your batman been emptying his bladder into it?"

Burgess laughed. The sound seemed unreal to him, detached and far away, as if it came from someone else's mouth.

"Come on then, Newcombe. Stop boring us with your wittering and tell us your fascinating news," Clarke urged with an exaggerated yawn.

"Well, cave dwellers. You are to have a new CO as you are aware. What you don't know is that he's a real-life, decorated hero."

Burgess and Clarke looked at each other and pulled faces of mock respect.

Newcombe saw it but refused to be thrown off course. "Yes, gentlemen. As of tomorrow you are to be commanded by no less a personage than Major Edmund Lucas DSO and MC."

Burgess's mood changed immediately. *That swine Lucas.*

Here? Wasn't that charade of a photograph they had posed for last winter enough? The dugout walls began to close in on him, his chest became heavy and his breathing became shallower.

"Burgess, are you alright, old man? You look worse than you usually do." Clarke's concern was evident. Newcombe took advantage of the distraction to pour himself another whisky.

"Probably just overcome with the honour of serving with a man who won the Distinguished Service Order for gallantry at the Somme last year, aren't you, Burgess? He won his Military Cross at Gallipoli, I believe," said Newcombe.

"Gallipoli?" asked Clarke. "Weren't you at Gallipoli, Burgess?"

Burgess licked his dry lips and forced himself to think. What should he say to Clarke? He couldn't tell him the truth. And besides, Lucas probably still trusted him. He might have forgotten that he knew what really took place. Perhaps it never even happened.

But it had. And Lucas was coming here. What should he do? React as if he didn't know the man. Lie?

At last his breathing returned to normal and he spoke. "That's right, yes, I was at Gallipoli, but I never met Major Lucas. Different battalion of the RMLI. When did you say he was arriving, Newcombe?"

Newcombe stood and picked up his cap. "Tomorrow. Probably very early if what I've heard is right. Around stand-to. He'll try to catch you two out. See if you're slacking then give you a good rollicking just to let you know he's boss. Be ready for him, that's my advice."

He plonked the empty tumbler down onto the table. The gas cape was flicked open again and Newcombe was gone. The candle guttered but remained alight and a silence fell between the two men.

Eventually Clarke spoke. "Look Burgess. I know you'll

probably tell me to shut up because you always do when I ask you about Gallipoli. But there's more to this than you were willing to tell in front of Newcombe, isn't there? You did know Lucas; I can see it in your face."

But it was too soon. "You're right, Clarke. I am going to tell you to shut up. Let's get some sleep and be ready for stand-to in a few hours. I don't want this brute catching us out."

Within minutes Clarke's snores began to echo around the dugout. Burgess lay on his back and turned a deaf ear to the world as he mulled over Newcombe's words. The ghost of Gallipoli was about to visit him again.

Gallipoli. The Third Battle of Krithia had opened on the 4th June 1915 and, when the artillery bombardment had ceased at midday, his battalion had advanced in the centre of the line. He had closed his eyes, screamed and charged at the Turkish positions, caught up in the madness of it all. They had captured the centre of the enemy front line trenches but the battalion took such appalling losses that it ceased to exist from thereon. By nightfall the British had lost a quarter of their troops, some 4,500 men. Men had been shot to pieces all around him and bodies lay everywhere, covered in swarms of flies.

Many of the survivors were ashen with shock, as was he. The remaining soldiers had looked around them, noting who was there and who was gone.

Burgess had written a letter home to his father that night. In it he wrote: *It is terrible to see men, who not so long ago were well and healthy, now with tired faces and haunted eyes, staring out of the trenches. Most of them should be in hospital. They are cheating death but only for the present. They are walking corpses…*

On 6th June they were still awaiting the order to advance. By this time more than half the battalion was troubled by dysentery, and within a couple of days it was an epidemic. The climate was becoming another enemy. The heat of the midday sun was intense and there was little or no shade. The water supply was insufficient and the sickening smell of bloated bodies filled the air. The flies buzzed around everywhere, feeding on the corpses, and if he tried to eat without a veil over his head it was almost impossible not to swallow flies at the same time as his food. As soon as a tin was opened it would become covered with the filthy creatures.

Burgess began to feel unwell. It started with a headache which grew rapidly in severity. He began to sweat as a fever took hold and a tickle in his throat soon grew into a full-blown hacking cough that left him feeling exhausted as each bout temporarily subsided.

Within a few days he had gone from the field ambulance to the stationary hospital suffering from intestinal haemorrhaging. The doctor told him he had probably picked up the illness through contaminated food or water and that the rose-colored spots which began to appear all over his skin were confirmation of enteric fever. He was invalided back to England on the *SS Runic* and at the beginning of October he was in Plymouth Hospital where his condition was deemed to be satisfactory, much to his family's relief.

However, he remembered thinking that he would have been happy to die. *How many times had he wished that?*

When he had at last recovered his physical health, he had been posted to Scapa Flow. *The backside of beyond.* After the horrors of Gallipoli, he had initially been grateful for a quieter life of routine Marine duties, and an uneventful period of several months had passed, eventually turning to boredom, until the bodies on the shore had begun to arrive.

He stared at the low ceiling of the dugout. *A grave. A bloody big grave.* Any minute now the metal would give way and tons of earth would come down on top of him, burying him alive. He would be entombed here forever with Clarke, whose nasal snores continued their regular rhythm. Here for eternity in the company of a man he barely knew. He smiled ruefully at the insanity of it all.

CHAPTER 6

Ypres Salient – Tuesday, 12th June 1917

B URGESS COULD SEE nothing beyond a few yards. The grey-white fog swirled and twisted, teased for a moment, opening a gap a few yards wide, and then closed in on itself again. He began to sweat despite the coldness of the morning. Dew lay in droplets on the sandbags piled up in front of him and the grip of his Webley revolver was cold even through the leather of his gloves.

The enemy were out there somewhere. *Why didn't they attack?* He called on his reserves of patience. The Turks had been the same. Quiet, stealthy, patient killers. One look over the top of a trench and *bang!* Another dead man to roll out of the trench before the bloated flies gathered upon him.

He heard a crack somewhere out ahead in the white gloom. Someone coughed nervously next to him. "Shh! Quiet!" he hissed, straining his eyes and ears, waiting for the next sign of the impending attack. The dense fog was so close now that they would have little chance to react in time. Within a few seconds of being spotted the German stormtroopers would be upon them.

Then they came.

There were about a score of them, each with a cloth bag slung across his chest and several were already delving into them to extract stick grenades as they ran towards the British trench. He fired one shot but missed and the green-grey figures opened up with sub-machine guns before leaping into the trench. Something struck Burgess in the face and he landed with a thud on the duckboards. Rough hands grabbed his throat and yanked him to his feet. Then came a hard blow across the back of the head and he felt no more.

Nearby Clarke was fighting for his life with another stormtrooper. He had killed two already with his revolver, one right through the heart, one straight in the head, clean shots both, but now the weapon lay empty and useless in the palm of his hand. He attempted to use it as a club, to beat to death the German in front of him.

Someone pushed Clarke aside and a figure he recognised as Sergeant Doyle lifted his trademark two-pounder hammer and smashed it into the German's face. The man screamed and dropped his machine gun, hands clutching at the huge dent in the side of his left cheek. Doyle moved on along the trench, dispatching other Germans who were engaged in hand-to-hand fighting with his men, scything them down from behind as the hammer crunched into bone.

Clarke turned to see two Germans pulling the limp body of Burgess over the trench wall. "Burgess!" he yelled and, picking up the still-screaming German's machine gun, he pushed and shoved his way through the throng of embattled men towards the disappearing group.

By the time he reached the spot they were gone into no man's land and Francis Clarke faced one of the biggest decisions of his life. Should he risk his life out there trying to save a friend from capture or stay with his men until the Germans were driven out?

His decision was made by an inner voice and Clarke reasoned, albeit briefly, that his men were holding their own, whereas Burgess was in dire straits. He levered himself out of the trench and allowed the dense fog to surround him.

His sense of awareness was increased at once. He stood still, concentrated and listened. Ahead of him he heard German voices and a dragging sound. But he had no idea how far away they were. The fog suddenly started to play tricks on his imagination. What if he ran into a German bayonet? Was that a figure to his left? He drew breath, tried to calm his pounding heart, and pointed the machine gun well out in front. He would take some of them with him anyway. *If the flaming thing worked, that was.*

Three shapes emerged up ahead. The two Germans were struggling with Burgess's injured body and were cursing him loudly. A captured British officer would be a great prize though and they kept at their task, oblivious to Clarke's presence.

Clarke closed on the group, then, when he was sure he was close enough to be heard, he shouted, "Hey, Fritz! *Hände hoche!*" His knowledge of German was rudimentary and he hoped that this would not turn into a dialogue.

The two Germans dropped Burgess's arms and whirled round to meet him. One began to raise his machine gun and Clarke knew that his life now depended on fate. *Well, perhaps it always does,* he thought. *So here goes.*

He pulled the trigger of the machine gun and jets of flame shot towards the German who grunted and slumped backwards like a rag doll. His companion turned and ran into the fog but Clarke pulled the trigger again; the man fell noisily onto the ground somewhere out in the murk.

Shivering with excitement, Clarke fought to control his breathing. "Right, Burgess, let's get you out of here," he said quietly to the groaning figure.

Burgess blinked and opened his eyes as Clarke turned him over. "What's all that bloody noise?" he muttered.

"Just me and a couple of Fritzes arguing over you like some prize pig. Do you think you can walk with my help?"

"Aargh! I'll try. What the hell happened?"

"Never mind that for the moment. Let's just get you and I back to civilisation before the Kultur boys come back," urged

Clarke as he slung Burgess's arm across his shoulders and dragged him to his feet.

They moved remarkably swiftly across the ground back towards their trenches. Burgess regained his strength with each step but Clarke became aware that the next few moments could be especially dangerous.

Peter Newcombe loaded several rounds into his Webley revolver, acutely conscious of the adrenalin that was still coursing through his veins. There was a scuffling sound to his right and a heightened tension spread instantly among the look-outs.

"They're coming back, sir! Ruddy Hun bastards want some more, do they?"

Newcombe jumped up onto the firestep and looked out into no man's land. The fog was clearing, with visibility up to about ten yards. He could see a figure coming towards him, but there was something wrong about the way the man moved. His actions were uncoordinated, jerky and without rhythm. There was a purpose in what he was doing however; he was headed for their lines. Grim determination was bringing him onwards.

"Hold your fire!" shouted Newcombe. "It's Lieutenant Burgess!"

Burgess came on. He tripped over his own feet and fell into the mud. Floundering now, he scooped the mud up in his palms and pushed it either side of him.

Newcombe turned to his men. "Get him in here. Quickly, before the Huns come back!"

Two men clambered up the wooden ladder propped against the wall of the trench and scrambled out into no man's land. They grasped Burgess under the arms and dragged his limp body into the trench.

Disorientated, dazed and too shocked to speak, Burgess's head twitched from side to side. His eyes stared crazily out at

Newcombe. *Neurasthenia*. Newcombe had seen it in other men. The last time he had seen Burgess he had been fighting in the trench not ten minutes before. What could have happened in such a short time to bring about a reaction like this?

"Burgess? Burgess, listen to me. You're safe now, do you understand?" He placed his hand on his shoulder.

No response. Burgess kept shaking like a man possessed.

Newcombe tried again. "Come on. Tell me what happened out there."

Burgess continued to stare at him. Newcombe saw that his very soul was in torment behind those vacant blue eyes. His body was here but his mind was somewhere else, replaying the events of the past ten minutes.

A private soldier who acted as Burgess's batman appeared with a tumbler and a bottle of whisky. He looked up at Newcombe for approval. "Hope you don't mind, sir. I went into your dugout. Thought it might help."

Newcombe shook his head and clenched his teeth. To see Burgess like this was pitiful; the man's self-control was gone. Whatever had just happened to him had scared him so badly that his mind had flipped in another direction and he knew that it was pointless giving him anything. The soldier held out the tumbler but Burgess's eyes were on Newcombe, unsettling him with their intensity of emotion.

"Thank you, Haveldar, but I think Mr Burgess will need more than a glass of whisky now."

CHAPTER 7

Kinmel Park Camp, north Wales – Thursday, 14th June 1917

"**A**ND THIS, GENTLEMEN, is the Number Five Mills Bomb. A particularly lethal invention of the good Mr Mills. I don't know if his wife had upset him that morning or what, but a short time later he had produced a piece of work capable of blowing Fritz to kingdom come – and a few of his mates with him as well, I might add."

Nervous laughter rippled around the group. The speaker was a war-weary sergeant-major with a neatly-trimmed toothbrush moustache the colour of old rope. He held out a grey, egg-shaped object with a large metal ring protruding from one side.

The group of young officers stared in fascination at the explosive device he held in the palm of his hand. Dark and sinister, they knew it contained enough power to kill or badly maim all of them should he make a mistake.

Second Lieutenant Albert Maskell shuffled uneasily in his new uniform. A week out of Officer Training School, he had been sent here to Kinmel Camp in north Wales to learn the lethal art of 'bomb throwing'. Surrounded by a mixture of fresh-faced ex-public schoolboys and experienced soldiers promoted through the ranks, whose dark-rimmed eyes told of previous battle experience, he felt uncomfortable and very much alone. He missed the companionship of the ranks, even its inherent danger. Instead, here he was, a trainee leader of men, and the responsibility did not sit comfortably with him. He was sorry now he had ever listened to Lucas and regretted being here.

He thought back to the photograph. In his officer's uniform

Lucas had preened and posed, while he had gazed down at the stains on his sergeant's tunic. But those three stripes had been won fairly. Well, up to a point. Up to that moment when…

"Now then, if you gentlemen, one and all, will pay close attention, I shall show you what Mr Mills had in mind when he invented this lovely weapon." The sergeant-major turned away from the group and lobbed the bomb some fifty yards into the distance.

"Get down!" he yelled and Maskell and the others threw themselves onto the ground. Three seconds later a mighty explosion shook the ground and small particles of earth rained down on them.

The NCO stood up, dusted himself down and walked purposefully towards the scene of the explosion. The officers followed, like so many unthinking sheep, and each gasped as they saw the hole in the ground the bomb had made. All except Maskell. He had seen bombs explode before and was beginning to find this whole performance wearisome.

"There you are, gentlemen. Imagine what that would have done to Fritz if he hadn't have been paying attention." Several of the group nodded in full agreement. "Right, let's give you a bag of bombs each and get practising!"

The sergeant-major led them back towards a table where a neat row of khaki bags were laid out. The officers stood in a line and were rewarded with a bag of a dozen bombs each. A corporal then called out a list of names and allocated each one a number.

Maskell sauntered towards the bombing bays which lay off to the right. He sought out bay number four and dropped down into the shallow hole which was surrounded by sandbags. Well-versed already in throwing bombs the previous year on the Somme, he sighed with the routine of it all and wondered what had possessed him six months ago. He had been a well-respected sergeant but then the jealousy of seeing others get on – one in particular – had aroused something within him and he had joined the ranks of the aspiring few. But he was determined to play the game and to pass this course, and steeled himself for the next few minutes. *It will soon be over*, he told himself.

The sergeant-major's voice boomed out across the bays. "Gentlemen, as you have been instructed, take the first bomb out of the bag."

Maskell obeyed.

"Holding the lever closed, remove the safety pin."

Maskell complied.

"Prepare to throw."

Maskell prepared.

"Throw!"

Maskell threw.

A series of projectiles arced out of the individual bays and looped across the firing range. A few seconds later a series of deafening explosions boomed out, so close that they almost became one.

Silence settled. Then another explosion shook the ground. Sergeant-Major Thompson wheeled to his right. A cloud of dust plumed up from bay number four. A sickening feeling stung at the pit of his stomach and he began running towards the billowing smoke.

He cursed out loud. Coughing and gagging, he swam through the dense smoke barrier and ducked and dived for a clearer view into the pit. Other figures emerged alongside him. "I say, what's wrong? What's happened? Has someone been hurt?" asked one.

Thompson didn't reply. He dropped into the pit and groped in the smoke – for what he didn't know. Eventually his fingers made contact with a sticky mess and as the smoke cleared he reeled at the sight of a torn, dismembered body oozing blood.

Second Lieutenant Albert Maskell would never return to France. He would never return anywhere.

Ypres Salient – Tuesday, 31st July 1917

Peter Newcombe lay face down in the mud; its dank smell slid into his throat and settled in his stomach. To move now would mean death, certain death. The hideous turmoil of combat, muffled sounds of explosions and machine gun fire ripped through the air all around him. Had the world gone mad? The ground shook; his body shuddered and, as his eardrums had been affected by the concussions, so the whole battlefield was undergoing its terrible transformation in a world one step removed from his own. It was as though he was no longer a part of it, cut off as he was by his hearing loss.

Smashed sections of the vicious German barbed wire lay ahead of him but as stones and mud rained down from the impact of the artillery barrage, he knew he could not move a muscle. He was pinned down, half-deaf and feeling the earth vibrating under the impact of hundreds of metal flails.

He thought back to the anxious faces all around him as he had stood at the bottom of the trench ladder. Nervous yet grimly determined, they had followed him up and out of the comparative safety of the trench when at last he had blown his whistle and given the order to start the attack at 3.50 a.m. that morning. How long ago was that? He dared not move a muscle to look at his watch; the machine gunner up ahead would see him, target him and kill him, as simple as that.

They had poured out into no man's land to join the hundreds, no thousands of men, as far as his eye could see. *And into what?* Shell hole after shell hole full of stagnant water and the grotesque, lifeless vestiges of what had once been men. Crouching, revolver in hand, he had led the way forward, encouraging his men by waving a brown gloved hand. *Futile. Pathetic. Courageous. Was this what leadership was all about?*

And then it had been over to the Gods of War. They would decide who lived and who died, whose body would be cut down by the lumps of whirling metal or the hurtling machine gun bullets.

Men had begun to fall. They fell into the cloying mud, into pools of water or just crumpled to their knees, some staring in horrid fascination at the red holes that had pitted their bodies, others just blown to pieces.

Still they went on, into a terrible landscape of violent destruction.

And now here he was, lying in the bloodied mud. Burgess and Clarke were both gone. He was the last one left. Yet up ahead death, or glory, or both, were waiting in the form of a concrete machine gun emplacement. He would need every ounce of his courage to raise himself up and charge the evil nest that was spitting lines of lead at him and his men.

It was time. His time.

CHAPTER 8

Barry, south Wales – Wednesday, 15th August 1917

ROMILLY PARK WAS awash with colour that August afternoon, the flowerbeds in full bloom. Families were out enjoying the summer sunshine, strolling along the meandering pathways, enjoying the cocoon of an environment far removed from the slaughter of war. Popular tunes rang out from the bandstand which was surrounded by a throng of cheery people. Couples were playing tennis – women constrained in their long skirts while more comfortably-dressed men laughed at the ease of it all. Children shrieked playfully as they ran in and out of the bushes lining the paths that cut between the sections of freshly-mown grass.

Assistant Provost Captain Thomas Oscendale sat on an iron bench, painted green in an attempt to blend it into its surroundings; its twisted metal lines bringing back to him memories of contorted, rusty metal and broken bodies. The images rarely went away, even when he was here, at home, on a week's leave. They had travelled with him from France, impossible to leave behind.

His family had moved here to Barry when he was eleven. To Barry Island to be precise, that exclamation mark at the end of the twisting sentence of coastline upon which the town sat. This was the place where his family's new roots had been put down after they had moved here from Cornwall. He recalled memories of twenty years ago: playing football in an untamed field, building dens in the woods with friends, some of whom he would never see again. The memories of his youth. *The things of childhood once seemed so permanent.*

It looked so different now, even in the time he had been away.

"Excuse me, is there anyone sitting here?" A voice brought him back to the present and he opened his eyes, squinting into the sunshine to see a woman clad in mourning clothes, her face shrouded behind a fine black veil, standing near him. He never got used to the colour of the widow's weeds; though goodness knows there were enough of them walking the streets of Barry or any other town these days. Their melancholia always entered his soul, leaving him depressed and all too aware of his own fleeting mortality. But there was no wife to dress in black and mourn for him. No, she had been taken from him several years ago.

He stood courteously and moved to one side out of the direct glare of the sun to allow him a better look at the woman who appeared to be in her late twenties or early thirties perhaps; pale beneath her veil but with large, hazel eyes that looked confidently into his.

"No, no, madam," he replied and he indicated redundantly the empty place on the bench.

"I'm sorry, I shouldn't have disturbed you. You looked quite peaceful there with your eyes closed. Would you care to sit again?" asked the woman, the crepe of her dress rustling as she lowered herself onto the bench. She smiled fleetingly at him then turned away, her eyes drawn to the children.

"The band, they play very well," he commented. Damn, couldn't he think of anything better to say?

"Yes, they are all local men who play here from time to time," she replied. And there the conversation ended for the moment. He had never been good at small talk, especially with women. *Too many games, so much left unsaid.*

He stole a glimpse at her profile as she continued to look straight ahead. She then turned her head so quickly that she saw him looking at her. Embarrassed at having been caught out, he averted his eyes but not before he had seen her smile again at him.

"Are you home on leave?"

He turned back to face her. The young woman was lifting her mourning veil and he saw her face clearly for the first time. She was attractive but looked tired, the weeks of mourning taking their toll and leaving her with the all too familiar hallmarks of a woman bereaved.

"Yes," he replied. "Home on leave until next Tuesday." The door had suddenly opened and a polite but relaxed conversation continued for a few minutes, about the music, the floral displays, but never about the war, a subject they both took means to consciously avoid. He felt a surge of pleasure; it was satisfying, sitting here in the sunshine, enjoying the company of a refined woman.

They introduced themselves. She was Mrs Hannah Graham. He clumsily introduced himself as Captain Oscendale.

"I mean Thomas, Thomas Oscendale," he corrected at once.

He cursed himself again for his gaucheness. He was awkward already in her presence, as he often was in the company of attractive women. It had always been this way. He had been tongue-tied and hesitant in the company of the girls he had known as a young man and the stumbling conversations and awkward silences in between had left their scars.

"To be honest with you, Captain Oscendale, I've spent rather a lot of time sitting indoors recently. What I mean is, sitting in the parlour receiving visitors."

She turned towards the sun, closed her eyes and breathed deeply. "It's lovely to be out here in the fresh air," she continued. "It is wonderful to feel the sun on my face. Well, I must continue on my walk and make the most of this lovely day."

"Would you mind if I accompanied you, Mrs Graham?" he asked, overcoming his hesitation. Compassion for her plight and an acute awareness of his own solitude merged in him instantly.

"Yes, I'd like that." She lowered her veil again and, rising from the bench in unison, they began to walk slowly along a pathway, commenting politely on the lively children all around them, the nannies scolding them while immaculately-dressed mothers sat chatting on the rows of benches, their physical and emotional detachment from their offspring plainly evident. In his mind he tried to decide on her character, her life. Composed, upright, dutiful. Childless, he thought, by the way she looked tenderly at the youngsters. A mother-in-waiting who would now have to be very patient.

She abruptly stopped walking. "My husband was also home on leave," she murmured, gazing out across the park. The words emerged as if part of a broken train of thought.

"Recently?" he asked because he could think of nothing else to say.

"Yes," she replied eventually, "he came home last month for a few days, prior to his returning for training for the latest offensive." She turned her head away from his enquiring eyes. "He didn't want to go back, you know. It had all become... too much." Her voice tailed away and Oscendale studied her face, the light piercing her veil. She sensed that he understood and raised her hands to lift it from her face, drawing it back over her broad-brimmed hat. Turning towards him, he saw once more her undiluted beauty and he was enraptured. He longed to reach out for her, to hold her in his arms, to comfort her and assure her that all this would pass.

But, to his disappointment, she said merely, "Well, thank you for your company, Captain Oscendale. After that brief interlude I must go back to my... my home and face my sorrow once more."

"May I escort you safely to your home, Mrs Graham?"

"No. Thank you all the same, Captain. I live just there." She pointed to a row of grand villas that ran along the fringe of the park.

It was impulsive and bold but somehow rather splendid, he thought later. "I wonder, Mrs Graham, will you be here again tomorrow?"

She shook her head but then surprised him by saying, "Not tomorrow. But I will come here again on Sunday. After church. Perhaps we could talk some more then?"

Oscendale nodded and she moved away. He watched her as she walked further from him. She was gone now, mingling into the crowds. *Sunday. Yes, he would be here. It couldn't come soon enough.*

A hand was placed on his shoulder and the rest of his surroundings snapped back into focus.

"Captain Oscendale?" The voice was male, young and not without some arrogance in its tone.

Oscendale turned to see a freckle-faced young man in an ill-fitting suit who touched the rim of his bowler hat in acknowledgment. Oscendale studied his face, hoping for some recognition.

A moment passed and the young man said, "Captain Oscendale, I'm Detective Constable Willis, Barry Police. I was told I might find you here." Oscendale decided he didn't know the policeman, though he had worked at the Barry Station for several years before the war began. One of the new batch brought in to replace the older lags like him while they were away on military duties, he supposed.

The man looked at the departing Mrs Graham. "A fine-looking woman. Don't suppose she'll have any trouble finding another husband." He turned back to Oscendale and winked.

Oscendale stepped closer to the policeman. "It's nothing to

do with you, sonny. Show a bit of respect for a poor widow, eh?"

The young man's awkwardness came to the fore. "Sorry, sir. I meant no offence. It's just… well… you know she is an attractive lady, that's all." He reddened and looked crushed.

The folly of the young, thought Oscendale, *and don't forget, Tom, you were young once. Anyway, aren't you getting a little too over-protective of the delightful Mrs Graham all of a sudden?*

He softened. "All right, Willis. Now we know where we stand, what can I do for you? I'm military at present as you can see, I don't do local police work anymore."

A note of relief came back into the young policeman's voice. "I was sent to get you by Inspector Woodfin, sir." He paused. "There's been a murder and as there's a military aspect to it, the inspector thought you might be able to assist him."

"Murder?" *Had death followed him here as well?*

"Yes, sir. Nearby too. Park Grove. Over there. Handy you being so close, if you know what I mean."

Oscendale followed his outstretched finger. On a nearby hill, Park Grove rose like a set of stairs opposite the main entrance to the park. Red-bricked terraced houses clung to its sides and immature shrubs dotted the front gardens.

"What number?" Oscendale asked.

"Number 25, sir. Last one. Right-hand side."

"And who's been killed? Military connection you say?" he queried, his curiosity aroused.

Willis fumbled in his suit pocket, took out his notebook and thumbed through the pages. At last he found the correct one. "An officer's wife, sir. Susan Maskell. The body was found by her maid this morning. Inspector Woodfin is at the scene."

"One last question, Willis. How did you know I was here?"

The young man's smirk returned. "Your landlady, Mrs Owen, sir. I'm not a policeman for nothing, am I now?"

CHAPTER 9

Barry – Wednesday, 15th August 1917

NUMBER 25 PARK Grove was a bay-fronted, newly-built dwelling with a neat and trim front garden enclosed within the utilitarian railings. As the last house on its side of the road, it appeared to be supporting the weight of all the other houses that leaned on it as they rose up the side of the steep hill. Oscendale lifted the latch of the iron front gate, closed it behind him and approached the stern-looking policeman who stood guard at the front door. Oscendale did not recognise him either. *My, my, the world has moved on since I left,* he thought to himself.

"Captain Oscendale, Military Foot Police," he announced. "I'm here to see Inspector Woodfin."

"Yes, sir," replied the constable. "He's in the front bedroom."

He stood aside and allowed Oscendale to enter a cool, airless house. The faint smell of beeswax polish hung in the air and he wondered what secrets lurked within as he walked through the rooms downstairs, leaving each one only after he had studied it, trying to search for any clues or impression of how this family lived their lives. It was a routine he had trained himself to follow before he became distracted by the sight of a dead body. Nothing struck him as unusual or out of place. The rooms were clean and tidy and very ordinary.

Corrick Woodfin was an old colleague, a friend even. The pair of them had worked on the Barry Police Force for several years before the war had intervened. He had always liked the man's sense of humour. Woodfin was direct, unpretentious and thus inclined to irritate his superiors – a trait that Oscendale empathised with – and he knew he would enjoy his friend's company, in spite of the circumstances, after the formality of military life. *And its loneliness.*

The moment had been put off for long enough. Death waited upstairs in yet another guise.

Oscendale climbed the stairs, turned to his left, went up a further short flight of stairs and stood outside a bright, sunlit room. His eyes blinked after the gloom of downstairs and it took him a few seconds to adjust. Before he could rest his eyes on anything else in the room, a large figure loomed in front of him, silhouetted by and blocking out the sunlight.

"Tom Oscendale! And looking smarter than he ever did when he worked with me."

The speaker was lean and dapper, clad in a grey flannel suit, and adjusted his attire of a silk waistcoat and maroon tie with mock humour while looking the soldier up and down. Oscendale knew the man had always prided himself on looking more than presentable and his deep voice resounded from beneath the neatly-trimmed moustache that totally covered his top lip.

"So the Hun hasn't got you yet, after all. Not heard a dicky bird from you in a while, Tom. Ah, you're probably too far behind the lines to get a scratch anyway."

His friendly face wore a broad grin as he spoke and Oscendale returned the smile. He held out his hand but it was knocked away and Woodfin enveloped him in a huge embrace. Pushing Oscendale away at last, he continued, "Good to see you, Tom. Glad you're still alive and in one piece. Unless that's a pair of wooden legs you're walking on?" Woodfin let out a chesty laugh.

"No, Corrick. I'm in one piece – for the time being anyway. Good to see you too. By the way, your young apprentice needs to learn some social graces."

Willis had decided to work on the rooms downstairs and to interview the maid, and for that Oscendale was grateful. He did not want him around when he and Woodfin were working together. This could be just like old times. *Except that he was a different man now.*

Woodfin snorted. "Kids, Tom. That's what they send me. Not proper coppers like you and me. Bloody kids. Wet behind the ears and with inflated egos to boot."

Oscendale smiled in sympathy. "Corrick, if they're any older they get sent to where I am and we have them bayoneted, shot or blown into little pieces. Be thankful you've got someone to make your tea and feed *your* ego with adoration for your outstanding deduction skills."

"True," agreed Woodfin rubbing his chin in mock cogitation. "You may have a point." He winked then said, "Well then, down to business. I need your help on this one. I heard you were around."

"Yes, just home for a few days on leave. Had nowhere else to go really," Oscendale replied.

"Well," teased Woodfin with a twinkle in his eye as he stood aside for Oscendale to enter the room, "I have something here you might be interested in. Tell me what you make of this."

A blanket had been placed over the victim who was lying on the floorboards. Oscendale bent down on one knee, lifted the covering and held his breath when he saw what lay underneath.

Woodfin shook his head. "A terrible death, Tom. Burnt her face off."

The woman lay on her back, her clenched hands by her sides. She was fully clothed apart from a shoeless foot and one of her white stockings, which had been removed and thrust into her mouth. But the most horrific feature was the black shrivelled skin covering her skull.

"What on earth – is this how you found her? Just like this?"

"Yes. Gagged first, then burnt. Her name is Susan Maskell. Aged 25. Her husband is Albert Maskell, a second lieutenant in the Royal Welsh Fusiliers. His battalion is in France somewhere. Unsurprisingly, we haven't been able to contact him yet. I assume this is them on their wedding day." Woodfin showed a framed photograph of a young couple to Oscendale.

Oscendale nodded and moved closer to the dead woman. What little remained of her long hair lay in thin, crisp strands on her blackened skull and there was nothing left of her face to liken it to the young woman in the photograph. A sickly odour filled the air.

He studied the white stocking protruding from the woman's mouth. "This wouldn't have stopped her crying out and alerting the neighbours. And it would have burnt anyway. This was added after she'd died. Strange, wouldn't you agree?" He reached forward without waiting for a reply and removed the stocking. *I wonder*, he thought and gently prised the black, crusted lips apart.

Woodfin knew better than to interrupt Oscendale and stood back and watched him work. He pushed his fingers inside the woman's mouth and removed an object, a crumpled piece of paper. He unfurled it and held it to the light. On it was written in blue chinagraph pencil a question – *Do you remember when in bygone days we mixed our blood together?*

Oscendale stood up and passed the note to Woodfin. "What do you make of that? And there's no sign of the original gag." He thought for a moment. "Do you know why you haven't been able to contact her husband yet?"

Woodfin furrowed his brow, still surprised at what he had just read.

"He may be on his way home on leave. I think he was meant to find this. The stocking is to signify silence and the note is obviously a warning to him. Where's the woman who found her?"

"Downstairs, in the back room," replied Woodfin.

"Was there any sign of a forced entry into the house?" queried Oscendale then added, "And is she the only servant in the house?"

"No, no sign of a break-in and yes, only the maid. She told Willis that Mrs Maskell had just returned from visiting her parents who live in Cheltenham. She's been away for a few days and wasn't expected home until this afternoon. She came to work at ten o'clock and found her like this. It was very distressful finding her this way, as you can imagine. The poor girl is distraught and we haven't been able to get much more out of her yet."

Oscendale's inquisitive eyes surveyed the room and his attention was drawn to a black, leather-bound Bible, its gilt-edged pages lying open between two figurines on a mahogany chest of drawers. He saw that the verses the dead woman had been reading recently were from the Book of Proverbs. One passage had been underlined. It read: *Favour is deceitful, and beauty is vain: but a woman that feareth the LORD, she shall be praised.*

He mentally filed the passage and then showed it to Woodfin. There were many strange elements to this murder and his pulse began to quicken. He realised this was what he had been missing these past months and set about re-examining the corpse.

CHAPTER 10

Barry – Thursday, 16th August 1917

A POSTCARD ARRIVED the following morning. He picked it up from where Mrs Owen had slid it under his bedroom door and read:

Dear Oscendale,
About to have a lovely time.
Loki

Oscendale turned the card over. It was a sepia view of Romilly Park, showing a scene not unlike the one that was still fresh in his memory. In the centre of the photograph was a line of benches – one with two figures on it – and a cold shiver rippled down his spine as he realised that he and Hannah Graham had sat on one of those benches the day before.

A mother pushed a pram while two women with parasols gazed at the bandstand that stood ready for a band to play in. It was uncanny, as if the photographer had been present yesterday to take a picture of them both talking on the bench. He had to look again to make sure it was not the two of them sitting there. But no, it was a woman in a white dress talking to a child.

He had absolutely no idea what the message referred to. The postmark was local – Barry 5.30 p.m. 15th August. *Yesterday. Who knew he was staying here for the week?*

Puzzled, he spent some time mulling over the possibilities of the card before finally deciding it was pointless. Someone was playing a trick on him. Woodfin perhaps? After all, Loki was the name of the Norse God of mischief. Willis might have told

Woodfin he had seen him with Hannah the day before. Good old Corrick. Always ready for a laugh. Perhaps Woodfin meant that he looked to be having a lovely time and, if so, he was right. The afternoon with Hannah had been captivating, unique and left him wanting more. And soon. *Well, he was not about to give Woodfin the satisfaction of responding to his puerile humour so he would just ignore it.*

Later that morning he called on Woodfin at the small local County Police Station in Harbour Road. There was no real progress with the enquiry and his former colleague was engaged in rustling papers and scratching notes in the margins of documents spread across his desk. *Routine paperwork*, thought Oscendale so he settled himself into an old chair in Woodfin's office that had seen more than several better days and picked up the newspaper that lay on a sun-faded table.

After flicking through a few pages and seeing that Charlie Chaplin was in the latest film to be shown at one of the local cinemas – the grandly named Adelphi Royal – he saw a story that immediately caught his attention.

VICTORIA CROSS FOR INVALIDED SOLDIER BARRY PATIENT THE RECIPIENT OF MANY COVETED DECORATIONS

He read on.

It was earlier this month that Edgar Harrington, an invalided soldier, a sergeant in the Leicestershire Regiment, whose home is in Heywood, was admitted as a patient at the Windsor Road Red Cross Hospital. He is a married man, a cotton spinner by trade, of diminutive stature and of by no means heroic appearance. It was on the 31st of July that Sergeant Harrington attacked a machine gun firing party of the enemy, near Ypres. He went forward and captured their machine gun, turning the weapon on the remainder of the attacking party with deadly effect. The brave young non-commissioned officer was reported for his magnificent courage and recommended for distinctive recognition. He has already gained four valued decorations, including the Distinguished Conduct Medal, the Croix de Guerre, the Médaille Militaire and the Russian Order of St George. On Wednesday last, the gratifying intelligence reached the Windsor Road Red Cross Hospital that his Majesty the King had been graciously pleased to confer upon Sergeant Harrington the highest honour, the coveted decoration of the Victoria Cross. The new VC winner, who is only 23 years of age, has served with the Colours since the commencement of the war, and it is owing to his having been wounded in the taking of the machine gun that he is now recovering at Windsor Road Hospital.

"Bloody hell!"

"What is it?" asked Woodfin, looking up from his paperwork.

"An unlikely hero, Corrick. A very unlikely hero. Mind if I use your telephone?"

Windsor Road Red Cross Hospital was situated at the rear of one of the local churches that stood as beacons of salvation and righteousness all across the town of Barry. The church hall, many of its former users currently away serving the war machine, was presently being utilised to save bodies, not souls and it had opened just a few months previously to cope with the growing demand for treatment of the wounded.

He entered the ward and saw dozens of beds lined up on either side. Some were empty but in others men lay quietly, immobile and in great pain. The smell of ether and disinfectant pervaded the air. A team of nurses scurried around, fastidiously attending to their patients' needs, their headdresses giving them a nun-like appearance. *Angels of mercy saving the bodies of the damned.*

Two soldiers dressed in blue hospital suits with red ties limped past him, talking in hushed tones. Oscendale looked across to the row of beds on the far side, catching the eye of one man who was staring at him. He noted a depression in the bed sheet where the man's left leg should have been. A pocket prayer book lay there instead. Another casualty with a shrapnel-damaged jaw held a white porcelain drinking cup to his lips and clumsily poured liquid into a twisted mouth, assisted by an attentive nurse.

"Yes, you can speak to Sergeant Harrington," Oscendale was told curtly, "but he's just started another interview. This time it's with a reporter from the *Cardiff Times* so you'll have to be very patient and wait for him to finish. He's quite the hero you know, and lots of people want to talk to him." The young nurse was awestruck, wide-eyed in the presence of such courage. *And patronising.*

He sought out Harrington who was sitting on the end of his bed talking animatedly. Pinned to his Hospital Blues, he was wearing the ribbon of the DCM, also the ribbons of two French medals – the Médaille Militaire and the Croix de Guerre, plus the Russian Order of St George. The burgundy ribbon of the Victoria Cross had joined them.

A reporter was sitting in a chair next to the bed, settling himself into the interview with the new hero. "How did you gain all these other decorations?" asked the reporter, pointing to Harrington's chest with his pencil.

The young man looked down, as if to check they were still there, and replied in a broad accent, "Well, I'll tell thee. It were while I were on active service in Salonika, early last year. I were awarded the Distinguished Conduct Medal for conspicuous bravery in the field and these three foreign decorations, well they just followed in its train. I were in a bombing post some distance in front of the trenches, when our force suddenly retired. I continued to fire upon the enemy with destructive effect for seventy-two hours until our men returned and I were relieved."

The words came with practised ease. Oscendale mused that the soldier was becoming quite adept at handling interviews with reporters. *How many of them had he seen? How many others had lapped up his heroics?*

"And how did you win the Victoria Cross?" asked the reporter, joining the nurse in the ranks of the suitably impressed.

"Well, it were on't thirty-first of July. Our officer, Lieutenant Dixon, mustered the men and asked for volunteers to snuff out an enemy machine gun which was giving us trouble. I volunteered and taking my rifle and a revolver, I crept into a ravine some distance away where I saw a machine gun in the charge of three of the enemy. I popped off at the men and, running forward, took charge of the gun which I turned upon a small farmhouse further in the distance and brought down three other men, who I thought were a relief party. The machine gun I brought back to our own lines and I were told I should be recommended for the Victoria Cross."

"And you were wounded during the course of this?" said the reporter scribbling furiously.

"Aye. As I were bringing machine gun back I were shot in leg by an enemy sniper. Right here in me left calf. Didn't stop me though. Just kept going till I brought machine gun in." He ended with a flourish and beamed at the reporter.

"That's truly astonishing. And you have attended a number of presentations locally I understand?"

"Aye. Been guest of honour at several dinners in the past few days and have also been presented with War Savings Certificates at a dance held in my honour last night by the

Barry Railway General Offices. I'm a bit jiggered this morning as a result."

The reporter smiled in sympathy and both men looked down at Harrington's bandaged calf.

"And what about your home town? Heywood isn't it? Near Rochdale?"

"Oh aye, they've written to me 'n all. The mayor says 'am to have a fitting welcome home, including a civic reception on Saturday week and a money presentation from the townspeople of nearly £400 'as been collected."

"So when did you hear you were to be awarded the Victoria Cross?" asked the reporter.

"When I got the letter. Here t'is."

Harrington passed an envelope to the young reporter who took it, opened it and read the contents before returning it to the delighted soldier, after scribbling yet more notes.

"And when will you be receiving the medal?"

"Any time soon. At the moment this'll have to suffice." He tapped the burgundy ribbon on his chest with his finger.

The interview concluded, the reporter thanked Harrington for his time, shook his hand and departed, leaving the chair free for Oscendale who approached the bed slowly. Harrington watched him approach, the broad smile on his face turning to a puzzled frown.

"Good morning, Sergeant Harrington," he opened. "I'm Captain Oscendale, Military Foot Police."

He paused and waited to see the effect his words would have. Harrington shifted uncomfortably on the bed and readjusted his position.

"And what can I do for tha, sir? Excuse me if I don't stand." He pointed at his injured calf.

Oscendale sat in the chair. He pointed at the Victoria Cross ribbon. "Just received that, have you, Sergeant?"

"Yes, sir," replied Harrington. "I were presented wi'it by Major-General Black at the Buttrills Camp here in Barry last week."

"I see. Shouldn't you have been called to receive the actual medal by now or presented with it here if you are still unable to travel? You must be anxious to get it, I'd have thought?"

"Ah well, it's been postponed, sir, in the light of the death of the King's son, Prince John, you see. Been told I'll have to wait a bit. Understandable under the circumstances. I'm a family man mi'sel, sir, and I can understand it. If it were one of my nippers I'd feel just the same."

Oscendale allowed the conversation to pause while he studied the man's face. There was something not quite right here, he was sure.

"Can I see the letter you received please?"

Harrington's dark eyes grew suspicious.

"What's this all about, sir?"

Oscendale said nothing but held the man's gaze. At last Harrington shrugged and passed the envelope to Oscendale who removed the letter and began to read. London postmark, brief statement of the facts and the signature of a Captain P. S. Roberts.

Oscendale returned the letter to the man. He began slowly, gathering pace in his delivery as he built up to the final accusation.

"You see, Harrington, I have a friend who works in the Army Records Office in Preston by the name of Lieutenant Stonehouse. When I read of your story in the local paper this morning I rang him. After all, winning a Victoria Cross is a big event. People want to know about it. The strange thing is that he checked your record and told me that you haven't been awarded the Victoria Cross. In fact you haven't been awarded any decorations for distinguished conduct and to top it all you're not even a bloody sergeant!" The revelation was delivered in a whispered hiss.

Harrington looked nervously either side of him to see if Oscendale's words had been overheard. But no-one looked up.

Harrington squirmed like a man with trench lice. "Look, sir. This has got a bit out of hand, tha knows. Captain Roberts put me up to it. He gave me the ribbons. He said no-one would know and that I deserved something back for all my service. I know… I know… I never done anything as brave as what I made out but I been in action, sir. I've shot a few Huns and nearly been killed mi'sel often enough."

"Who is this Captain Roberts?" Oscendale fumed.

"I dunno, sir. I met him in a shop a few weeks ago, after I arrived here in Barry. He told me he had been in the army and that you never got proper treatment after you was demobbed. He said I should look out for mi'sel and make sure my future was bright."

"So he gave you those ribbons?"

"Yes, sir. Well, not the VC. That was my idea. I wrote to my brother in Stepney. He typed the letter in the office where he works and signed it in Captain Roberts's name. I thought seeing as how no-one questioned the other medals, they wouldn't question this one."

So Harrington had become greedy for the limelight. Wanted more adulation and more money.

"How did you contact this Captain Roberts?"

"I used to meet him in Charlie Yeoman's shop. You know, the photographer's in Dock View Road."

Oscendale leaned closer. "You're a bloody sham, Harrington. Braver men than you have lost their lives without anyone giving them a medal. You take those ribbons off now, do you hear me? And that money goes back to the people who gave it to you here in Barry. You tell the Mayor of Heywood you don't want any money or a civic reception and that there's been a mistake. Be sure you do it otherwise I'll have the MPs here this afternoon and you'll be arrested and charged. Understand?"

"Yes, sir. Sorry, sir." By now Harrington was thoroughly miserable and deflated, his world caving in about him.

Oscendale stood up and glared at the cringing man. Bloody false heroes. Was there nothing people wouldn't stoop to in wartime?

CHAPTER 11

Barry – Thursday, 16th August 1917

CHARLES YEOMAN – Photographer. The words had been hand-painted neatly above the shop front at number 19 Dock Road. A display of cabinet photographs of servicemen and their families stared out at him from behind a plate glass window. Men with chests puffed out in pride, encased in starch-stiff new uniforms, showed faces naively unaware of what lay ahead of them. He pushed open the door and a bell rang above his head to announce his entrance.

"Good morning. My name is Captain Oscendale. Is Mr Charles Yeoman about?" he asked of a youth who was dusting the surface of the high wooden counter.

"I'm afraid not, sir. Mr Yeoman is with the troops in France. Official war photographer, he is. His father's taken over the business 'til such time as Mr Yeoman returns. Will he do, sir?"

A voice came from a doorway at the side of the counter. "What is it, George?"

George turned towards the source of the disembodied voice and said, "An officer here wants to see Mr Yeoman. I've just told him he doesn't work here no more."

An elderly man with a full head of silver hair, wearing a wing collar shirt and a bow tie, emerged from the room at the back of the shop, wiping his hands on a cloth as he did so. "*Any*more, George. I've told you, *any*more." He looked at Oscendale and said, "If you'd like to take a seat, sir. I'll be with you in a moment. Just seeing to a few plates at present. I'll be back in a jiffy." He beamed genially at the prospect of another customer. Business was apparently good. Hundreds of soldiers must have had their photographs taken in this shop before they set off on the troopships that regularly left Barry Docks for the ports of France.

The old man began to turn away but Oscendale raised his voice and said, "I don't want my photograph taken. I was wondering if I could ask you a few questions about one of your customers."

The eyes grew suspicious and the smile was gone. "Questions about my customers? I don't know, sir. Confidentiality and all that, you know."

Oscendale's voice hardened. "Actually, sir, no I don't. This is a photographer's shop not a doctor's surgery. You don't have confidentiality."

The man's demeanour changed and he glared at him. He paused, considering his response. "Very well, Captain. What do you want to know?"

"Sergeant Harrington, our local Victoria Cross winner. He came in to have his photograph taken recently, yes?"

The old man sniffed. "Yes. Sergeant Harrington wanted a photograph taken to send to his wife up north somewhere. Why?"

"Was he with anyone when he arrived?"

Yeoman thought for a moment. "No. No. I don't think so. I remember him being alone."

"Did he meet anyone while he was in this shop?"

Again the old man dithered before he replied. "He might have done. Why?"

"Who was it?" Oscendale pressed.

There was a pause. "A military gentleman I think. Was it Captain Roberts? Yes, yes, Captain Roberts, that's who it was. Why?"

"Is Captain Roberts a regular customer of yours?"

"He pops in now and then," replied the man cautiously.

"And what did they talk about, do you remember?" Oscendale asked.

"Captain Oscendale, I don't make it my business to eavesdrop on my customers' conversations. I wasn't listening – far too busy setting up for the photograph."

"And where does he live, this Captain Roberts? Do you know?"

"No," Yeoman replied irritably, running his hand through his hair, but Oscendale noticed the lad, who had been almost immobile up to this point, dart a look at his employer.

Oscendale pounced. "Then I'd like to see your list of customers."

The photographer shook his head. "Now you really are asking too much, Captain Oscendale. That list *is* confidential."

Oscendale took a step towards the man. "Show me the list or I'll go into that back room and check exactly what photographs you're developing and if they are anything like the ones some soldiers get hold of, I'll impound them and take you straight to the police station. Do you hear me?"

The old man did not hesitate. He turned immediately and scurried away into a back room. Seconds later he emerged with a marbled accounts book which he set with a thump on the counter before Oscendale.

"Good," said Oscendale. "Now we're making some progress." He opened the stiff front cover and began scanning the list of customers whose addresses were written neatly alongside the date of their sitting and the cost due of their photographs. He soon found Harrington's name dated the 6th August and on the same day that of Captain P. S. Roberts, but there was no address listed.

Oscendale flicked through the pages of the ledger and was about to hand back the book when his eye caught sight of a name he recognised. A name from the past. Edmund Lucas.

He allowed his eye to stray to the names above and below it. He recognised another one of them. *Albert Maskell.* He paused, noted the information and closed the book with gusto.

"Thank you for your co-operation, Mr Yeoman, much appreciated." Oscendale opened the door again, the bell ringing his departure this time. He glanced up at it and then back at the old man who looked at him with utter disdain, his ordered world of photography having been disturbed by this bully of a policeman. Oscendale took his cue from that look and deliberately swung the door shut as hard as he could, and was pleased to hear the jingling bell fall from its mounting onto the floor with a crash.

Songs of praise rang out within the Seamen's Mission Hall, deep voices rising up, praising God in the highest. Sinful souls sang for redemption while outside the world carried on regardless. Oscendale waited by the entrance, leaning one elbow on a railing and smoking yet another cigarette, relieved that he was not one of the faithful who had been drawn inside by the hope of instant salvation.

A uniformed figure emerged from the Barry Docks police station next door. His head was raised, gazing up at the heavens as if either gauging the weather or expecting a sight of the Almighty himself in response to the singing. He adjusted his leather helmet strap and placed the headgear on his head. Looking across at the Docks Offices opposite, he then noticed Oscendale and raised his hand in a gesture of recognition.

Oscendale nodded. "Fred Warren. How are you?" He dropped his cigarette, stubbed it out with his army boot and walked towards the policeman with his arm outstretched. They shook hands warmly and Warren clapped him on the shoulder.

"I'm glad they've had the sense to promote you. Needs a bit of order over there from what I hear."

"You shouldn't believe everything you hear, Fred, you know that. It's grim and bloody but it's on a huge scale and mistakes are bound to happen."

"Yes, I suppose you're right, Tom. I hear you've been helping Inspector Woodfin with this murder. Any rogue seamen involved do you reckon?" He turned towards the Seamen's Mission, the singing intensifying in emotion and rising to a pitch of religious fervour.

"Could be," replied Oscendale, unwilling to give anything away. He liked Fred Warren but knew the good-hearted policeman could not keep anything to himself and a loose word now could hinder a later step in the investigation. "And how's life here on the docks?" he enquired, changing the subject. "Busier than ever?"

Warren gazed across at the rows of ships waiting to load coal, the black gold from the Welsh valleys, before transporting it abroad to feed the furnace of war. "You know how it was before the war, Tom, a seething mass of different nationalities, emotions and personalities. Throw in some alcohol on payday and a 'here today, gone tomorrow' philosophy and the next thing you know there's a fight and a stabbing for us to deal with." He shrugged his shoulders. "Nothing's really changed, has it?"

Oscendale sighed sympathetically in agreement. He had not yet been in the army long enough to forget his civilian duties prior to his enlistment in the summer of 1914. He recalled one foreign seaman lying in a pool of blood on the pavement in Thompson Street on a cold, autumn night. His frightened eyes had been wide open while he muttered something in a language Oscendale had not understood. Eventually he had stopped speaking, his eyes had become still and he had died. His assailant was never caught, his ship sailed without him and the man whose name Oscendale still remembered, Ali Nagi, was laid to rest in the town cemetery in an unmarked grave. The only mourners had been a local minister and some employees of the funeral home that took the corpse to the cemetery. Oscendale had stood over the grave long after the others had gone about their other duties, and watched the gravediggers throw lump after lump of sodden earth onto the cheap coffin, until the mound rose like a huge molehill.

The door of the Seamen's Mission Hall opened behind him and a stream of sailors flooded out. Warren wished him luck with the investigation before he set off on his beat around the docks. Oscendale waited patiently, knowing the man he sought would see him first.

At last the crowd of men began to thin out as the sailors made their way back to their ships, their lodgings or to one of the town's many public houses or brothels.

A man of about thirty pulled a flat cap low over his forehead, said goodbye to the group of men and, with a slight shiver, stuffed his hands into the pockets of his reefer jacket. He approached Oscendale with the rolling gait of a sailor who long ago acquired his sea legs. Oscendale remembered his father walking the same way. He remembered his mother telling him it was to compensate for the rolling of the ship's decks. He had asked her why Dad thought the earth was rolling as well and she had returned to her washing with only a laugh as his answer.

As he passed Oscendale the sailor muttered, "Follow behind me." Oscendale complied. They went under the railway bridge as yet another coal train rumbled overhead. Turning a corner they entered a narrow culvert which obscured them from view. The sailor turned to stand in front of him. He looked furtively over Oscendale's shoulder.

"Mr Greenwood, the message you left for me at the police station said you had some information I might find useful?"

Greenwood looked around him again before replying. "I saw the article in one of the local papers about the soldier in the hospital in Windsor Road who claimed he had been awarded the Victoria Cross. My brother-in-law is an officer serving with the Leicestershire Regiment. His name is Lieutenant Burgess. I think you should speak to him."

Burgess? Where had he seen that name recently? Then he remembered.

Oscendale took out his notebook and wrote down the officer's name. "And where would I find him? Which sector of the Front? Do you know?"

Greenwood grimaced. "He's not at the Front, Captain Oscendale. That's why I contacted you. He's been in a hospital in London."

"Has he been wounded?"

Greenwood grimaced again. "Yes, he's been wounded, but not physically. He was admitted to the Maudsley Hospital suffering from neurasthenia."

"How bad is he?"

"Very," replied Greenwood. "He was brought home recently after the fighting at Ypres. I've had a letter from him. You might want to read it first." Greenwood put his hand into the inside pocket of his jacket and pulled out an envelope. "It's very disturbing. I remember the Ossie Burgess who was an intelligent young man, full of life and hope for the future. This man," he tapped the envelope, "is someone else." With that he passed the envelope to Oscendale.

Dear Jim,

How are you and Iris? As you can see from the address at the top of this page I'm in hospital. I'm well looked after and I want for nothing but the night times are the worst. I stay awake for hours, frightened of the dark. They tell me it's nothing to worry about but they are not there with me when the nightmares come. The noise in my head builds and then fades.

I can't stop thinking about the last few weeks at Ypres. It was horrific. Unreal. At least I'm back in Blighty now. It's all ragtime though, isn't it? Ragtime. Sometimes I can't stop laughing, at other times I just burst into tears and cry and curse until some sweet angel appears to soothe me.

They said I should get a medal after what I've been through but I know what medals cost, Jim. I know how much you have to pay. And I don't mean just courage. Ask Lucas, he knows. Bloody Lucas and his racket. I'll show him for what he is. And I thought he was my friend.

It's late, Jim and I'm tired. Too tired to write any more.
Ossie

Oscendale raised his head after he had finished reading. Greenwood was watching him carefully, drawing heavily on a lit cigarette. He said, "When I saw the article about that sergeant in the hospital I remembered what Ossie wrote. I thought you might be interested."

"I am interested," replied Oscendale thoughtfully. "Very interested."

"That's a relief to me, Captain." Greenwood was nodding, his face creased by a crooked smile. "And you're in luck because he's made a little progress. He might be willing to talk more about it now. I hear he's at home in Claude Road, Cardiff. Number 61." The seaman paused and sniffed the air. "Smells like rain. Time to go. Good evening, Captain Oscendale."

"Just one more thing, Mr Greenwood," said Oscendale. "Why the nervousness? You don't strike me as a man who is scared of very much."

Greenwood stared deep into Oscendale's eyes. "When someone starts asking questions of my wife about her brother, someone who refuses to give his name and who only calls round when I'm out, then I get worried, Captain Oscendale. Particularly when my wife is told to keep her mouth shut. I'm off to sea again in a week or two and I don't like the thought of my wife being threatened. You see to it that this bastard is caught, eh?"

Oscendale thanked Greenwood, noted the address and made his way back to Harbour Road. *Edmund Lucas again. Twice in one day. A ghost from Gallipoli kept reappearing.*

CHAPTER 12

Cardiff, south Wales – Friday, 17th August 1917

IT WAS EARLY morning. The rain had cleared and a fresh new day had dawned; he felt optimistic once more. This was leaving and yet not leaving. He was glad about that. He felt a tug in his stomach as he mimicked the emotions he would have felt if this truly had been a parting. And there was still time before his leave ended to make more happen. *The citadel of his hopes and fears.*

At Barry Railway Station he paid for his ticket and strolled onto the platform. There were several dozen people milling about, which was by no means unusual for this busy station. Many of them were soldiers returning to the Front after being home on leave, or those leaving for the first time, being waved off by their loved ones. The anxiety and sadness was palpable. Last, lingering embraces and then they would have to go.

At last the trail of smoke from the locomotive pulling the passenger train came into view, crawling along the tracks from Barry Island, and he made his way to the edge of the platform. The train slid along towards him, its wheels screeching and disappearing into clouds of steam. People began to move forward, eager to board. Others made their final goodbyes before parting. He settled himself into an empty compartment and was relieved when he heard the stationmaster blow his whistle and the journey began.

The compartment door slid open and two soldiers entered. One pulled down a window and leaned out, clearly excited as the great steam engine jerked slowly out of the station, gradually gathering speed. It trundled past the rows of terraced houses built to accomodate the thousands of workers pouring in from England and the south Wales valleys. Behind each door, both the bright hope a boom docks town could bring and the grim daily struggle which fuelled it.

As the stations on the line to Cardiff passed one by one, Oscendale began to reflect. Meeting Hannah Graham had been followed by another exposure to the seedier side of life. Death had been a daily occurrence over the past three years, but to be reminded of the inhumanity of mankind on a return to his home town was appalling and had left him feeling depressed. His opinion of other human beings was tarnished through his experiences of the past few years, even before he had gone to war, but there was precious little respite, even here. He had enjoyed Hannah Graham's company and had felt attracted to her, hopeful that perhaps something might develop. But then he was always hoping, always willing something to change in his life, to allow him to have the happiness that he desired but had experienced only rarely.

Carriage doors slammed as more passengers boarded and he did what most stimulated him at a time when melancholy threatened – he turned over in his mind the facts of a current case. He closed his eyes, lost in his thoughts for the remainder of the journey, until he sensed that he must now be close to his destination and roused himself. He checked his watch and was pleased to see that the train had arrived on time. At last it jolted to a halt at Roath Branch Junction on the east side of Cardiff. Oscendale hastily jumped down from the carriage, eager to get through the bustling crowds and out of the station. Crowds irritated him, particularly noisy ones.

The Burgess family home stood on the corner of a crossroads at 61 Claude Road. A three-storey house with a high gable, the year 1899 was carved into a lintel. Two huge angled bay windows protruded, as if to protect against the threat of the outside world.

The heavy damask curtains barred external eyes from the secret lives within.

Obeying the sign beneath the bell pull – *Out of order, please use door knocker* – he duly gave the heavy brass lion's head three loud, firm raps. He waited at the doorway, studying the embellished Portland stone that surrounded it and in due course he was confronted by a well-presented housemaid who dutifully asked him his name and business. He obliged. "Wait here please," she said before adjusting her starched apron and retreating into the house again. *Middle-class grandeur aspiring to better.*

She left him to peer into the tiled hallway furnished with a hallstand bedecked with coats and a pot of umbrellas, a painting or two and the pungent whiff of cigar smoke.

A short time later the housemaid reappeared, opened the door wider and ushered him inside. He saw that the painting was a print, the stair runner almost threadbare and that there was a shabbiness about the place. *Fast disappearing money?* he wondered. The signs were unmistakable.

He was shown into the drawing room where a confident-looking man in his fifties sat smoking a cigar, thinning hair swept across his forehead, legs crossed and elbow cocked on the arm of a brown leather wing-backed chair. He rose and folded the newspaper he had been reading as Oscendale entered and shook his hand.

"Good morning, Captain Oscendale," greeted the man in a thinly-disguised West Country accent. "Frederick Burgess. How may I help you?" He gestured for Oscendale to sit, which he did, removing his cap as he did so.

"Good morning, sir. Thank you for seeing me. I'd like to speak to your son, Lieutenant Burgess, if that's possible. I understand he's staying here at present?"

Burgess's brow had creased slightly in anticipation of the expected questioning and he inhaled thoughtfully on his cigar before replying. "What is this about? He's here on official leave, you know, as a result of his being…" He paused, then stubbed out his cigar before adding, "wounded."

Wounded. Far more socially acceptable than shell-shocked.

"Yes, sir. I'm aware of that. I think he may be able to assist me in an investigation I'm currently undertaking."

Burgess thought for a moment, his sharp eyes never leaving Oscendale. At last he spoke, his voice much quieter than before, as if afraid of being overheard. "Captain Oscendale, my son has served his country for three years. Osmond enlisted in September 1914 with the Royal Marine Light Infantry. He saw action at Gallipoli and was evacuated home two days after his nineteenth birthday. Can you imagine that, Captain Oscendale? Then he was posted to Scapa Flow where he endured desolate conditions and a terrible winter sleeping on the floor of a wooden hut. He then sought promotion to be an officer, attended officer training school and took part in this latest show at Ypres. But something terrible happened to him there, Captain Oscendale, something so awful that it has disturbed the balance of his mind and has turned my convivial, gregarious son into a shadow of his former self."

He paused and suddenly looked crestfallen. Oscendale could only speculate as to the inner turmoil and anguish he was experiencing. A father's love for his son. The emotions in the room were raw now and he knew better than to interrupt. Instead he waited for the man to continue.

There was a silence for a time as Frederick Burgess struggled to regain his composure. His eyes were glistening and Oscendale knew how difficult it must be for him to show feelings of this sort. He was sure that a man like Burgess would consider such displays of raw emotion unseemly. He turned away in deference and studied the paintings and photographs on the wall. When Burgess spoke again he knew that his gesture had been seen and understood and, more importantly, appreciated.

"I will allow you to see Osmond, Captain Oscendale. But I ask that you don't upset him. Any recollection of that incident could throw his recovery back several weeks. It's been hard enough as it is." He shook his head murmuring, "His mother…"

But Oscendale interrupted with, "Thank you, sir. For what it's worth, I was at Gallipoli too. I lost my best friend over there."

Burgess smiled a wan, sad display of understanding before standing up and summoning the housemaid. "Renee, please ask Mr Burgess to come downstairs."

Renee set off on her errand. Oscendale heard her knock on a bedroom door. A short time later, footsteps trod warily down the stairs and the door to the room slowly opened.

The man who entered had a young man's face but heavy, dark bags hung under his eyes. His unkempt black hair was swept back from his impassive, unshaven face. Dressed in a robe, pyjamas and slippers, he shuffled into the room then sank slowly into an empty chair. He stared lifelessly out of the window as if there was no-one else in the room.

"Ossie, this is Captain Oscendale," said his father, rising out of his chair to pat him on the hand. "He has come here to ask you a few questions. He needs your help with his investigation. Are you happy to talk to him?" Then to Oscendale he asked, "Do you mind if I stay, Captain? I might be able to settle him if he becomes anxious."

"Of course." Oscendale turned to Burgess and said, "Good morning, Lieutenant Burgess. I'd like to ask you a few questions, if that's alright." He waited for a response but there was none. "I understand you were at Gallipoli, as I was. What beach did you land on?"

The young man did not move his gaze from the light coming in through the window. "Kum Kale in March, then Y Beach," he answered in a quiet, husky voice.

"Y Beach," Oscendale repeated. "I was also at Y Beach. In April of '15."

With that the young man broke away from the sunlight and turned his head towards Oscendale but his eyes were looking through him to someone or something very far away. Oscendale had seen that stare before and knew what it meant. "I was there in April," muttered Burgess. "Twenty-fifth. Landed on the peninsula. RMLI."

Oscendale felt his pulse quicken. He had hoped Burgess would tell him something quite different. "You were under the command of Lieutenant Lucas on that morning?" he asked.

"That's right. Lucas." He fell silent and returned his gaze to the sunlight streaming in through the window, catching golden dust motes like dancers performing in a beam of light. "My friend Edmund Lucas," he said at last, "who killed one of our own men. You see, you and I have met before, Captain Oscendale."

Oscendale was making hurried notes but his hand began to tremble as the words came out of Burgess's mouth. His mind had soared from this room in a house in Cardiff. He and Burgess were both there again, in that gully leading from Y Beach to the cliff tops, where the Turks were waiting.

CHAPTER 13

Penarth, south Wales – Friday, 17th August 1917

POLICE CONSTABLE NATHANIEL Ayliffe was not a happy man. The heavy rain was cascading down his helmet and running onto his scrunched-up face. He quickened his pace hoping to escape the damned weather, but speed only seemed to increase the amount of water which fell on him and make a wet Friday in Penarth even wetter.

The main street was quiet, the good townspeople of this ancient settlement, now a thriving docks town, preferring to stay inside, in their houses or in the pubs. *How sensible.* He was not on duty tonight to chase burglars or arrest drunks, he reflected. No, he was following a tip-off that if successful would give him great personal satisfaction.

There was no view of the Somerset coastline today. Flat and Steep Holm islands had disappeared behind the dark, stormy clouds. He hurried through the waterlogged roads, along the rows of terraced houses, their stone frontages turned inky black by the rain. He had walked this beat for several years – no elegant, elaborately gabled or turreted houses stood in this part of town. This was the side of Penarth reserved for the labourers, mariners and coal trimmers. Turning a corner he entered Pilot Street, where a row of squashed terraces jostled side by side for the best view of the houses opposite. *Inward-looking. Prying.*

Anonymous and self-deprecating, number 34 stood compressed by the neighbouring houses; one of many rented two-up two-downs for workers at Penarth Docks.

Ayliffe drew himself upright, letting the rain teem down his face as he surveyed the property. A dull light shone from behind a curtain in the upstairs window. He knocked hard on the door.

No answer.

He knocked again, harder this time. Still no reply. He looked up. The light had been extinguished. *Too late, my son.*

Ayliffe lifted the tarnished brass letter flap, bent down and called out. "Police! Open up!"

The door was eventually opened by a woman in her mid-twenties whose lank hair hung down untidily around her gaunt face. She flicked some out of her eyes and spoke. "Yes? What do you want?"

Old before her time, she was worn down by the endless toil to eke out an existence here on the breadline. Her voice was thin and nervous and Ayliffe's experience told him she was on edge. He smelt success.

"Mrs Elsie Phillips?" he asked. The woman nodded. "I'd like to speak to one Lloyd Phillips. Is he here?"

"Lloyd? No, haven't seen him for months. He's in the army, you know," the woman replied, scrutinising his policeman's uniform as if to say *why haven't you joined up?* He held her gaze until she lowered her eyes.

Lying, thought Ayliffe.

"Really? Your neighbours tell us your husband has been home recently," he countered.

"What? The nosey beggars. They're just trying to make trouble," she replied and leaned out of the doorway to look up and down the street, as if her neighbours were congregating in an accusing host outside. "Well I haven't seen him if he has. He's in France!" she bawled, loud enough for the whole street to hear.

The policeman tried a less official approach.

"Mind if I come in, Mrs Phillips? I'm getting soaked out

here." He pulled his best *pity me* face. She rolled her eyes but thought hard.

He knew it was a crucial moment for her. If she refused to let him in it might confirm that she had something to hide. If she did and there was a man in the house, he would be discovered.

She decided to brazen it out. Standing aside, she reluctantly allowed him to come in.

The hallway was cold and stark, and told of a woman with little spare money to spend on the fripperies of life.

"You live here alone, Elsie?"

"It's Mrs Phillips to you. And yes," she replied defensively, "since my mother died last year and Lloyd enlisted I've been on my own."

"That must be difficult with only you to pay the bills and the rent, what with your husband at the Front."

She stopped in the doorway to the living room. "What are you saying?" she asked suspiciously. "I work long hours and I manage. All right?"

"I just imagine that times are hard," he said casually. "What with the war and all."

She gave ground and retreated into the living room. A small fire burnt low in the grate but the sparsely furnished room was warm and cosy.

He felt there had been another presence in here recently and checked for the obvious signs – two glasses, two chairs having been sat in – but he could see nothing. The drying clothes strung below the mantelpiece were obviously female items. Either she had covered the tracks very well or his information had been wrong.

"Mind if I sit down?" he asked and she shrugged and pointed to one of the two worn armchairs.

"Okay, Mrs Phillips," he began pleasantly, "I need to confirm some facts. Just for the records, you know." She shrugged, so he continued. "You say you haven't seen Lloyd for some time, is that correct?" She nodded and he paused before asking his next question. The smell of cooking reached his nostrils. "Were you about to have your supper?"

"Er, yes. Yes," she replied. "Pie tonight."

"Smells lovely. Might be burning though. Do you want to have a look at it?" He pointed towards the range.

She hesitated. "No, no, it'll be fine."

"Believe me that smells like burning."

Elsie Phillips smiled nervously again as she bent down to open the oven door. The smell of burnt pastry billowed out in a cloud of smoke. This pie was more than cooked. She had obviously been distracted before he arrived.

He followed her into the scullery where she placed the pie on the draining board. Small and cramped, there was hardly enough room for the pair of them.

"That's a large pie. You could feed an army of soldiers with that. You going to eat all that tonight?"

The woman was angry. "It's ruined. No-one will be eating that. Look, what do you want? I've told you I haven't seen Lloyd for months. He hasn't been home on leave so how could I? Check with the army. They haven't sent him home for ages. Right?"

Just then there was the sound of a slowly creaking floorboard upstairs. Elsie Phillips looked up, her face full of alarm.

"Just the house breathing," she said unconvincingly.

Ayliffe waited. The creak came again. "Who's upstairs, Elsie?" he asked, eyes raised to the ceiling.

"No-one. I told you, it's just the house breathing. Creaks all the time."

"Rubbish!" shouted Ayliffe as he bolted out of the room. Taking the stairs two at a time he headed for the front bedroom. He placed his hand on the wooden door knob; it was locked.

"Phillips!" he yelled, banging on the door. "I know you're in there. Give yourself up, man. Don't be stupid."

He pressed his ear to the door and listened. Silence. Then he heard it. Just the faintest sound of a window being raised.

"Phillips!" he yelled again. "Open the door!"

There was no subtlety now. The window rattled loudly and Ayliffe knew Phillips was on his way out. He turned and raced down the stairs, along the passageway and out into the rain again, just in time to see a man in civilian clothes running away along the street and swiftly disappear down an alleyway between the houses.

Ayliffe drew out his whistle and blew hard while heading off into the driving rain after the deserter, the sounds of Elsie Phillips' banshee-like cries echoing between the houses on either side of him.

CHAPTER 14

Barry – Friday, 17th August 1917

"GET OFF ME! You've got no right to pull me in here. I've done nothing!" The shouting could be heard all along the corridor, emanating from the cell in which Elsie Phillips had been placed. Thin, boney hands grasped the iron bars and she screamed in frustration. Oscendale winced as he stood near the main desk, talking to Woodfin.

"That's quite enough, Elsie!" shouted the exasperated Constable Ayliffe. "There'll be someone along to talk to you again shortly." Ayliffe had lost his quarry in the warren of side streets that made up that part of Penarth – and had lost his patience with Elsie. He had endured her constant tantrums from the moment he had returned to Pilot Street and arrested her, all the way to the Harbour Road police station.

Woodfin's initial interview with Elsie Phillips having progressed no further than short, clipped responses, Oscendale asked if anyone had searched her. Woodfin said he knew just the person, which did not surprise Oscendale, but what did surprise him was the female figure who reported to the main desk some thirty minutes later – by which time Constable Ayliffe was ready to resign.

"Corporal Banfield, sir. How can I be of assistance?" she asked with surprising confidence of the open-mouthed sergeant behind the desk.

"Good evening, Corporal." Oscendale was taken aback at the sight of a woman in the uniform of the Queen Mary Auxiliary Service. They were still a rarity on the Western Front, though he was aware that women were now becoming part of not just the civilian police force but the military police force as well. *Needs must in changing times,* he mused.

She turned to Oscendale, fixed him with her glittering eyes and saluted him smartly. "Sir, I was asked to assist with a female prisoner." *Organised. Methodical. Straight to the point without any frills.* He was already impressed by this young woman.

"Yes… well, Banfield. Er… she's in there. You can probably hear her screaming."

Oscendale was unused to giving orders to a girl of this age. Fresh-faced, perhaps in her late teens, her attractiveness threw him out of his stride, particularly as she tucked a loose strand of auburn hair underneath her cap.

Banfield looked confused. "Do you want me to question her or search her, sir?" she asked. Once again Oscendale felt flummoxed. *Grow up,* he told himself.

"Yes. Search her please." He saw Woodfin grinning at him from over the woman's shoulder. He was enjoying Oscendale's moment of discomfort and made no move to help him.

"And what am I looking for, sir?" she asked, tilting her head a little, well aware that her femininity was unsettling him. And enjoying it as much as Woodfin.

One person teasing him was enough. Two made him recover his wits. "The woman is Mrs Elsie Phillips. She was brought in here two hours ago for harbouring a suspected deserter. He made a bolt for it and I'd like to talk to him. The constable who brought her in saw her slip something into her… er… undergarments and I want to know what it is."

"Yes, sir," said Banfield. "I see. Well, if you'll let me into the cell please, Constable." She spoke to Ayliffe who was standing next to the cell door.

"You watch her, Corp," he advised. "She's a real firecracker." He winked and unlocked the cell door.

"Who the hell are you? What do you want?!" shouted Elsie

Phillips as Banfield entered the cell. She uttered nothing in return, merely closing the cell door behind her.

The three men gathered at the main desk once more, decorum preventing them from peering through the bars to see what was going on inside. They heard Banfield talking quietly. Phillips screamed some foul-mouthed abuse before a scuffle ensued. Oscendale made to move to the cell door but Woodfin tapped him on the shoulder. "She'll be fine."

There was more of Phillips's shrieking and then silence. A short time later Banfield emerged, straightened her cap and smiled at the assembled men. In her hand she held an envelope that she proffered to Oscendale.

"Is that what you were looking for, Captain Oscendale?" she said and handed the envelope to the admiring captain of Military Police.

Mr and Mrs Newcombe,
17 High Street
Cardiff

But there was no stamp or any postmark to be seen. He turned once more to the letter. It was dated 1st August 1917:

Dear Mother and Father,
I'm writing this letter to you from my hospital bed. You will not recognise the writing because a kind chap named Phillips is actually writing it for me as my hand is shaking too much even to hold a pencil.
We attacked strongly fortified German positions yesterday and I'm afraid I came out of it rather badly. I was in a tight corner with danger all around and my men falling like leaves on either side of me. I did something rather stupid, trying to be brave and all that. I felt I had to do something to get us out of the trouble we were in and ended up getting myself wounded.

You will remember my writing of a man named Burgess who joined our section recently. Well, he was cut up pretty rough in a German trench raid a few weeks ago. He managed to get in okay from no man's land but he was so badly affected that Major Bennett had him shipped out. I believe he's in hospital in London somewhere. Poor Clarke was killed as well.

You may have read in the papers of a so-called hero, Edmund Lucas. Well, he is here with us. The thing is, Lucas is not as grand as he likes to make out. Burgess knew it and I know it. With Burgess gone I'm the only one left. I hope to God I'll be able to come through this okay and return home to tell the truth but I fear it may be some time.

Take care of yourselves and pray for me.

Your loving son,

Peter

Oscendale read the letter again. He was puzzled. Why had Elsie gone to such lengths to conceal it? There had to be more.

"Banfield!" he called.

Oscendale passed the creased photograph to Woodfin. "Tell me what you see."

Woodfin took the photograph, noticing that his friend's hand was trembling slightly.

The photograph was a moment captured for all time. Four men in army uniforms, all in their twenties by the look of them. He peered more closely at the badges on their caps. "Different regiments," he said aloud. "Three of them are of the Leicestershire Regiment and one Royal Army Medical Corps. Officers. No, hang on a minute. Two officers, one sergeant and a private. One officer has the ribbons of a DSO and an MC. Brave man. Strange mix of ranks though."

He looked up at Oscendale who asked, "Go on, what else can you see?"

90

"'Wind up' tunics on the officers and an economy tunic on the private soldier, so it was taken this year or last year. Studio photograph." He turned the card over. On the back were written the words *C. Yeoman, Photographer, Dock View Road, Barry.* "Hmmm," said Woodfin. "Local chaps maybe, home on leave. Do we know who they are?"

Oscendale tapped the photograph with his finger. "Corporal Banfield found this when I asked her to go back and search Elsie a second time. She had hidden it under the bed. She handed over the letter to Banfield, as we know, but it was this photograph she was really trying to hide. Elsie says her husband is the private. Have another look at the man in the top right-hand corner."

Woodfin held the card closer and examined it carefully.

"Well, it reminds me of someone. Hang on a minute! It's that fellow whose picture was in the *Cardiff Times* last month. Won the DSO on the Somme. Chap from Cardiff. Lewis? No, Lucas. Lucas, that was it."

"Correct. We know the names of two of the men in this photograph. Now have a look at this. It could be the reason why she wanted to hide the photograph so badly." He passed the letter to Woodfin who read it quickly and whistled.

"We need to have another word with Elsie, don't you think?" said Oscendale.

Elsie Phillips was sitting quietly on the bunk in her cell. Corporal Banfield sat in a corner watching her closely. Oscendale and Woodfin entered and placed two chairs either side of Phillips who looked up at them with defiant eyes. *Not totally tamed yet then*, thought Woodfin. He threw Banfield a look of admiration. Oscendale was quiet, Woodfin noticed, relishing the thought of another display of embarrassment by his colleague in the presence of an attractive woman.

But Oscendale was quickly down to business this time. "Elsie, you need to talk to us. For Lloyd's sake. At the moment you are looking at several years in prison for protecting a deserter. Do you understand?"

"Yes, sir," she replied sulkily. "Though my Lloyd isn't a deserter, sir. He's just afraid."

"All soldiers are afraid, Elsie." Oscendale was softening a little. "You can't just run away though, can you?"

Elsie Phillips lowered her gaze and shook her head. "It's not like that, sir. Lloyd's no coward. The Germans don't frighten him. Lloyd's seen too much to be afraid. Anyway his job is saving lives, not taking them."

"He's got the best job in this war," said Oscendale quietly. She stared at him.

"You're right, sir, Lloyd's saved dozens of lives. That's all he talks about when he comes home on leave. How many boys he's saved. Tells me their names and how grateful they were." She stopped. "He tells me about the other ones too." Her voice tailed away.

Oscendale produced the letter. "This letter Lieutenant Newcombe wrote to his parents. Why did Lloyd have it and why did he give it to you?"

Phillips sniffed and wiped her nose in the sleeve of her grubby blouse. "He was afraid, sir."

"What was he afraid of, Elsie?" asked Woodfin.

She refused to lift her head and just shook it quickly.

Oscendale looked at Woodfin who shrugged.

A sympathetic female voice spoke. "Elsie love, if you want to help Lloyd I suggest you tell these two gentlemen the answers to their questions. Right now they may be the only people who can help him." Oscendale turned to see that Banfield had brought her chair closer to them.

Elsie Phillips looked up into the young woman's face, thought for a while and then spoke. "Alright then. Lloyd was given the letter by Lieutenant Newcombe," she began. "He was dying and wanted his family to know what had happened to him. And what he knew."

Oscendale held out the photograph he had found. "Which one is Lieutenant Newcombe?"

Elsie Phillips did not need to look at the photograph. "He's not in that photograph, sir. That's Lloyd and his friends. They had it taken earlier this year when they were all home on leave." She sniffed. "At least he thought they were his friends."

"What do you mean?" asked Oscendale puzzled.

"They was all friends in Cardiff before the war, when he took up his job in the railway offices. They all played football for the same church team." She smiled at the memory. "That's when I first saw Lloyd, sir." She pursed her lips in a sad smile.

"So this photograph wasn't given to Lloyd by Lieutenant Newcombe?" quizzed Woodfin.

"Good lord, no, sir." She paused. "But Lloyd didn't want anyone seeing it. Said his life was in danger and it was his insurance."

"What are their names, Elsie?" asked Oscendale.

Phillips tapped the figure standing on the left. "That's Ossie Burgess, sir. Lovely chap was Ossie."

Burgess!

"Was? You said was," asked Oscendale.

"Yes," answered Phillips sniffing again. "He's dead, sir. Well, he might as well be, that's what my Lloyd reckoned. One of the Ghosts of Gallipoli, he said."

Oscendale sat back with a start. *Gallipoli again.*

That's why my Lloyd brought the letter home. He was going to give it to the parents so they could do something about *him!*" She jabbed angrily at the image of Lucas in the photograph.

"You know who this is?" asked Woodfin.

"Of course I do," she snapped, her ire roused again. "That's

Edmund Lucas. He was a conceited pig before he joined the army and he's a bloody sight worse now, that's what my Lloyd says anyway."

"And who is the other man, Elsie?" queried Oscendale. "Who is this?" He pointed to the figure seated alongside Lloyd Phillips at the front.

She did not need to look at the photograph. "That's Albert Maskell, sir. They killed him as well."

They left Elsie Phillips sobbing in the cell. Woodfin went to his office and Oscendale sat on a chair in a corridor and opened the envelope Banfield had recovered earlier. The letter was written on YMCA-headed paper. He turned the envelope over.

Oscendale and Woodfin walked home from the sombre little police station in drizzling rain.

"Do you think that's feasible, Tom?" asked Woodfin after a time. "That Lucas had this Albert Maskell killed at Kinmel Park because he knew something? And then he had his wife murdered as well? But why murder Maskell's wife after Maskell was already dead? What was the point of the warning message you pulled out of her mouth in that case? What does it mean anyway? *Do you remember when in bygone days we mixed our blood together?*"

"I don't know," replied Oscendale. "I really don't know. It seems damned odd to me but it's a real enough thought to Lloyd Phillips to send him on the run in fear of his life." He stopped walking. "And what if it's worse than that, Corrick? What if Lucas is responsible for the mess Burgess is in now? That man may have the blood of two of his friends on his hands. One thing's for sure. We need to find Lloyd Phillips and quickly."

"So where do you think he is?" asked Woodfin.

"I think he's gone home, Corrick, to where he was born and brought up. He's a frightened man and no doubt he's gone where he feels he'll be safest. Home."

CHAPTER 15

Carmarthen, south Wales – Saturday, 18th August 1917

A FEW YARDS after the signpost that indicated they were approaching the small village of Bronwydd Arms, the farmer stopped his cart at the foot of a long, rutted track that snaked its way up the side of a hill. What it led to Oscendale could not see, but at least the track was dry. Oscendale jumped down from the cart. *"Da bo chi,"* he said shaking the farmer's calloused hand.

The man responded in Welsh as he had done throughout the slow journey from the railway station which had naturally limited the conversation, though he had understood Oscendale's English well enough. *"Pob lwc,"* he muttered and urged the plodding horse forward once more.

The farm he sought stood on the top of a hill that commanded far-reaching views of the surrounding countryside. Down in the belly of the deep valley a steam train was hissing its way forward, heading east. Clouds of smoke belched from its chimney and the dark green livery of the Great Western Railway Company gave it an almost military empathy with its surroundings. He watched the train until it disappeared into the fold between two hills, then turned his attention to the hike that now confronted him. His boots crunched on the gravel track and was the only sound that disturbed the tranquillity of this idyllic location.

Several minutes later he arrived sweating at the top of the track. Lifting the bar on a gate, he opened it and entered a farmyard. A white-painted, two-storey stone farmhouse stood as still as it ever had. To the right another track led to two squat wattle and daub barns and a cart house, next to which

Oscendale noticed a weathered and rusted, semi-derelict, corrugated iron shed. The air was thick with the smell of freshly-deposited manure and he trod carefully to avoid the wet pats scattered across the ground. An aged black and white border collie limped up to him and sniffed his trouser leg suspiciously before finding something more interesting to do.

The front door of the farmhouse opened well before he reached it and he guessed his approach had been observed for some time from the kitchen window. A grey-haired, buxom woman stood in the doorway, drying her hands on the pinafore that was wrapped around her stout figure. *"Bore da. Ga i'ch helpu chi?"* she asked anxiously.

He shook his head and replied, *"Bore da.* I'm sorry I don't speak more than a few words of Welsh. My name is Oscendale." He pointed to a tap on the wall of the farmhouse. "I'm parched. Would you mind if I have a drink of water?"

The woman nodded after a moment or two and uttered something he did not understand. He turned the tap on and held his mouth under the flow of cold spring water, swallowing in gulps. After he had quenched his thirst he wiped his mouth with his hand. *"Diolch.* I'm looking for Lloyd Phillips. Is he here?"

She hesitated before nodding again and pointing towards a field at the far side of the farmhouse. Oscendale touched his cap in gratitude and opened another gate that barred the entrance to the field, conscious of the woman's watchful eyes. He saw that the ground rose to his right. He could see no sign of Phillips in the direction the woman had indicated, so he began the climb to the top of the hill. The dog escorted him briefly but was soon tempted by the cool shade of a bush.

Birds wheeled and scouted overhead and cattle eyed him laconically as he passed, lifting their heads briefly to stare with large, bulbous eyes, chewing mechanically in a steady rhythm before turning their attention once more to the food beneath their feet. His presence did not intrude into their world.

He crested the brow of the hill and the high summer sun beat down upon his tanned face. His mouth was dry again already. Flies buzzed obstinately around him and he flicked them away irritably. He removed his cap and wiped his forehead, pausing to observe the view. A series of small farms nestled on the hills of the valley. The large open fields were populated with sheep; so far away they appeared as mere specks. Golden wheat shimmered under the blue sky, their ripening almost done. Not a breath of wind stirred in the quiet stillness. Unsullied countryside. *Peaceful countryside.*

He still could not see Phillips and Oscendale wondered if the woman had been mistaken. He might have finished his work in this field and moved on to another one, so Oscendale began to walk down the far side of the hill towards a dry stone wall, the obtrusive insects still attempting to land on his face.

A red and white sheepdog was sitting by the gate into the next field. It watched him as he approached, bared its teeth and growled. There was no-one else in sight and, as Oscendale approached, the dog leapt up and began barking at him. Making himself as big as he could by spreading his arms, he walked steadily forwards and extended an open palm. The dog whimpered then fell silent, licked his hand and lay down on its belly, panting.

It was then that Oscendale caught sight of the body of a man, partially hidden and lying in a dry ditch, a shotgun by his side. He was dressed in a grey working jacket and trousers. A flat cap had fallen off his head and lay alongside him. Oscendale knelt down and felt where the pulse should have been below the man's jaw but his fingertips met only stillness. The way that the man's head was positioned indicated that his neck had been twisted and was probably broken.

Even from the profile of the face Oscendale could see it was Phillips.

He reached across and picked up the shotgun. Single-barrelled, the sort farmers used for vermin control. He flicked open the breech and saw that there was still an unfired cartridge inside. Replacing the gun in exactly the same spot, he considered again the position of the body relative to the gate. Had Phillips slipped while climbing over it, lost his footing and fallen awkwardly somehow because of the gun he was holding, breaking his neck? Was it just an accident?

There was no-one else around and the only witness was the dog, still on its belly, which stared at him, head dropped mournfully onto its legs, waiting for him to give the next command; there would be none forthcoming from its dead master.

It appeared as if it were an accident, the sort that happened occasionally on farms the length and breadth of Britain, but if his wife said Phillips was already on the run in fear of his life, Oscendale could not help but think this was a cruel twist of fate.

But there was something that did not sit right in Oscendale's mind about the whole scene and he walked several paces away before turning round and looking at it again from a fresh vantage point. Then he realised what was puzzling him. Why would a farmer who knew his land climb over the gate with a loaded shotgun? He would have broken the breech if he was going to do anything that might result in the gun going off. And what was he doing with a gun anyway? Perhaps he had been looking for vermin but the chances of him finding any rats here on the hillside during the daytime were small: they would be gnawing away voraciously at the last of the winter hay stored in the barn. *He had brought the gun for another reason.* If a man carried a loaded shotgun with the breech closed while he was walking, he was expecting to fire it at something. *Or someone.*

And why would Phillips have wanted to climb over the gate? Why not merely open it? Oscendale examined it more carefully. There was no sign of any dirt on the bars and looking at Phillips's boots, they were caked in dirt. No, perhaps he had not even begun to climb over.

Oscendale drew his Webley pistol and began to walk alongside the dry ditch. It eventually became hidden by thickets of undergrowth. Someone could have easily lain in wait for Phillips for some time before attacking him as he paused by the gate; someone who wanted to silence Phillips before he could tell anyone what it was he knew.

Whoever it was had gone and the young farmer's son who had survived the carnage of the Western Front was lying dead in his own farm field.

CHAPTER 16

Carmarthen – Saturday, 18th August 1917

O SCENDALE WAS AWARE that at any one time there were tens of thousands of deserters on the run throughout Great Britain but the chance of another military policeman pursuing Phillips here, resulting in a terrible accident, was remote. And any MP worth his salt would not have left the dead man lying where he was. No, this had been well thought out. Calculated.

He scoured the ditches and hedges of the field beyond for the next few minutes, revolver in hand, but there was no sign of the killer. Whoever it was who had broken Phillips's neck had then fled, leaving no other tracks or traces. Holstering his revolver, he made his way back.

As he approached the gate again he saw a figure hunched over Phillips's prostrate form. He was stroking the man's hair, choking back the tears and repeating his name.

Oscendale approached quietly, not wishing to disturb the man's grief but he opened the gate so as to make some noise to alert him to his presence. It squeaked with the decades of rust on the hinges, and the man looked up.

Beneath a worn flat cap, a thick mat of grey hair sat on top of a round, ruddy face that spoke of years in the open air in all weather conditions. Oscendale judged by the pain in the man's eyes that he was indeed the father. Mrs Phillips must have told her husband that a military policeman was on their land and he had come to see what the fuss was about.

"Mr Phillips? My name is Captain Oscendale. I am so sorry about your son. You are his father, I assume?"

He rose, reaching at the same time for the shotgun that lay on the ground. The man's reprimand took Oscendale aback. "You interfering bastard! You couldn't leave him alone, could you? Had to come here after him. And when he wouldn't go quietly back to all that bloody madness you had to kill him. Don't you realise he'd had enough?!"

"Mr Phillips," he replied desperately, "I didn't kill Lloyd. This was how I found him. He was already dead by the time I got here."

"*Celwyddgi!*" shouted Phillips and raised the gun to his shoulder. His guttural voice betrayed his deepest emotions and from the look on the man's face, Oscendale feared he would pull the trigger at any moment.

He thought desperately. "Look, you've seen how he died. A broken neck. If I'd wanted to kill him, I'd have used this, wouldn't I?" Oscendale slapped his pistol holster.

"*Rhedeg*, you bloody redcap!" came the voice of the distraught farmer.

Oscendale took a step back. "Listen to what I'm telling you. Put that gun down please. There's already been one murder on your farm today. You don't want another one, do you?"

"Keep running 'til I catch you, then I'll blast your brains out!"

The farmer lifted the shotgun and fired over Oscendale's head. This was going to be revenge.

"Don't be a fool!" Oscendale saw that he was reloading the shotgun.

Oscendale was damned if he was going to have a hole shot in him by a grief-crazed father. The notion of shooting the man flashed across his mind. He dismissed it as fast as it had appeared and in the same instant launched himself at his startled adversary.

He connected full-on with the startled Phillips who fell

backwards, spilling the shotgun to the ground. Oscendale clung on to the farmer's jacket and levered himself on top of him. He pinned the man's arms to the side and squeezed as the farmer heaved and bucked in an attempt to dislodge him from his torso shouting "*Llofrudd!*" over and over again.

Phillips was strong, a strength honed by many years of hard manual work, and Oscendale had his work cut out to keep him pinned down. At last, however, he felt the man's strength start to weaken as he gasped for air, until they became cries of despair and knew he was in control.

"Right!" he shouted into the man's face. "Do you want to keep struggling or do you want to hear the truth? Because I didn't kill your son, got it? Like I said, he was already dead when I found him." He moved his face closer to Phillips's and glared into it, with eyes wide open and teeth clenched.

Phillips's look of hatred faded into disbelief. Oscendale waited a few minutes until he was absolutely sure the anger was gone, and then he rolled off and retrieved the shotgun.

The farmer sat up, breathing heavily and Oscendale realised he had been pressing too hard on the man's chest. He was rubbing it painfully and looking at Oscendale with a mixture of puzzlement and grief. Oscendale picked up his cap, said nothing and waited for the man to speak first.

"You say you didn't do it?" He coughed out the words.

Now they could make progress. "Correct. I'm afraid your son was dead by the time I got here. Oh, and contrary to popular opinion, Mr Phillips, we try the deserters and if they're guilty we usually imprison them, not execute them!"

"Look, you must understand. The shock, you know. I… I can't believe it. I didn't want my boy to go back. Not after what he told me. Not to all that." The man buried his face in his gnarled hands.

"Well, I wanted to talk to him about something that

happened over there that he witnessed. Something involving a Major Lucas."

He had been watching Phillips carefully as he spoke and he saw a faint sign of recognition cross his face as he lowered his hands.

"Lucas? Yes, Lloyd told me about Lucas alright. Told me what someone had seen him do. Or not do. And they gave him a medal as well." He spat out the words and shook his head slowly.

"What did your son tell you, Mr Phillips? What did he tell you about Lucas?"

"Look, mister, I'll tell you what my son said. But not here, not at the moment. I want to bring my boy back to the house. I've got to tell his mam. And his brother. Will you help me please?" Oscendale felt the pity rise up in him. Had he forgotten the effect of sudden death on a family? Was he really becoming that inured to it all?

He held out a hand to Phillips to lift him up. "Of course, Mr Phillips. You tell me what you know and I will go after the man who did this to your son."

CHAPTER 17

Carmarthen – Saturday, 18th August 1917

THE LOCAL UNDERTAKER brought a temporary coffin on a cart whose iron wheels ground noisily up the steep gravel path to the front door. The young man's body was placed inside the wooden box and laid out in the parlour, two of the mahogany dining chairs being used to support the weight. He lay there, as his ancestors had before him, a familiar scene within this museum of a room. At each end of the oak mantelpiece sat two large Staffordshire dog ornaments, then two tall brass candlesticks and, in the centre, a picture of Lloyd in his uniform. A long case clock stood to attention and continued to mark the passage of time, clunking as the pendulum swung back and forth.

Family and neighbours began to arrive, their eyes glaring suspiciously at Oscendale as soon as they saw the red cover on his cap, before they were ushered into the dining room next to the parlour. Here the Welsh voices rattled out, emotions spilling over, sustained by cups of tea.

The local bobby arrived on his bicycle with his solemn condolences for a family he also counted among his friends, and then recorded in his notebook the sparse amount of information that Oscendale was prepared to divulge. They watched as Mrs Phillips approached a young boy whom Oscendale took to be Lloyd's brother. Wide-eyed and disbelieving, he listened to his mother's words while gazing at the faces gathered around the room.

Although he did not understand the language falling from the woman's lips, he did not need to in order to understand her grief. Oscendale's thoughts drifted back twenty years to the time when his mother had told him of his own father's death. The sequence of events was still painful even after all these years.

He had been sent to a neighbour's house to play with a friend. The boy's parents had kept the secret safe. For the whole morning he was there, they had not given even a hint of what had taken place during the night and he had played happily with his friend's toys until the time had come for him to go. He had run along the side lane that led to his home, oblivious of the tragedy that awaited him within.

The living room had been full of neighbours drinking tea. He had entered the circle and was confronted by his mother who bent down and whispered, "Your father's gone to heaven."

That was it. No more, no less. No embrace, no comfort. Just the circle of probing eyes watching for his reaction. A young boy alone in a ring of adults. And not one rose to comfort him. He had moved to the window and stared out at the garden his father had loved, had tended so well. The roses were fading now. His world was dying too.

They expected tears but he was not going to give them tears. He held them back, took several deep breaths and saw the mist appearing on the window pane. He drew a single cross and turned back to face them all.

He had been kept away from the funeral, sent packing again on that terrible day. There had been no last goodbyes, only a lifetime's grief.

And in this farmhouse, all these years later, the memory was replaying itself with complete clarity. Oscendale rose and went to the boy. He put his arms around him and consoled him, drawing him close. The boy did not resist. Although this man was a stranger, at that moment they both shared the same grief, separated as they were by two decades. The boy knew and sobbed. Children always know.

"You know about Lieutenant Newcombe, of course," said Phillips later as he and Oscendale sat together on the old stick chairs in the kitchen, looking out across the valley through a window whose centuries-old glass twisted and distorted the view of the world outside. The neighbours had gone and so had the body of his eldest son. "After all, you were there at the end." There was still a glimmer of scepticism in the farmer's eyes, something that Oscendale could not yet fathom.

"At the end? I wasn't there at the end. I never met Lieutenant Newcombe," he replied.

Phillips frowned suspiciously, thought for a moment, then continued in his lilting accent. "Well, this is what Lloyd told me anyway. The barrage lasted for six hours. The shells flew over our lines and smashed into the German positions. Then when zero hour came the shelling grew in ferocity. Lieutenant Newcombe waited in the front line trench with Major Lucas alongside him. They were both very nervous about an enemy counter-barrage which could have caused havoc amongst the trenches packed with our soldiers.

"Lucas got jumpier as zero hour approached. Newcombe said he had never known him so edgy. The whistles were sounded and the men left the trench. The ground is sodden, as I suppose you know, so their progress through the mud was slow.

"There was a wood directly in front of them, also a huge pillbox that had not been destroyed by our guns. Lucas stuck closely to him as they advanced and was not as forward in leading the men as you might have expected. The machine guns opened up and the men around him began to fall. Lucas cried out and fell. Newcombe thought he'd been shot so he just kept going, leading the rest of his men.

"Lieutenant Newcombe moved from shell hole to shell hole, crawling in and out of them, until he had outflanked the position. He then rushed forward when he was behind the pillbox and threw bombs through the openings until he'd silenced the machine guns. Then he ran in through the entrance holding a rifle he had picked up on the way and bayoneted the surviving Germans.

"He came back outside again to wave his men forward but was shot in the stomach by a sniper and collapsed. He was brought into my son's Advanced Dressing Station, more dead than alive. Lloyd knew there was little the doctors could do for him so he just kept him company in his remaining hours on God's earth. When he discovered that Lloyd's wife was from Penarth he said he wanted to tell his parents something and asked Lloyd if he could trust him. He wrote down what the officer dictated to him in a last letter to his mother and father, and I was amazed at what he told me.

"Apparently, Major Lucas is claiming the credit for storming the pillbox and with the lieutenant gone there's no one to challenge him. To tell you the truth, Captain Oscendale, he was afraid of having this letter in his possession. He knew there's them that would have liked to have taken it from him. That's why he gave it to Elsie and came back here. Poor Elsie. She'll have to be told…" His words tailed off as he wiped his eyes and blew heavily into a crumpled handkerchief.

Oscendale put a reassuring hand on the man's shoulder. "Your son carried Newcombe's letter all the way home from Belgium. Believe me, these people who want it are no fools and are very dangerous. He had every right to feel afraid."

Phillips fell silent for a time then added. "And Lloyd said it wasn't the first time that his friend Lucas had made out his part in things was greater than it actually was. He said that another friend of theirs was with Lucas on the Somme last year. It wasn't like he said it was there, either. But he took the credit, took the medal too. Lloyd's friend told the truth to his officer, a man by the name of Hughes."

Oscendale felt his own heart rate quicken as he spoke the words. "But tell me. There's something more, isn't there?"

"Yes, sir," said Phillips morosely. "You see, Lieutenant Newcombe had some visitors just before he died. Lloyd was asked to leave the ward while they talked. They said it was secret military business. When he returned the lieutenant was dead and the visitors had gone."

"How many of them were there?" asked Oscendale.

"Two, sir. Grim-looking men, Lloyd said."

"And did they give Lloyd their names?" asked Oscendale, hardly daring to ask the question. The answer shook him to the core of his being.

"That was the funny thing, sir," replied Phillips. "One said his name was Oscendale."

Oscendale took his leave of the grieving family. He shook hands with Phillips and thanked him for the information he had provided. As he strode down the rutted path that curved around the hill, he recalled the optimism with which he had climbed it. One dead man later he was in possession of the facts he sought but felt hollow, drained by the turn of events. Lloyd Phillips had survived hell on the Western Front only to be killed by an unknown hand. Unknown maybe, but Oscendale felt sure he knew which source had sent the killer out to do his dirty work. He now had to tell Elsie Phillips that the man she loved was dead.

CHAPTER 18

Barry – Sunday, 19th August 1917

THE SECOND POSTCARD was waiting for him when he awoke the following morning. His landlady was her usual whingeing self, greeting his return with a grumble about the state in which he had left his room. Never the tidiest of tenants, preferring to abandon his military orderliness when off-duty, Oscendale had to admit that she did have a point on this occasion, but if he wanted a housekeeper, he would pay for one and he was certainly not happy about her poking around in his room.

Hiding his irritation, he apologised with all the sincerity he could muster and she seemed to accept it, though with this obnoxious woman it was difficult to spot any emotion other than downright surliness in her face. It was the visage of a woman for whom men were the enemy. Oscendale imagined her as a young woman, but found the image too difficult to sustain so he abandoned it as futile. The sooner he was out of these lodgings the better.

She handed him the postcard apathetically. It was another photograph of Romilly Park, this time also showing Park Grove where Susan Maskell had been murdered. On the back was written:

Dear Oscendale,
The game commences.
Loki

He frowned with bemusement. Someone was evidently having more fun at his expense. A macabre joke by Woodfin again? No, somehow this was no longer a joke. This was not Woodfin's playful humour. This was almost a warning, sinister and threatening. He placed the card in his pocket and vowed to examine it more carefully later. For now, there was other work to be done.

Oscendale needed time to think so he took a circuitous route to his destination, which took a good half-an-hour. Entering the police station, he spoke to the sergeant manning the desk and asked if Inspector Woodfin was in. He was told that he had been called to an accident in the town but that Detective Constable Willis was in his office. The sergeant corrected himself and said, "I mean, your old office, sir. That is…"

"It's alright, Streeter," interrupted Oscendale, raising a hand. "I understand." He said as much but in his heart he knew that he resented the presence of the young detective in his office. A part of him was aware that it was a case of time moving on and the office needing to be filled, while another, darker side of him felt that the office should have been mothballed until his return from the war. *The question was, would he return?*

He knocked on his old office door, which gave him a strange and uncomfortable feeling, and waited until he heard a voice calling, "Come in!"

Willis was lounging in his chair with his legs crossed on the desk. When the young man saw the look in Oscendale's eyes he quickly lowered his feet to the floor. Willis knew that this was the second time he had irritated Oscendale in the past twenty-four hours. He stood up and came around the desk towards him, his hand outstretched.

"Morning, sir. Good to see you again. I hope that I may be able to apologise for my remark the other day. No hard feelings, eh?" He smiled genially at Oscendale and tilted his head slightly waiting for his response.

Oscendale was not convinced but was prepared to give the young man another chance. His father had once told him that the man who makes no mistakes makes nothing, so he decided to put Willis's inappropriate comment down to the folly of youth and he shook his hand.

"Inspector Woodfin not here, then?"

"No, sir. A poor chap was run over by a bus in Thompson Street this morning. Soldier on leave apparently. An accident on his way home. Tragic. Inspector Woodfin has gone to identify him, recover his identification tags and that."

Oscendale pondered again the sad irony of warfare and how death was so arbitrary. *It's either got your name on it or it hasn't.*

"What about Susan Maskell's murder? Do we have any more leads on that?"

Willis turned back to his desk and picked up a brown file of papers. He extracted one piece and handed it to Oscendale.

"Well, sir, these are the statements taken by our lads from the neighbours in Park Grove. One of them saw a man at Susan Maskell's door on the morning of the murder."

Oscendale took the statement and began to read it. "Interesting," he said when he had finished. "No further details taken because the copper who took this thought Mrs Geddes an unreliable witness."

"Yes," replied Willis slowly. "Actually, I was just on my way to talk to the lady. Would you care to come along as well, sir?" The young man had mellowed from the brash upstart he had first appeared to be and Oscendale wondered once more whether he had misjudged him. Willis took his bowler hat from the stand near the window and held the door open for Oscendale.

Minnie Geddes was a rotund spinster who announced proudly

to Oscendale and Willis that each afternoon she liked to go into her front bedroom, take a chair across to the large bay window, place her spectacles on the tip of her powdered nose and spend several hours watching the comings and goings of the inhabitants of Park Grove. She knew all her neighbours by name and could give them a potted history of any one of them. She could also furnish them with dates and times of anything they wanted to know, all stored away. "Up here," she stated conceitedly and tapped the side of her head with an arthritic index finger.

She invited them into the front parlour and offered them refreshments, but they soon realised that this was a token gesture only. Having two detectives in her house was far too exciting to allow herself to be distracted by serving tea. She was a woman who would listen briefly to any story she could but would start talking over the speaker if she had a story of her own that was far more interesting, in her opinion. *Listening and speaking at the same time. A remarkable gift,* thought Oscendale.

But she was a treasure house of hearsay. She loved to relate gossip and had an inexhaustible capacity for receiving it. After half-an-hour's frustration, during which Willis became increasingly agitated at her inability to stay focused on the events of the previous Wednesday, Oscendale's patience was rewarded when Mrs Geddes gave him a detailed description and, finally, even the name of the visitor.

"Oh yes, Captain Oscendale. Of course I know who it was. It was Mr Mepham, the minister at All Souls Church on Porthceri Road."

"And how long did he stay, Mrs Geddes?"

The old lady frowned and thought for a while, drawing a permanently crooked finger up to her chin. "I think it was about ten minutes, no longer. It was just before the young lady in number 18 came out of her front door and tripped on the step. She's adopted you know. Taken in by a very nice couple and given a good home. Yes, about ten minutes I would say."

"And what can you tell me about Mr Mepham?" asked Oscendale, leaning closer and giving the old lady his fullest attention.

After bidding many farewells to Mrs Geddes, they eventually made their way up the steep rise of Park Grove.

"Minnie Geddes is an old gossip. Just because she saw this Mepham character enter Susan Maskell's house it doesn't mean he murdered her. After all he's a churchman," said Willis to Oscendale as they reached the top of the hill. "I wonder why he visited her though?"

Oscendale shrugged. "It could be any one of a number of reasons. Mrs Geddes mentioned that Susan Maskell was a member of his church, as is she, so it's possible it was just church business. He was only there for ten minutes, but that's enough time to kill someone."

"Should we pay a visit straightaway to Mr Mepham?" asked Willis.

Oscendale smiled at the young man's naivety.

He was put through to the Records Department within seconds.

"Lieutenant Stonehouse. How may I help you?"

"Morning, Harry. Tom Oscendale again."

"Well, blow me down. Two enquiries in just a few days. You're keeping me busy."

"Indeed. Listen, Harry, have you a file for one Archibald Mepham? I believe he was a regimental chaplain sometime in the last five years. Not sure which regiment though."

"Hmm. Pretty vague, Tom. I'll look into it and ring you back."

Oscendale drummed his fingers impatiently to the rhythm of the clock ticking on the wall and waited for the phone to ring. The call came back about twenty minutes later. "Interesting fellow, your Reverend Mepham," said Stonehouse. "Quite a thick file on him. Unusual for a chaplain."

Oscendale smiled at the other end of the phone. This was exactly what he had hoped for. Minnie Geddes might be a gossip but there was nothing wrong with her memory, despite what Willis thought.

"Why did he leave the army? Does it say?"

There was a pause as Stonehouse flicked through the file some two hundred miles away. Oscendale could picture the scene in his mind: drab military office, orderly piles of paperwork.

"Hmmm," said Stonehouse at last. "He was rather fonder of the ladies than he should have been, him being a chaplain and all. Allegedly made advances towards a fellow officer's wife. Dishonourable discharge in fact. Contested it but the CO insisted he leave the regiment."

"Thanks, Harry. Just what I wanted."

CHAPTER 19

Barry – Sunday, 19th August 1917

Archibald Mepham, the latest in a short line of ministers at All Souls Church, displayed his best non-committal, pious face when he opened the door to a military policeman and a detective. It appeared that not many things in life threw the Reverend Mepham, and policemen were obviously not one of them. He bade them enter, offered tea, he having just started his mid-morning intake, and asked them how he might be of service.

He was the very embodiment of middle-class respectability. Seated in a cosy armchair, he sipped from a pure white bone china teacup, delicately dabbing his mouth with a linen napkin after each mouthful, while his dormouse of a wife scuttled from Willis to Oscendale, refilling their cups with quiet efficiency from the silver teapot, as if in an attempt to delay the questioning that was evidently to come.

Oscendale declined the peace offerings of fancy biscuits, while Willis made up for a missed breakfast by consuming several ginger nuts and a slice of Mrs Mepham's Victoria sponge cake.

"How well did you know Susan Maskell?" Willis asked Mepham while dunking a ginger nut biscuit and dropping numerous crumbs onto his lap.

Mepham replied that Mrs Maskell and her husband, prior to his being posted overseas, had been valued members of his church and Bible class, and that her untimely death had left an irreplaceable gap in the church community. The congregation was devastated. It would take a long time for the pain of Mrs

Maskell's dreadful demise to pass but the Lord would give them strength to carry on.

He was unflappable, so after Willis had tried several other angles around the same question, Oscendale indicated that he would like to ask a question of his own, irritated both with Mepham for his obsequiousness and with Willis for speaking with his mouth full.

"I believe you served in India, sir, with the army, prior to settling for civilian life."

Mepham's eyes narrowed a fraction but his response was cool and neutral. "That is correct, Captain Oscendale. Nesta and I were in India for five years."

"And why did you leave the army, sir?" he pressed. He noticed that Mrs Mepham was fiddling nervously with her pearl necklace. To his surprise she answered before her husband could. Her teacup was replaced on its saucer less than delicately and, for the first time since they had been seated, she spoke about a subject other than tea and biscuits.

"It was a beastly business. Jealousy, that's what it was. People were jealous of Archie's success. He was very popular with the troops and some of the other officers resented it so they fabricated a ghastly story about him. It was really most unfair. Yes, a beastly business."

"There, there, Nesta, forget all that," soothed Mepham. "It's all over now. It's true, Captain Oscendale. I was forced out by vicious tongues and spiteful lies. We had no option other than to come home and start again. But I did nothing wrong, I can assure you. *If I regard iniquity in my heart, the Lord will not hear me.*"

"I see," he said. "And why did you visit Susan Maskell at home on the day she died, sir?"

It was there, he felt sure. Just a slight hesitation and the way an unsettled Mrs Mepham stole a furtive look at her husband,

116

as if old skeletons were rattling their bones in the closet. *Or cloisters*, thought Oscendale.

"It was parish business, Captain Oscendale. Private business between the late Mrs Maskell and myself. I see no need to relate it here." He smiled.

Willis, finally sated with ginger nuts and tea, pounced. "Ah well, you see everything is relevant to a murder investigation, Mr Mepham. I suggest you answer the question properly, otherwise we might have to continue this conversation another time at another venue."

Mrs Mepham interjected again. "It was my suggestion, Mr Willis. Susan had offered to bake some war cakes, as we call them. Our church members are working tirelessly, fundraising for the war effort in a variety of ways. Archie was out and about that morning so I asked him to call in and remind her. Nothing wrong with that is there?"

"And what time was this, sir?" asked Oscendale.

"About ten o'clock wasn't it, dear?" replied Mepham, saved, his jovial face beaming at the two men.

"Yes, that's about right. But she didn't answer the door, did she?" confirmed Mrs Mepham smiling in support of her dear husband but Oscendale had noted the glistening moisture appearing above her upper lip.

He would make no progress even if he stayed until Judgement Day, so after a while he and Willis allowed themselves to be shown to the door where Mepham wished them well with their investigation.

"Dreadful, simply dreadful. And such a nice lady too. Ah well, such is life. And death of course."

"Did you see the way she stuck up for him, sir? She supported him every step of the way. She knew what he was up to in India as well, I bet. Why are some women like that?" asked Willis when they were outside on the pavement. "They just put up with all sorts of nonsense from their husbands. She's the forgiving type. He probably gave her a sermon on forgiveness anyway!"

"I don't know," replied Oscendale. "All the same, I think we'll pay him another visit later, at the church perhaps, when his guardian angel is not around." He glanced at his wristwatch. "But I have another appointment. Tell Inspector Woodfin I'll call in to see him later."

He had been counting the hours to the time when he hoped that Hannah Graham would be true to her word and visit the park again. She had been invading his thoughts, distracting him from his work. Oscendale sat and waited on the same bench that they had shared just a few days before. It was overcast and his mood shared the colour of the day. He checked his watch yet again. Perhaps she would not turn up. He was surprised at how lonely he felt at the thought, when a recognisable voice quietly shook him out of his malaise "Hello again, Captain."

He looked up at her. She had appeared wraith-like, out of nowhere. The gloom was brightened, though the widow's clothes reminded him once more of her present position. He sprang up from the bench and touched the peak of his cap. "Good afternoon, Mrs Graham. I'm so glad you came."

"Did you think I would not, Captain?" Had he taken a step too far, too quickly? He noticed a slight smile at the corners of her lips. She was teasing him.

Oscendale suddenly felt calmer and his mood lifted. He put the terrible, horrifying thoughts that tormented him away in a cupboard in his mind. For a short time, at least.

As the clouds predicted, it began to drizzle. Fine and gentle, the summer rain fell on them, lightly tapping their hats as they hurried to reach the cover of the green shelter where others had gathered too. She smiled encouragingly as he awkwardly asked her if she would like to go to the cinema instead. It was somewhere less conspicuous. He was becoming sensitive about the appropriateness of his feelings towards her. *Lusting after a dead officer's wife.*

They hired a brake to the grandly-named Phoenix Palace in Broad Street. He had always wondered which member of the royal family had deigned to visit this place of entertainment with its mock Corinthian pillars and could only conclude that it was a symbol of a town reaching out and above itself. *Nothing wrong with that,* he thought. After all, what would his late father have made of his son's success?

On the hoarding was displayed the title of a new film: *The Battle of the Ancre and Advance of the Tanks.* Oscendale had seen *The Battle of the Somme* in the same cinema the previous year. He was curious to see what story the latest film told but did not think that this was of interest to Hannah and was prepared to walk away when, to his surprise, she walked into the foyer, turned to him and beckoned him in. He pondered for a moment and asked if she was sure. She replied that she thought it right that she should see what he and her late husband had been forced to endure.

He spoke to the large woman who was impossibly squeezed into the ticket booth and asked for two circle seats. They entered the dimly-lit auditorium which was packed with curious customers anxious for the film to start. An usher guided them to a row containing two empty seats, along which they manoeuvred with difficulty, stepping on toes and issuing several apologies. Seated at last, the lights went down as the velvet curtains separated to expose the screen and the organist sat poised ready to heighten the real-life drama that was about to unfold before them.

They passed the next sixty minutes in silence while all around them the audience responded with exclamations and sobs as the dreadful events of the film unfolded.

He made no attempt to speak to her as the images rolled by: the mud, the shells, the dead bodies. She squeezed his arm on several occasions as if signalling her connection with his alien world. But what he saw on the film was remote, detached. Thankfully, there was no sound so she could not experience the screams of the shells or the inglorious cries of the wounded. She could not smell the stench of rotting flesh and chloride of lime, mixed with cordite and cooking. The film could capture and display none of these. And not a rat was to be seen, not a louse to be scratched at, even though the trenches were infested with vermin and disease. It was his world but it was something else too. It was a window pane to the battlefields but the comfort of the cinema meant that the window between the viewer and the reality of life on the Western Front was always closed. When the house lights came back on at the end they stood for the national anthem, then sat still, waiting for other people to leave. In all this horror, a part of him was glad that there was so much more that was missing.

The knock on his bedroom door had an urgency about it. Oscendale put aside Newcombe's letter, which he had been re-reading, and rose from the iron bedstead. The room was warm, despite the open window. He walked to the door in his bare feet and opened it.

Corrick Woodfin stood there, a black hat in his hands. His face was puce and his breathing was laboured, as if he had run the distance to Oscendale's lodgings.

"Tom, you're not going to believe this. There's been another murder."

"What?" replied Oscendale frowning uneasily.

"Yes. Soldier's wife again. Same cause of death. Face burned right off this time." He lowered his eyes and shook his head sadly. "It's horrific, unbelievable."

Oscendale was shocked. So his initial thoughts had been wrong. He had assumed that Susan Maskell had been murdered because of her husband's link with Edmund Lucas. However, if this was another killing of a soldier's wife it was just possible that he and Woodfin now had a multiple killer to deal with, or was there a connection between this latest dead woman and Lucas?

"And there's a link to Susan Maskell. They were both members of All Souls Church," added Woodfin, as if reading his thoughts.

"Give me a few minutes and I'll meet you downstairs," said Oscendale. He stretched to ease the stiffness in his back and cursed the less than comfortable mattress.

On their way to the terraced house in Cannon Street, Woodfin related the details to Oscendale.

Jennie Lake's husband had been serving with the Army Service Corps in France until he had died of his wounds a fortnight ago. Ensconced in the ground floor rooms at number seven, she was trying to make ends meet as best she could while working as an office clerk during the week and raising two young children. As a member of All Souls Church she took Sunday School classes each week.

A neighbour had helped her put the children to bed at around 7 p.m. before leaving to tend to her own family. Jennie Lake was next seen at around 8 p.m. when her lifeless body was discovered by a fellow tenant who always called in at that time of the evening for a chat before bedtime. The woman, Dolly O'Hare, had knocked on the door of the sitting room without reply. The door had been slightly ajar so she had entered the room, calling quietly for her neighbour so as not to disturb her sleeping children. She noticed a strange smell in the room that made her feel queasy.

She had found Mrs Lake lying on her unmade bed with her face turned to black jelly, the remnants of a charred gag tied around her mouth. Dolly had clutched at her own throat, almost unable to breathe or swallow, and with tears streaming down her hollow cheeks, she ran screaming hysterically from the room, alerting the whole neighbourhood to her gruesome find.

Oscendale put the blanket back over the face of the victim. "A question, Corrick: was it Mepham or someone working for Edmund Lucas? Because either of them could be involved here."

"I'm still not convinced about Mepham, Tom. Just because you found a scandal in his military record doesn't mean he's going around murdering women and leaving them like this."

"Which brings me to my second question," said Oscendale. "How do we know this is Jennie Lake and how do we know it was Susan Maskell that we saw in Park Grove?"

Woodfin frowned and was silent for a time. "From their clothing and the timings. Jennie Lake didn't leave her house and was seen an hour or so earlier. These are her clothes."

"Who found Susan Maskell's body?"

"Her maid. I told you that when you first came to the scene," replied Woodfin who was slightly annoyed by his friend's questioning.

"No," replied Oscendale. "She saw a dead body. She told me she didn't go too close as she was so terrified."

Was it possible he was playing a game of disguise with his victims? And if so, who was his real target in all of this?

"And look at this, Corrick." Oscendale gestured towards an item on the only table in the room. A small Bible lay open, its almost translucent pages stained by the sweat and dirt of generations of readers.

"A family Bible," replied Woodfin. "Nothing strange in that. It is a Sunday, Tom. Maybe she was reading a passage or two after she had put the nippers to bed. Preparing for next week's Bible class?"

"But it's the passage, Corrick," pressed Oscendale. "Look at it. Underlined like the one in Susan Maskell's bedroom."

Woodfin lifted the tome and began to read. "*So shall the king greatly desire thy beauty: for he is thy Lord; and worship thou him.* Psalm 45. Tom!"

Oscendale's fingers were inside the dead woman's mouth. He withdrew them after a few seconds. "No note this time, just a verse from the Bible again. *So shall the king greatly desire thy beauty.* Did someone find himself rebuffed?" He looked down sadly on the deformed face of the woman. "Possibly someone whom she turned down? Thought she was fair game as her husband was away. Murdered her for that maybe?"

"Seems a bit tenuous, Tom."

"Well I know who my money is on. We need to bring Mepham in for questioning," stated Oscendale confidently. "Now."

CHAPTER 20

Barry – Sunday, 19th August 1917

THE DAMP, MUSKY smell of the interior of the church hit Oscendale as soon as he pushed the door ajar, evoking familiar memories. Oak and old, the huge door presented a formidable barrier, yet when he lifted the black enamelled latch it had yielded easily. He had opened it cautiously.

He and Woodfin had called at the Mephams' home only to be told by the ingratiating Mrs Mepham that her husband was still at the church, tidying up after that evening's service and preparing for next week's Bible class. Woodfin had remarked on the lateness of the hour, but Mrs Mepham, her face a picture of religious honesty and trust, had responded that God's work did not have set hours. *Sanctified and sanctimonious.*

Oscendale's military boots tapped on the uneven flagstone floor, the clicks echoing around the church. A high, vaulted ceiling rose above his head and long, stained glass windows displayed saints and martyrs kneeling in the act of penitence. The late evening sunlight streamed through the panes, throwing a myriad of colours all around. As he walked through the changing hues, he caught sight of the effect on his khaki uniform until he entered the blood-red light which soaked right through him.

He shook off the thought and checked the aisles. Seeing no-one, he returned to the doorway and waved to Woodfin.

"Doesn't feel right, carrying a loaded gun into a place like this," Woodfin muttered, looking at Oscendale's drawn Webley revolver.

"You're right. I very much doubt Mepham will be armed. Old habits dying hard, I'm afraid. But this man *is* the killer," he said with conviction. He returned his revolver to its well-worn, brown leather holster.

"Look, Tom, if it is Mepham, and I'm still not convinced, he only preys on defenceless women and a gun isn't his choice of weapon anyway," added Woodfin and Oscendale looked at him without speaking as the anger rose within him again. *Defenceless women.* Woodfin was right. *This man was not just a killer but a coward. It was time to make him pay.*

The two men separated, Oscendale motioning Woodfin to the far side of the church while he advanced towards the nave, past the plaques, dying flowers and memorials to past worshippers.

The man was in here somewhere; he had seen him come out of the main door a few minutes ago and then go back inside, as if he had forgotten something. There had been nothing in his movements that suggested he knew that he was being followed. But now he had disappeared.

A door to one side of the choir stalls stood slightly ajar. Had it moved just then or were his senses playing tricks on him?

There was a moment of stillness and anticipation when time seemed to close in upon itself. Then it happened. A flame burst from the direction of the choir stalls and a deafening roar reverberated around the church. He heard Woodfin cry out and fall heavily to the floor.

"Woodfin!" The gun rang out again and a heavy bullet ran through the wood of the pew not far from where Woodfin had fallen, sending rippling echoes all around the walls.

From behind the cover of one of the carved stone pillars that flanked the pews, Oscendale slid quietly to the floor and tried to engineer a position where he could see the doorway from beneath the pew. It was impossible so he began a retreat back along the aisle, taking out his revolver as he did so. He reached the rear of the church and skirted round the edges of the rows of pews towards the stricken policeman.

Woodfin was groaning and trying to stem the flow of blood from his calf. Glancing quickly around for any signs of movement from the choir stalls, Oscendale took off his tie and soon had an improvised dressing wrapped around Woodfin's leg. The wound was not as serious as he had first thought; the injury had been caused by the splintered wood and not by a bullet. Woodfin gasped, "You were right. There's evil here today, Tom. Be careful, my friend."

Oscendale crept quietly to the edge of the choir stall and looked along the row to see an arched doorway where the shots had come from; the door was closed. He approached it cautiously, twisted the wrought iron handle quickly before springing back to one side, then, hearing nothing inside and seeing the door swing open, he threw himself on the floor and fired two random shots into the void.

Nothing.

Silence.

He crouched. *Ah well, Tommy Boy*, he thought to himself, *it's now or never. Just keep your finger on that trigger. If he gets you at least you can send one back his way.*

And he went through the door that led down to the depths beneath the church.

The church crypt was in complete darkness. The dank, eerie, blackness seeped into him, enveloping him like sin itself. His eyes were useless – he might as well be blind. But was he alone in here?

He kept his breathing low and shallow, Oscendale was convinced that a quarry could always hear the hunter breathing. Mepham was in here somewhere, entombed in the eerie, shadowless void. He could be twenty yards away or just beside him. Oscendale listened intently but could hear nothing. If he stepped forward he might walk straight into him. The seconds passed and still no sound.

Then something stirred in the room, so close that a slight movement of air touched his right cheek. Breathing! Faint but recognisable. A man walking very slowly close by. But which direction? Oscendale raised his Webley and stretched his arm out in front of him. As he did so it touched someone.

There was a slight rustling of clothing followed by a loud explosion in front of him. A blinding light and the acrid smell of smoke, then the darkness rolled in again. Oscendale moved quickly and lowered himself quietly to the floor. If Mepham fired again it would be high and this time Oscendale would be able to see the direction the shot had come from without being blinded by the muzzle flash.

But there was no second shot. Instead he heard the sound of footsteps then a clang as a door latch was lifted. To his left he saw the illuminated rectangle of a door opening and a silhouette move through it. Mepham did not look back but slammed the door shut with a thud, its ironwork clattering behind him. Seconds later Oscendale opened it a fraction and poked the barrel of his Webley through the gap.

Blinking away the dazzling flashes of light beyond, he inched the creaking hinges wider and swept both sides of the corridor with his pistol. There was no sign of Mepham. Cautiously, Oscendale stepped out, his pistol barrel pointing up a set of stone stairs that led to another floor.

He heard footsteps running across the wooden floor above his head and using the handrails at the side of the stairs he vaulted up them two at a time.

He found himself in the vestry staring at the array of white, black and purple robes. An oak cupboard stood in a corner and mounds of dog-eared hymn books had been stacked neatly on an old table. He turned to look for a way out when suddenly, a voice rang out behind him, cold and chilling in the thin air as Mepham stepped out of the cupboard.

"Stand completely still, Captain Oscendale. I have my army revolver pointing at your back and if you turn around I will shoot you. Do you understand?" The tone was measured, clipped.

Oscendale complied. He shifted his weight onto his right foot and leaned his right shoulder ever so slightly forward.

"Thank you. Now please drop your revolver to the floor."

Oscendale moved his right arm as if to comply but then threw his weight down and to his right. As he fell, he twisted his body, brought up his revolver and fired.

Mepham was stunned. He looked down and in disbelief muttered, "The sins of my soul and body, forgive…" But there was a red circle of blood growing on his chest where his hand rested. He felt cold, then hot, then cold again. The walls of the dingy little vestry began to spin. The floor became the ceiling and he tumbled forward onto the ground.

Oscendale stood up and stepped towards him, his revolver outstretched in case another shot was required. Oscendale noticed that his lips were still moving; he stood over him and crouched down to catch the inaudible whisper.

"Wo… kill more, I…"

"What?" snapped Oscendale, full of loathing.

"I… would… kill…" But that was all. Mepham's head lolled to the side and his lips ceased to move.

"So how were you so sure it was him? You know I was never convinced," said Woodfin, grimacing as Oscendale lifted him to his feet.

"Mepham had to be the link. His two-faced religious piety came across when I first met him and what better way to meet lonely women looking for solace than at a Bible class? It's a smaller, more intimate group. Much better to get to know someone, to get closer to them."

"Susan Maskell probably appreciated his tender ministrations but Mepham saw them as something else," added Woodfin.

"Yes. So when he went to her house to take advantage of what he thought was encouragement and she rejected him, he lost his temper," replied Oscendale. "All his frustrations with what happened in India probably came out and he murdered her."

"Well, she was an attractive woman by all accounts so he decided to remove the one thing that had attracted him – her face. He burnt it off." Woodfin winced in reply

"That's right. Jennie Lake the same. He gagged her to stop her screaming being heard by her children and neighbours," continued Oscendale. "By this time he probably had a taste for seeing a woman suffer. Wanted to see her in agony as her face burnt. He left the Bibles open as a reminder to others. He added a message in his first victim's mouth but probably didn't have time to do anything similar to Jennie Lake. Remember, there were other people in the house at the time."

He paused as Woodfin grimaced with the pain in his leg. "Keep your chin up, Corrick. I'll soon have you in the hands of the Red Cross where you can join another great wounded hero I met recently, so if you can hang on a bit, I'd be much obliged. A corpse is that much heavier to carry." He winked at Woodfin and together they made their way out of the church.

CHAPTER 21

Barry – Monday, 20th August 1917

THE SAME RECURRING images appeared to her on this warm August night as she lay in bed, sleep proving elusive.

She had been eighteen years of age. Her mother, so ambitious for her eldest daughter, had been anxious for her to look her best for the visit Hannah Williams was to make.

James Graham. Handsome James Graham whom she had met while paying in the day's takings at the bank. She had been drawn to this smartly dressed and polite young man from the moment she had first seen him. She became more than willing to undertake this chore every day, even waiting in the longest queue just to be served by him. They would make polite conversation while he counted the money she passed across the counter, noting the amount of each coinage in a meticulous hand in a large, leather-bound ledger.

And then the roles had been reversed. He had become a regular customer at her parents' general provisions store and their paths quickly intertwined. He had stared repeatedly at Hannah, making it perfectly obvious he would also wait his turn to be served by her, even if there was another assistant available. Their fingers had touched and lingered, momentarily locked together as he had passed the money for his purchases to her. The warmth of one human being touching another.

He had done all the right things in the proper manner. The courtship was progressing well and her family had been delighted to receive an invitation to meet his parents. After all, his father was the bank manager and his job had served the family very well, living as they did in an imposing villa on Porthceri Road.

Her mother was fussing about the new summer outfit to which she was just adding the final touches. The frilly, white, high-necked voile blouse with tiny blue and pale green embroidered flowers suited Hannah's perfect figure. It draped softly down to the pale blue silk sash that encircled her tiny waist. The full skirt had been trimmed here and there with the same blue and green flowers. Her mother and her younger sister Alice remarked that she looked wonderful.

Alice sat at the table, drawing with her coloured pencils. And for a moment Hannah saw the three ages of woman: her younger sister with all her innocence, more interested in colours, shapes and lines; her mother, tired and irritable after a day's work in the shop, all her ambitions now transferred from herself onto her daughter; and she, Hannah, being dressed, gift wrapped. *Available for purchase.*

She recalled how she had felt: anxious, excited and nervous. This was such a significant moment in her life. James Graham had shown an interest in her and now she had to make sure that his mother approved of her suitability as a prospective wife.

It had all gone so well. Two years later they had been married and she had become the new Mrs Graham. She had everything she was supposed to want: an affluent husband, a new life in a large, beautifully furnished house, albeit her in-laws' home, and a social standing higher than anyone in her family had ever known.

James had been attentive at first, loving even, but then the fissures had grown. First the silences, then the absences, as he spent more and more time at his work and was promoted to a higher position in the bank, leaving her to play the role of devoted wife.

But not that of a mother. There had been no children to complete the increasingly shallow idyll. Mrs Graham had repeatedly asked politely when she could expect to be a grandmother, asking Hannah if there were any *developments*. She had felt a failure, a disappointment. *Abandoned.*

When the war came, James had been one of the first to enlist. His father had remonstrated with him that he could not run the bank alone, but James had insisted he would join up. It was time for him to leave everything behind. Even Hannah.

He had paraded before his family, dressed in his brand new officer's uniform, looking striking and self-assured. Off he had gone to war, a vision of well-tailored manliness in khaki and leather.

And now he was gone. Forever. Dead. Lying somewhere in France or Flanders. She was alone. Alone in a house inhabited by two other people who were nothing but strangers to her. The doors of communication, closed long ago, were now locked with the key of grief.

Mr and Mrs Graham had been sympathetic to her distress but they had their own emotions to deal with. His father had shut himself in his study and his wife often joined him there. Hannah could hear them talking as she passed the closed door but she knew better than to intrude. James was their son; she was merely his wife.

But now she had met someone else. This man Oscendale intrigued her and she found that James's memory had begun to fade as she thought about the shy, awkward captain who had been so attentive on the two occasions they had met.

There was something more. She knew that she needed love, wanted a man to fulfil her needs and desires. James had no longer wanted her after those first few months. His desire for her had become a routine with one end in mind. She wanted more. *She wanted to fill the void that she felt inside.*

She got up and walked to her dressing table. After pouring water from a jug into a large china bowl, she dipped her hands in the water, running the cooling liquid over her face and neck. The touch of her own fingers made her skin tingle and she looked in the mirror at her reflection.

It was time to think about herself. Over these past twelve years she had become the very model of middle-class respectability and duty. But now she wanted something else. Someone else.

The screaming of a seagull woke Oscendale before dawn. Beginning as a repetitive series of staccato sneers, the sound was so akin to that of a machine gun that he awoke startled, his pulse racing. More gulls joined in with the lone bird and soon a cacophony of screaming and screeching filled his room. He pulled a pillow angrily over his head but the din still penetrated and he knew as his mind began to work and his temper grew that sleep was over for the night.

He turned to lie on his back and stared at the curtains: thin and faded, through which sunlight began to intrude, lapping away at the vestiges of sleep. He rubbed his eyes and watched the floaters in them dance and dart across the rays of light.

Sighing and muttering to himself, he got up and washed with the stale water he poured from a chipped jug perched apologetically on a chest of drawers. He dressed then made his bed, for once obeying his military training. *Routines.*

He tramped heavily down the steep stairs and out through the front door, closing it noisily behind him.

The early morning was a wonderful time. At least it was here, far from the noise of battle, and he soon began to feel calmer. He strolled along the tree-lined street, occasionally softly whistling no particular tune as he went, without the faintest idea of where he was going. He needed time to think, to explore the possibilities and probabilities of this latest series of events.

His walk took him to Cold Knap beach, a spot with bittersweet memories, yet it had been one of his favourite places many years ago. At least until a boyhood friend had drowned in a bathing accident in the sandy waters known for their dangerous undercurrents. The boy had been swept out to sea by the strong, swirling waters that lurked just off the coast and Oscendale had stopped coming here as often from that day onwards. The youngster's time had come sooner than it should have done. And others he had known had now joined him. The carnage going on across the Channel was seeing to that. He quietly whispered the boy's name in memory and added a eulogy. *You were a good friend.*

The sun was breaking through the indigo sky over Steep Holm, that featureless lump of black rock set in the Bristol Channel, and Oscendale pictured the same sun rising for the men in the trenches in France and Flanders that morning. For some it would be the last dawn they would admire. Men on both sides would die during another day of the latest, greatest offensive. But the beauty of nature's palette arising from its night's sleep took his thoughts from the death across the Channel to the glory of the new dawn.

Pools of scarlet formed and then dissipated as the water swirled and surged into the shoreline in the early light. A vast vermillion tear, a gateway to another world, had been ripped in the sky, as if by an invisible hand. New and bright, the sun began to emerge from its slumber, cutting great slashes into the dark night sky, urging it onwards and away.

He felt almost pagan sat here on the pebbles banked up in tiers on the ruby-red shore, gazing at its majesty, at one with the seasons and the timings of day and night.

A lone gull circled overhead, mocking him each time it opened its beak. Then a movement in the distance caught his eye and he watched as a solitary figure dressed in black walked slowly towards him. Given the distance, it was hard to make out. Perhaps it was a fisherman out early to catch the high tide.

He turned back to the sea, lapping and flowing gently,

methodically caressing and cleansing the rocks. *Washing his soul clean.*

And the figure drew closer. It was a woman. Oscendale frowned. A lone woman walking along the seafront at barely six o'clock in the morning? *Very unusual.*

But then he recognised her. It was Hannah. His curiosity grew as she came nearer. She saw him looking at her and waved. Puzzled, he raised his hand to wave back. A thousand thoughts flew back and forth in his head. Had she come here seeking him? Was she troubled or was this an impetuous venture on her part? And how did she know he was here? Perhaps it was just a coincidence, another link in the chain between them.

He stood up and dusted the white powder of the pebbles from his uniform.

"Good morning, Captain Oscendale." Slightly breathless, she greeted him with mock formality and smiled at him, her pale skin marble-like in the early dawn.

"Mrs Graham," he replied, doffing his cap. "Well, good morning to you." There was a look of expectancy on her face so Oscendale matched her mood and asked, "May I have the pleasure of an early morning stroll in your company?" He offered her his elbow. She slipped her arm though his and they began to walk.

"I saw you wandering through the park from my window and hoped – thought – I might find you here. I don't sleep too well," she said, as if answering his thoughts. "I'm usually up with the lark these days. Such a beautiful sunrise don't you think?"

He agreed. They stopped and watched the depth of colours and breathed in the salt air. After a while she spoke about the film they had seen yesterday; the time had not been right for it on their walk home. It was too close, too raw and they had avoided the subject by talking of other things.

The subject led on to her late husband. It was a moment

Oscendale had dreaded. He knew they would have to discuss it sooner or later but he had been happy to postpone the moment. It was awkward and embarrassing. It was also painful for him to think of her in love with another man. *In another man's bed.*

He could not conceal his surprise at her next statement as she clenched his arm.

"You see, Thomas, we… well, we had an understanding. I was not the woman James really wanted to marry but it was mutually convenient and it turned out to be more of a successful business deal between our parents. He gave me a home and now he had a wife. But he loved someone else. Someone he couldn't marry. I found that out later. Our parents came to an agreement and an arrangement was made. We were just pawns. Oh, it was so romantic at first but it soon became clear he was never going to love me. It didn't turn out the way it had started. He was kind but not loving. Have you any idea how lonely that can be? To have someone so close but so far away?"

They sat on a bench, a little apart. She stared out at the sea and he watched her, transfixed, the glow of the morning sun adding depth and colour to her perfect complexion.

Her hand came down upon his. Neither of them moved again or spoke for a time. It was that defining moment between a man and a woman. One of them had broken down the wall, had turned thoughts to deeds without the words as a signpost. It was the moment he had longed for, and yet one surrounded by taboo. She was an officer's widow, in mourning. *And only recently widowed too.*

How could he resist? Her profile was captivating and so beautiful. Her mouth was slightly apart, breathing in the freshness of the dawn air. She turned her head towards him, her eyes searching his mouth, her full pink lips parted further, soft and inviting. He lifted his left hand to her face and caressed her cheek, drawing a line with his finger from her brow to her jaw.

Her eyes closed as he moved his face towards hers, hesitating as he did so.

He watched her as he drew closer. Their lips met, warm and moist in the cold air, and he was gone. Gone from the horrors of his life, the death and the misery, the problems and the uncertainty. All that mattered was being with this woman.

They kissed lovingly, slowly, until at last they gently and hesitatingly pulled apart. Their eyes opened and she smiled, raising her face to his and willing him nearer. Her hands cupped the back of his neck and drew him to her once more, urging him closer. He kissed her again, this time with a passion that swept away all sense of reason.

They were both bathed in yellow light. He drew back. At last he spoke. "Hannah, this is… this is something I want but…"

She reached out a hand and touched his mouth. "Thomas, I know. But sometimes common sense makes no sense." He stroked her neck, loving the feel of her skin. He began to gently kiss her throat, moving across the hollow of her neck to her ear. "Thomas," she whispered, the longing pulsing through her.

They stood up together, listening to the noise of the waves against the pebbles, rumbling them up and down the slope of the beach. "Can you hear the sound of the sea breathing?" she said. He could feel her warm breath against his cheek as she nuzzled up to him.

To Oscendale there was something else, something that would not go away despite the way he felt at this moment. And he hated himself for it and he hated the war for it. A line of infantrymen breaking in assault on the Germans on their high ground, the rifles and shells driving them back. The discordant sound was the roar of battle, the crash of the guns and the thump of the shells. The calls of the gulls above were the screams of men dying in agony. Even the light breeze that blew past their ears became the sound of machine guns bullets zipping past his head.

"The seventh wave, Thomas. Look!" She pointed as a wave, greater and more powerful than the rest crashed down onto the beach, smashing the pebbles together, shattering them like human bones.

He tried to dispel the thoughts that were plaguing him. How could he think like this? The last few minutes had been exquisite and yet there it was – the damned war filling his head again.

She sensed something was wrong and pulled away from him. "What is it? You're quiet."

He turned to her, her face lovely in the morning sun. He pulled her to him and kissed her full on the mouth, seeking the escape that only she could provide. This would wipe away everything.

They realised that they were too public here. Even given the earliness of the hour, there were people starting to go about their daily business. A short, stout fisherman was crunching his way along the beach, looking for exactly the right spot to set up his camp for the day. A cyclist wrapped up well and wearing a scarf wound around his neck, shoulders hunched and cap drawn down against the early morning chill, was awkwardly weaving his way along the seafront, his bicycle heading one way while his head was positioned as if it were locked permanently to his right, entranced by the sunrise.

As he passed them he touched his cap and called out, "Morning, young lovers!"

Oscendale intended to take Hannah home, when the first drops of rain began to tap out their rhythm. They both saw an ominous black cloud spreading over the sky. He noticed that she had no umbrella so he removed his overcoat and wrapped it around her. She came willingly into his arms. They hurried along the seafront and made their way around to the Old Harbour on the other side of the promontory that jutted out into the Bristol Channel. The rain was falling relentlessly, the taps had become prods and he knew they had to find shelter soon.

Nestled into the corner of the beach, partly obscured by dense vegetation, he saw the stone watchtower. Rugged and weather-beaten, the solid structure sat at the highest point of the beach, perched on rocks where it had gazed out at the boats and ships that had entered and left the port for decades. Built like a miniature medieval castle, it was a two-storey building with a horizontal roof. A window overlooked the silted-up harbour and beyond to the immense stone breakwater jutting out from Barry Island, then to the sea, testimony to its former use as a lookout post for approaching ships. Beneath its stoic gaze lay the wrecks of two wooden ships, their ribs poking up out of the mud and sand. Oscendale mused that the watchtower's inhabitants had failed in their duties sometime in the past.

He knew it would be empty; the growth of Barry Docks at the turn of the century meant that it was now redundant. The seagoing craft had gone elsewhere and time had moved on. He pointed and they hurried towards it, his overcoat drawn over her head. The door was locked but not secure; the hasp was rusted and brittle so he easily flicked it apart with his jack-knife.

They were inside, out of the rain and alone. The solitary window gave some light into the room and a view across the Bristol Channel where the sun shone on the patchwork of fields across the water. *England. Raining here and sunny over there. How could that be? Sunshine and darkness. Peace and war.*

She touched his strong, firm hand and raised it to her mouth, softly kissing the fingers one by one and then his palm. Outside the rain still fell, heavier now, and a single bolt of lightning flashed across the headland opposite. A few seconds later thunder rumbled in the distance and he drew her closer to him and stroked her hair. She discarded his overcoat and laid it on the floor, pulling him towards her. He kissed her again. Was there anything better than this? Their eyes met and they knew their destiny.

They lay together for some time afterwards, wanting nothing more than to stay close to one another, lost in their innermost thoughts until she shivered in his arms. "Cold? Come closer." He spoke in a voice that cracked with emotion. He held her tightly. She felt safe. Wanted. Loved. Just their rhythmic breathing and the melodious sound of the sea filled the room.

When Oscendale opened his eyes, he saw Hannah was standing at the window. As she turned she was silhouetted in the sunlight that streamed into the building and he was transfixed by how beautiful she looked. It was a moment he wanted to hold forever yet the rain had stopped and they knew it was time to leave.

The air was damp outside, the last of the rain clouds moving away over the sea. They strolled hand-in-hand down to the beach, the dark sand still full of water from the receding tide. Hannah impulsively removed her shoes, lifted her dress and stepped onto the glistening metallic sheen – purple, azure and yellow – shining brightly in the newborn sunlight.

She squealed suddenly as one foot began to disappear into the brown ooze that lay below the surface. "Thomas, help me, please!" He laughed and placed his arms around her waist, feeling the firmness of her body, and lifted her clear of the mud. Her feet were now dark brown so he guided her to a pool of water and watched as she ran her hand over her feet and ankles, washing the mud from her skin, absolute silence between them. They had reached that stage already where thoughts were passed between them without words interfering.

But he inwardly cursed himself as his thoughts again went back to other mud on other bodies. *Would it never go away?*

CHAPTER 22

London – Tuesday, 21st August 1917

A FELLOW PASSENGER sneezed loudly and he awoke with a start. For a moment or two he was in that place between sleep and consciousness where dreams and reality mix and the distinction is worryingly unclear. His heart beat furiously, gaining momentum, and his head swam in murky whirlpools while he tried to focus on the present, the here and now. The journal in which he had been writing was on the floor, splayed open, his thoughts exposed for anyone to read. He hurriedly picked it up, his mouth bitter with the staleness of sleep.

Oscendale looked out of the carriage window, its griminess almost obscuring his view of the world outside and he tried to place where he was. Watching the brown waters of the Bristol Channel flow past, his feelings became more melancholic. This first part of the journey back to France was always the most difficult. The further he travelled from his home town, the more he altered. The whole event was a process of loss. Each mile of the long journey saw him losing and gaining something along the way, becoming someone else. A man apart.

Was he less of a man for it? He certainly felt different. This time he had been cleansed, refreshed and renewed. As the weak sun disappeared behind each grey-black cloud and re-emerged a few minutes later, he realised a part of him had changed. He now possessed once more his humanity, his soul – even his conscience – and it had been some time since he had felt like this.

How precious those moments with Hannah Graham had been! He felt again that awareness of the world, even of himself, that he had last experienced many months ago. Years, even. At last there was hope at the end of the horror. If he could live through it, survive, there was a part of him that could be saved, be revived by this.

The opaque clouds that had lingered too long eventually gave way to more broken pockets of sunshine and his spirits soared for a time. He promised himself that he would return soon to see her again. But Hannah was gone for the present, each passing mile putting more and more distance between them, and he was alone – on his way back to the carnage.

But there were more pressing matters to attend to that fed the other hunger in his soul.

The train continued on its rumbling journey and as he began to read the notes he had started making, he realised that what he was considering doing was highly dangerous. But he had no choice this time. It had to be done.

Oscendale had never got used to the hustle and bustle of London. He had visited the great city several times since his enlistment. Another opportunity that joining the vast apparatus of the British Army had presented to him, he mused as he alighted at Paddington Station. Before the war started he had not travelled further than the west of England.

It was not the noise of the sprawling, dirty mass of the capital city; he was used to that from working the docks area in Barry. The din as the workers loaded and unloaded the dozens of ships that crowded into the Welsh port was not something for the faint-hearted. No, London was a far busier place than his hometown could ever be, despite its aspirations. Here on the streets, horses, carriages, motor vehicles, trams and pedestrians all made their way at speed to important rendezvous of some kind or another. It all took some getting used to. It was soulless, impersonal, a gigantic human machine.

The night attempted to close in on the citizens who hurried

142

along the streets and they appeared to him to be lonely figures, each intent on a race against an invisible clock. He felt uncomfortable, another isolated figure among so many.

Oscendale then became aware of another sound merging with the hubbub of everyday London life when, from out of the darkness, came a deep droning that gradually increased in intensity. It was a set of powerful engines and he gazed up into the night sky. A black, cigar-shaped object was visible high up in the darkness. *A Zeppelin!* He had read about the menace of the Zeppelins but this was the first one he had ever seen. Its sinister torpedo shape appeared to be a true portent of death.

Then the monotonous, throbbing noise ceased. In its place came only the whistling of the wind. The Zeppelin continued to move, drifting like a huge finger above his head. The engine had stopped. *No, there it was again.* The wind brought back the remorseless rumble as the huge engines drove it onwards, its course plotted by the crew ensconced in the gondola slung beneath its belly.

A bright, searing light came first. Then the shock wave pushed him hard in the chest, the ground moving and rumbling beneath his feet, like some giant animal groaning in pain. The air was knocked from his lungs as he was flung into the wall at the side of the street. With a grunt he fell onto the cobblestones, his breathing harsh and laboured. A hot gust blew on his face and he closed his eyes instinctively to protect them.

A shrill scream, then another, and soon a wailing tide of unremitting noise was all around him. He tried to get his bearings but could think only of his own survival. *Keep breathing, see it out. Get back to normal. Live.*

He inhaled a cloud of dust which immediately dried up his mouth and throat. Spitting out the grit, he fought to inhale fresh air. His throat felt scorched. His body was wracked with coughing and he bent over, falling onto his hands and knees, then crawled forward to some imaginary place of safety, all the time struggling for breath. The minutes passed and there seemed to be no end to the torture.

Looking up at last, as his lungs began to clear themselves and his breathing began to return to normal, he saw that the night sky had altered to crimson red. Fires were burning. The city was burning. People rushed past him, fearful, voices yelling.

And still the screaming came as if shrieking in alarm at what they saw so-called civilised people doing to each other. Bedlam broke loose all around him.

With considerable effort Oscendale levered himself to his feet and steadied himself against a wall. He coughed and spat again as he looked along the road to the source of the light – a fierce red and yellow glow.

The end of the street was ablaze. Anxious silhouettes were gathering outside a burning house. Figures were pointing and buckets of water were being thrown uselessly onto the flames that were consuming the house.

A fire engine, then another, hurtled past along the road, bells sounding furiously, almost hysterically. Firemen leapt from their vehicles to begin their well-practised drill. He watched, mesmerised, as these brave men unfurled the hoses and connected them to water supplies, releasing a powerful jet of water onto the flames.

The Zeppelin was caught in the searchlights of the city's defences as it hovered above, looking demonic in the glow. It was another grisly example of the terrible ends to which the human mind was being put during this ghastly war. An invention that could bring peaceful travel to other countries was now being used to destroy.

His arm was grabbed fiercely and he turned to face an elderly woman, whose crinkled, dirty cheeks were streaked by tears. She looked up at him, imploring him to help.

"Officer, please! There's no one come out of there yet."

The firemen were doing their best but the blaze was out of control, ravaging the building and licking across to the house next door. He stood stupefied. This was outside his experience. The woman pleaded with him, her hand tugging on his arm. For a moment all thought left him and he was unable to move. He should do something heroic like rush into the building and save a life, but the scene was out of his control. The machinery of war had overpowered him like a gigantic wave and he felt crushed, his breathing laboured and noisy.

"Please help me!" The woman shouted again. Still he did nothing. It was as if he was paralysed.

At last he responded. With a feeling of utter frustration and helplessness, his mind almost totally shut down, he shouted, "Quick!" at the woman.

The woman stared at him but now her expression had changed to one of bemusement and then utter incomprehension. Why would this soldier not help her in her time of need? She dropped her hand from his arm, pulled away and shook her head as she stepped backwards and moved off to find someone else who would help her.

The public house across the street had suffered a direct hit. The bomb had travelled through the roof and detonated in the cellar, blowing out the front wall of the building. From the outside, beer barrels could be seen on the remains of the shattered bar. The floor above had collapsed and a bed lay incongruously in the middle of what had been the saloon. Smashed timbers lolled from the ceiling and broken tables and chairs had been hurled out into the street. Oscendale saw an arm poking out from under a pile of dusty rubble. Nearby the pub's piano stood upright, seemingly untouched in the middle of the street.

He slumped to the ground. What was happening to him?

Quite suddenly he was unable to think or act. He pounded his fist into the dust around him in frustration. *Think!* he urged himself. *Help these people!*

But nothing happened. No thoughts or actions came into his head. It was blank. A piece of white paper with no words on it. Closing his eyes and willing himself to think again, his thoughts at last returned to him as his breathing had done. The paralysis had passed and he set off determined, but still feeling sick in the pit of his stomach, towards the burning house to help in any way he could before it was too late.

CHAPTER 23

London – Wednesday, 22nd August 1917

THE FOLLOWING MORNING Oscendale made his way to the Maudsley Hospital on Denmark Hill. He had slept fitfully that night and he was still turning over the sequence of events in his mind, searching for a reason why he had reacted to the bombing raid in the way that he had. He sought for answers but found none and the irrational way he had behaved worried him deeply.

Arriving at the hospital, he passed through its impressive portico and between two columns that stood like sentries guarding the patients within. Opened two years previously, the hospital had been immediately requisitioned by the government for the duration of the war to cope with the surge in casualties from the Front.

He was directed towards the ward that contained the man he sought. Encased in a wheelchair, a disabled soldier with a hideously disfigured face came along the corridor. Oscendale stood aside to let the maimed man pass. He could choose to look away and ignore the man's very existence or he could stare at him, knowing that curiosity would be mistaken for mawkish, guilt-ridden fascination.

He chose a mixture of the two. Glancing quickly at the man's twisted features, he saw defiant eyes staring unblinkingly into his. Oscendale turned away, embarrassed, then felt pulled back to witness first-hand what terrible injuries hot metal could cause. Still the man was staring at him. In that moment the roles were reversed. Who was the more curious? Who was the voyeur of another man's suffering?

The remnants of the man's jaws moved and a sound came forth but it was nothing that Oscendale could recognise.

He said nothing in reply, his awkwardness increasing. The man repeated the same incomprehensible noise. Oscendale leaned closer, assuming proximity was the problem, though in his heart he knew it was not. Clearly frustrated, the man grumbled and angrily spun the wheels of his chair until he was a disappearing figure along the endless corridor.

Oscendale searched the lines of perfectly-made hospital beds until he found the soldier he had come to see. "Hello, Burgess. Good to see you again."

The man tried to block out once more the constant whine in his head by pulling the white linen pillow tightly to his ears but without success. He released his grip, opened his eyes and tried to focus on the figure standing over him.

"I'm sorry," Burgess murmured quietly. "Did you say something? I… I didn't quite catch it."

Oscendale saw that youth had gone, leaving deep lines cut into sallow skin. Puffy eyes surrounded by dark skin looked up at him but were focused on a spot some distance beyond.

"Oscendale, it's Captain Oscendale. Do you remember me?"

He always felt uncomfortable around the shell-shock cases. They were too unpredictable in a world that already held far too much uncertainty for him. He had known men lunge at him, shout out, shake, fall to the floor or begin crying uncontrollably. They unnerved him, unsettled him.

Because most of all they reminded him of himself.

Burgess was subdued for the moment, almost lifeless. Maybe it was the morphine. *Or the calm before the storm.* Oscendale waited for a reply.

The whine in Burgess's ears decreased and he stared again at the man: flecks of grey in his dark hair. A contrast between young and old. Youth and middle age. *Aren't we all?* he thought and smiled. The man's voice was soft and deep, almost lilting. Songs and music passed through his head and he felt himself sinking back into the softness and emptiness.

"Lieutenant Burgess?" The voice came again and the vision scurried away. He was here. Here and now. A broken man in a hospital bed. With a visitor. *Where were his manners?*

"Yes, yes, of course. I'm sorry, Captain Oscendale. I find it hard to concentrate, you know. Please, sit down." He indicated a plain wooden chair placed at the side of his bed. "Forgive my manners," he continued. The clarity of thought had come back. "Comes with the condition. Am I being assessed again?"

"No," replied Oscendale. It was evident that Burgess had no recollection of their previous meeting. "I'm not a doctor. I'm with the Military Police." He paused and waited for a reaction. This was crucial; it would indicate whether Burgess was well enough to help him or not.

There was none. Burgess waited for Oscendale to say more. As he did so the whine in his head started to grow into a buzz. His eyelid began to twitch and he rubbed it in an unsuccessful attempt to stop it.

Oscendale watched the grimace cross Burgess's face but he knew it was unrelated to his own words. The man was obviously suffering some awful inner torment, something he could not convey to Oscendale.

"We spoke at your home in Cardiff. Do you remember?" There was no reply.

He had pushed him too far last time. But as soon as Burgess had started talking about that day on Y Beach, Oscendale had wanted to know more. Burgess's father had urged caution several times but Oscendale had been relentless in his questioning, driven on by the anger he felt at his friend's death.

At the end of it he knew that Parry had seen Lucas in the

Turkish house at Gallipoli where Oscendale had found his body. Parry had witnessed something Lucas had done, that was clear. Oscendale had asked Burgess what that was several times, but he kept saying that he did not know.

Eventually it became too much and Burgess had put his head in his hands and sobbed. Burgess's father looked tenderly at his son and had asked Oscendale firmly to leave, which he did, and he had been genuinely sorry when he had received the message yesterday that Burgess had collapsed and was being taken back to the Maudsley Hospital here in London.

"Would you prefer me to come back another time?" he offered between coughs, his throat still raw from the events of yesterday. He started to rise from the chair. *Perhaps this had been a bad idea.*

Burgess shook his head again. "No, no, that's fine. I… I just have this noise in my head. Comes and goes. Some days it's better than others. It's not so good today. Perhaps talking would help it a little. Military Police, you say. How can I help you? I wasn't aware I'd been involved in any crime?"

Oscendale returned to his seat. "Thank you, Burgess. I know this isn't easy but I think you have some more information that I want. Something you may not actually be aware of."

Burgess adjusted his position so he could face Oscendale directly and said, "Information? Information about what?"

"Tell me about when you first joined the Leicesters in April."

First arrived? He felt he had never left.

In a clear voice but with a halting manner, he told Oscendale his story. He began slowly at first, hesitating over facts and details, and then gaining in confidence as the stream of consciousness burst through the dam.

At Folkestone he had boarded a troopship to Boulogne, landing on 11th April, where he was greeted by lines of locals, endeavouring to sell him fruit and chocolate. From there he had travelled to the huge British military base at Etaples, *Eat Apples* as he had heard it called, before he boarded a train for Flanders.

Oscendale tried to suppress his irritating cough so as not to disturb Burgess's recollections. A nurse appeared with a jug of water and two glasses and plumped Burgess's pillows for him, smiling all the while and then disappearing without uttering a word.

"I left rest camp after receiving my orders to travel to the Front. There was quite an air of confidence amongst the officers I joined in the trenches. They were all excited about fighting off a recent German attack. They couldn't talk about much else that evening."

He paused as he recalled Clarke and Newcombe. Something was nagging away at the back of his mind.

"Conditions were pretty bad in the trenches that month, I'll wager," said Oscendale, trying to continue the flow.

"Mmm. Water covered the floor of the dugout. Damp, cold, miserable. The men slept in the open on firesteps or in funk holes dug out of the sides of the trench. At least I had a lousy straw bunk to sleep on." *Sleep without dreams.* "Haveldar, my batman, a decent sort of chap, saw to my creature comforts. Probably dead by now."

He shuddered as he remembered the rats. Constant companions, as were lice. He soon adapted to having vermin scuttle over him, inhabiting the dugout as they did, but lice were more of an irritation.

"I was like some sort of nocturnal animal, staring into the blackness of no man's land each night, knowing that the German infantry in the trenches opposite were doing the same. At night everyone was kept busy doing the routine work maintaining the trench. If I wasn't leading a patrol, I'd organise working parties, with men bringing up planks of wood, duckboards, and everything else needed to maintain a trench. The weather made little difference – work continued as ever."

Oscendale could picture the scene. He knew how relentless life in the trenches could be. He could see the men repairing the parados at the rear of the trench and parapet, the sides of the trenches, replacing duckboards that ran along the bottom of the trench to keep their feet as dry as possible. Then digging saps – shallow trenches just deep enough for a soldier to crawl along – projecting out from the front line at ninety degrees towards the enemy lines, manned at night to provide safer access to the listening posts.

Burgess's voice continued. "At stand-to I'd issue the rum ration. It was a tense time. Dawn. The time when most German attacks begin. Breakfast was then taken at 9 a.m. I can taste it now. Bread, boiled bacon and a mug of tea. Sometimes Newcombe would receive a hamper from Harrods or Fortnum and Mason. It was bizarre. Luxury provisions in a squalid dugout." Burgess gave a half-hearted laugh.

"Then sentry duty. The men were tired. We were all tired; awake all night, craving sleep. They knew a court martial would result if they fell asleep whilst on sentry duty. It was relentless for us all; the rota was two hours on and four hours off. For the men not engaged on sentry duty, there were more trench repairs, drainage improvements and any damage to our dugouts was also repaired."

Oscendale saw how the routine of trench life had become fixed in Burgess's mind. It was like throwing a switch. Prompted by short questions, it had all come out. He resisted the temptation to hurry him along to the part he was really interested in and let the young man continue at his own pace.

"When it was my turn to be orderly officer of the day, there would be scores of letters to censor and stamp. Given the casualties that were occurring, I'd write the dreaded letter home, knowing that within three days of posting some mother, father, brother or sister would be clasping the letter in disbelief. Do you smoke Captain Oscendale?" Not waiting for an answer, Burgess continued. "I hate the damned things. I suppose it's a comfort to the men in the front line; it quells the nerves, relieves the stress. No wonder chain-smoking is common. But it's dangerous in the dark – third light and all that. Water supply was a real difficulty."

Burgess swallowed as he remembered the taste of the water and Oscendale sipped from his second glass of fresh water knowing exactly what Burgess was recalling. "If we were lucky we would be supplied with water from a nearby well, otherwise it would be from a bowser brought up to the front line by nightly carrying-parties in petrol cans, which left it with a taste never to be forgotten."

Whether Burgess and the other officers washed depended on water supply and his relationship with his men. Often if the men had no water to wash in, then Burgess desisted too. "Shaving from the last dregs of a cup of tea," he motioned, feeling his chin.

Self-deprecating or not, Oscendale began to picture a young, inexperienced officer who nevertheless cared about his men and was probably respected by them for it.

Burgess paused in his litany of duties, as if that had been the end of the story and he was uncertain where to go next.

"What about Major Lucas?" prompted Oscendale. "Tell me about him."

"Lucas?" The young man thought for a moment then continued. "Major Lucas. The great hero of Gallipoli. Major Lucas DSO of the Somme. Except some of us know the truth," he sneered.

"He was in command of that section of trench, yes? Tell me about the night patrol he organised for the 11th June."

As Burgess was new to the line, he was sent out with a party of men led by an NCO to test his mettle and give him experience. The men had removed any insignia and personal items to prevent identification by the Germans if they were captured or killed.

"Lucas told us the enemy guns had blown a gap in the wire so we had to take new rolls out into no man's land and repair it. We knew what a filthy job it was. The barbs on the wire are so vicious that even though we all had gloves on we knew we would return scratched and bleeding. But that was the least of our worries. Any noise and the German machine guns would have opened fire on us. A single Very light could illuminate a wide part of the battlefront, leaving my men and me lit up in the darkness.

"Anyway, we left our trenches at about midnight and pretty soon we were in trouble. The Germans were sending up plenty of flares and it became clear that we would never get to the wire so I ordered the men to turn back. When we got back into the trench Lucas went berserk. Called me all sorts of things, loud enough for everyone to hear. Bad form, don't you think? Claimed I was a spineless effing coward." Burgess paused and drew breath, the events he was recalling becoming all too clear. Oscendale debated whether to draw a halt before the man became too upset but he knew he needed the information.

"The following morning the fog descended. All was quiet for a while and then, suddenly, all hell broke loose."

He told Oscendale how he found himself in no man's land with Clarke standing over him and a dead German alongside. He paused and struggled again to remember what had happened out there but it would not come. Instead his head began to throb again so he fell silent and waited for it to pass.

Oscendale watched the young officer close his eyes and struggle to recall. He tensed as he waited for Burgess to get to the vital details. He had been so blinded by the revelation of the circumstances of Parry's death in their initial interview in Cardiff that it was only later he realised that Burgess might have more to tell him. A minute or so of silence passed before he began speaking again.

"Somehow I made my way back to our front line, avoiding being shot by either side as the soldiers exchanged rounds in the fog. I don't remember any of it though. I lost the capacity to speak and could hear nothing. Traumatised, they tell me."

He told Oscendale he had been tremulous and deaf and could remember nothing of what had occurred in no man's land, either through the awful experience of what he had witnessed, or perhaps through a blow to the head, which could also account for his deafness.

"I was transferred by field ambulance to a casualty clearing station, where I was assessed and finally sent here for treatment. Cold baths, swimming, being out in the open air. They encourage you to take up a new interest or hobby. It's all on offer here: tennis, bowling, badminton, gardening and golf. Must say, I wouldn't mind a round of golf or a game of tennis with some of the other officers." He thought for a while then said quietly, "Maybe next week if I'm up to it."

Oscendale probed deeper. "Tell me about no man's land. About what happened out there in the fog." Oscendale chanced his arm. "Tell me about Lucas."

Oscendale's words triggered the memory. The room disappeared and he was out in the blackness of no man's land, the Germans pulling and pushing him towards their own lines. Rats, fat after gorging themselves on his comrades, took on the appearance of familiar faces.

One of the Germans turned to him and spoke in perfect English…

"Burgess?" The man's voice cut into his thoughts again. "Tell me about you and Lucas in no man's land."

Burgess was there once more but this time he found the words for the horror he had witnessed and it all came out in a headlong rush. Everything.

When it was over he was exhausted. He laid his head back on the pillow and his breathing came in great wracked sobs. The Germans were gone and the room came back into view. A nurse appeared at the bedside. She took his pulse and started to rub his brow, speaking in a soft, familiar lilt to him. As she did so she turned to chastise the military policeman who had caused so much pain and anguish to this brave young man but Oscendale was already on his way back down the ward and she glared at his retreating back as he left.

CHAPTER 24

London – Wednesday, 22nd August 1917

THE FOYER OF the Lanchester Hotel was a place full of glitz, glamour and gaudiness. A wide staircase swept up to the rooms above and dinner-jacketed men in starched white shirts accompanied women in long, flowing, elegant gowns up and down the concourse. His military uniform attracted stares as if he were from an unpleasant other world which rudely interrupted their sharing of the pleasures of life. There was the scent of money in the air and Oscendale shifted uneasily at the reception desk until a thin-faced clerk with an even thinner air of patience asked him if he could help. Oscendale gave the name of the man he was looking for and the clerk, with a dismissive tone, gave him directions to a room to the right.

Curious women, powdered and rouged, and haughty, inquisitive men watched Oscendale until he reached the dining room. The maître d'hôtel stepped quickly in front of him and asked for his room number. Oscendale asked for Captain Hughes and the man raised a hand and told him to wait. He turned and steered his way between the furniture and diners until he reached a large table around which sat a collection of middle-aged men. The waiter bent down and whispered something to one of them.

On other tables, women's attractive faces shone as brightly as their jewels in the candlelight coming from the silver centrepieces of their tables. A string quartet, its members also impeccably dressed, played softly in another corner of the room, their efforts largely ignored.

The glamorous dining room was designed to confuse the senses. It seized his perceptions of how a room should appear and threw them out of its long, wide windows framed with silk brocade. The walls were decorated with landscape scenes, but not as they might appear in a vast collection of paintings, expensively obtained and ostentatiously hung; these scenes were designed to make one believe that the internal was external and the outside world had entered through the walls. It was a place of fantasy, where unreality barred reality.

Africa and the Orient were both here. Images of muscular black warriors and Chinese emperors stared down at him with dull, mock interest. The wildest beasts of those two great continents bared their teeth and sprang at him. *A world in conflict.* Around the blood-red marble fireplace, swathes of leafy green creepers and palm trees rose from the varnished floor to the sky blue ceiling. Suspended in mid-air was a twinkling glass and gold chandelier, a confection of pear-shaped droplets. The *trompe-l'oeil* Hellenic urns leapt from the corners of the room, bemusing and bewitching with their artistry.

Oscendale felt his head swim, the effect complete. He attempted to restore his composure by looking out of the windows which ran the full length of the room. Ranks of trees and shrubs lay in military parade fashion before him, bathed in the burning colours of the dying sunlight. He blinked to block it all out and did what he always did at such times, he thought of the reality of his life, of Hannah.

The maître d'hôtel had finished speaking confidentially to the man whom Oscendale sought and scuttled away. After exchanging a few words of apology to his companions, the man rose from the table and walked towards Oscendale, continuing to draw heavily on his large cigar, blowing the smoke upwards to the blue sky of the ceiling, apparently unconcerned by this intrusion into his evening.

"Good evening, Captain Oscendale. Come this way and we can talk in private."

Captain Hughes led him to an ante-room where he closed the door behind them before leaning on the mantelpiece and flicking cigar ash into the hearth.

"It was about Edmund Lucas, wasn't it?" queried Hughes. He was a square-faced man with brown hair and there was something about his bearing that spoke of hard work and ability. He had taken Oscendale's telephone call earlier that day and had agreed to meet.

"Yes. I understand you have served with him in the past, were with him when he won a gallantry medal."

"That's correct," said Hughes. "It was a bit of a surprise to us all when the news came through about his DSO. To tell you the truth there were a few comments passed in the mess about it. Bit of backbiting, you know. Inevitable really when a chap gets a gong out of the blue as it were."

Hughes paused and his brow furrowed. He pretentiously cleared his throat as if he were conscious that he had already said too much. The loyalty of the mess was usually fiercely protected. However, Oscendale put on his open face, waited and knew more would follow.

"You see," obliged Hughes, "Lucas is a decent enough fellow. Always good company in the mess, but, well, I don't know, there's just something about him that isn't reliable. Not dependable. Wouldn't leave him alone with your wallet or your sister, so to speak."

"But you served with him at the Somme didn't you? What's he like under fire?"

Hughes hesitated. "Well, every fellow's different. We're all afraid of being afraid, if you know what I mean, aren't we?"

He looked at Oscendale for some reassurance. *The bond of the soldier perhaps*? But Oscendale wasn't interested in whatever inner demons plagued Captain Charles Hughes.

"Maybe," he said non-committally. "But you *were* in action with him?"

"Yes," replied Hughes, becoming more matter-of-fact. "It was at Lesboeufs, during the battle for Morval last year. We were ordered to take a fortified farmhouse. Lucas was with me in the front line trenches during the early hours. We were due to attack at dawn. The artillery barrage came down as anticipated, really churning up the Boche positions.

"We went over the top and advanced across no man's land. Our men opened up with Lewis guns, rifle bombs and Stokes mortars from our trenches. The noise was terrific." Hughes sat down, leaning his elbows on his knees and stared at his clasped hands. "Rifle sections moved around the flanks of the farmhouse, which was more a collection of ruins by that time than anything else. When the artillery and trench mortar fire ceased, the attack went in, we from the front and the other sections from the sides. The Huns had been driven deep into their dugouts so there was little resistance, if the truth be told. We ran up to the entrances and bombed them. Lucas was like a man possessed though. He was stupefied. I had to practically drag him along. Look, you *are* Military Police, aren't you?" he asked, looking up suspiciously and studying Oscendale's uniform.

Oscendale was puzzled by the question which had arrived suddenly. "Yes, of course, Hughes. Why? What's the matter?"

Hughes looked concerned. "Well, it's just that this was where Lucas won his DSO and it wasn't quite like he recalled later. I mean, I was one of the chaps throwing bombs into the German dugouts and I don't recall any German attack that was beaten off. Thing is, nobody I spoke to afterwards recalled it either. I know we were preoccupied in dealing with the dugouts but dash it all, if the Huns had been firing at any of us above ground I'm sure we would have noticed."

"And Lucas reported later that there had been a counter-attack?"

"Yes. Claimed the Huns had come in from the east and had

shot several of our men before he grabbed a Lewis gun from a dead machine gunner and drove them off. Saved our bacon, he reckoned."

"Were there any witnesses to what he was supposed to have done?" asked Oscendale.

"Yes, there was as a matter of fact. A man who was my sergeant until I recommended him for a commission. Chap called Maskell. Albert Maskell."

CHAPTER 25

Wytschaete, Belgium – Thursday, 23rd August 1917

THE 23RD OF August was a special day for David Loram; it was the day of his sixth wedding anniversary. After washing and dressing, he made his way quickly towards the headquarters building in the middle of Wytschaete. If the army postal service was up to its usual high standard, he felt certain that there would be a letter waiting for him in the morning post.

He approached the wooden opening in the rows of pigeonholes that held the mail for their office – one among many in the reception area – and noticed that there were several envelopes placed inside. His pulse quickened as he removed the envelope with his name on it, raised it to his mouth and kissed it. Julia's scent had travelled hundreds of miles and yet it was as fresh as when she had posted it at Tewkesbury Post Office two days before.

Loram pictured the scene: the prim and proper postmistress, as fussy and meticulous as ever, peering at Julia over her horn-rimmed glasses, her boney, beak-like nose perfectly suited for her occupation, reading the address with interest and raising her sharp eyes to Julia.

He carefully opened the envelope, placing it in his left breast pocket, leaving a little poking out and the flap undone so he could still inhale the smell of her scent every time he breathed. Then, unfolding the letter gently, he eagerly began to read the neat script.

My Darling David,
Happy Anniversary, my love! Six years ago you and I became

one. I miss you so much, my sweetheart, my one and only love. Most of all I miss you next to me in our bed at night, holding me tightly in your arms. Sometimes I feel so alone but I know you must be over there and I must be here, looking after our little Peter. You tell me you are far behind the lines, well away from the fighting but I know you too well, David Loram. I know you write those things to comfort me. Please, please take care of yourself, my darling. Don't take any risks by putting yourself in harm's way and come home as soon as you can. Thinking of you all day on our special day.

> *Devotedly and forever,*
> *Your wife Julia xxxxx*

Loram read the letter four times before putting it away again inside the scented envelope. He thought of her face as she read the silk postcard depicting an embroidered rose inside a heart that he had sent her, on the back of which he had clumsily attempted to describe his love.

Julia Bowles had been the love of his life since the day he had first caught sight of her across the room at the local church dance. She was his wife at nineteen and the mother of his son a year later. And he missed her greatly.

Loram had never felt an outsider until the war began. He had been a gregarious, popular member of the police force that had become part of his life from his early twenties.

He was a good shot too, a skill honed on misty mornings, lying in wait for the foxes that roamed the fields around the farm where he had once worked. With an ancient .22 rifle lent to him by an elderly farmer, he had lain in wait until the creatures had appeared and he had prided himself on taking no more than two shots to kill his prey. As he grew more proficient he had allowed himself only one shot and if he missed then the lucky animal would be allowed to escape.

Loram had left school at fourteen and had drifted from one

farm job to another before he bumped into his old schoolmaster one afternoon in town. Loram easily recognised Mr Jefferies with his red hair framing his red face, and he in turn had remembered the young rascal he used to teach.

It had always appeared to Loram that his old schoolmaster was everything beginning with the letter R. Apart from the obvious visual attributes, he taught the three Rs and could not pronounce his 'r's although this didn't stop him enunciating his views on life to Loram now. Jefferies was always right and seemed to him, even as a young man, to possess the wisdom of Solomon. At the seventeenth-century Bear Inn, over the course of several pale ales, he had told young David why he was wasting his life and that he should put his skills to a more practical use by catching bigger game than foxes.

The direction of Loram's life had been altered irretrievably as a result of that meeting. He had been won over by Jefferies's advice and, leaving the public house, he formulated a plan that would eventually see him patrolling the villages around Tewkesbury on his regulation police bicycle.

The war had interrupted a job he was growing to love, but he had no intention of being left behind. Besides, in common with others, he felt duty bound. He had applied for the Military Mounted Police, feeling his skills and knowledge as an excellent horseman from his days on the farm would be welcomed, and he was bemused when he was rejected. He had sulked at that point, in a way he had not done since he was a schoolboy, and joined the infantry instead.

His proficiency with a rifle had become immediately apparent and he had been singled out for sniper training. He had undergone instruction in weapons handling, concealment, tracking (which he took to, naturally), map reading and, above all, patience.

He had then gone to the front line on his first tour.

It was different, he had to acknowledge. There was no companionship, something that he did miss – snipers were reviled, not encouraged as friends.

And then there was the cold, calculated act of killing. He soon grew weary of that and began to play tricks. Allowing himself just one bullet a day, he would aim to shoot a cup out of an enemy soldier's hand rather than put a bullet in his head. The man probably took it as a slice of luck but Loram laughed when he saw the look of relief on his target's face. Sniping was fine but he enjoyed the duels with enemy snipers the most. Dog eat dog.

He was presently a guard, assistant… well what exactly was he? He could not say. All he knew was he had enjoyed working for Oscendale over the past year. It was so different to the loneliness of his previous role. It was not without its ups and downs but there were more ups than downs it had to be said. His officer could be unpredictable, could withdraw into himself. And at times the strain showed. He knew the nervous signs, knew when to back away and when to leave him to another brooding silence. But Oscendale was a good man and an excellent detective, and Loram knew that he valued the work that he did.

The map lay spread out on the table. Lines traced in blue and red criss-crossed a flat, featureless landscape. Smudges showed the rapidly changing face of the current battle, the struggle that was to be the prelude to the end. Everywhere the British were making gains. The British line bulged with salients and the phones rang constantly with details of these new areas of taken ground. More and more information was babbled by excited clerks to junior officers who then relayed the tidings up the chain of command until they arrived on the desk of Field Marshall Douglas Haig himself.

"Morning, Captain Oscendale sir. How was your leave?" The

NCO breezed into the room and picked up the half-full mug of cold tea from among the papers, files and reports on Oscendale's desk. His enquiry about Oscendale's leave was an obligatory question and he did not anticipate much in reply.

"Fine." The response was as he had expected.

Oscendale appeared deep in thought, staring at the map in front of him, studying the progress of the latest offensive. He knew his boss rarely took such a strategic interest in the war. His life revolved around the minutiae of human behaviour, in particular the psychology that led men to murder their fellow human beings. Investigating murders when so much killing was going on around them always struck Loram as incongruous.

"Good. Pleased to hear it. Cup of tea, sir?"

The voice of reality and reason. He lifted his head reluctantly from the plan of Golgotha to the cheerful face of his orderly. Sergeant Loram had joined his office the previous year after they had both been involved in a murder investigation in the town of Albert. He had replaced a one-dimensional, particularly dim-witted clerk who had spent his whole time searching for chinks in Oscendale's armour. The man was still assigned to Oscendale's office but had withdrawn into the background – the spectre at the feast.

"Yes, why not? And no sugar."

"Today's post too, sir," said Loram, adding yet more envelopes to the neat pile at Oscendale's elbow. "Oh and Major Avate rang earlier. He asked if you could ring him as soon as you can."

An air of office efficiency hid a whole host of Loram's qualities, Oscendale knew. There were few men cooler in a dangerous situation and if there was a better sniper in the area than Loram, Oscendale would like to meet him – as long as he was on the right side of no man's land.

If Provost Avate wanted to speak to him urgently at a time like this then something must be up. He lifted the receiver from its cradle and gave the operator Avate's number. After three rings Avate's deep, authoritative voice answered. "Avate."

"Oscendale here, sir."

"Ah yes. Morning, Tom. This Major Lucas you asked me to look into. Well, it seems you have your eye on a pillar of military respectability. Career soldier from a family of the same ilk. Gained his commission in 1912. Slow progress before the war. Didn't shine at all. But since the war started, a meteoric rise, shall we say. Served at Gallipoli with the Royal Marines, as you know, and won the MC there. Promoted to captain as a result and assigned to the Leicesters. Served on the Somme around Morval last summer. Won the DSO for his role in resisting a Boche counter-attack. Promoted again to major and recommended for a bar to his DSO earlier this month for distinguished service in your sector. Took a blockhouse single-handed."

He heard a reaction of disbelief from Oscendale but continued. "Nothing's appeared in the *London Gazette* yet though." He paused. "Something in all of that you're not happy with?"

Oscendale wrote quickly on a notepad. "Just pieces of a jigsaw, sir. Much obliged to you." It certainly was an impressive record, littered with official approbation. *But his mind went back to a farmer's son in a field in Carmarthenshire.*

The phone went dead. Oscendale felt no slight; he was used to Avate's abrupt ways and the two men had an excellent working relationship. Avate would defend Oscendale's sometimes cavalier actions because he knew he usually delivered. He tore the sheet of paper from the pad and placed it in his pocket.

The yellow-grey smoke wafted up lazily into the still air, hovered for a while and then faded. Lounging back in his office chair, he inhaled once slowly, raised his eyes upwards and stared at the flies sparring with each other.

"What do you want from your life, Tom?" Jack Parry had asked him one night as they sat opposite each other on the transport ship making its way across the Mediterranean to Gallipoli.

"What do I want?" Oscendale had replied, thrown by the depth of the question. The evening thus far had consisted of too many whiskies and tall stories, as well as a certain amount of discussion regarding the possibilities of being wounded once the fighting started. Their laughter and voices had resonated around the walls of the cabin. Here was Jack asking him something so intense and meaningful. It was a startling thought and for a time he could not adapt his mood to respond.

"Come on," Jack had said at last, his patience wearing thin. "What do you want your life to bring you?"

He had leaned forward, elbows on the table, scattering a pile of paper to the floor. He was drunk and he knew it. A future, he thought. He just wanted a damn future and not to die…

"I don't know, Jack. Never really thought about it. Usual things I suppose. Happiness. Money. That sort of thing."

"What about love? Have you ever been in love with a girl, Tom?"

Once. Just once. Before she had gone.

But he was back in the Salient now, the huge bulge reaching out from the British lines, where the Germans surrounded them on three sides. A place of death and destruction. The eternal, infernal Salient. And Lucas was here somewhere. Perhaps it was time to turn to the demons of the past to point the way to the future. He looked again at the letter he held in his hand.

Dear Captain Oscendale,
I hope you won't mind me writing to you as I know from Mrs Owen, who you stayed with recently, that you are a very busy man, what with this terrible war and everything.

Oscendale paused. *Mrs Owen.* Strange how the unpleasant incidents in one's own life are always there, lurking in the corners of the mind. Even this recent unfortunate experience had refused to leave his memory. *Possibly the worst lodgings I've ever stayed in,* he thought, *and Lord knows there have been enough of them.*

His life had become transitory. He was an itinerant, he realised, moving from place to place, from one crime scene to another. And it was grinding him down, wearing away at the heels of his life. He shrugged away the self-pity and returned again to the contents of the letter.

The scrawling hand continued its journey across the paper.

I hoped you might have time to look into a terrible wrong. My boy Edward may be in the arms of the angels by the time you read this, God bless him. But it won't be the Germans who put him there – it will be his own side. That's right, Captain Oscendale, the British Army will kill him at a prison in a town called Poperinghe. They say he is a coward, that he ran away and left his pals to their fate. But I know my own son. Any mother knows their son and I know my boy didn't run.

Oscendale felt the mother's pain emerging from the page but what she was unaware of was that he had read this letter before. Or at least one that was remarkably similar to it. A British soldier shot at dawn to set an example to the others. Oscendale had seen a firing squad at work once and the memory of it gave him a sense of revulsion even now.

The youth, for that was all he had been really, was carried kicking and screaming from his cell to a chair in a French yard, tied fast to it with rope and a piece of cloth pinned to his chest. When he reacted so violently to this that he rocked the chair until it toppled over onto the cobbled ground, the sergeant in charge of the firing squad had shaken with a mixture of anger and sorrow. The chair had been righted and the youth had tipped it over a second time. That was enough for the sergeant. He had refused to carry out the order to fire so an officer had impatiently strode across the courtyard and shot the still-screaming soldier in the head.

Oscendale sighed and turned again to the letter.

His last letter to me spoke of an officer he was afraid of, a man he neither respected nor trusted. He said that the man was not what he appeared to be. This was the officer who demanded my Edward be court-martialled for cowardice in the face of the enemy. But I know he was no coward, Captain Oscendale. Please find out what he did and set my poor grieving mind at rest. He is a brave boy who loved his pals and would not have left them alone.

The next line made Oscendale's blood run cold.

His name is Edward Copeland of the Leicestershire Regiment.
Yours in hope,
Emma Copeland

Could it be Lucas again? Oscendale read the details the mother had provided of her son. *Leicestershire Regiment.* Lucas's regiment. It had to be the same man.

"Loram!"

Loram opened the office door from behind which the voice had bellowed.

"Sir?"

Oscendale told Loram about the letter. He listened carefully then asked several questions, some of which Oscendale was able to answer, others he was not.

"And what do you make of this?" Oscendale passed the letter to Loram who read it and shrugged.

"Could have been written by any mother whose son is held in the cells at Poperinghe, sir. Why do you think it's any different?" He looked quizzically at Oscendale, noting the concern on his face.

"I don't know. It's odd that she knows about her boy. The families aren't usually made aware of these things, as you know. Maybe it's a coincidence, but it is Lucas's regiment again." Oscendale then added resolutely, "I'm going to Poperinghe. If I get there in time I can at least talk to the man, find out what he did and write something to his mother. I also need to talk to a man named Haveldar who is stationed up there as well with the Leicesters. Burgess told me he knew something. Something that could help us nail Lucas."

CHAPTER 26

Ypres Salient – Friday, 24th August 1917

HIS EYES REMAINED closed but he knew that he was lying in mud, thick and clinging; it felt gritty in his mouth and tasted foul. As he started to come to his senses, he wondered exactly where he was. It was all so vague. He had been in Poperinghe, not here. He attempted to determine what was real and what was an illusion. But it was not easy. Thoughts and memories began to blur. There was Poperinghe and there was here. Poperinghe was safe and this was… Well what was it?

The pain in his head thumped remorselessly and even though he attempted to open his eyes, the eyelids would not respond. He forced himself to spit out the metallic tasting muck. Like iron. Was it blood?

He tried to think. Why was he lying here and where exactly was 'here'? The fog within his mind made clear thoughts elusive. How to make sense of it all? He fought hard against the urge to give in and just go back to the deep abyss as a lurking sense of danger encouraged him to remain conscious.

Slowly, the tangled, hazy recollections appeared. Blurred scenes of him speaking to a soldier in a cell. Poperinghe. What was his name? The man had been frightened, ashen and gaunt. But then most men facing certain death would have appeared the same way. His demeanour had changed when he had asked him about what he had done. He had seen pure hatred in the man's eyes.

He had bidden the condemned man farewell and gone out into the summer rain, confused and bewildered. But why? He tried to recall exactly what had transpired since that moment.

At least that was what he thought had happened as he lay on the ground, his head throbbing. Except it had not worked out quite like that. He tried to separate reality from his wishful thinking but clouds of obscurity kept getting in the way. It was the man's face. It kept reappearing in his mind. The look of incomprehension had been clear.

Bright lights. A village square. Wet cobbles. A café with people eating, drinking, singing. *Didn't they realise there was a war on?* He had felt thirsty. Two MPs patrolling the local streets had saluted. The next thing he knew he was here. He tried to remember more. *There must be more.*

His head ached as if he'd been hit with a metal bar and when he tried to push himself up, the pain spiralled down to his neck and shoulders. Had he been knocked out? He tried desperately to clear his head and to think. Unconnected fragments of memories came back to him in fits and starts. There had been another man besides the MPs. Who was it? Lucas? He had gone into a café. A man had wanted to talk to him. The MPs had waited outside. There had been a drink. Two drinks? Then nothing. Then here. What had they talked about? Oscendale could not remember. There was nothing else.

And that was it. Now here he was, lying in the mud. The pounding in his head grew louder and the earth began to vibrate. He realised something heavy and noisy was approaching. The sound triggered the memory. There was something else. The German artillery had come down in great crumps and the men with him had been shattered into pieces. One had fallen screaming to the ground, his face chewed away by a shell fragment.

Oscendale had blundered on, quickly losing his sense of direction until he had passed out. His ears were still ringing and he could only guess that a concussive blast had floored him, knocking him out for a while.

He now became fully aware of the noise that was growing in intensity. Another barrage of artillery fire, coming closer?

Then he saw it.

Like a vast metallic beast, it lurched and crawled towards him. He watched its approach, awestruck that man had produced the ultimate mobile killer. Impregnable, remorseless and deadly, this was the latest manifestation of the British vision of how to destroy the Germans.

And it was heading straight for him.

Lengths of barbed wire had caught in its tracks and were being whipped in circles as they continued to rotate around the huge lozenge-shaped body. Threadlike yet lethal, they emitted a high pitched whine as they flicked out at everything around them like angry snakes.

Oscendale also saw something else being picked up by the powerful steel tracks – human limbs. As the tank ground forward it minced the bodies of the dead. Sometimes crushed arms and legs became trapped in the plates, were raised from the earth and tossed up in a macabre dance of death where they took on lives of their own, cartwheeling through the air before returning once more to the mud. Oscendale watched, mesmerised at the insanity of it all. There was no semblance of humanity here. It was as if an agricultural flail was traversing a graveyard. He felt sick of it all, sick to the pit of his stomach.

The machine ground to a halt, its tracks squealing as it did so. Oscendale watched as a hatch at the side of one of the pontoons was flung open. He attempted to stand but could only stagger and fall once more into the cloying mud. Footsteps hurriedly splashed across the ooze and he looked up to see a grimy face peering into his.

"Now then, sir, looks like you've been in the wars – or one at least. Time to get you out of here before the Huns try again. Men! Over here!"

Two soldiers, one wearing a piece of cloth tied around his face, immediately leapt out of the tank, forcibly grabbed Oscendale and bundled him inside.

The driver of the tank turned around and Oscendale saw that below his helmet he wore a chainmail face mask. His features were totally obscured and he shouted something incomprehensible before turning back to his appointed task of getting them all out of there. The door was slammed shut and the tank lurched forwards again.

By now the Germans had found their range and bullets clattered into the far side of the tank, sending white hot pieces of metal spinning through the air above him.

He felt he had died and gone to hell. His body temperature rose in seconds and he began coughing immediately. Encased in the belly of a monster, he struggled to breathe in air that was hot and full of carbon monoxide exhaust fumes and cordite. The roar of the engine was deafening. He gritted his teeth in an effort to cope with the pain sweeping through his head.

One crew member's stomach could not cope with the stench any longer and he turned from his position at the side of the tank and retched before vomiting over the floor of the tank.

As there was no suspension system, Oscendale was tossed around like a cork in a barrel and more than once banged his head on the sides of the tank. The mixed odours now included the smell of rapidly warming vomit and he wondered how long it would be before he added to the stench himself.

A downpour of lead hailstones battered rapidly against the exterior of the tank, loosening sparks of splintered metal that flew across his line of sight as the German machine gun bullets hammered on the outside.

Oscendale breathed in as shallowly as he could; still the noxious fumes permeated his nostrils and seeped down into his lungs. The noise and the inferno-like heat meant that he felt giddy and woozy with the madness of it all. He knew he could no longer stand so he crouched on the steel floor of the tank and watched blurred forms, partially lit by the observation slits, pouring gunfire into the German positions.

He heard the man who had rescued him scream out, "There's another one – two hundred yards to the left! See it?"

One of the crew roared something in return, swung his machine gun to the left and opened fire. Gunners were frantically loading the six-pounders and firing at an enemy somewhere ahead.

The tank jolted along, lifting and falling with the rise and fall of the ground. After hitting his head on a piece of metal again he curled up into a foetal-like ball with his hands over his head and waited for it all to stop. He knew he was safer in here than he had been lying out in the open but he was aware he was still in mortal danger.

There was a loud bang on the right-hand side of the tank and he felt it slew to the left, but to his relief they kept going. Seconds later another anti-tank round hit the right-hand side again and a piece of metal as big as a fist flew across to the other side, catching one of the crew in the head. He saw the man fall screaming to the floor, his hands covering the bloody pulp of what had been his face.

Another explosion, this time louder than the last. When he opened his eyes again he could see that part of the front of the tank had disappeared. There were bodies groaning all around him. The officer was on his feet, attempting to pull one of the men out of an open side door. Enemy machine gun bullets began peppering the gap and Oscendale knew he had only seconds to live if he did not move quickly.

He wrenched himself to his feet and threw himself out of the side door. He rolled onto the ground and raced to a shell hole just as the ammunition and fuel tank blew up. Blue, purple, orange and red flames raged from the stricken monster. The plates at the sides begin to groan and buckle as they twisted and curled viciously with the glowing heat of the furnace inside, as if they were mere pieces of paper.

The tank slumped to one side, beaten and cowed. A huge jagged hole was gored into the right-hand side of the front. He saw that a track had been ripped off and lay like a snail trail behind the shell of the immobile and dying beast. Of the crew of eight, it appeared that only a few had managed to get out in time. The others, if they had not died in the initial explosion, were suffering agonising deaths inside the tank.

There was screaming on the far side and around the front of the tank staggered a crewman who was ablaze. He waved his arms above his head as the flames licked and danced all over him, consuming him until he fell to the ground. He twitched and then lay still, the flames continuing to eat away at his prone form.

Grey figures were scurrying towards them through gaps in the barbed wire. They would disappear from view into shell holes for a few moments before reappearing much closer. He could try to run but felt certain he would be cut down in a hail of bullets, so he resigned himself to capture and lay still.

The officer was some yards away with one of the crew, both lying on the ground. Seconds later they were surrounded by German infantry. He watched as the two men slowly sat up, raising their hands in submission. His own capitulation was only seconds away.

The first few seconds of surrender were always the most dangerous. One twitchy German soldier and he could be run through with a butcher bayonet before an officer arrived, so he was relieved when the first person to enter his shell hole was a figure with a peaked cap who pointed a revolver at him.

Oscendale raised both his arms in surrender and staggered

to his feet. The officer did not speak but motioned him towards the German lines with the barrel of his Luger pistol. Oscendale complied, knowing that this was all he could do in the circumstances. He saw the tank officer lift the wounded crew member to his feet and begin a stumbling journey towards the German lines under the watchful eyes of several enemy soldiers who held their bayoneted rifles out towards the two men. The weapons in the front line were silent now as the parties made their way to the German positions and Oscendale felt a strange sense of relief, as though he was out of the danger that had been his constant companion for the past few hours. His body ached all over as the adrenaline and energy began to recede and evaporate from his pores. But at least he was still alive.

CHAPTER 27

Ypres Salient – Friday, 24th August 1917

O SCENDALE WAS FULLY aware that they would soon be searched and their possessions taken, ready to be gambled over later, so he had removed his watch and dropped it into the top of his left boot while he was in the shell hole. *That's not going anywhere,* he thought. He had also crumpled up his packet of cigarettes and pushed them into the earth. *I'm damned if I am going to let some Hun have them.*

His wallet was tossed back to him after being relieved of most of its contents by a soldier who was apparently already pleased with his bounty from the other two prisoners. Oscendale, the officer and the limping crewman were given an escort of two German infantrymen and instructed to go further back to the reserve trenches. They kept moving at the wounded man's pace. He was occasionally prompted with the butt of a rifle to walk faster by the impatient escort, before they eventually reached a solidly-built section of trench. They climbed down into it and were roughly ushered towards a dugout entrance.

A young soldier wearing a cap stared at them in fascination. To Oscendale's eyes he looked about sixteen. At the end of the trench older, far more experienced eyes were scrutinising them. Three German officers watched their progress, one holding a cigar between gloved fingers. Another, with his arms folded, scowled at them while the third spun on his heel and went back into the dugout.

They descended a long set of wooden steps. The smell of sweat, unwashed bodies and tobacco smoke hung heavy in the airless chamber where their arrival was observed by the emotionless stares of several other sullen-looking Germans.

They proceeded along a corridor until they reached a second set of steps. The wounded man went down first, wincing in pain as he clambered down to the lower level. Here in a small room an officer sat writing at a sturdy-looking table. He looked up expectantly, removed his spectacles and smiled. "Good afternoon, gentlemen. Welcome to German territory."

There followed a series of questions, each amiably put, to which the three men politely replied, and then they were asked for their documents. Oscendale produced what little he had left and the others did the same. The wounded man was having difficulty standing, his wound causing him great pain, so once the questioning was over, the officer called for a guard who took him away for medical treatment.

Hauptmann Michael Bernhofer asked the man to repeat what he had just said.

The previously assured young lieutenant who stood before his desk reading the latest report became flustered. His smooth delivery interrupted, he was thrown. Anxious to retrieve his composure he mumbled, "Repeat it, *Herr Hauptmann*?"

Bernhofer continued to frown and stared intently into the distance. "Yes, you heard me. Repeat it all," he ordered. Bernhofer was not listening anyway. He just did not want any new information distracting his thoughts so he asked the man to start his report once again. His mind was whirling. *Oscendale. Captain Oscendale.* A name from the past had just reappeared.

The previous summer, during the British offensive on the Somme, and in particular, the attack on Mametz Wood, Bernhofer had come out second best in an encounter with this man he had never met. It had been a battle of wits fought across no man's land and he had lost. The memory still rankled with him, as did the humiliation he had endured from his fellow officers. He had no idea what Oscendale looked like but he had caused the death of one of his best operatives – one he had been particularly fond of – and Bernhofer wanted revenge.

Paying later is always the dearest option, he mused, and this time it would be Oscendale who paid.

In the intervening twelve months an irritated Bernhofer had fumed at the way a great prize had been snatched from his hands by this Englishman. Now here he was again. And this time he had been captured. *Another foray behind German lines?* Bernhofer smiled. This time it might be different. He knew just the right person to find out. Someone who was already in that sector. A man who had recently switched loyalties. Expensive, but after all, talent did not come cheap.

After a few hours, a new escort arrived and Oscendale was told by the German officer that they were being sent further behind the lines to be allocated to a prisoner of war camp. The escort led him and the tank officer to where three other British officers were gathered, sitting on the wooden floor of a small room off the main gallery. A Tank Corps captain lifted his head, remained seated and stared blankly at Oscendale. A second lieutenant of the Cheshire Regiment politely introduced himself as George Newell and a dark-haired lieutenant with the Manchester Regiment called Millward relayed to him how he had been separated from his men after being captured earlier that afternoon. Oscendale sat next to the captain who said brusquely, "Polain", with a quick nod of his head, clearly not in the mood for conversing with anyone.

As they were about to set off, the tank officer pulled Oscendale to one side out of earshot of their new companions. "Listen, Oscendale, I may be barking up the wrong tree here, but I was briefed yesterday that the Germans have been using infiltrators of late. You know, dressing their fellows up in our uniforms, and penetrating our lines to gather gen on our defences before returning to their own side. Those three may be kosher but I don't remember seeing any Cheshires or Manchesters in our sector of the Front, do you?"

Oscendale looked again at the three men. They were plausible enough. He ran his eyes over their uniforms. All their badges were right. No, there was nothing wrong there. In fact, there was nothing that was immediately obvious to betray any man as an undercover German spy. Perhaps he was over-reacting. Or maybe it was better to be cautious. Anyway, they could not do any harm at present as they were behind the wrong lines. If any of them was a spy then why remain in disguise?

Leutnant Otto Ziegler of Department IIIb, the German Intelligence branch, stole a look back at the military policeman. *Yes, Captain Oscendale, I recognise you. How could I forget July 1916? It was so easy taking the map from your office as you slept so peacefully in your chair. When your name was passed through to our office someone noticed it was familiar. I am here to see why you have allowed yourself to be captured. I wonder what business you have behind our lines. Yes, Captain, I recognise you but you don't have a clue who I am.*

The tank officer and he were then separated, barely having time to wish each other luck in the captivity to come. Oscendale suddenly felt a failure at the prospect of being sent to a prisoner of war camp. He would be powerless to assist the war effort and it would mean that Lucas would be free to carry on with his nefarious activities. A guttural shout rang out and the party of four were joined by three grim-faced German soldiers who urged them on their way. They were being marched off to spend the rest of the war behind a wire fence.

Later that evening, unexpectedly, like an apparition, Bernhofer's thoughts returned to Oscendale at a most inappropriate moment. The light from the fire shone on the side of the woman's cheek, illuminating the profile of her face and neck. Bernhofer leaned forward and began to gently stroke the soft, warm skin. Such loveliness in his hands among such vileness in the world seemed entirely incongruous but then things of beauty were a wonder to him at any time. Here and now it was female beauty but at other times it was architecture, art and nature.

Nature! When he thought of the carnage of the front line and the desolate landscape of Ypres his smile concealed a heavy heart.

The woman was an escape from all of that. An officer should have a mistress to distract him, and his current lover was a gem, even by his very high standards. It was truly amazing to him how beautiful women were – and this one in particular.

But tonight his mind was not wholly focused on carnal pleasures. There had been interesting news of an old adversary and Bernhofer was intrigued by the possibility of locking horns with a former foe. As the woman nuzzled into his chest, he felt her eager warmth but was unresponsive to her kisses as he thought back to the previous year and how the British policeman had robbed him of a prize. A prize valuable in financial terms but more so in terms of his career.

But he had also lost one of his best agents to the man. Not just an agent but another former lover too. She had provided Bernhofer with regular details on Oscendale's investigation at Mametz Wood, then the communication from the agent had stopped, which probably meant that she had been compromised. Whether she was alive or dead – executed by the British as a spy – he had no idea. But he did care and it had filled him with apprehension.

So the policeman Oscendale had been captured here at Ypres, according to the report. But why here? He was uncertain what was being investigated but if it was in his area then Bernhofer was curious to know.

Thoughts of revenge began to recede as the woman whispered his name and gave him even more attention, biting his earlobe and making her desire for him more urgent. He slid his hand inside her unbuttoned blouse, felt her warm breasts and decided that he had done enough military work for one day.

The girl departed just after midnight, leaving Bernhofer alone in his bed. The warmth and comfort she left behind soon began to fade, the bed grew colder and he began to reflect on this latest encounter.

What had he grown into? He would never have behaved in such a manner before the war. As a young schoolmaster in a small town school he had given everything to his charges. Their development, their enthusiasm, their love for the literature he introduced them to, had been the fuel that drove his life.

Alone with his melancholic thoughts, he realised what he had become: bitter, hardened and selfish. His physical relationships were cynical, momentary gratifications of his physical needs that left only temporary satisfaction. He had become someone else: a stranger to himself – and someone he did not really like.

But the man who had cheated him of his career advancement last summer was on his side of no man's land, being accompanied to his office before being sent on to a camp. He would be here in the morning and he would finally be able to look into the eyes of the man whose memory had tormented him for over a year.

He rolled onto his side. Tomorrow he would plan his revenge. And this time it *would* be different. After all, Oscendale was very close and getting closer.

CHAPTER 28

Poperinghe, Belgium – Friday, 24th August 1917

OSCENDALE HAD NOT returned by the time morning came but Loram was not unduly concerned. A town like Poperinghe held much of interest to a soldier. He assumed that Oscendale must have met up with some acquaintances and had probably spent the evening in an officers' club, downing a few stiff drinks and sharing some ribald off-duty stories. He had never struck Loram as a man to frequent the Blue Lamps – the officers' brothels of the towns they had been stationed in. In fact, he never spoke much about women, though Loram was aware that something had happened on his last leave that had left him morose at times, distant at others, as if turning over some great problem in his mind. Only a love affair did that to a man, in Loram's opinion. Cases such as the one they were engaged on meant more immediate action.

But by mid-afternoon Loram was concerned enough to telephone Military Police headquarters at Poperinghe where he was told that Captain Oscendale had briefly visited one of their prisoners the previous evening but had left around 7 p.m. No, he had not returned nor had he said where he was going, and yes, the prisoner Edward Copeland was due to be executed the following morning.

Loram kicked his heels for a while then decided to make a few more telephone calls.

Thirty minutes later he informed North, Oscendale's obdurate clerk, that he was on his way to Poperinghe and that Captain Oscendale was now officially absent without leave.

The gateway to the Salient, Poperinghe had been a base for

the British Army for several years. Surrounded by a collection of soldiers' camps, hospitals and supply depots, it was just twelve kilometres from Ypres. The hop fields surrounding it had been commandeered to provide the locations for a multitude of military hospitals, barracks and training grounds.

Being further back than the main target – Ypres – it was a place of comparative safety for troops out of action on a few days' leave. It had the usual array of *estaminets* and brothels, as well as a few officers' clubs. Its railway station had been the target of German artillery for three years and while parts of it were damaged, the majority of shells aimed at it had instead fallen into the town of Poperinghe itself, devastating houses, shops and public buildings. Loram had heard a rumour that the local stationmaster had been arrested, tried and then shot as a German spy and that was why the station was such a regular target for the German guns. However, it was more likely that the railway station was a target because of its importance to the British line of communication and resupply, representing as it did the main thoroughfare for arriving and departing troops.

The Salient had an atmosphere all of its own. To Loram it was bleaker, more sinister and certainly more dangerous than other parts of the Front. It was the British Army's toehold in Belgium but its significance was political and moral rather than strategic. Surrounded on three sides by the German lines, it was a place of death and destruction.

And death sometimes came from bullets fired by soldiers in khaki rather than grey. The *Stadhuis,* or town hall in the *Grote Markt,* was the place where condemned soldiers were held before they were taken outside, tied to a post or sat in a chair, blindfolded and shot.

Loram disembarked from the train, breathing in the steam cloud as it blew back along the platform from the resting locomotive hissing contentedly in front, its work temporarily done. He hurried along, noting the shell damage, handed in his travel pass to a fellow military policeman then headed into the shattered town of Poperinghe.

With Oscendale missing he knew it was his duty to take up the current case. Oscendale had shown him the letter and Loram knew that he had travelled here to talk to the imprisoned soldier. Since that time nothing had been heard from him. He was growing worried. This was not like his boss; he was dogged and persistent and was also an officer who kept his subordinates in touch with what he was doing and thinking.

The soldier sitting on the bare wooden bench, his blankets folded neatly at one end, looked up at Loram as he entered the small, stone-lined cell. The heavy metal door was closed firmly behind him and the peep hole slid open.

Loram saw a pallid, haunted face and wondered if it was true that condemned men were given morphine to dull their senses as their hour of execution drew near.

"Good morning, Copeland. My name is Sergeant Loram, Military Foot Police."

The soldier did not respond. His expression was one of hope, as if he were expecting a reprieve and Loram had come to supply it.

"I believe you had a visitor last night," Loram continued. "A Captain Oscendale."

Copeland's disappointment showed when he realised that his longed-for reprieve had not come. His shoulders dropped and his gaze returned to the stone floor of the cell as he mumbled something.

"I'm sorry, son," said Loram. "I didn't catch that. Captain Oscendale has gone missing and I'm trying to find out what happened to him."

Copeland scratched himself. "What's it got to do with me?" he said at last.

Loram tried again. "I was hoping you might be able to help me. What did you and Captain Oscendale talk about?"

The soldier stood up and went to the window. Five metal bars prevented all hope of escape and the light threw the shadows of five lines on the floor. Outside the rain fell heavily.

"He asked me about my case. He asked if I knew someone called Lucas." He paused for a few seconds and his shoulders moved as if he were trying to contain some strong emotion. "I told him what I was accused of and he seemed confused. I thought… I thought when you came in you were bringing me a message from him."

"What did you tell him about your case?" asked Loram.

The soldier turned to him, his face contorted. "I told him about that bitch. About how she led me on. How I got a court martial and now they're going to shoot me. Bastards!" Copeland spat venomously on the floor.

Loram fell silent. Nothing seemed to be making sense.

"What are you in here for, son?"

And instead of the tale of desertion which Copeland's mother had hinted at in her letter, Loram was obliged to listen to a horrific account of rape and murder. The crazed look of sheer pleasure on the young soldier's face as he boasted how he beat and abused a local prostitute shook Loram to the core of his being.

There was no way out at all for this young man. Clearly insane, he was to be shot by men from his own side and Loram could not help feeling it was the least he deserved for such a heinous act. He was a man of violence – all good soldiers were – but the gratuitous cruelty of Copeland's crime revolted him.

Loram stood up and took his leave without a shred of

pity. "Goodbye, Copeland. Oh, one more thing. Did Captain Oscendale say where he was going?"

Copeland replied gruffly, "W-H. You know, that bloody do-gooders' club."

Loram smiled grimly in return. "I'll do one thing for you. I'll write to your mother and tell her I've spoken with you, if you want."

Copeland frowned. "And why would you do that, Sarge? She's been dead and buried these past five years."

Loram was stunned. His grim smile had dissolved and it had nothing to do with Copeland's ingratitude. So the letter had been part of an elaborate trap and it appeared that it had been sprung. But why had Oscendale been lured here and by whom? Loram was determined to find out the answer and he would begin at W-H.

He was just leaving the building when he had a sudden thought. He entered the main office and asked for the latest casualty reports. What he saw on the first page shocked him. He numbly gave the paper back to the orderly and went outside. Under the heading *Missing in Action* he had seen the name *Oscendale, T. Captain.*

CHAPTER 29

Ypres Salient – Friday, 24th August 1917

THEY TRUDGED ON. The light had begun to fail now and the shadows lengthened. The guards were in no rush to be anywhere and they took frequent breaks, grunting at the four British officers to stop and sit while they threw themselves to the ground and lit up a cigarette or a long wooden pipe. It seemed they were more than happy to be away from their front lines and were determined to make the most of a few hours' rest from the carnage.

After a time they all grew used to the routine and it became Polain's habit to motion to one of the guards that he was tired and it was time for a break, to which the three guards gladly acquiesced for fifteen minutes, or sometimes more.

The journey was long and tedious. Minutes grew into hours and the yards into miles, and each mile took them further away from the British lines and closer to incarceration. Oscendale dared not remove his watch from his boot so he could only guess at the time.

It was in the early hours of the morning and they had just started their next march, when Millward tapped him on the arm. He and Newell had said little throughout the journey and for much of the time Polain and Oscendale had been the only ones talking. He had listened with feigned interest as Polain told him of the inner and outer workings of his tank, now another smouldering wreck some miles behind them. Oscendale found he could not care less. He had been in one tank and never intended to ride inside another one again. *Ever.*

Millward was gesturing towards a shape in the gloom to their left. Oscendale strained his eyes and managed to pick out a small cottage a hundred yards or so off the road.

He understood. If they were to convince their captors of the need for shelter then maybe they would have a better chance of escape when the Germans decided on a rota for sleeping. After all, it would be easier to escape from one man rather than three. Besides which, he was growing tired himself now – hungry too. The others must be feeling the same. Maybe they would get something to eat at last.

Nudging Polain in the back, he pointed left with an exaggerated gesture. As he had hoped, the largest of the Germans saw the movement and his eyes too were drawn towards the building. He spoke to his fellow guard, slung his rifle onto his shoulder and called to the third German who was leading the group.

"*Moment mal!*" shouted the leading German and the three enemy guards grouped together, discussing exactly what Oscendale had been hoping for. They then turned to the four British officers and one of them spoke in English for the first time. "We will spend the night here. Go." He prodded Newell with his rifle barrel and they all began to walk towards the building.

As they got closer, they could see that the cottage appeared to be deserted. They halted outside and one of them knocked hard on the timber door. The two other Germans looked at each other, clearly aggravated. He was pushed aside by one of them who used the butt of his rifle to shatter the lock and then kicked the door open with his booted foot.

There was no response so he entered, emerging again a short time later with a pleased look on his face. He gestured to the prisoners to enter and they soon found themselves in a single room that had been some kind of dwelling and store before the war. The earth floor was covered in places with straw though the occupants had obviously not been back for some time, judging by the cobwebs.

One of the Germans set to work in the dusty hearth while the prisoners, under the watchful eyes of the other two guards, collected armfuls of kindling. A fire was soon blazing away and the German drew back from the heat, pleased with his efforts. In the meantime one of his fellow soldiers had brought out some bread and meat from his knapsack and the three of them began to eat their supper, voraciously tearing off strips of bread and devouring them after holding them up to their prisoners and grinning.

The four British prisoners watched in envy as the Germans ate and talked loudly. One of them drew a bottle of what Oscendale assumed was schnapps from his bag, and the three of them toasted each other before drinking. They sang songs intermittently, gesturing towards their captives as they stressed particular lines. Oscendale knew enough German to realise they were marching songs that heralded Germany's victory over her enemies.

After a time the heat of the room made Oscendale sleepy and his eyelids began to droop, despite the loud banter and raucous singing of the alcohol-infused Germans. He noticed that Polain was already asleep on a filthy pile of straw, as was Millward, while Newell sat cross-legged on the floor, watching them eat and drink with ill-disguised malice.

He forced himself to stay awake, thinking of anything to keep his mind working – Hannah, what Burgess had told him about Lucas, but soon found his thoughts drifting away on a sea of sleep.

Some time later he was awoken by someone hissing into his ear. He opened his eyes, angry at having been dragged from this warm, comfortable state, to see Newell's face in front of him. "Sir," he whispered, "two of the Huns are asleep and the other one is dropping off too. Now's our chance."

Oscendale looked across the room. Newell was right. Two of the guards were snoring, stretched out on the floor. The large German was sitting with his rifle propped up in front of him, the evil-looking serrated bayonet catching the glow from the fire. But his head was dropping, just as Oscendale's had done earlier and he was clearly having trouble staying awake. The food, schnapps and the warmth in such a confined space were all combining to do their soothing work and send him off to sleep.

Polain and Millward were still taking deep, regular breaths so it was clear that only he and Newell were awake at present. He nodded at Newell, who began a slow, silent advance towards the guard.

Just as he came within a yard of him, the man's head jerked up and he opened his eyes, some sixth sense warning him that danger was approaching. But it was too late. Newell caught him clean on the jaw with his fist and the man grunted once and fell backwards, his head hitting the stone wall behind him with a crack.

Oscendale, now fully awake, leapt across the room and seized the man's rifle. Newell detached the bayonet from the end of the barrel and kicked one of the sleeping Germans in the side. The man moaned and stirred but did not wake so Newell kicked him harder. "Polain! Millward! Wake up. We've got a bit of a surprise for you!"

Polain opened his eyes and sat up with a start, while Millward blinked furiously before focussing on the scene. By now both of the Germans were wide awake and in a state of disbelief.

"But... but what are we going to do with them?" asked Polain. "We can't drag them around Belgium with us."

"Well this one's dead anyway," said Newell ruefully, looking down at the man he had attacked. "Looks like I hit him a bit too hard."

Blood was oozing from the man's nose and ears, a sure sign that the fall against the wall had fractured his skull and killed him. They now only had two Germans to worry about.

"If we find some rope we can tie them up and leave them here. They'll be found eventually by their own side," replied Oscendale and turned away to look for something suitable with which to bind the men.

"Oh, I don't think so," snarled Millward and with that he fired two shots from the rifle he had taken from one of the Germans.

Oscendale spun round in time to see the two men slumping backwards onto the earth floor.

"What the hell did you do that for?!" he yelled at Millward. Polain stood staring at the bodies, his mouth open.

"I'd have thought it was obvious," replied Millward. "Look, sir, if we are ever to get back to our own lines, we'll have a better chance without two Hun barbarians in tow. And if we left them here there's no guarantee they wouldn't have broken free and raised the alarm. This is a war."

Oscendale was furious. Killing was one thing but killing men in cold blood was another. "I know it's a bloody war, Millward. Probably better than you do! But if we behave like that then it's not a war worth fighting. Barbarians? It's bloody obvious who the barbarian is at the moment! And how far do you think that rifle noise just travelled, eh? This is dangerous enemy territory and any minute now we could have Hun soldiers arriving at our door! You're an idiot so just shut up and let me do the thinking from now on, understood?"

Ziegler frowned to himself and looked around the room. This was not turning out the way it had been planned by

Hauptmann Bernhofer. Events had taken a quite different turn. All he could do now was stay with these men and look for an opportunity to fulfil the second part of his mission. *To kill this man Oscendale.*

CHAPTER 30

Poperinghe – Friday, 24th August 1917

L ORAM COULD HEAR the sounds in the distance heralding
more death and suffering. *Another day, another
bombardment. Welcome to the Salient.* He walked along the
maze of cobbled streets of Poperinghe until the road narrowed
and he became lost. He asked directions of a passing soldier
coming out of a café and was shown the way to his destination.
He drew his trench coat even tighter around him as the rain
poured down from the gloomy sky.

At last he stopped outside a three-storey building. Once an
elegant Belgian town house, it now had a sign above the double
front doors that read 'Wyndham House 1915 – Every Soldier's
Club'. Well known to soldiers serving around the battered
fortress of Ypres, it was the haunt of men of all ranks who found
their way here to share company and conversation, brief periods
of solace before their return to action. Loram could think of
nowhere else to go at present, given the devastating news he had
read at the *Stadhuis,* so he pushed open one of the panelled doors
and stepped inside, past the welcome sign, into the hallway. He
could hear someone tapping out notes on a piano, an occasional
boisterous laugh and the sound of men talking.

The hallway was tiled with large buff-coloured squares of
terracotta. Some were broken and cracked, testament to decades
of occupants and especially the increased volume of visitors since
1915. Wall lights and a bronze chandelier of moderate size hung
from an ornate plaster ceiling rose and radiated a yellowish-grey
light. An arched opening to the right pointed the way to an oak
staircase that led to the first floor. A brighter light seeped into

the hallway from a door at the far end, while to the left were more doorways to several other rooms.

Khaki-clad soldiers stood around in groups, smoking and conversing. What struck Loram was the mix of different ranks. Officers and other ranks were sharing tales and jokes. Boundaries were blurred here, and there was little insistence on formality. It was as though the war had ended and peace had been declared. *Perhaps it had, perhaps it was all over.*

But there were house rules, as one might expect with a military institution. On a sign on the wall, stained brown, grim letters pronounced: 'Keep your temper. Nobody else wants it.'

He looked at a picture on one of the walls. The leaders of the enemy states were playing a game of dice at the scene of the crucifixion. Christ hung on the cross, pierced and bleeding. 'Humanity' was written across his loincloth. The background showed churches burning and black crows circling. The skulls of the dead were piled up in heaps at the foot of the cross.

Loram wondered whose side Christ was on. 'Bloodshed brings redemption', said the caption. But whose? What was evil and what was goodness? Was it really laudable to kill? And to what end?

On another notice board was a poem:

The Bishop tells us: 'When the boys come back
They will not be the same; for they'll have fought
In a just cause: they lead the last attack
On the Anti-Christ; their comrades' blood has bought
New right to breed an honourable race,
They have challenged Death and dared him face to face.'
'We're none of us the same!' the boys reply.
'For George lost both his legs; and Bill's stone blind;
Poor Jim's shot through the lungs and like to die;
And Bert's gone syphilitic: you'll not find

A chap who's served that hasn't found some change.'
And the Bishop said: 'The ways of God are strange!'

Loram entered a room in which around thirty soldiers sat
reading. The faded décor gave a hint as to its salubrious past,
but the peeling wallpaper, flaking paint and cracks in the ceiling
showed a terminal deterioration.

The next room he entered was still in touch with its past.
Expensive wall decorations, showing colourful tropical birds in
even more mysterious foreign landscapes, framed the sides of a
crisp white door. The men seated within ignored him, so intent
were they on listening to one of the soldiers reading a poem:

"Through wood and dale the sacred river ran,
Then reached the caverns measureless to man,
And 'mid this tumult Kubla heard from far,
Ancestral voices prophesying war!"

There was a pause in the speaker's delivery and not a man
moved. The hubbub of conversation in the hallway he had just
left faded. Each man knew the significance of the lines and each
retreated into his own private thoughts. Loram stood still too,
caught in the web of it all, that moment when a group of human
beings are feeling just one emotion to the exclusion of all others.
It was magical, momentous and maudlin.

"Go on then, Kubla. Get on with it," interjected an impatient
voice and the moment was lost forever. Other voices joined in,
glad that it was gone. Too painful to keep, it was time to let go.

"Yes, come on, Ted, next line! Before we all die of boredom!"
Men laughed and the spell was broken. The recital continued.

He left the group to their mock happiness and was drawn
towards the long windows at the rear of the house where a door
led out onto the garden.

The building had narrowly survived the attentions of the German gunners. Located down a side street, it was still within range of their guns and a shell had landed in its garden leaving a huge, gaping black and brown hole in the earth.

The garden which should have been in full bloom had been hammered by the incessant rain that came down like bullets fired from the heavens. He leaned against the open door and sympathised with the tulips smashed flat by the force of the rain. They lay, blood-red and fiery-yellow, like stricken bodies on the ground. Rivulets of mud ran down the stone path and meandered their way towards him.

"Dashed awful weather," said a voice. Loram turned to see a short, bespectacled, wispy-haired military chaplain, who peered myopically out at the forlorn garden and sighed. "I worked so hard to plant that up in the spring too. Sometimes God tells you not to waste your time and to do something different eh?" He removed his round-rimmed glasses and began to polish them. "I'm Carlton by the way. I run this house."

Loram examined the face of the speaker. There was a softness of demeanour, weighed down by a deep compassion. A man you could instantly trust.

"Yes, Father. I suppose he does. Perhaps it's time for us all to leave and do something different. Maybe it's time to go home."

"Have you lost something, my son? Or should that be *someone*?" asked Carlton.

Loram grimaced. Was this the sympathy coming that he did not want? There was no-one who understood the pain he was suffering at present. Losing Oscendale was like losing a brother.

"Yes," he replied slowly. "My officer, Captain Oscendale. I believe he came here yesterday… " He could say no more.

The padre furrowed his brows and thought before responding. "Oscendale? An unusual name. I would have remembered that. No, he hasn't been here."

Loram fell silent. After a time Carlton motioned at the garden again. "I've lost friends and even relations too in this ghastly war. And when I'm gardening I wonder what the point of it all is. The flowers grow and decay and people I know die with increasing regularity. The men who once came here, many of them haven't come back. And I like to think it's not just me. Or my sermons." With his head tilted to one side he smiled at Loram who appreciated the black humour of the remark.

"No-one will know when you are old that all of this happened. No-one will ask you about it. Time will have moved on, new people with new lives in a new era will take their own place in the world," said the padre sadly. "They won't care about what we have all been through. They will just see us as silly old men who have lost our marbles and can't have ever done anything remotely interesting. Ever. We will live in that sort of society. It will denigrate the elderly and what they did. Remember your friend, my son. Don't you ever forget him." He pointed to the staircase. "We have a small chapel, you know. Sounds grand but it's really just a few benches for the boys to sit on and an old table we use as an altar. They take some comfort from my rudimentary efforts. It might help." And with a broad smile he was gone.

Loram lit a cigarette and smoked for a while afterwards, leaning against the door frame, thinking about Oscendale, the past, the future. *The future.* What did this war hold for him? Another lost friend and no end to the killing. He threw his cigarette into the garden in disgust and turned back inside as the rain continued to fall.

He climbed the twisting stairs to the first floor. At the top was an even steeper set of wooden stairs with a note attached. 'Jacob's Ladder', some wag had written. Loram smiled to himself. There was humour in this house, which he expected of soldiers, but also an informality that was quite at odds with military life.

Grasping the worn handrails, he levered himself upwards until he emerged into a room that was filled with light, despite the dark clouds that now lay overhead. Immediately he sensed peace, tranquillity and even spirituality.

This converted hop loft was humble, even basic, as the padre had intimated, but there was something here, the evidence of a presence. There was sanity here, as there had been below, amid all the madness. There was also a sense of being watched in a kindly way which became manifest when a voice behind him said, "I told you it wasn't much, young man, but we do our best."

Loram turned to see Carlton mounting the last few steps. In one hand he held a wooden cross and a white cloth. When he reached the top he walked between the rows of benches and placed the cross on the altar.

But Loram did not see the cross of Christ. What he saw was the cross of a battlefield grave. It threw him from the place he was in to one that was far more uncomfortable.

Carlton was followed by a stream of soldiers. Each one mounted the steep stairs and took their place in the chapel. They placed themselves in rows and sat in silence, heads bowed, facing the front. Carlton was dressed in his robes of office – the white surplice contrasting vividly with the black of the cassock. *Darkness and light. Blindness and sight. The way forward and the way back.* He intoned the order of service and the voices of the lines of khaki backs in front of Loram responded in kind.

His mind travelled back to another time when he had stood in the confines of the great abbey at Tewkesbury each Sunday with his family. First as a small boy, flanked by his sisters and brothers, with his mother and father keeping a careful watch on their offspring, seated at each end of the row of thin wooden chairs that they occupied. Then later, with his own family, his wife and young son. There in the long nave and Romanesque tower he had first experienced the power of man's vision of a house of God. The light had flowed through the medieval and the more recent Victorian stained glass windows and he had looked in awe at the colours and forms of the glass panels. He had lifted his eyes upwards and picked out the roof bosses of gilded angels and saints that gazed benevolently down on him.

But here in this low-ceilinged room, with death and destruction so close and so immediate, he read antiquated words that seemed remote and distant and he had no heart to join in.

Swift to its close ebbs out life's little day;
Earth's joys grow dim, its glories pass away.

He felt the raw tension in the room, experiencing the collective will of men praying for survival. There was an energy here that sought to rise above the fatalism that was so prevalent while they were in the trenches. That hopelessness had become distant, remote yet omnipresent. Now there was a determination to try every means to survive.

I need Thy presence every passing hour;
What but Thy grace can foil the tempter's power?

And Carlton's persona shone through it all like a beacon, a symbol of hope and inspiration. His very presence soared above this motley congregation. He was one of them and yet not. His soft, sonorous voice was lulling them all into an almost hypnotic state, where Heaven met Earth, where death met the living, and each soldier felt blessed, unique, destined to escape the approaching cataclysm, setting aside the devil in each of them.

Loram saw and felt it all. Carlton drew him in, offered him succour, absolution, hope and even forgiveness for what he had done. Then the image of the poster on the hallway wall came back to him once more. The crucifix on the altar in front of

Carlton became again a wooden grave marker and the spell was broken. He was somewhere else. The skulls of the dead were piled high and unseen forces threw dice to decide who would live and who would die. And above it all the suffering of Christ on his cross and man beneath became intertwined and were one, tortuous whole.

I fear no foe, with Thee at hand to bless;
Ills have no weight, and tears no bitterness.

He wondered why a path to God must be through a man, yet if a room was an extension of one's personality then this attic chapel truly was an extension of Carlton's. Snatches of phrases came to him as his mind drifted away from the past to the present.

The debris of humanity was here, the desperation of the individual, the decay of the human spirit, the collapse of society and the depression of his own existence. He felt a great wave of sadness well up inside him.

He looked down at his hands holding the pages of the hymn book apart and noticed the brown staining to the paper. Hundreds of other hands had held open these pages as he did now. Hundreds of eyes had gazed at these words. Numerous voices had been raised to the heavens in song. The cry for redemption and survival.

Shine through the gloom and point me to the skies
Heaven's morning breaks, and earth's vain shadows flee.

He lost himself in his gloomy thoughts and was still looking up at the ceiling as the prayers concluded. Closing the burgundy cover of the book, he placed it in the wooden rack on the back of the chair in front of him.

The congregation was still standing, at one with Carlton, following his every word. Yet Loram was detached, on the periphery of this, lost on a journey somewhere to the heavens. Life, death, it was all without relevance here. The clergyman was attempting to open the portal, to connect the mass of fighting men with God himself, but Loram felt it was all false hope, all without purpose or end. The soldiers would go on believing that God had picked them out from amongst the living, had chosen them to survive. The eternal finger had pointed and they would live. Or die. And if they died they would be martyred here in the mud of Ypres. Remembered for a time and then forgotten. Gone for all time.

"Sit down, sergeant and join the rest of us." It was Carlton. A sea of faces was looking at him, some with amusement, some with annoyance. He was the last man left standing. Alone. No, not true. He and Carlton had lifted themselves above the congregation and faced each other above the clouds.

He sat down quickly, feeling very conspicuous, his face burning while the muffled sound of several comments travelled around the room. Rubbing a hand over his face, he realised he was tired, that was all. He could not remember the last good sleep he had enjoyed. His mind was flying off in odd directions and he was losing touch with reality. *That had been quite a journey just now.*

The rest of the service passed in a blur and he felt his heavy eyelids droop as Carlton recited yet more prayers and the service reached its conclusion. As he was leaving Carlton touched his arm. "You were gone there for a minute or two, Sergeant Loram. Was my service really that dull?"

Loram gazed into Carlton's cheery face. He was smiling at him and Loram felt ashamed of his earlier thoughts. But it was not Carlton's actions or tender ministering that had angered him. It was the whole juxtaposition of religion and killing. It was difficult to fix in a world as unsettled as this. He realised that religion was as much about individual human beings as its trappings of churches, hymn books and strange garbs. He smiled at the man, shook his head and replied, "No, father. It's not you, it's me."

Carlton nodded and said, "A soldier can find that the God inside of him is not the one he was expecting. Get some sleep, Loram. Try in there." Carlton leaned forward and pointed down the ladder to a door at the side of the floor below. "That's a spare bedroom. Put your head down and I'll make sure you're not disturbed."

Loram felt the tiredness wash over him and he accepted the offer gratefully. He descended the steep stairs and opened the door.

Whatever is troubling that sergeant is growing, thought Carlton. *I hope he finds absolution soon otherwise it may destroy him.*

CHAPTER 31

Ypres Salient – Saturday, 25th August 1917

A S THEY MADE their way across the fields that encircled the abandoned cottage, steering their course west by the position of the moon, Oscendale mulled over the events of the last few minutes. If any of his current companions was a German spy then the man had missed a prime opportunity to save himself from what was going to be a very hazardous journey over the next few hours. At any time he could have told the guards who he was and been saved. Oscendale and the others would have been quickly dispatched to keep the man's identity secure and their bodies hurriedly buried in anonymous graves. Instead he had chosen to continue to be part of the small group. Perhaps it was a convoluted attempt to infiltrate the British lines. Or did he hope to gather further information from the other three officers?

Oscendale considered Millward's actions. He had seized a rifle from the astonished Germans and fired two rounds into them in quick succession. There had been no time for anyone to protest. Had he killed them to prevent them exposing him as the spy? But there again, Newell had dealt a savage and fatal blow to the dozing guard. Had he done that deliberately or had it been a tragic accident? Would a German spy really kill one of his own countrymen in cold blood? Or perhaps he was reading too much into it all. He rubbed a weary hand over his face. The strain of the past few hours could be getting to him. It was, of course, entirely possible that each of the other three officers was genuine. Without that poison in his ear he would be seeing the situation exactly as it was – four British prisoners on the run.

He had watched all of their faces closely in the aftermath. Millward had been sullen after Oscendale's rebuke, whereas Newell had been disdainful and had commented that all Germans deserved to die. Had there been a glint of excitement in his eye as well? Perhaps that had just been the residue of the tension he had felt in approaching the sleeping guard. Polain had just been stunned by the savagery of it all.

So far then, it was inconclusive. If one of them was a spy then he was hiding it well. *But then that was what spies were trained to do.*

They had reached a railway line. Polain was standing on one of the sleepers, looking up and down the track for any sign of a train, but all was still and quiet and the moon came and went as scudding, bluish-grey clouds grew in number above them. Just at that moment Oscendale felt the first drops of rain fall on his face. He checked the time and saw it was just after 2 a.m., about three hours away from dawn.

Moving across open fields behind enemy lines in daylight was out of the question so they had to make as much progress to the west as they could during the hours of darkness. They headed along the railway line until it began to bend northwards so they abandoned it and continued along a track towards a wood that appeared black and sinister ahead of them. They were reluctant to enter it but Oscendale pointed out that there would be paths to follow which would speed up their journey.

The next stage of their trek was spent almost in silence as they followed an uneven muddy track that ran straight through the wood, listening to the rustling of the trees above their heads and halting only when they heard movement among the dark, closely-packed trunks – tense and then relieved on each occasion that it was merely an animal moving around in the tangled undergrowth.

When they emerged from the wood they found themselves

on the edge of a battle-scarred village. As they looked down on the gaping holes in the roofs and the broken walls, they felt a sense of dread. This was all that remained of what had once been a sleepy Belgian village – death and decay, illuminated by the bluish tinge of the moon. Tangled piles of wooden boards lay in heaps either side of what was, strangely, still recognisable as the main thoroughfare. Twisted shapes of splintered trees stood amid piles of rubble. The chewed remains of a church, eaten away by the remorseless effect of shellfire, rose up behind the jagged outlines of bricks and masonry. A solitary damaged signpost indicated the way to an indecipherable destination, as if pointing a sad finger at the destruction all around them.

They walked cautiously into the gloomy outskirts before Oscendale raised a hand as he saw something moving ahead. An enormous rat scurried across the track in front of them, disappearing into a hole beneath a mound of broken bricks. Lying incongruously in the middle of the main street was the swollen corpse of a cow. A gigantic hole was cut into its stomach and as they approached, a legion of vermin poured forth and frantically scurried away into the distance. All four men halted at the sight and none of them showed any willingness to proceed.

"I think it's probably best if we wait here until the sun rises," suggested Newell quietly. "We don't know who's in the village and it's too dangerous to go nosing around for food in the dark."

Polain grunted. "If there's any food those bloody rats will have been at it by now. I think we should move on."

Silence fell momentarily on the group before Newell took the lead and sat himself down on a grassy verge. Oscendale, too tired to argue anymore, followed suit and sat down with his back to a tumbledown wall. Reluctantly, Millward and Polain did the same.

As the milky-white dawn swept away the shadows all around

them, they began to see more of the wrecked village. The twisted, skeletal shapes of the night became clearer and they saw the damage that had been wrought on the once-peaceful village by the force of successive artillery bombardments.

They agreed to proceed cautiously into the village. Polain was in the lead, with Newell on his left and Millward on his right. Armed with captured rifles in enemy territory, they knew they were extremely vulnerable. An attempt at capitulation to any armed Germans who might suddenly appear would probably mean death, and sooner rather than later. Oscendale brought up the rear as he had decided he did not want either Newell or Millward behind him, armed with a rifle. He was still circumspect in his opinions of the two men but he felt confident he was not revealing any of his suspicions in his dealings with them.

They progressed guardedly up the main street, checking the remnants of buildings as they went. Doors and windows were now superfluous as each building was open to the skies and few had any complete form. The decay all around them indicated that this had been an area fought over some time ago.

They came to the village church, took a quick look inside then went off to check other buildings but Oscendale remained. He had never been a very religious man but appreciated the beauty of what had once been a fine building, even if he had stopped going to his local church many years before the war began.

There had been too much posturing and one-upmanship in the church he had been forced to attend as a boy. His grandmother vying with the other ladies for the wearer of the best Sunday hat had left him remote from the central purpose of the occasion. He had joined the choir, and then left in acrimonious circumstances. His mother had insisted he join and the choirmaster had insisted he leave. Talking during the vicar's sermon was not allowed, he had slowly intoned to the young Oscendale, and laughter had no place in church.

In that desolate place it was as if God still remained, but battered and bloody. An image of Jesus on the cross passed through his mind. Heaven and Earth. All that remained of the physical manifestation of God were the jagged edges of the walls, the piles of broken wood on the floor and the ruined altar. Still, he now had a clearer view of Heaven perhaps, he thought, through the gaping hole where the roof had once been. He pictured the congregation coming here to worship. But the shells had come and destroyed their church. Such a pity. He admired the faith of those who had come here. It was not for him, that single-minded belief in a greater being, a higher entity, but he knew how it could shape and form a life, drive a person on, give them strength. Not a pale imitation of it. *An imitation, a veneer...*

Then he understood. He knew now he had been much mistaken over the identity of the Barry murderer. It hit him like a punch. How could he not have seen it when it was staring him in the face? Yet here he was, trapped behind enemy lines. And when their guards did not report in at headquarters, the alarm would be raised. The bodies of the dead Germans would be discovered and a manhunt would begin for the four of them, if it had not already done so. They had become fugitives and could expect only summary justice if they were caught. Having dispatched three of their comrades, their captors would exact swift revenge. But he knew that catching the murderer still at large hundreds of miles away would depend on his returning safely to the British lines, and it made him even more determined to survive.

Eventually they were all satisfied that the only living beings that remained in the village were themselves and the rats, which appeared all too frequently at the smell of this fresh meat. They found a building that still had walls high enough to hide them from the enemy and settled onto the remains of the wooden floor. It was not safe to light a fire to dry their damp clothes, so they positioned themselves so that the morning sun would dry them naturally.

They agreed a sentry rota and Polain took first shift. Oscendale felt reassured and allowed himself to relax. Within minutes he was lost to sleep.

It was not a restorative sleep, but then again what did he expect? His vivid dreams were a fertile area for the irrational and bizarre, and he was relieved when he awoke to a bright sun bathing his face in warmth. Bleary-eyed, he watched smoke rising from the sleeping figures of Newell and Polain. For a moment he thought both men were smouldering and he laughed inwardly at his folly when he realised it was merely the heat of the sun drying their damp clothes.

"Sleep alright, sir?" asked a voice behind him. He turned round to see Millward on guard duty, his captured German G98 resting on a window ledge, the barrel pointing down the main street.

"Not really," replied Oscendale. "Bad dreams. Sometimes it's good not to dream." He felt nervous that Millward had taken over sentry duty from Polain without his knowledge and that he had slept through it. The man could have killed them all. But perhaps he was wrong about Millward. Maybe none of them were German spies. Perhaps he just needed more sleep. After the discomfort of the previous days this was pleasant. And warm.

When he awoke again it was Newell who was leaning over him. He would have given anything for a few more minutes of rest. "Your turn, sir," he said and Oscendale groaned as he slowly dragged himself up from the depths, stretched and stood ready to take his turn at the fractured window.

Nothing stirred all day and the rotation of sentry duty went on until dusk. With each passing hour Oscendale grew more and more uneasy about the devastated village. There was a brooding menace that came over it as the light began to falter. A disturbing sense of death began to seep into his soul. It was something intangible, something unspecific, yet something told him it was there. He sniffed the air like an animal but smelt nothing out of the ordinary. What was it then? They had searched the buildings and found nothing unusual. The village was still deserted so why did he feel like he did?

Then in the distance he heard it: a faint rumbling. He strained to listen again and the indistinct noise repeated itself. It was the sound of horses' hooves. He turned away from the window and woke the others. "Quick, wake up! Someone's coming."

The men roused themselves immediately and all four were soon at the ready behind the walls of the house and several tense minutes passed during which they listened to the approaching horses, plus the tramp of marching feet, accompanied by shouting. His mind raced. An enemy patrol dispatched to look for them? A column of advancing infantry? It was not too late to run. They could slip out of the back door and be into the fields beyond in a matter of seconds. But would that be any safer than staying hidden here? He urged the others to wait for a few more minutes. If it was a column of reinforcements then the information might be useful to headquarters when they eventually crossed back to their own lines. Perhaps it was a unit of their own men, part of the great advance. Had they broken through the German lines?

So they waited. A rider appeared at the end of the road. An *Uhlan*, a German cavalryman, resplendent in his uniform and seated on a large black horse, led a column of marching men. But there was something irregular about the men. They were not marching like disciplined ranks of infantrymen. They were in disarray, weary, bedraggled, out of step and Oscendale wondered for a moment if they were walking wounded being taken to a field hospital. Then he noticed other *Uhlans* at the sides and eventually one at the rear. *The men were prisoners. British prisoners.*

His heart beat furiously. Here was a chance to set free a number of British soldiers. They had three rifles between them and there were how many *Uhlans*? Six. They should be able to deal with six *Uhlans*, especially in territory like this where they could not use their horses to charge them down. He turned to look at Polain.

He was nowhere to be seen.

Only Millward was alongside him. Newell too had gone. The anger began to boil up inside him. This was a chance to release a score of British prisoners and his group had been halved in a few seconds.

"Where the hell are the others?" he hissed. Millward turned away from the Germans and looked around him. He shrugged and shook his head.

Oscendale signalled to Millward to stay where he was and crawled backwards from the open window frame until he was certain he was out of sight of the *Uhlans* who were getting closer by the second. He skirted around the wall at the rear of the building and looked left and right for a sign of the two men. There was none.

Trusting his instincts, he turned right, jumped what was left of the collapsed wall and entered the next broken-down house. Creeping quietly and trying not to scrunch on broken glass, he rounded the last wall and peered along the remnants of a row of small gardens that abutted onto the line of ruined houses.

The sight that greeted him stopped him dead in his tracks.

Newell was kneeling amid the ruins of a broken outhouse. Polain was several yards away pointing a rifle at him. He turned around as Oscendale approached then returned his aim quickly to the kneeling Newell.

"Oscendale, this man is a traitor."

Oscendale's mind whirled. The world had gone backwards and was standing on its head.

"Keep your bloody voice down. What do you mean *traitor*?"

The rifle barrel was shuddering. Polain was evidently under great stress.

"Tell me what's happened? What's going on?"

Polain took a deep breath and lowered his rifle. "I noticed him sloping off just as we spotted the *Uhlans*. I decided to leave you and Millward to watch them while I followed him to see what he was up to. He's been behaving a bit suspiciously for a while. I'm surprised you haven't noticed, if you don't mind me saying."

"Suspiciously? What are you talking about?"

"Well, do you recall when we first arrived here? Do you remember how he was keen to spend the day here? It was a lunatic decision to my mind, and I said so at the time. If this village has been shelled it's obviously of some importance to the Germans. Our best move would have been to press on until we found a more isolated place."

Newell, who had said nothing up to this point, spoke for the first time. "Don't listen to him, sir. He's talking nonsense."

"Shut your mouth, Newell!" shouted Polain.

"Quiet!" demanded Oscendale. "Get down, Polain. The Germans will see you in a minute and we'll all be done for."

Polain dropped to the ground in a squat.

"Look, sir," pleaded Newell, "it was not like that at all. I was the one who saw Polain creeping off so I decided to follow him. I gestured to you but you were too fixed on the *Uhlans* to notice me. I couldn't let him get a head start so I set off after him. Got a bit too close and he sprung on me. Now he's trying to twist the story and shift the finger of suspicion on to me."

Oscendale looked at Polain who raised the rifle again. Oscendale batted it down with his hand. "Nobody's shooting anybody on our side, so put the bloody thing down. We have bigger fish to fry. The Germans are getting away and you two have mucked up our chance of releasing those British prisoners."

There was a scurrying of feet behind them and Oscendale and Polain whirled around, rifles at the ready. Millward leapt the wall and nearly landed on top of them. He was edgy and out of breath.

"Got fed up of waiting for you, sir. Thought I might be the only one left so I left them to it. They didn't spot me and are continuing down the main street," he said before adding despondently, "I think we've lost our chance of freeing those boys. Looks like they'll be spending the rest of the war in a prisoner of war camp."

The four men said nothing for a few seconds until Polain piped up. "So what are we going to do about him, Oscendale?" he asked flicking his rifle towards Newell.

"What the hell are we going to do about you, more like," responded Newell. "Bastard! You have to believe me, sir."

Oscendale bit his lip and thought for a few moments. At last he spoke. "Look, at the moment I don't trust either of you. One of you is lying to me but I can't tell which. I'm just going to have to keep an eye on both of you for a while. Meanwhile, the *Uhlans* have gone and so have those poor prisoners. If it wasn't for you two we'd have been able to kill the Boche and release our men. As it is we're stuck behind enemy lines with a traitor in our midst and it's one of you two. Millward, take the rifle."

"What?" hissed Polain. "You think it's me?"

Oscendale was close to losing his temper. The events of the past few minutes were shredding his nerves. *This is the time to prove you're a leader, Tommy boy,* he said to himself.

"I don't know yet," he said irritably. "It's one of you and until it becomes clear who it is, Millward and I will take the rifles and you two can just trust us to behave." He looked grimly at both men.

"This is ridiculous," sighed Polain. "I'm no spy, he is… I saw him… the bastard tried…"

"Shut up, Polain!" cut in Oscendale. "I've just about had a bloody gutful of this. Get up. We're leaving. It'll be dark soon so we'd better get on with it."

CHAPTER 32

Ypres Salient – Saturday, 25th August 1917

T HE STRAW WAS piled in untidy heaps around the perimeter of the barn, bale upon bale, winter food for animals that was now being used as bedding for men. Some of the soldiers lay on their sides, resting on one elbow and chatting away to their pals while a few were already asleep, mouths agape, snoring loudly and oblivious to the activity around them. Others were just settling into their new billets, wandering around, looking for a comfortable spot among the detritus of an infantry battalion at rest and out of the front line.

The barn had been abandoned by its owner, probably since the first weeks of the war. Amid the debris was discarded farming equipment, rusting through lack of use. A wheelbarrow was propped against the huge wooden doors that were barred shut on the far side of the barn, perhaps in a vain attempt to prevent the forces of war from barging in. The machinery of the military had taken over and replaced the tilling of the ground with the tilling of men. More crops for Death's rich harvest.

A soldier had made good use of the nails protruding from the wooden posts which supported the ancient roof. On one side he had hung his boots, on another his steel helmet; his webbing and pack hung on a third and on the fourth, his rifle. His companions saw what he had done and began appropriating other posts and nails for themselves. Others were less fastidious. Tiredness having overcome them, rifles had been laid on the hay matting and packs and webbing soon joined them.

Games of cards and dice began, formed as if on command, and men stood in circles to watch or offer advice. It was noisy with the hubbub and banter of men's voices. Most of the soldiers had removed their helmets and donned their trench caps instead, a smattering of old-style caps for the survivors from the first years of the war mixing with the softer, untidier 'Gor Blimey' caps of the latest recruits.

Some men had acquired old, patterned blankets somewhere on their recent travels and pulled these from their packs to draw around themselves to ward off the chill in the night air. Those without buttoned their greatcoats to the throat, while fires began to burn and flicker in cleared areas of the earth floor.

Tobacco smoke hung heavy in the air, creating a haze that rose up into the gloomy heights of the barn. A black and white cat leapt over one set of legs to another in search of food, while a group of men in a corner tried to attract its attention by whistling and calling out. They had evidently spotted a rat whose demise would give many of them and their colleagues a less interrupted sleep that coming night.

The men's spirits were good, noted Loram, but they usually were. He had known gloom and despondency whether in or out of the line. The soldiers were always pessimistic, but the camaraderie of the front line bred a black humour that was encouraged and enjoyed.

A kneeling, bespectacled soldier was endeavouring to coerce life out of a smouldering pile of hay. Loram watched his cheeks balloon as he blew and cursed in equal measure until a spark became a flame. A cheer of approbation went up from several figures to whom he gave an exaggerated bow, and Loram realised that he was missing the comradeship of a military unit. His new job had taken him away from all that. He had a much smaller circle of acquaintances now and for a moment he hankered after a return to his previous existence. But then he recalled his days as a sniper, lonely days, shunned by his pals as an unwelcome centre of enemy attention from shellfire and opposing snipers.

He realised that he had been more of a solitary figure than he had imagined.

He spoke briefly to a nearby soldier who, between scratching his flea bites, glanced around and pointed to the rear of the barn. Loram weaved his way through the throng of mostly prostrate figures and finally saw the man he had spent most of the day endeavouring to track down. Ossie Burgess's erstwhile batman, Private John Haveldar, was sitting with his back to a wall of the barn, legs outstretched, smoking contentedly on his pipe.

Loram sat down next to him and began a conversation. Within minutes the subject had turned to Haveldar's recent role as a stretcher-bearer. "We soon used up our official supplies of dressings. There were so many men to treat that there was never enough of the proper material, so we resorted to whatever we could find. I tore up anything, whether it was a sheet, a shirt, socks. We needed dressings so we used all this stuff, anything really. We tried to find clean material but usually we used whatever came to hand. It was either let the man bleed to death or take a risk with gangrene as the result of a dirty dressing. That's not much of a choice is it?"

Haveldar looked at Loram as if daring him to choose the wrong option but he knew better than to argue with a stretcher-bearer. He sat quietly and let the man continue.

"I was soon covered in mud and blood, soaked through from the sodding rain, and hungry, damned hungry. I'd be there out in the mud attending to a man who was screaming his lungs out and the fighting and shelling was going on all around me. Sometimes the casualty would be hit again and he'd die right in front of me. Then I'd have to move on to another one, all the time wondering if I'd be next, if I'd have to treat myself." He shook his head sadly at the absurdity of it all. "It was like a nightmare. I'd bawl and curse at the Huns and shake my fist at them for all that wasted effort."

The rain continued to hammer down on the roof of the barn and having found Haveldar at last, Loram was determined not to lose him. Haveldar, deep in thought, took a slow, steady puff of his pipe before exhaling a swirl of aromatic grey smoke.

"Sometimes there's no sign of a road or path up there." He gestured with his thumb to somewhere over his left shoulder. "The rain has obliterated it all. Six men to carry a stretcher. Slipping in and out of the mud. It sucks at your legs and your strength. Sometimes you're up to your waist in it. You make two journeys and that's all you can do. You're knackered. All you want to do is lie down and rest.

"And you can hear the shrieks in no man's land. Yelling, screaming. Voices begging and crying for help. Those poor sods who've crawled into shell holes and can't get out. They're stuck. The bloody rain fills the crater with water and drowns them."

He paused again, his eyes staring across the barn, his mind far away.

"That day I was treating one poor blighter who had his head all smashed in by a lump of shrapnel and yet he was still alive. His lips were moving and a horrible gurgling sound was coming out. I could see his brain, all pink and corrugated through the hole in his skull. His terrified eyes were bulging with the pain. I worked on him for ten minutes with all hell breaking loose around me until his lips stopped moving and his eyes went glassy. I sometimes wonder what his last few thoughts were, and if he saw me at all."

At last the man finished. As he drew on his pipe and drank from the bottle of beer Loram had provided, he was not there. He was somewhere else in his recent past, out there on the battlefield with the dead and the dying.

"Anyway," Haveldar said at last. "There's time enough for all that when we have to go back. For the time being let's just drink beer, eh?"

Loram clinked bottles with Haveldar and they both downed large mouthfuls of the Belgian beer.

"I suppose you must have seen some sights, though. I mean, the bravery of our lads," opened Loram.

"Oh aye, there were some mad bastards too. The bloodlust got into them and they just charged forward, screaming and yelling like sodding madmen. Sometimes it worked and they got there and other times they didn't and they were shot. It's all fate really, isn't it?"

"Yes, you don't know what's coming next. Whether that bullet has got your name on it or someone else's. And officers, eh? Mad beggars some of them."

"Yes, good ones too." Haveldar nodded. "Brave ones. Some didn't last, though." He raised a finger to the side of his head and rotated it.

"Cracking up you mean? I know. I've seen plenty of those. Poor sods can't help it. There's all sorts of courage. Not every brave man gets a medal."

Haveldar leaned forward conspiratorially. "Well, Sarge. It all depends on what someone wants."

"How do you mean? You think some of them are cowards?"

"Could be," replied Haveldar. "But sometimes an officer might not want the truth to get out. Someone might be… sort of sent away… to keep them out of the way. You know what I mean? The lieutenant I was batman to, for example." He tapped the side of his nose.

"Really? Tell me more. Tell me about your lieutenant," said Loram and brought out another bottle of beer from his pack.

CHAPTER 33

Ypres Salient – Saturday, 25th August 1917

T HE GIRL WAS young, about fourteen. She sat on a chair next to the fire which she attentively poked with a metal rod, making the flames leap up and spark. The light from the glowing wood flickered on the skin of her face and she looked back at Oscendale, confidently holding his gaze before her perceptive eyes took in the details of the three other British officers. To Oscendale she had immediately seemed an innocent among all this depravity. But now he saw there was an older, harder edge to her face and he wondered how that experience came to be there in one so young.

Seeing what the men were engaged in, the girl took the decision to assist them. Leaning to one side, with a movement born of years of practice, she placed her hands on the wooden arms of the chair, levered herself out and stood up. The movement was stiff and awkward, as if she were in pain, and Oscendale noticed for the first time since they had entered the room that one of her legs was wrapped in a metal brace which protruded beyond the hem of her skirt. The young girl saw that he had seen it and she merely smiled. A smile, he thought, that spoke of sadness and suffering. He felt a pang of guilt at bringing more into her home.

Chorin said, "This is my daughter, Isabelle. She will help me tend to your wounded friend. Quick, lay him on the table and take his tunic off."

They picked Newell's static body up again and laid it on the table. The blood had soaked a large, dark red stain on the front of Newell's tunic and his breathing had turned into a rasping sound, punctuated by the bubbling of liquid deep in his lungs. Isabelle gently held his bloodied hand between her two small hands. His eyes remained closed and his face had taken on a deathly pallor, visible even in the semi-darkness of the room.

It had all been so sudden. There had been an explosion that had lit up the gathering gloom of the evening. A *potato masher*, a German stick grenade, or something similar had gone off with a loud thump. Oscendale had thrown himself flat on the ground and whirled around to see a cloud of black smoke rising up from the side of the road. The other three men were lying prone behind him. He had sighed with relief as each one had raised his head in turn. Bewildered, his eyes had flickered from side to side, looking for the German who had just thrown the bomb.

Then he had heard Newell's voice calling out to him. "Sorry, sir!" he shouted, "but it was a *pickelhaube*. Just lying there by the side of the road. I thought it would make a good souvenir. Always wanted one," he had added lamely, his voice dropping as he realised the foolishness of what he had just done. "Must have been booby-trapped. Lucky I threw a stone at it first otherwise…"

But it had not ended there. The *Uhlan* had come on them in a flash. A straggler from the main party they had seen earlier had appeared a few moments later just as they emerged from the ruined village. Oscendale and Millward had opened fire and one of them had shot him dead, but not before he had stabbed his lance into Newell's chest.

They had fled the scene, concerned that the other *Uhlans* would return at the sound of the shooting and the explosion. Several anxious minutes had passed but there had been no sign of the others so they had carried the injured Newell until they chanced upon a farmhouse. The farmer had opened the door to them immediately and ushered them inside. He had introduced himself as Philippe Chorin.

They did what they could for Newell but after a time Chorin looked up at Oscendale and shook his head sadly and murmured, "I am sorry." They lapsed into silence, waiting for Newell to die.

The young girl's eyes were fixed on Newell for a long time, then she turned to Oscendale and said, *"Ce soldat a un regard d'honnête homme."*

Oscendale turned over in his mind what to do next. Polain and Millward were silent, offering no advice on their next steps. He knew they should leave Newell here with the Belgians and carry on with their journey but he was unwilling to leave the stricken soldier. There was still no proof he had been spying for the Germans.

The tension and the sadness overcame them all and they became resigned to their fate. Chorin gave them some bread and soup and hard lumps of cheese and urged them to rest. Tiredness flowed over Oscendale after he had eaten the food and eventually he decided to stay until Newell died. He told the others that the Germans would be looking for them in daylight and there was still plenty of time to rest and then press on. It would make sense to rest while they could, and they agreed.

The next thing he knew he was being shaken gently by the shoulder. He opened his eyes blearily and saw the girl leaning over him.

"Capitaine, capitaine," she whispered. *"Le pauvre homme. Il est mort."* She made the sign of the cross on herself.

Oscendale got up and languidly walked across the stone floor to the table. In the early dawn he saw there was no sign of life and when he felt for a pulse the body felt cold. Newell was dead. Polain and Millward were still sleeping. There was no sign of Chorin.

"Where is your father?" asked Oscendale, his mind a mix of emotions and still drowsy. The girl looked at him uncomprehendingly. *"Ton papa. Où est-il?"*

The girl pointed to a closed door. *"Dans son lit."* It appeared Monsieur Chorin had decided he could not forsake the comforts of his bed any longer. Oscendale did not really blame him. *"Va le chercher tout de suite!"* The girl limped off and made her awkward way to her father's bedroom.

His eyes were drawn again to Newell's dead body. As in many cases he had seen, the agony was gone from his face. He looked marble-like and serene. *And too young to die.*

A few minutes later the girl and her father appeared, the man tying his belt around an aged woollen dressing gown. He walked straight up to Newell and listened for a heartbeat. *"Mort,"* he announced simply. *Practical,* thought Oscendale. *A man who has seen many deaths, animal and human.*

As she had done to Oscendale, the girl gently woke Polain and Millward and sadly pointed to the body of the deceased man. Oscendale and Chorin carried Newell's body outside and they dug a hole in a nearby field. They split the digging between them, the older man making light work of his shift.

Newell was laid to rest as the sun rose in the morning sky and Oscendale said a rudimentary prayer over the body before Polain and Millward began to fill in the grave. It felt strange, saying a prayer at the graveside of a man who might have been an enemy spy. They had lost a night's march because of Newell and for a moment Oscendale resented that. They would have to risk moving in daylight. It was dangerous, but their pursuers would be closer now and they would surely be captured if they stayed here. Besides, he could not allow the farmer and his daughter to suffer punishment, even death, for harbouring them if they were caught at this farmhouse. And the body of the dead *Uhlan* in the nearby village might soon be discovered.

Oscendale told the others it was time to move on and they bade farewell to Chorin and his daughter. He saw again the sadness in the young girl's eyes and wondered, not for the first time, if the price they were paying for victory was far too high.

CHAPTER 34

Ypres Salient – Saturday, 25th August 1917

L ORAM STEERED THE motorcycle past the columns of troops that marched along the road into the town. Ypres itself was quiet by day. The Germans held the high ground on three sides so movement was inadvisable but at night the town took on the character of a bustling British conurbation. The roads out of the town were full of artillery units moving up, gun teams pulled by six horses with three riders and the crew on the limber. They were strung out to prevent the shelling causing even more catastrophic effects. Though the Germans continued to bombard the town, their aim was blind and the shells landed randomly.

He rode along Elverdingestraat until he reached the less than intimidating presence of Ypres Prison. A high brick wall with a fairytale turret sat on the corner of two of the main walls. It carried no menace, unlike a prison back in Britain. This one gave off an air of gentle admonition rather than severe punishment. Ypres Prison was the main straggler collecting post and it was just possible that Oscendale had been brought in here during the past twenty-four hours. He had planned to start with this and then try the dressing stations.

The guard checked Loram's pass at the main door and from there an MP promptly escorted him across the crowded courtyard. Loram stared at the grey men in grey uniforms, the hundreds of captured German prisoners huddled together in the courtyard, weary-eyed and filthy.

"That lot were brought in yesterday. They'd been captured but abandoned by their escort so they'd drifted on like a load of sheep until they'd crossed our lines. Our men are through here," said the MP, indicating the gate to another courtyard.

Scores of men were waiting patiently to be interviewed by a group of NCOs sitting at a line of desks. Loram knew these men were not deserters. In the fog of war men became detached from their units on a regular basis. They would then drift back towards the rear where they would be picked up by the MFP and, in this sector, brought here to Ypres Prison to be fed, watered and given rest before being reassigned to their parent unit.

He spent an unproductive hour scanning the lines of faces for any sign of his officer. He then took to asking randomly if anyone had seen him. It was a long shot, he knew, but Oscendale was such an unusual name he hoped it might be a case of once-heard never-forgotten, but each enquiry was met with a shrug or a shake of the head.

He was just ready to give up and leave when a soldier tapped him on the shoulder. "Oscendale, did I hear you say?" he asked. "There was an officer by that name in our trenches a day or two ago. A bit unwell, as I remember. Drop of the hard stuff perhaps." He mimed a drinking action and winked. The man gave him the sector he had been in and Loram thanked him and returned to the motorcycle he had commandeered earlier.

He rode along the lines of men travelling in both directions along the Menin Road out of Ypres. The incomers were generally quiet, while the men who made their way back into the town were brooding, sullen and agitated. They had done their bit, for the time being anyway, felt they had paid their dues and were expecting to gain their reward of time-off miles behind the lines.

There were five traffic control posts along the Ypres-Broodseinde and Ypres-Menin roads. Each one was manned by four men of the MFP who became the objects of loathing for men who were tired, hungry and battle-fatigued and eager only to be out of the hell of the front line.

Loram's motorcycle excited much curiosity from the newcomers while his red cap cover attracted only derision from the veterans, particularly when the line was halted for yet another check hundreds of yards ahead. He manoeuvred the machine along the lines, showing his pass at each of the five traffic control posts until he arrived at the front line.

From regimental headquarters on the Birr Crossroads he rode as far as he could and then left his motorcycle with 6th Battalion headquarters before continuing on foot to the front line trenches.

The dugout was about as comfortable as he had expected. A sector of German trench had been captured in the last advance and when he entered a snug, timber-lined area he saw that the reputation of the German dugouts was justified. Three British officers were grouped around a table, poring over a map.

"Sergeant Loram, Military Foot Police," he announced, saluting smartly to gain their attention.

A captain answered him with a quizzical look. "Good evening, Sergeant Loram," he answered. "Not often we see the Military Foot Police twice in a few days."

His information had been correct. "Really, sir?" he queried.

"Yes. One of your officers was through here the other day. Oscendale, I think his name was."

"And have you seen him since, sir?"

The man thought for a moment. "No, can't say I have. What about you, Brown?"

He turned to a heavy-set lieutenant who was already shaking his head and replied, "No, sir. I know that he was going forward with some of Major Lucas's men for a reconnaissance yesterday morning. He did seem rather unwell too. Groggy. An officer said he'd had a rough night and wasn't feeling up to par." He laughed and the other two joined in.

Loram frowned. *Lucas again.* "What happened to the other men, sir? Did they return?"

Lieutenant Brown thought for a while before replying. "No, now you come to mention it. I haven't seen them since yesterday. Don't know that they even went through with it. No sign of your chap since then, I'm afraid."

Loram thanked the three officers and went back outside. *Oscendale going into no man's land with some of Lucas's men?* It did not make sense. And then they had not returned. So that was why he was posted as missing. But that report had been filed during the morning. There was no way that Lucas's men could have sent in that report if they were still here in the front line in the afternoon. The telephone lines would not have been laid by then. So where was Oscendale? Loram gazed across no man's land and knew instinctively that his boss was out there somewhere.

The third officer, who had remained silent throughout the discussion, took his leave and left the dugout. He looked along the trench and saw Loram gazing out across no man's land, oblivious to him as he then entered another dugout. Asking the signaller to leave, citing confidential business, he lifted the telephone and asked to be put through to Hazebrouck.

"Hope? It's Lieutenant Eaton here. Is Major Lucas there? Oh. Well, inform him that the MP he was asking about is here. Yes. Enquiring about a missing officer called Oscendale. Ask him what he wants me to do."

CHAPTER 35

Ypres Salient – Sunday, 26th August 1917

THEY CONTINUED THEIR journey westwards through the early morning light, moving carefully along the sides of lanes and pathways. Oscendale was up in front with Polain and Millward following. Newell was gone but the threat remained of being discovered by a German patrol and being recaptured. They had come too far to fail now but had decided to take the risk of travelling in daylight. Endless detours added to the miles as each time they saw German troops they took a long, circuitous route around them.

By mid-morning they could hear shellfire in the distance. They were close to the front line at last. Their spirits rose – so far in fact that they became careless. Rounding yet another bend in a meandering lane, Oscendale suddenly came into view of a German patrol resting on the verges. There was barely time to react before a German soldier, a piece of bread raised to his mouth, gave a spluttered alarm to the rest of the dozen or so men.

Oscendale retreated, bolting as fast as he could back along the lane. As he ran towards Polain and Millward he waved to them to get out of sight as quickly as possible. All three dived through the hedging at the side and landed in the field beyond.

Behind them they could hear the tramp of boots as the Germans gave chase. Fortunately for the three men there was a small copse about a hundred yards away.

Oscendale looked into Polain and Millward's anxious faces and made up his mind.

"You two head for that copse. I'll give them something else to think about." Oscendale checked the breech of his rifle then said, "Go on then. Get out of here!"

Both men set off across the field towards the copse. Oscendale watched them go and wondered how he was going to distract the Germans so that Polain and Millward could reach the cover of the trees.

He could see nothing of the Germans on the other side of the hedge that bordered the farm fields and they were still running past him along the lane by the sound of it. There was nothing for it; he would have to reveal his own position if his two comrades were to escape.

A German raised his head over the top. It was the last thing he ever did. Oscendale's bullet hit him in the neck and he fell backwards into the lane. The other Germans paused and Oscendale took advantage of their hesitation to run further away from the hedge line into the field. Part of it had been ploughed and he took up a prone position some fifty yards away, behind a low bank of earth.

Just as he did so he saw another soldier break cover and fire a shot at the figures of Polain and Millward. They were nearly into the copse. Then another crack and a bullet zipped past him. He lined up his rifle sights on the second figure, now frantically reloading, and fired. The man flew backwards into the lane, his rifle following him.

Oscendale sprang up and put yet more distance between himself and the lane. He threw himself down on the furrowed earth again and fired two more shots, this time into the hedge itself as the Germans were making gaps in it to aim through. A glance to his right. No sign of the other two. Pulling back the rifle bolt, he saw there were no more rounds in the magazine so he flung it to one side in disgust. He set off, zigzagging towards the far edge of the field. Fortunately it cambered and it was not long before the lane was completely out of sight. He had lost contact with Polain and Millward, for a time at least. He was on his own, unarmed and he was heading in the wrong direction.

He journeyed in fits and starts for the remainder of the day, keeping under the cover of woods and hedgerows as frequently as he could. Each time he attempted to head west again, he sighted German patrols or columns of marching men heading to the front. The skirmish with the patrol meant that his whereabouts were known and the Germans were not going to let British soldiers rampage around behind their lines.

As the day wore on he found himself starting at each noise he heard, his body stiffening with escalating tension. He came across the body of a dead German lying in one of the woods and, with repugnance, removed his greatcoat. It was too large and smelt of the mustiness of death but he wrapped it around him in an effort to keep out the cold and the rain that now coursed down.

Night fell at last and he began to shiver despite the rancid greatcoat. He felt weak with hunger but forced himself to ignore the tightening in his stomach. The clouds were low and black and he had no moon to guide him so he gave up trying to make progress and spent an uncomfortable night in the lee of an old wall in a wood, straining his ears to listen to every sound of movement. Most of the time all he could hear was the rain falling through the leaves and branches above him.

It was still dark when he opened his eyes; he could smell the sodden earth and the cold damp air in the wood clung to his very being. Then he heard voices. And they were close.

CHAPTER 36

Ypres Salient – Sunday, 26th August 1917

MARK BOWEN WAS twenty-two years old and considered himself one of the veterans of the war. One year in any other occupation would not have been classed as such, but in the grim process of survival as an infantryman on the Western Front a year was a lifetime. He had experienced his first taste of action at Delville Wood during the summer in the Somme and had seen killing at close hand many times since then.

His experiences had taught him caution. Bowen had learnt the signs of danger and had become almost animal-like in his responses to them. He listened for the sounds of the shells and knew what each one meant. He could detect the first odours of gas and his keen eyesight could survey the ground around each new section of trench he came to and decide from which direction the threat of a German attack or night-time trench raid would come.

It was therefore with a certain sense of confidence that he had returned once more to the Salient in June. Not over-confident, he was far too wily a soldier now for that, but he knew he possessed a level of experience that, properly adhered to, would give him a better chance of surviving than the new drafts that had recently joined his battalion.

Bowen was not averse to passing on the benefits of his wisdom and some men listened and learnt; some did not. He was able to tell with some certainty therefore who would live the longer. It was a matter of reducing the odds through care and attention to detail.

He had of late, though, found that a certain change had come over him and he could pinpoint this feeling too. It was after the first attack of this latest battle had taken place on the 31st of July. The stoicism and dogged resolve to survive this war had begun to seep away from him, like water from a leaking bucket. Instead he found that he was becoming more carefree, more willing to volunteer for those tasks that in previous months he had avoided as being too risky and the pursuit of fools intent on an early grave. It was almost as though he could not stop himself and it troubled him.

It was therefore without amazement that he found himself raising his hand when Lieutenant Bonsall asked for volunteers to accompany him and a grim-faced man with a sniper's rifle, whom he introduced to the platoon as Sergeant Loram, to go out into no man's land as soon as it was dusk to search for a missing officer.

Overcast, murky and saturated with incessant rain, the daylight soon ebbed away. Bowen checked his kit once more and ensured that his homemade trench knife, fashioned from a broken French bayonet, was lodged securely in his right puttee. Grasping its ridged, brass handle gave him reassurance, though he knew if he were close enough to any enemy soldier to be able to use it then he was flirting more closely with death than he would previously have thought wise. It was a degree of war weariness, he was convinced, but it was also that sense that he could not continue living at such a high pitch for much longer. His phlegmatic approach, coupled with a certain degree of fatalism, was a product of his brain's search for relief from a prolonged period of extreme stress.

At the appointed time he joined Loram, Bonsall and three other men from the platoon on the firestep. Bonsall checked his watch. He waved his revolver and the men waded out of the stream that had formed above the duckboards below their feet and climbed the trench ladders, cautiously poking their heads over the top before peering anxiously at the desolation they were about to step into.

The enemy guns were quiet tonight so Bonsall judged it was as safe as it ever would be to continue. They climbed out of the trench and into the pitted waste of no man's land, Bowen's internal survival mechanism automatically switching to full alert.

The ground captured on the first day of the battle was littered with collapsed pillboxes. They struck Bowen as being like the remnants of an abandoned village after a storm had swept through. Tree trunks that held only a few withered branches stood as sentinels to the natural landscape which had been tilled by thousands of hands for centuries past before war had carved its way through. It had left the landscape bleak, consisting merely of broken concrete and smashed trees. The only minor undulations were those caused by the lips of shell craters. It was so flat that Bowen could see for hundreds of yards in every direction by the moon which appeared and then disappeared behind the clouds, illuminating and then hiding the scene in front of him, like curtains between acts in a music hall.

And he knew that the same moonlight would enable the Germans to see him and the others very soon.

In common with many soldiers, in fact most in his experience, Loram had been newly converted to the ancient religion of superstition. Before the war he had been a reasonably enthusiastic Christian and a regular churchgoer, but on coming under fire in action for the first time he had found himself a willing convert to the doctrine enshrined in his fellow soldiers, and had gladly embraced anything that, he was assured, had been proven to keep a man alive when the bullets started flying and the shells started dropping.

It was the latter that he was most fearful of. When you

stuck your head up over a parapet to see what was going on, in Loram's well-considered opinion it was your own fault when a sniper, who had been waiting for you to do exactly that, put a bullet between your eyes. When you left the trench at the start of an attack and walked across no man's land – walked because you were laden down with seventy pounds of kit and because the mud of Passchendaele or the Somme meant that it was hard work putting one foot in front of another, let alone running – then it was fate, luck, divine intervention, whatever you wanted to call it that prevented an enemy rifle bullet or machine gun round finding you in its path.

As the bullets had hurtled towards him on one occasion the previous year he had found it impossible to believe that he would survive, so he decided there and then to throw himself in the nearest shell hole and then progress from one to the other. If you tried to crawl rather than walk you were told by officers and NCOs that you were making yourself more of a target as you were spending much longer in no man's land. He followed the logic to some extent, but knew that his way, fire and movement, gave him at least a fighting chance of surviving the rest of each day.

Artillery shells, on the other hand, were quite different. Whether they were 77mm shells or *Minenwerfers* – trench mortars – those often-silent killers were exactly that and he had seen their devastating effect at close quarters too often.

Loram was lying in another shell hole. The party of men he had persuaded to accompany him out in no man's land in a mad, dangerous and probably futile search had run into trouble immediately. The German machine gunners had spotted them and they had tumbled into separate shell holes. Loram was now alone.

If he was to try and make his way back, he could be picked off immediately by any German with a rifle who happened to be peering over the top of his parapet at the time. Yet he couldn't stay there for much longer. The Huns were bound to counter-attack soon to try and recapture the ground they had lost recently.

He felt the first drops of rain coming down again and thought to himself, *great, here we go again.*

A furious Bernhofer looked down on the corpses of the three guards. When they had not reported in with the four British prisoners they had been escorting, the alarm had been raised. He had ordered an immediate search of the surrounding countryside. A party of *Uhlans* had also reported that one of their men had been found shot well behind the lines on the outskirts of an abandoned village.

Their faces were cold and grey, their mouths and eyes wide open, as if in protest. One man's head had been struck a violent blow, his hair a matted clump of dark red strands stuck together by the glue of his blood. The other two had been shot. Propped in a seating position against the wall as they were, they could only have been killed in cold blood. He felt anger rise like bile in his throat.

"Schmidt!" he called to a sergeant who hurried up to him.

"Yes, *Herr Hauptmann*," replied a man with the strain of years of fighting etched into his face.

"Schmidt, I want these men caught. Do you understand?" The man stood there and listened to his orders. "But I want them alive. I want to look into the eyes of this Oscendale. I want to see what drives a man like him to kill men like this. This is not how we fight a war. This is murder! And not for the first time."

Bernhofer was used to death. Yet he was determined never to become callous about the taking of another man's life. He fought for his country and he fought to survive. But to him there were still unwritten rules regarding warfare, still a code of ethics that all good soldiers should live by. This man Oscendale had broken one of them. He had killed unarmed men in cold blood.

Loram sprang up and moved as fast as he could through the teeming rain and across the waterlogged ground towards the hoisted British helmet. No gunfire rang out, which he put down to the lack of visibility, and in a few seconds he threw himself into the hole.

"Well, Loram," shouted Bonsall's voice through the rain, "I think the Boche have put a stop to our little enterprise." He pointed towards the grey figures that were advancing towards them through the downpour.

"You're right. Time to get out of here before they arrive," agreed Loram, working his way towards the far side of the shell hole. He grimaced. *Why did the bloody Germans have to choose this precise moment for a counter-attack?*

Bonsall followed him and together they squelched out of the shell hole and began a zigzagged, crouched run back towards their own lines. It had been an idiotic idea but at least he had tried.

They passed several dead soldiers in the blasted waste, but one was of particular interest to Loram. He stopped beside a young British private and knelt down. He removed the man's papers and then reached inside his tunic at the throat and pulled at one of his identity tags. Attached to the pink fibre roundel was a farthing, drilled at the top to allow the string for the dog tags to pass through. A lucky charm from a girl or his mother? Like all such objects it was superstitiously worn by the owner until its luck ran out.

"I'm sorry to say I didn't really know that chap at all," said Bonsall sadly. "There just wasn't time I suppose."

Loram clenched his lips together. "No, sir, but we can't let him die unnoticed."

Loram gazed down at the lifeless face, the rainwater coursing down the forehead into unblinking, glassy eyes. He reached forward and closed the eyelids with his fingertips, saying silent thanks to the soldier whom he hoped now had peace and freedom. Bonsall grabbed his arm and pointed back to the grey shapes that were beginning to loom ever closer in the mist of the rain and they resumed their furtive journey back to the relative safety of their own lines, with Loram tightly clutching one of Mark Bowen's identity discs in his hand.

CHAPTER 37

Ypres Salient – Monday, 27th August 1917

PEERING CAREFULLY OVER the crumbling wall, Oscendale looked down into a lane below and froze. A German transport column had halted on the track. There appeared to be some sort of problem with one of the horses shackled to a cart laden with what he took to be supplies and ammunition: boxes upon boxes of them, all partially covered against the rain by a brown-green sheet. Soldiers were attempting to persuade the horse to continue its task but the animal was evidently at the end of its tether.

An officer rode up on his bay horse and shouted to the soldiers, pointing to the wheel and to the other carts that were backed up behind, having to slowly manoeuvre around the stalled column.

There was a noise behind him. Was someone or something there? Oscendale turned around quickly to check but was satisfied that he was alone. He looked again at the scene below him. The soldiers eventually unloaded the stricken cart and the supplies were packed onto another one. The recalcitrant horse was tied behind a cart and the officer was satisfied enough to order the column to move on and continue their journey to the west.

He heard the sound again – a scrabbling of rocks behind him, but he was too late this time. A hand was clamped to his mouth, a knee was rammed roughly into the small of his back and he was pinned. He tensed his body and waited for the bayonet thrust but nothing happened. He remained absolutely still, hoping it would be taken as a sign he was willing to surrender. He tasted dirt on the man's hand and longed to be able to spit it out but he could not move at all.

The seconds passed and Oscendale became confused. If this was a German who held him in his clutches why had he not signalled to the troops below that he had captured an enemy soldier?

The transport column gradually made its rattling, tortuous way up the road and when the last wagon disappeared out of sight, the pressure in his back was eased and the filthy hand removed from his mouth. Oscendale gasped for breath and spat several times before turning round.

Squatting on his haunches behind him was a German soldier. Grubby, unshaven and grinning at him to display several broken teeth, the man said, "English, you take me back with you. I fight no more."

Oscendale was stunned. The German spoke again before Oscendale could reply. "We go. You with Andreas. Now! *Kommen*!" With that he scrambled down the bank into the lane. The man was apparently unarmed and Oscendale knew he could refuse to follow if he wanted to. He got up and followed his new companion down into the lane.

He was heading back to his own lines in the company of a German deserter and he wondered if his life could get any more bizarre.

As daylight broke gloomily, the heavens opened again and rain started to fall. They were in a labyrinth of small tracks that ran between tangled undergrowth when Oscendale stopped. In front of him two enemy soldiers were sitting on a fallen log. Holding their rifles upright, with their backs to him, they were engrossed in their conversation and oblivious to the rain as it dripped down their helmets onto their tunics, leaving dark stains that had grown into huge black patches.

He kept absolutely still as the rivulets of rain ran down his own face, impairing his vision and tickling his upper lip. He fought the urge to shake his head or wipe his eyes. Oscendale could only hope that Andreas was doing the same.

One German appeared to move. Oscendale dared not breathe but could not resist the temptation to blink furiously in an attempt to dispel the water. His misty vision cleared a little and he saw to his relief that the two men were still preoccupied and remained unaware of his presence.

He wondered what to do next, fearing that the panicky Andreas would not exhibit the same patience as he had shown and would betray their presence at any moment. His joints were beginning to ache and he knew that he would have to make a move towards cover soon.

At last, one leg at a time, he backed into the bushes, watching the Germans carefully. He breathed a huge sigh of relief as the branches wrapped themselves around him once more.

He felt a hand grip his arm and turned quickly to look into the dirty, unshaven face of his new companion who motioned that they should pass to the left of the group and Oscendale nodded. They were making their detour when a metallic clang rang out, clear even through the sound of the rain. Andreas, who was in front, looked back and then immediately began running away in panic. He had accidentally kicked a half-hidden petrol can that was protruding out of the ground.

Puzzled that the Germans had still not reacted at all, Oscendale stepped out of the thicket into the clearing. He heard a strained voice pleading, *"Nein! Nein!"* but he kept walking towards the seated soldiers.

When he reached them he saw that his suspicions had been right. Lifeless eyes gazed beyond him from white, ashen faces. The men were dead and had been for several hours, probably killed by the concussive wave from a nearby shell blast. He looked around. There were enough shell holes to choose from and it could have been any one of them that had led to their strange, instantaneous death.

He stood for a while, looking at the two men, transfixed by the presence of death and yet the total absence of marks on their bodies.

At last the deserter's urgent hissings became too much and Oscendale waved an impatient hand at the German and left the corpses to the mercy of the elements. The guises of death were undeniably very curious.

The ground was churned up and uneven, rising and falling with the shell holes that pocked the face of the land. Andreas would disappear and then reappear in front of him but Oscendale knew their luck would run out soon. One of the machine gun bullets chasing them across this ground would find its mark and they would feel its searing red-hot impact before falling down into the mud.

Then Andreas disappeared and did not reappear again. Oscendale thought for a moment that he had been shot so he threw himself to the earth and lay still for a time. The firing continued and he decided that to stay where he was could be fatal so he levered himself up and began to run once more before flinging himself to the ground as a second machine gun joined in. He crawled to the lip of a shell crater and saw a yawning hole beneath him. It was the entrance to a German dugout: a vast pit sunk into the earth with carefully constructed wooden steps and handrails. It fell some thirty feet below him before levelling off onto flat ground and an open space. A dark entrance on the left indicated a subterranean tunnel beyond.

Oscendale glanced around once more before deciding that whatever lay below was safer than being up here with the bullets.

He rolled forward onto the top step, careful not to expose himself to the machine gunner.

He stood up when his head was below ground level and, grasping the wooden hand rail, descended uneasily down the steps. He kept his eyes on the opening below him, expecting a group of German soldiers to appear at any moment.

When he reached the bottom, Oscendale paused at the entrance to the tunnel. To enter it would be a leap of faith, as he could see nothing inside and for all he knew there were several armed soldiers just waiting for him as soon as he stepped out of the light. There was no sign of that thieving Boche bastard Andreas either. He was reluctant to call out to him for fear of alerting a sentry, possibly dozing just inside the doorway.

If he failed this test of his courage he would lose his trench watch forever. It was a gift that had meant much to him, evoking many cherished memories, and he was reluctant to part with it. He had looked at it a few minutes earlier to check the time and the bloody German had reached out and ripped it from his wrist. He had then taken off like a startled rabbit.

At last Oscendale summoned all his courage, took a deep breath and stepped inside the doorway.

He was surprised to find the entrance so small and walked straight into a wall directly ahead of him. The light faded almost immediately as he turned the corner. He listened but could hear nothing – only the drip of water. His senses began to play tricks on him. Was there something moving in the darkness ahead? What sort of game was the swine playing?

As he stood still and let his eyes adjust to the gloom he saw that there was in fact a faint light glowing somewhere ahead. He drew out the box of matches that were among the few possession he had taken from Newell. He had no choice. It was either that or blunder around in the dark.

A timber-lined passageway stretched in front of him, with

a faint yellow light seeping into the inky blackness from an opening somewhere up ahead.

He peered through a doorway as his match petered out. The room was illuminated just long enough for him to see several forms lying on the bunks.

Oscendale dropped the match immediately, which fizzled out in a pool of water. Crouching down, ready to leap on anyone that came towards him, his breathing was rasping loudly now with the tension.

But nothing stirred. No voice spoke. Had he just imagined it? At last he was confident enough to light another match. There were clothes strewn everywhere as if someone had been going through the men's possessions, searching for souvenirs. The figures had not moved. There were five of them, all with blankets drawn up over their bodies. Cautiously, he prodded one of the figures. There was no response. He moved closer and flicked back the edge of the blanket.

What he saw made him drop the match in horror. The face was grey and dead. But the eyes were two dark, empty sockets and the skin was full of gaping holes where the vermin had already begun their work.

He stood unable to move and counted to ten, struggling to regain his self-control. As he backed out into the passageway once more he noticed a holster and belt slung on the end of one of the cots. He picked it up and extracted a Luger pistol. It was loaded.

He proceeded along the narrow, drawn inexorably towards the yellow light. More than once he paused as something scuttled along the floor in front of him. *Rats, they're just rats. Keep going. That bloody Hun must be here somewhere.*

The darkness played havoc with the senses. At times he felt cold, at others feverishly hot. He inhaled smells he had never experienced before. Strange sounds reached his ears and then disappeared as quickly as they had arrived. The water continued to drip from the beams above his head.

He came to the source of the light and hesitated before peering inside. It was a space about ten feet square. Remarkably, it was completely wood panelled and more than that, the wood had been whitewashed. A thick pillar propped up a central wooden beam that held the roof intact, and would probably do so despite the fiercest bombardment by the British artillery. A candle twitched inside a lantern placed on a small roughly-made table and it cast a pale glow around the room.

There was a cupboard of some sort built into an alcove and on it was a washbasin and jug. A German officer's cap hung on a peg driven into the wall and his coat was on another peg next to it. But the most astonishing thing about the room was the sight of a brass bed in the centre. White pillows and sheets gleamed in the candlelight and, to a man who had not slept in a bed for some days, it looked inviting. A wave of fatigue came over him with the thought and he had to resist the temptation to give in.

There was no sign of the officer whose quarters they were, so he turned back into the eerie tunnel once more and inched slowly through the darkness, carrying the lantern in his left hand and the Luger in his right.

At last he came to a junction. *Left or right?* What did it matter? He plumped for left, the shadows receding with each step he took. He looked at the candle, burning low. *Remember to leave enough to get back.* If the lantern failed him he reckoned he could get back to the entrance with the remaining matches. *Keep going.* Still no sign of life and no sign of any other light.

Suddenly, he was sent sprawling as he tripped over something large on the floor. The pistol flew out of his hand. The lantern smashed and the candle's flame was snuffed as it drowned in yet another puddle of water. He cursed himself. His lifeline had gone. He groped around in his pocket for the box of matches. They were gone as well.

For a moment absolute fear overtook him. He was underground in a tomb. Could he remember his way back?

He groped around on the floor but the fingers of his left hand met only a puddle of water.

Finally his fingers met the cold metal of his pistol. *Thank goodness.* He grasped it and heaved a sigh of relief. What now? He thought for a moment and then fired one shot along the corridor in front of him.

The roar in such a confined space was deafening and his ears began ringing immediately but the light of the muzzle flash had shown him two important things. His box of matches lay on dry ground about a yard ahead. He memorised the spot and was certain he could find it again in the dark.

He had also seen the Germans.

CHAPTER 38

Ypres Salient – Monday, 27th August 1917

THERE HAD BEEN dozens of figures lying on the floor ahead of him, illuminated by the flash of light that had momentarily lit up the tunnel. For a second or two he allowed his brain to assimilate what he had just seen in this hellhole.

Some of the soldiers had been staring at the ceiling of the passageway, and others had been sitting up against the walls. For a moment he thought they must be sleeping in readiness for an attack.

His breathing was shallow and he was trembling. There was no shouting or scuffling. No one stirred. Again he heard the drips of water falling into the silence somewhere in the passageway, louder now, echoing along these long caverns. *They were corpses that he had seen.*

He sniffed the air, smelling the mouldy, damp scent of earth and that other peculiar smell that he had encountered when he had first entered the dugout. But the air was breathable.

Retrieving the box, he lit another match and gazed down upon the corpse of a soldier. The mouth was open, displaying two rows of yellow teeth; a dreadful gash was ripped across the stomach. The blood had seeped from the tunic and was congealed in a pool beneath the body. Ahead lay more of them. It was like a charnel house and he questioned, not for the first time, how men could do this to one other. He imagined the shrieks as men cut and stabbed at each other down here in the tunnel. He saw British khaki mixed with German *feldgrau*, men from both sides who had hacked and torn at each other. And only the dead remained.

So mesmerised was he by the sights on the floor in front of him that he failed to notice the flame burning down the length of the stalk and he was jolted from his thoughts by the sharp pain in his fingers. He winced and threw the match down.

There was only one way to go and that was backwards. If the thieving Hun had gone further along the tunnel then he was welcome to it. The German could keep the watch; he still had the memory it represented.

He picked up the candle from the lantern and lit it again before beginning the walk back, becoming increasingly conscious of a burning sensation in his left fingers. First rubbing them on his clothing and then scratching them, he proceeded cautiously back the way he had come.

His head began to throb again and he rubbed his temple. His mind felt dream-like, as in that state before sleep when strange, vaguely-connected thoughts swirl around.

Sin. The original sin should have been the taking of another human life, not what he had with Hannah. How was the act of love more sinful than the awful sights down here? The light in the dark. The human condition. His condition.

He stopped and listened. Had he heard something? Rats? Footsteps or scurrying rodents? He was the sole living man among so many dead. Down among the dead men. He thought he heard another sound. A laugh. He brushed it aside. His mind was playing tricks again. He was the only living man here. Well, he and the German. Good old Hun. The only sane one among them all. All he wanted was to surrender and serve out the rest of the war in captivity, then go home to his family and pick up the pieces. Pieces. Pieces of men. Pieces of eight. Eight pieces of a man.

What was happening to him? He was becoming delirious. Why? The concentration? The fear? The dark? He heard the sound again. He stood still. The only thing he could hear was his own blinking. Blinking? Since when had he started to hear that? Where was his heartbeat? Perhaps he should sit down. *Rest. Sit down.* Then he would feel better. *Yes, sit down.*

Then the noise came again. It was there. It was real. He forced his eyes open and pushed away all thoughts of rest. There was someone or something down here with him. To the front or behind him? He could no longer tell. *Bastard thief!*

"Is that you?" he called, his voice hollow. He listened to the echo of his question repeated as if in mock humour. A faint breeze stirred and its gentle touch ran across his face. Hannah. Here? The candle went out. He shook his head again involuntarily. Something was causing him to lose concentration. What was it? That smell again. The dead? Perhaps it was the smell of the dead. There were bodies here after all. Rigid, decaying bodies.

He had smelt death many times in the past three years. It was a smell that settled in the nostrils, crawled down the back of the throat and clung to the stomach. It would remain there for hours afterwards – days sometimes – and it was a smell he would never forget. The bodies in the water were the worst, floating on the surface of shell holes filled with rancid water. The blue-grey swollen corpses. The waxy appearance of the bodies. He had watched men die. He had seen bodies being taken out of dressing stations and piled up behind a hedge so as not to unsettle those waiting their turn to be treated. Bad for morale.

There was only one dead body he would never see. His own.

Time to light another match. Time to see the dead.

As the match he had struck to light the candle fell to the floor and died, he heard the noise again, this time much closer. It was as if something was being dragged along the floor. Then he heard another sound, like air escaping from a leaking pipe, but in bursts. He stood stock still for a moment listening keenly for the hiss to come again, straining his ears, but it had ceased. No, there it was again. He blew out the candle, allowing the darkness to hide him, and took the Luger out of his pocket once more. He resisted the urge to run, knowing that he would just stumble and fall over, perhaps onto another line of corpses.

It was coming closer. He tried to judge how far away it was but could not tell. He was being hunted. Was it a German or something more sinister? The ghosts of the dead? Death itself perhaps, coming to greet him.

A rat scuttled by below him, running over his foot. Then another, then another. Whatever was back there was causing even the rats to flee. His mind raced. Any second now it would be upon him. Raising his arm, he held out the pistol again in front of him and gently squeezed the trigger.

Just a click. No explosion of gunfire. Just an impotent click. The pistol was empty.

The hissing sound began again. How far away now, twenty yards, less? In an instant he recalled what else he had seen in those last few seconds of light before he had allowed the blackness to hide him. He had seen a can some two feet away from his feet. Carefully and slowly, he dropped down and groped around until his hands closed around cold metal. He lifted it and twisted the top which, to his relief, unscrewed easily and silently. He sniffed the contents. *Petrol.* It was as he had thought.

Closer. He was coming much closer. The figure was probably close enough now, maybe just a few yards from him. He drew back the can and swung it forward with all his might. He heard a thud as it connected. The clang of the can hitting the floor was followed closely by the thump of a body. Oscendale frantically pulled his box of matches from his pocket and lit one.

Lying on the floor not ten feet from him was a German soldier wearing a skull-like gas mask and dragging a sack of loot from the scores of corpses that littered these tunnels and rooms.

He was scrabbling around for his rifle which was on the floor some feet away.

Oscendale threw the match onto the German's tunic. The petrol ignited immediately, turning the German's uniform into a flaming mass. His body twisted around in agony as the intense heat seared his body and muffled screams came from behind the gas mask as it melted onto his face. He rolled on the floor in an effort to put out the flames and continued to writhe in panic. Oscendale snatched the rifle from the ground and fired five rounds into the stricken man until he made no further move. He gasped with relief and threw the empty rifle to the floor.

Oscendale took a few steps backwards, staring at the burning corpse. Then he spun around quickly and began to make his way along the tunnel towards the opening, the light from the still-burning German behind him illuminating the way. He turned a corner and the way ahead was once more plunged into darkness so he was forced to relight the stump of the candle. The urge to cough was overwhelming, a slight irritating tickle at first which grew in intensity and burned the back of his throat. The strange smell had begun to grow stronger as well.

Then he realised. *Gas!* Some of the pools of liquid he had been splashing through were liquid gas which had condensed on the cold floor of the tunnel. The matches he had dropped had started to react with it and turn the liquid into vapour. There was a sense of urgency about his movements now. He had to get out of here before the gas turned his lungs to froth.

The blackness was playing tricks on him again; the tunnel was familiar but then again it was not. Had he just not noticed things when he came along here a few minutes ago or had he taken a wrong turning and would never be able to find his way out? He could feel the urge to vomit as the gas crept its way down his throat but still he pressed on. He lifted the bottom of his greatcoat and pressed it to his nose and mouth. It would help but only for a short time. He forced himself to breathe slowly.

Keep going, keep going. It's around here somewhere.

His eyes started to film over with tears and the gas began to attack his lips and nose as well. He kept going, the candle, his beacon, held out in front of him. Then he saw what he was looking for – the sleeping quarters. Trying to ignore his revulsion, he stumbled inside. If he was wrong about this it would be all over in a few seconds. He would fall to the floor into another deadly pool of the liquid which would burn away at his hands and face as he choked to death on his own stomach contents.

There it was, hanging on the end of one of the bunks. He ripped open the bag and put the gas mask over his face, sucking in the filtered air.

He almost cried with relief. The air was stale but clear of gas. He took several breaths then lifted off the mask and spat on the floor, clearing his mouth and lungs of the foul vapour. He did this repeatedly until he was sure he was not going to be sick into the gas mask and that he had cleared as much of the gas he had breathed in as he could. Then he forced himself to relax and to regulate his breathing. After several more minutes he felt ready to return to the entrance.

He found Andreas in a recess further along the tunnel; he was dead. The gas had done its deadly work and he had died in his sleep, suffocating on his own vomit. Bending down, Oscendale took his watch from the man's pocket. He clasped it tightly in his clammy fist. He had so nearly lost it but now it was his again. Briefly, the memory of the woman who had given it to him came flooding back. She had given him so much but it had all been taken away so suddenly. And all that had remained at the end was this watch. The strap had snapped as it had been yanked from his wrist so he put it into his tunic pocket and carried on.

Climbing the steep steps he emerged into a world of light

and air. He pulled off the gas mask and lay on his back, allowing the damp air to fill his lungs. He rolled over and pushed himself up, still coughing and spitting, until he was sitting with his knees pulled up and his head in between them. Eventually, he looked up. At the top of the dugout steps he saw the contorted bodies of two Germans hit by shellfire just before they reached the sanctuary of the underground world. Lying alongside them were several helmets, discarded or blown off, he could not tell. He became aware once more of a burning sensation in his legs and left hand and looked down. He saw that his tunic and trousers were wet with the liquid gas and it appeared the vile substance was soaking through onto his flesh. He knew that if he did not remove the items quickly then the skin would ulcerate and turn septic. The pain would be excruciating.

The thought that came into his mind revolted him but it was the only thing to do.

The Germans had been dead long enough for their flesh to begin to decompose or be consumed. The face of one of them was already eaten away and there was a suspicious bulge in the stomach of the other. Something was moving beneath the clothing and Oscendale unbuttoned the man's tunic with some trepidation. The rat sprang out of the chest and scuttled away towards the dugout entrance. The soldier looked about the same size as him so he tore off the tunic and the trousers, donning both in quick succession.

He knew that if he were caught he would be shot as a spy, but was still hopeful that he could make his way to the British trenches. The trick would be not getting shot by his own side. He saw a trench knife poking out of the German's right boot and extracted it, tucking it into his own.

Oscendale set off, crawling when he was on the surface and scrambling around the insides of shell holes when he knew he was out of sight. Slowly he traversed the ruined landscape, hiding behind the occasional stump of a tree, leafless and lifeless. The sensation in his legs was abating somewhat but his left hand was getting worse.

CHAPTER 39

Ypres Salient – Monday, 27th August 1917

THE ARTILLERY BARRAGE ceased at last. Oscendale peered over the lip of the shell crater, one of dozens all around him, and saw with some relief mixed with unease the remnants of a shattered blockhouse ahead of him. It had been struck by at least one shell and half of its exterior had been demolished. Lumps of concrete lay strewn around, while a thicket of metal reinforcing rods poked like new growth out of the ground.

Part of the structure still remained intact and he began to pull himself towards an opening blown in the wall, conscious that a machine gun embrasure still gaped menacingly above his head in the afternoon light. If there was anyone left alive inside he knew he was a perfect target, alone and lightly-armed. He held the trench knife he had taken from the corpse more firmly and rolled inside the opening.

The interior was cool and quiet. He crouched, ready to throw himself at any attacker and plunge his blade home, but nothing stirred. As his eyes grew accustomed to the dim light, he began to discern the outlines of many lifeless men sprawled on the ground. Most of the roof had collapsed and he saw that several halves of bodies were crushed beneath the huge slabs of fallen concrete, while others lay intact, as if sleeping on the ground. He approached cautiously and prodded some of them with his knife. Satisfied that they were all dead, he propped himself against the wall of the blockhouse and stared at the bodies for a long time.

Eventually, he approached them once more and began searching their clothing for clues as to their identities, more out of idle curiosity as much as anything else as he saw no real benefit in knowing which regiment they belonged to now that their position had been destroyed.

Two of the men were officers so Oscendale began with them, searching their pockets for any identification. Besides the *soldbücher* – their paybooks – he found a letter and some photographs, stained and damp with sweat and blood. He unfolded the letter and by the evening light still seeping in through the opening he began to read in German:

My Dear Darling,

It is impossible to explain the awful conditions we now find ourselves in. The shellfire from the English guns is truly terrifying. It flays the ground all around us, huge geysers of earth thrown up in columns all about. Reds and yellows are the colours I see during the long hours of the night. I think I shall go out of my mind if it does not stop. Our blockhouse has been hit dozens of times. Shells rain down on its roof and it seems to lift and settle each time a large calibre one hits it. When that happens we raise our eyes fearfully up and anticipate it crashing down and crushing us all. We cannot speak, the noise is too great and we are all almost deaf to normal human levels of conversation. We make wild exaggerated gestures to each other to communicate. And all around us the torrent and the torment continues. I have issued opium to us all to calm our nerves. The men are in danger of becoming hysterical; some try to run outside to escape by being hit. This is not just drumfire – it is diabolical Hell. Even the rats try to escape by coming in here. They run up the walls and we kill them with our spades. No food or water has reached us in days. I do not know if I will survive all this to post this letter but I send my love to you and the children in the hope that God will spare me and we will be together again soon.
Your Josef

Oscendale looked up from the damp piece of paper into the face of the dead German. The *Oberleutnant*'s blue eyes were open but lifeless. His uniform, once probably so immaculate, was covered with debris. *Josef, so that was your name, but you won't see your family anymore, my friend and enemy. Your God didn't spare you.*

There were no wounds apparent on several of the bodies Oscendale had examined and it was evident to his sadly experienced eye that they had been killed by one gigantic concussion as a heavy calibre shell exploded on the roof of the blockhouse, its Greys fuze set to do its fiendish work on impact with the concrete. These were not the duds of the Somme. These shells would explode with great force and power on contact and the effects, as he was witnessing first hand, were truly terrible.

When he had finished searching the bodies, some of which were still warm, he had twelve paybooks and twelve sets of assorted papers which he carefully placed inside each one. He studied the names and their places of birth, dates of enlistment and all the other details these military papers provided him with, then set them aside in a cloth bread bag he took from the belt of one of the bodies. These could be retrieved later by their colleagues, he decided, before the rats scattered their contents in their fervour for food.

So he sat with his dead companions, the madness of the war brought home to him once more. He had time to pass so he took out his own brown leather wallet from his tunic pocket, opened it and extracted a sheet of cream coloured paper. He had found a pencil in the pocket of one of the Germans so, resting the paper on the wallet, he began his homage to his newly-found friends. *His dead circle of friends.*

The forms of the bodies, their twisted, unnatural postures, soon began to appear on the page. As he sketched, a skill he had been taught as a boy by his father, he gave the men personalities and lives. One was the storyteller, one the academic, another the fatalist, one the innocent and so on until all twelve had been given a character.

The minutes passed and the shadows lengthened. When Oscendale had finished his drawing he sat back and contemplated the sad heap of human remains he had transferred to the piece of paper. There they all were; he had captured this moment forever. Their bodies were already beginning the process of decay and would rot to mere bones but he knew he had saved these hours for the future. He sighed at the futility of the scene before him and lifted his eyes to the opening. The sky was changing colour and the rain was beginning to fall again. The droplets soon began to gather and the remorseless sound of the drips stirred him out of his ennui. It was time to think about heading back to his own lines. The machine gunners and snipers would have less chance of seeing him at night, and the counter-attack he had feared, had not come.

Over the past hour each external noise had caused him to stop his sketching. Again he wondered if this was the time? Was this the moment that the Germans had chosen? Any second a soldier could appear in the doorway. But nothing had happened and he had returned to his work, heartbeat subsiding once more.

He folded the drawing and placed it inside his wallet, putting the pencil into his pocket. Removing his water bottle from his belt, he held it up to the remnants of the concrete roof where the rain was running off the edge and falling onto the mud. He partially filled and drank from it several times, his thirst impossible to quench.

"*Wasser.*"

A cold trickle ran down Oscendale's spine.

The voice came again. "*Wasser. Bitte.*"

It was coming from behind him.

He turned to see that one of the two German officers was looking at him.

Bernhofer had watched the German soldier crawl through the hole in the wall of the blockhouse some time ago, seen him search the bodies of the men who had died alongside him when the British shell had exploded. He had felt him remove his *soldbuch* to add to those of Schmidt and the others and then calmly take out some paper and draw the bodies of his dead men.

The lump of concrete that had shattered his left leg meant he was unable to move. The blood he was losing made him slip in and out of consciousness and he had lost all track of time. He remembered that he and Schmidt's section had first spotted the British officer he sought as he emerged from the deep dugout in no man's land. They had seen him change into a German uniform and had followed him through the mist and rain, losing him in an artillery barrage that had compelled them to take cover in this cursed blockhouse which had been ripped apart moments after they had joined the machine gun crew already stationed inside.

One of his soldiers was here, taking cover. Bernhofer wanted water, a drink to soothe his parched throat.

"*Wasser*," he groaned again. The soldier came across to him and lifted his head gently. He poured cool water between his cracked lips. Bernhofer almost wept with relief. He opened his eyes and looked into those of his saviour.

The man's face wore a look of concern.

And then he spoke. In English.

"Well chum, I'm afraid you're in a bad way, there's no denying that." The soldier unbuttoned the collar of his tunic and lifted out his identity disc. "*Hauptmann Bernhofer, ja? Ich heisse Oscendale.*"

Oscendale! The Devil was mocking him now. Laughing at him

indeed as he slipped into his grave. Bernhofer looked into the face of his despised enemy and was powerless to fight back.

Oscendale looked at the piece of the blockhouse roof that lay across the German's leg. It was too heavy for him to move and the man had lost a great deal of blood. The limb was crushed and death would not be long in coming. He pressed his water bottle into the German's hand but saw no gratitude there, only a sudden look of hate. He assumed that delirium was setting in and he was relieved when the man's eyes began to close as the life ebbed from his body.

When at last he felt satisfied that he had done all he could for the dying man, Oscendale said a mental farewell before squirming out of the blockhouse opening. He was going back to the madness. *Or was it coming to him?*

CHAPTER 40

Ypres Salient – Monday, 27th August 1917

THE BLEAK LANDSCAPE appeared more sinister under the black night sky than he recalled a few hours earlier. Livid Very lights soared and fell in sad decay, throwing pools of light onto the featureless ground as far as the eye could see. The ground stretched in front of him as undulating waves of grassless, sodden mud. The rain increased in intensity as soon as he left his brief tenancy of the ruined blockhouse. He buried his head deeper in his shoulders and scurried from shell hole to shell hole, stopping to listen at regular intervals.

He had gone no more than about fifty yards when the first shot came. The crack rang out against the noise of the driving rain and he threw himself down, his hands and forearms disappearing into the brown ooze. It seeped into his mouth and he spat it out in disgust.

Oscendale had no idea from which direction the shot had come but he lay still, hoping the night would cloak him if the mud did not. He had lost his sense of direction and turned to look around for the blockhouse to recall the direction of the German lines. He blinked and forced his eyes to stay open as the rain teemed down. Visibility was now decreasing but he thought he could just about see it over his left shoulder.

He started as he saw shapes swarming around it, dozens of them. To his right there were yet more figures moving towards him, this time in their hundreds. *The counter-attack!* The Germans had decided to take advantage of the torrential downpour to move forward to attack the newly-held British positions.

A bizarre sight caught his eye as he looked forward again. A helmet was being waved atop a rifle barrel from a shell hole some thirty yards away. He wiped the water from his brow. Yes, there was no mistake, someone was signalling. Looking back at the advancing Germans, he saw they would be upon him in the next minute. There was a chance they could miss him in the deteriorating conditions or that he could feign death, but he knew his best option was to get to this friendly shell hole as soon as possible. He kept still, shaken by his train of thought. Friendly, but what if it was not? What if this was a signal to the Germans from one of their observers in no man's land?

Oscendale could not make up his mind. He lay perfectly still, at one with the shifting ground beneath him, suddenly powerless to move. It was all coming to an end.

A thick mist was all around him, wrapping him in swathes, restricting his field of vision to a few dozen yards. The Germans had gone. *Were they ever there?* He shook his head vigorously in frustration.

An artillery gun sat at a crooked angle, half-in and half-out of the mud and a dead German artilleryman lay close, a piece of jagged metal protruding from his chest. Nearby, a distressed message dog lay whimpering. Oscendale crawled across to it and extended a hand but it bared its teeth and snapped at him, its jaws clicking together on empty space. He saw that one of its front legs was missing and all that remained was a raw stump of red flesh.

It was as if even the dead were rising up out of the ground on this mad, distorted Judgement Day. He spied two filthy soldiers pick themselves up from the earth and proceed to set up their machine gun. They checked the mechanism, cleared the barrel and began feeding in a belt of ammunition. He was no more than twenty feet away and yet they had completely ignored him.

Just as they settled into position to fire on the British lines, he drew his trench knife and charged.

The loader turned around at the sound of his boots splashing through the mud. His face turned to a look of terror in the last few seconds before Oscendale stabbed him in the throat, blood spurting into his own face. He then turned his attention to the machine gunner, driving the knife into the man's chest. Oscendale felt a rib break with the force of the impact and the man's eyes stared into his until he thought he felt the precise moment that life left the body. Grunting with satisfaction, he slumped down into the mud once more before using his sleeve to wipe the blood out of his eyes. He looked at the two bodies, men he had just killed in this ghostly, spectral world of mist, and felt nothing. The blood on his hands was thick and sticky and he wiped them on his overcoat, noting the smears they painted on the cloth.

A shell fell nearby and a huge pressure wave punched him in the back. He gasped for air and tentatively ran his hands over his body, terrified he would find a piece of hot, torn metal sticking out of his flesh somewhere. There was no pain but there never was at first. His anxiety grew then turned to relief. He had not been hit. Dropping his head down to his chest, he waited until his breathing returned to normal and pulled himself up to his knees, crawling, then falling down again. *Homewards.*

He laughed out loud. *Homewards?* This was not home; it was hell on earth. *Another descent into hell.* More gunfire crackled somewhere to his left and he threw himself down. A wave of melancholy came over him like a black tide. *Firing at his laughter.* Didn't they get it? For three years strangers had been trying to kill him and here were more, firing at him because he was laughing, because he could take none of this seriously. *Because he understood the joke and they did not.*

The rain fell ceaselessly through the mist and he was soaked through, dirty, hungry and clad in a looted German uniform which was splattered with mud and blood. His shirt and heavy serge trousers were so wet they were sticking to his skin. The mist showed no sign of lifting and he felt he could go no further. At any moment grey figures would emerge from these earthbound clouds and it would be his turn to be run through with a metal blade.

His heartbeat had ceased to be a barometer of his fears. The thumping in his chest had stopped. He felt calm, relaxed. There was only the present. He knew he was close to the end. It would be easy just to give up. The rain, the hunger, the killing and the tension of the past few days had eaten into his soul. He was serene, ready to move on and leave this world. He would just close his eyes, descend into oblivion and let death take him away. The mist was his shroud. It was time to let go. *Death was no longer his enemy.*

Another shell landed close by with a deafening roar. A nearby corpse exploded into dozens of pieces which flew towards him and splattered his face and chest with blood and flesh. In a state of madness now he cried out and wiped off the putrid mess. He rubbed his eyes furiously and when he opened them he saw half a grinning face staring up at him. Covering his eyes, he turned and stumbled and staggered, crying out like a child, until he tripped over an old barbed wire piquet and fell sprawling into the mud. He rolled onto his back and squinted up at the roof of cloud that hung over him.

"God Almighty! Where the hell are you?!" he called out with a passion that startled him. But his only answer was another angry tirade of shelling, this time further away. He listened and waited for a response but God had no answer.

The pools of water shone like fallen stars in the shell holes that stretched across no man's land. At times the moon emerged as if on a whim from behind the bustling clouds that hurried across the ocean-like night sky on their infinite journey. In the moonlight ghostly figures marched in their hundreds across the battlefield. *The legions of the dead.* Then the drifting clouds would obscure the silver moon and the ghostly vision was gone. Only the scarred, ripped landscape remained, utterly desolate, barren of life, an enormous graveyard for the dead and the dying.

A desultory shell whined overhead and plunged down about a hundred yards away. It exploded with a roar and flung thousands of clods of earth high into the air. Oscendale watched transfixed as the earth tumbled then fell, settling itself, rearranged, onto the ground again, lazily disinterested once more in the affairs of men.

Calm had returned. The war had gone away. Perhaps the fighting had moved on, leaving this terrible landscape to die in peace beneath his feet.

He lost his footing and slipped into a shell hole. The horror and dread of sliding into the murky pool at the bottom overcame him. If he entered it there would be no way out. It would suck him in; drown him slowly with each gulp, inch by inch suffocating him in mud and water. Digging his fingers into the mire of the shell hole he slowed his progress until just his feet entered the pool. It cooled the burning sensation in his legs and he sighed with relief. Peering back into its murky depths, he recoiled as he saw a grinning face. A white skull with bared teeth and empty eye sockets leered back at him from beneath the surface of the water, its flesh all gone. *Life departed.* Unburied and yet mourned by a family hundreds of miles away at home. And what would they think of him here like this? Oscendale reached into the cold, foul water and pushed his fingers through the eye sockets. Gripping the skull, he pulled it free of the mud. Water ran from the orifices, splashing down onto the surface of the pool. He began to smile, then laughed out loud at the absurdity of it all and pulled it to his chest. *Another dead head.*

CHAPTER 41

Ypres Salient – Tuesday, 28th August 1917

"Here's another one, Corp. This one's still alive. Want me to bayonet the bastard?"

Oscendale opened his eyes. It was dark. He closed his eyes again, feeling the rainwater patting his face. Or was it the stars falling down gently from the peaceful sky? He felt warm and secure, tucked into a soft bed of mud. It surrounded him, held him in its embrace; the voice had woken him from his serenity. *Go away!*

A face was thrust into his. The mouth spoke. "No, let's take him in. See what he has to tell us. Pick him up."

"Yes, Corp," replied the first speaker, evidently disappointed.

Oscendale felt himself being lifted roughly by several pairs of hands. He was prised free of the clinging mud as it held him tight, as if not wanting to let him go. He was encouraged to his feet by shoves and kicks. Feeling feeble and dizzy, he fell and the sea of mud rose up to catch him, welcoming him back.

Once more he was levered to his feet and he heard distant voices as he felt arms hold him upright this time. His head felt as if it were about to explode and liquid of some sort – blood or water, he was not sure which – trickled down across his eyes and cheeks. He tasted something metallic in his mouth, a familiar fetid taste, and he spat it out. Still more ran down his throat so he spat once more.

"Eh, you dirty Hun bastard. Stop spitting on my uniform!" a disgusted voice shouted at him and he felt a sharp pain in his side.

Through a haze he saw the ground moving though he could not feel his legs. He was being taken somewhere but he had no idea where. Who were these men and what did they want of him? Why couldn't they just leave him alone to die? It had been so close. He had been comfortable in the mud, warm and content, and now he was being forced to go somewhere. He knew something felt wrong about all of this but the pain in his head that had started as soon as he was standing meant that he could not, for the life of him, work out what it was, however hard he tried.

He awoke to find himself on a stretcher. Struggling to open his tired, heavy eyelids, he was mystified by the flapping roof of a canvas tent which billowed and fell in intermittent rhythms while he struggled to orientate himself. He tried to remember why he felt concerned and anxious, but could not. How had he got here? In the end he gave up and continued staring through half-open eyes at the juddering material. There was something about it that he recognised. Something about the pitter-patter of the rain as it beat down on the outside of the tent.

"Oh, so you're awake then are you? About time too," said a face to his side that reared into his line of sight. He tried to respond but the words would not come. His tongue felt huge and useless in his mouth, like a foreign object placed there to silence him. Every bone and muscle in his body ached, his skin felt raw. He felt confused again. Why couldn't he speak? Why couldn't he remember? *Did he want to?*

The orderly drew up a chair and sat at the side of his bed. "Right then, chum. Let's see if we can find out what you have to tell us. *Wie heisst du?* No? Do you speak English? What is your name?"

He stared blankly at the man. Then a fearful dread set in. He could not even remember his name. *Who the hell was he?* There was no clarity of thought. He tried to sit up, frantically searching around for something that he could set in context, but there was nothing. Why could he not think of the words? A nurse with a yellow-tinged face stopped at the foot of his bed, coughing loudly into a handkerchief. What was going on?

"Yes, that's what your gas shells have done to our nurses. You can see for yourself now. Pleased with your work?"

It was incomprehensible. What the devil was he talking about? Gassing the nurses? What was going on here? Perhaps he was still asleep and this was just a ghastly dream. Yes, that must be it. He was still sleeping.

Accusingly, the orderly spoke again. "Yes, your gas. Mustard gas. They had to remove the gas-soaked uniforms as our men were in no state to do it themselves. Pretty soon they were coughing their guts up, their eyes streaming through the effects of the gas. That's why they've turned yellow-skinned. Even their hair has turned yellow – just from the fumes that arose from the clothing. More like canaries than nightingales, I reckon. And you lot call that civilised behaviour. What a way to fight a war. Anyway, come on chum, what's your name? You must have a name."

He tried hard again to remember who he was but could not.

"I see," sighed the orderly, putting away his notebook. "Cat's got your tongue has it? Ah well, we'll treat that head wound of yours anyway and sort out your hand and legs, then pack you off to a POW camp back in Blighty. Get some rest and I'll see you again later. Hopefully you'll be willing to tell me your name then. Oh, and don't try to escape otherwise he'll have you." He nodded towards an armed sentry who stood chatting to a nurse at the entrance to the tent.

Through the tent flap entrance he could see that night had fallen. Fallen since when? What had he been doing before he was brought here? He was unable to make any sense of his world and they wanted him to *rest*?

His head was thumping. His quivering hand reached up to touch the source of the pain and touched a bandage that swathed his head. When had that been applied? The panic returned once more. Things were happening to him that he was unaware of. It was an alien sense of not knowing who he was, let alone where he was. There was something that he needed to do and it filled his mind with anxiety.

"Yes, sir. That's him over there." Oscendale recognised the orderly's voice and a moment later an officer's face came into view.

"Ah the *soldat* is back in the land of the living eh? Do you speak English?" the officer asked, his questioning eyebrows raised with suspicion.

Oscendale nodded. He understood the words this time but could not summon his mouth to reply.

"Good. Now see here, Fritz, you are quite a mystery man. A German soldier captured in no man's land with a British officer's trench watch on him. Handsome watch it is too, even if I say so myself."

The officer spoke again. "So it appears that you have robbed the body of a dead British officer. Were you planning to pass yourself off as him? What did you do to him? You were covered in blood, weren't you? His blood."

Oscendale heard the words but knew they were wrong. *No, he wasn't pretending to be someone else.* He was someone else. Someone who was not here. He struggled to make his mouth move but could not. *Pretending to be someone else.*

The officer saw him struggling to speak. "Trying to say something, Fritz?" He turned to the orderly. "Why can't he speak, do we know?"

The soldier looked in sympathy at Oscendale. "The blow on his head might have rattled his cups and saucers a bit, sir. The doctor says he's sure it will come back eventually but we don't know how long it will be."

Oscendale dropped his head back onto the pillow. He needed to speak, to tell them… To tell them what? He closed his eyes once more. He did not know who he was or where he had come from. What was he going to say anyway?

Rainwater dripping from the roof of the tent began to lull him back and drowned out their babbling voices until he felt himself slipping once more into oblivion.

"He's gone again, sir. You won't get much more out of him for a few hours at least. He's been sleeping like a log since he got here."

The officer rubbed his chin thoughtfully. "Hmmm. I really want to know where he got that trench watch from. If our Captain Oscendale is out there in no man's land we want to know where the body is or where the Huns buried him."

CHAPTER 42

Poperinghe – Wednesday, 29th August 1917

S ITTING QUIETLY IN his hospital chair, he watched the nurses calmly going about their blessed business as they ministered to the wounded men who lay almost motionless in their beds. Some would cry out pitifully for them or for their mothers. The canvas continued to twitch above his head but now that he was upright or at least not horizontal, he felt he could think and was able to mull over what this all meant.

Occasionally the pain in his head broke through the layers of morphine in his system. Like sharp thorns, it would cut into his brain. He would close his eyes and wince, raising his hands to his aching temple. Then his breathing would settle once more and he would open his eyes.

As the hours passed he became more aware of an unconnected, random and sometimes inexplicable series of events seeping back into his consciousness. At first he had been relieved; it appeared his memory was returning. Then he became anxious again. This was a replay of what had happened to him, but in what order was it all supposed to be and what would happen at the end?

There was an Irish nurse who spoke to him whose face changed from calm and serene to drawn and tortured; a man with a rugged face to whom he knew he was indebted but did not know why; and always there was a feeling of something he should have done, something that still needed doing. He remembered too a man called Burgess who would understand how he felt just now.

But the more he struggled to grasp the memories and hold

on to them, the more they drifted off into the shadows, leaving him so frustrated he banged his fist angrily on the arm of the chair.

"Now then, Fritz, steady on there," came a familiar voice. "No need for that is there? We'll soon have you up and about and on your way to a nice, warm prison camp. No more fighting Tommy for you, right?" the orderly gently chastised him. "Have you remembered your name yet, eh?"

His name. Something as basic as his name and still he could not recall it. Was he called Burgess? His eyelid began to twitch again and he rubbed it in annoyance.

"No? Ah well, there's someone here to ask you a few more questions, Fritz. Be a sensible fellow and try to answer them, eh?"

The orderly stood aside and a man with a vivid, blood-red cover to his cap stood staring at him. The man's mouth had fallen open and the piece of paper he had held in his hand found wings and gently floated to the floor. "Captain Oscendale? Sir? What the bloody hell are you doing here?"

The message was waiting for a miserable Loram when he returned to regimental headquarters at Birr Crossroads after another fruitless search along the front line for any information regarding Oscendale. Thoroughly depressed, he had slumped down on the ground and leaned against the wall of the dugout just as an excited telegrapher rushed up to him and babbled something about an urgent message. He snatched the paper from the soldier's hand without speaking. What he read there caused him to sit up immediately.

To Sergeant Loram MFP. Major Avate needs to speak to you urgently.

They must have found the body. Loram sighed and ran a hand over his face before lifting the telephone from its cradle and waiting for the operator's voice on the other end.

"Major Avate's office please." There was silence. This was a telephone call he did not want to make. After three rings it was answered.

"Avate here."

"Sir, it's Sergeant Loram. You left a message to call you. You've found Captain Oscendale?"

"Yes, Loram. One of my men on a routine assignment found him in a field hospital. And after we'd almost given up hope."

They had found the body. His heart began to sink.

"Where is he, sir? I want to go and see him," asked Loram anxiously.

"Of course. I knew you would. Casualty Clearing Station 583 outside Poperinghe. Can you get some transport to there?"

"Yes, sir. Shouldn't be a problem, unless someone's pinched my motorcycle."

"Good. Oh and while you're there give him my regards, eh? And cheer up, Loram, for goodness' sake."

"Sir?" asked Loram confused.

"And tell him I expect him back to work as soon as possible. This Lucas case needs sorting out fast before the man causes any more havoc."

Avate hung up. Loram was dumbstruck. He replaced the receiver slowly in its cradle, missed it and it fell off the table. He thought again of the poster in W-H in Poperinghe, of the game of dice at the feet of Christ. The dice had been thrown again but this time Oscendale had not lost. And Loram was thankful to whatever entity or deity was protecting Oscendale, at least for the time being.

"Everything alright, Loram?" asked Lieutenant Bonsall who had joined him in the dugout.

"Yes, sir, everything is perfectly alright," he beamed, the anxiety of the day fast dissipating. "I'm off to visit a miracle of resurrection and salvation."

Oscendale turned his head towards the sunlight.

The last few days had been a journey into the forbidden recesses of his mind where all the memories he had thought merely hidden seemed to have gone forever, at one stage he had worried never to return. It was a journey into his consciousness that had traumatised and tortured him. Then the memories had returned, come to the fore and blasted away his thoughts.

Seeing the red cap cover had been the trigger. Like some huge beast awoken from its reverie, his mind had suddenly begun to stir at that moment and a drop of awareness had become a torrent within minutes and here he was, choking back the tears in a canvas hospital with the relief of it all. The doctor had warned him that he would start to feel increasingly emotional as the memories returned and things got back to normal. But he had not expected this. He was wrung out, exhausted, yet determined not to lose his thoughts again.

He also felt younger, younger than he had ever done. He had been given a gift. The gift of life. And yet he had felt so old recently. Old and alone. *A vision of the future?* His soul had been split and then restored. He had looked into black holes and piercing, lidless eyes had glared out at him. And he had seen the scars of life in a face so young. He had turned and cried for a love that had died as if it were yesterday, and the feelings were raw and new. Ill-fortune had reached out for him and then scuttled away.

He had waited. He was always waiting. Alone and nowhere to go. *Nowhere to go. To go nowhere.*

And then the training and experience he had gathered over all his years as a policeman saved him. The black visions had slithered back into obscurity. A bell had tolled and here he was. He was back where he wanted to be, where he had to be. It was time to return.

And he was ready for the steps he had wanted to take days ago.

The doctor refused to discharge him from the hospital for the next two days so Oscendale grew increasingly irritable. Only Loram's visit softened his mood and he spent some time briefing him on what he planned to do next. When Loram left he spoke with Avate who sanctioned the plan.

At last the doctor was satisfied and allowed him to leave but only on the condition that he would take a complete rest. Oscendale lied and agreed to follow the sternly delivered instructions, having no intention of doing so in reality. *This was more important than his health.*

CHAPTER 43

Ypres Prison – Saturday, 1st September 1917

THEY WERE GATHERED in one of the cellars of the old prison. Thick stone walls hemmed them in and the lack of daylight made the room oppressive, enclosing and heightening the atmosphere. The debriefing of the returning prisoners had already commenced when Oscendale and Loram entered. Millward was sitting, eating like a dog starved of food for days. Polain was talking to the officer who was conducting the interviews. He was saying, "What a blessed relief it is to be back. You have no idea what a joy this is," he added, pointing at his mug of tea. "We can have a proper drink later, eh? All those days on the run makes a chap thirsty."

Oscendale noticed that something had immediately caught Loram's attention. He was staring at Millward and Polain with a puzzled look on his face.

"What's the matter, Loram?"

He turned to Oscendale and murmured, "Can I have a word in private, sir?"

When they returned five minutes later, they heard Polain say, "And to see Oscendale again, safe and sound after we thought he'd been killed or captured by the Huns. We blundered around for days trying to find our way back. Not a clue where we were going. Well, it's all turned out splendidly, hasn't it? Apart from poor Newell that is, of course."

"Excuse me, sir," said Oscendale to Major Goddard, the officer who was conducting the debriefing. He had been chatting convivially with Polain up to that point. "Sorry to interrupt, but I think we all need to get something clear here. One of us is not exactly who he pretends to be. The thing is, we have an infiltrator in our midst." Millward looked up from eating his food and his furtive, brooding eyes met Oscendale's.

There was a short silence as each of the five men in the room tried to take in the implications of what Oscendale had just declared.

"What on earth do you mean, Oscendale?" Polain asked in disbelief.

"I mean," replied Oscendale, "that one person in this room is a German spy."

Ziegler twitched. What? How could this be? How did this man know that he was still alive? He was sure that he had covered his tracks well and no-one, absolutely no-one, could possibly know that he was the one. He had carefully shifted the blame and was sure that the other men were convinced. Had he missed something?

Polain was clearly shocked and spoke again. "Do you mean one of us? I thought we'd decided that Newell was the spy and it was rather good news when he was killed by his own side."

Oscendale thought back to the young girl's words. *"Ce soldat a un regard d'honnête homme."* The young girl had seen the truth. *This soldier has the look of an honest man.*

"For a time I thought so too," replied Oscendale, "and it shows how appearances can be deceptive. Newell wasn't the spy, although until a few minutes ago I thought he was. In fact, I don't even think he died as a result of the lance wound from the *Uhlan.* I think he was probably finished off by someone in this room during the night in Chorin's cottage.

"You see, our man was very clever; moving the focus of suspicion onto poor Newell was convenient. The state he was in that last night he was unable to defend himself; we all thought of him as being the infiltrator. No, it wasn't the unfortunate Lieutenant Newell. He was innocent. He was also a loyal British officer and I am glad we were with him when he died, rather than abandoning him to the Germans. Isabelle Chorin was right when she said to me that he had honesty in his eyes. He wasn't the spy. You are, Captain Polain."

Polain paused, the mug of tea halfway to his lips. Millward put his plate of food to one side, finished chewing and spoke for the first time.

"Polain? Are you sure? How do you know it's him?"

"Yes, I'm sure. Of course, we all thought it was Newell because of the incident with the *pickelhaube* as we were leaving the village. But that was really just a genuine accident. Newell couldn't resist the souvenir and it had been booby-trapped. Besides," he paused and turned to Polain before saying, "somebody in this room has met you before, haven't you, Loram?"

Loram stepped into the light. "Yes, sir. I saw Captain Polain, as he calls himself now, when he crossed over into our lines last year. Except that you called yourself something else then. You remember that, don't you?" He spoke directly to Polain.

Polain stood up from his seat, smiling nervously, his fingers playing with his cuffs. "Me? Oh, no, Oscendale. You have made a mistake. I'm not your man."

"Sit down!" shouted Oscendale, his patience coming to an end. Lies, like lack of food, made him very irritable.

"I don't understand," said Major Goddard. "You said that Captain Polain and Lieutenants Millward and Newell joined you behind the German lines. How do you know for certain it's Captain Polain? It could be any of them. Your man Loram could be wrong, you know. A case of mistaken identity perhaps? After all, it was over a year ago when he last saw him and time does strange things to people's memories, doesn't it?"

Oscendale sighed. "Sergeant Loram was, like me, a trained policeman before the war, sir. We tend to have good memories for faces." He raised an eyebrow and Goddard fidgeted and looked back at Polain. "Besides, the really strange thing was Polain's behaviour," continued Oscendale. "I wondered why he was the only one of us who didn't want to take the risk of rescuing the British prisoners. He knew that Newell was suspicious of him and he wasn't sure how much longer his disguise would last. He thought he could make contact with the *Uhlans* guarding the prisoners but Newell confronted him in the village when they first appeared."

Millward piped up, "So Polain was the one who was going to signal to them to betray our position?"

"Correct. After all, he couldn't have us running around behind the German lines, gathering goodness knows what sort of information before we made our way back, could he? I believe he was planted amongst us to find out what I was doing behind enemy lines. During my interview with the German officer he was insistent on confirming the spelling of my name, so much so that I noticed him glance to one side to check it against another list. I have no idea why I was on that list. Of course, escaping from the guards really threw a spanner into the works. He had to make a decision to stay with us. When the *Uhlans* came along he tried to pass a message to them somehow but Newell's appearance prevented him from doing so."

Polain was watching the whole scene play itself out without moving a muscle.

"But why was he in one of our tanks heading towards the German lines?" Millward asked.

"I had Loram check on that just now," replied Oscendale, "and it appears he wasn't. There is no Captain Polain of the Tank Corps, not one who's alive anyway. This man had the perfect cover, pretending to be an escaped prisoner of war alongside us."

"But he would have been discovered as soon as we checked his name against the casualty and missing returns," said Goddard.

"I don't think he wanted to hang about very long," said Oscendale. "He probably intended to disappear from here shortly and make himself scarce for a few days. With that uniform he could walk into any officers' club, glean some information and then make his way back through the lines. The hardest part would be getting into our lines in the first place. And once that had been accomplished…" Oscendale's voice trailed off and the men in the room turned their attention from Polain to him. "Good grief! So that's it." His eyes widened as the revelation came to him.

Polain saw at once the connection Oscendale had made and quickly snatching the knife from Millward's plate, he lunged straight at him. But Loram moved faster and threw him to the stone floor, wrenching the knife from his hand and deliberately breaking the wrist as he did so. Ziegler yelled out in pain and Loram twisted the injured arm up behind his back. "Shut up, you whining German bastard or I'll break the other one." When Polain complied, Loram released him.

Oscendale glared with disdain at Polain who was crouching on the floor, rocking back and forth, holding his swelling wrist in agony while Loram pointed a revolver at his head. "The captured tank crew would have known Polain was not a tank officer. He had them removed. Another way of ensuring he wasn't exposed."

"Well done, Oscendale," said Goddard. He turned to Polain. "A Hun spy indeed!"

"Yes," added Oscendale, "but you're more than that, aren't you, my friend? You're here to kill someone. An assassin behind our lines, free to murder senior officers. I expect our becoming separated when we ran into the German patrol was most inconvenient so you changed your plan and decided to stick with Millward, hoping you could find me before I crossed over to our lines. The last few days recovering in one of our hospitals must have been useful too. You probably picked up all sorts of information. Just a shame no-one thought to check your identification before this moment."

Ziegler, his eyes burning with hatred, now spoke. "Captain Oscendale, the last time we met you allowed me to just help myself to a map. You talk of your police training but it was easy. You didn't stir at all. I wish I had slit your throat there and then when I had the chance. I regretted that soon afterwards. And when we discovered you had infiltrated our lines with your lie about being picked up by a tank crew we knew you were here for a reason. My officer wanted to know what it was. Once I had found that out for him, well, then it was up to me what I wanted to do next."

Oscendale shuddered inwardly at the memory of a year ago. He remembered the night well. The German had stolen a map from his tunic pocket whilst he slept and he recalled how close he had come to death at this man's hands.

"Yes, you'll regret it up to the moment you are put up on the scaffold and hung by the neck until you are dead. And I hope the last thing you see is poor Newell's face." He turned to Loram. "Call the guards in and hand him over. We've got something else to do."

CHAPTER 44

Hazebrouck, France – Sunday, 2nd September 1917

THE MAN'S BALD pate shone with a thin veneer of grease, though he did not appear to be the sort to work up a sweat about anything. Above his ears two black patchy remnants of hair struggled for life. He raised his head half-curiously as Oscendale entered, dismissed him mentally for a moment and returned to the letter he had been typing, determined to finish it. *Clerk. Officious. Pedantic.* The words went through Oscendale's mind like tracer bullets. *Work done. Paper cleared away. Revisit something? Never. Job completed. Filed. Put away.*

The corporal finished typing as Oscendale drew closer. He drew out the piece of paper carefully, the cradle of his typewriter clicking like an empty rifle. He finally acknowledged the visitor and stood to give him a salute.

"Can I help you, sir?" he asked in a voice as dry as the paper he was still holding.

"I am here to see Major Lucas," Oscendale replied, already feeling his hackles rise.

"Do you have an appointment, sir?" It was a reasonable request from anyone else but something in the tone of the word 'sir' lent it a patronising edge that Oscendale did not intend to take from a junior man.

He leaned forward and rested his knuckles on the table before hissing, "Tell him I want to see him about Lloyd Phillips. His friend." He flicked his head towards the closed door to the rear of the room. "Go on," he ordered.

"Who, sir?" the clerk asked bemused, without taking a single step towards the door.

"Nobody you'd know but your officer will. Phillips. P-H-I-L-L-I-P-S. Just go in and tell him, eh? Oh and if you can keep more than one thought in your head at a time, say it's also about his other friends, Burgess and Maskell."

The clerk gave a pained expression and pushed his spectacles up to the bridge of his nose before moving quickly to the door – his body suddenly invigorated by a sense of irritation. He rapped on the door and waited. A voice called out "Enter!" and the man shuffled inside, closing the door behind him. Time passed. Oscendale noticed the pictures on the walls. Belgium before the war. *Very nice.* Unspoilt and unmarked. And dry. Sunny and dry.

The door opened again and the clerk emerged.

"Major Lucas will see you now, sir. Please go in." He removed his spectacles and a false smile flashed quickly across his face.

The clerk feigned courtesy by holding the door open for him. Oscendale brushed past the man without acknowledgement. He entered an airless room. Lucas stood up from behind the papers strewn on his desk.

"Captain Oscendale. Good to meet you."

Oscendale scanned the face of this military hero whose crisp, newly-laundered uniform displayed the purple and white ribbon of the Military Cross and next to it the unmistakeable red and blue of the Distinguished Service Order – one step removed from the Victoria Cross.

"Really?" He paused. "I was just looking at your ribbon bar, sir. A fine display."

Lucas looked down at the ribbons as if they had suddenly moved. "Yes, rather proud of these, I must admit." He tapped them with his index finger as if reminding Oscendale who he was and what he had done.

"Yes, a testament to your bravery at Gallipoli and on the Somme, aren't they?" He studied Lucas's face. Impassive.

286

Obligatory moustache finely trimmed. A touch of vanity about the man.

Lucas's brows furrowed with suspicion. His reply was a little more hesitant, his earlier bravado slightly receding.

"That's right. Have you been out here long?" *The barbed comment.* Military policeman to some equalled Home Front, guarding docks and the like.

"Yes, sir, as a matter of fact I have. Enlisted in the summer of '14, served at Mons. On the Somme as well, with a few distractions in between. Oh and including, you might be interested to know, a couple of weeks at Gallipoli."

Oscendale's reference to Gallipoli aroused troubled thoughts in Lucas's mind.

Silence fell for a few seconds as both men weighed up the other. Lucas broke the silence first. "So you were at the Dardanelles as well, were you? I see. With the Military Police?" he asked.

"That's right. With the Military Police. At Y Beach."

"Y Beach, do you say?" replied Lucas. "I was also at Y Beach."

"I know," said Oscendale instantly. "You were there on the 25th April."

"How do you know that? Wait a minute." Realisation spread quickly over his face as he recalled. "That's right. I know who you are. You're the idiot who went ahead up that gully from the beach against my express orders. You and…" Lucas's voice tailed off as he began to comprehend the reason for Oscendale's visit.

Oscendale leaned forward across the desk and made his move. "Yes, that was me. And I see you remember the other person who was with me on that day. The person whose courage you later misappropriated for yourself." Oscendale was conscious of the anger returning as he spoke.

The door opened and Hope stood there. "Is everything alright, sir?"

"Get out!" shouted Lucas and the startled soldier beat a hasty retreat.

"Don't take that tone with me, Oscendale. I'm your superior and don't forget it otherwise I'll have Hope march you out of this office quicker than you came in."

"You'll do what? Listen, Lucas, I know what you did at Krithia. And it's not the version you gave to your commanding officer later or the version you've been peddling around for the past two years. Parry rushed that Turkish house and took it, not you. But when you saw him die you decided you'd claim the credit for his actions and get yourself that!" Oscendale flicked his fingers contemptuously at the purple and white ribbon on Lucas's left breast and shook his head dismissively.

Lucas pressed his hand protectively against his medal ribbons. His eyes narrowed as he listened to Oscendale continue.

"That should have been his, not yours. You stole the glory because you knew if you didn't, questions would have been asked about your fitness to command that day or any other. You're a coward. You showed me that in the gully and at Krithia. You're vermin, Lucas, and a bloody disgrace to the British Army. Men have died in this war carrying out acts of bravery that were never seen by any survivors. Bravery that should have been rewarded but never will be, and you have the sordid indecency to steal another man's gallantry medal. And you did the same thing on the Somme a year later. You disgust me!"

Lucas had grown redder in the face by the second. "Be very careful, Captain Oscendale," he threatened through his clenched teeth. "Any more of these… lies and I'll have you arrested by one of your own men. My actions that day were witnessed and duly recorded later. There is no truth in your assertion."

"Oh it was witnessed all right," said Oscendale nodding. "Witnessed by a friend you persuaded to lie for you. And who threatened to tell the truth, so you arranged an accident with a Mills bomb at Kinmel Park. You blew him to smithereens to stop him talking."

Lucas did not reply but his lips had disappeared to leave the edges of a thin line in his face. He stood up and walked across the room to the window to gather his thoughts under this tirade of accusations.

"Albert Maskell was a decent man," continued Oscendale. "You bullied him into making a false statement just so you could advance your career with the advantage of another gallantry award. Your commanding officer at Morval wasn't convinced and entered it as a Mentioned in Dispatches recommendation. Albert Maskell ensured that what was entered into your CO's report was something a bit stronger. When your CO was conveniently killed before he was able to check the final draft of this report, your immoral act was safe."

"Where's your proof, Oscendale?" snarled Lucas, whirling round to face his accuser.

"When Maskell realised what he'd done, prompted I think by his suspicions over the officer's death, it gnawed away at him for a year. He said he was going to expose you as a charlatan and a liar. But because he was such an honourable man he gave you one last chance to redeem yourself by coming clean. That was out of the question of course, but Maskell didn't realise that so you had him posted to Kinmel Park for training and then had him killed, probably by the odious Captain Roberts."

"Absolute nonsense! You're deranged. This has gone far enough. Get out of my office!"

"No, Lucas, not far enough," replied Oscendale. "I've got more to say to you than that. You heard that somebody was getting a bit suspicious about some recent recommendations for gallantry awards so you thought you'd use an old contact that you'd known at the Somme. Roberts. You decided to shift the blame onto poor Harrington lying in a hospital bed. Harrington wasn't bright enough to see through your charade so you thought you'd concoct some ham-fisted plan to sell decorations that would be quickly exposed. That would leave you free to sell your service to any corrupt officer who wanted to hasten his movement up the tree by buying a gallantry award to which he was never entitled. Captain Roberts would just disappear, leaving no trail behind. I know because I tried to find him."

Lucas was dumbfounded. He sat back down in his chair and reached for a silver box on his desk. Opening it, he took out a cigarette which he held without lighting as he listened to Oscendale.

"And of course there were the witnesses. They had to be removed to keep the trail clear. After Albert Maskell, you had Lieutenant Newcombe killed just in case he had suspicions about something else you did. And then you heard his hospital orderly might know more than he was letting on so you sent Roberts to Carmarthen to kill him as well. I imagine that was quite a surprise when you discovered it was your old friend Lloyd Phillips. Bloody hell, man, where was it all going to stop?"

"Stop? I'll tell you. It was going to stop with you," replied Lucas, composed again. He turned the cigarette over slowly between his fingers and his eyes narrowed. "Once I had you out of the way, there would be nobody left."

"There's always somebody else," said Oscendale. "If it hadn't been me it would have been my sergeant."

"Ah yes. The devoted Sergeant Loram. Your faithful little sidekick. His foolhardy foray into no man's land should have finished him if somebody had done their job properly."

"And then there was Ossie Burgess," said Oscendale, ignoring the remark. He was determined to get Lucas to say more, whatever insults flew from his mouth.

"Burgess? What about him? Basket case I heard," sneered Lucas.

"Burgess was your friend, Lucas. Another friend you decided to remove to protect your precious reputation. But do you know what? He told me everything."

"Everything? Everything about what?" said Lucas.

"About last June. About what happened in no man's land."

Lucas fell silent. Oscendale knew it was time to pounce.

"When you joined the Leicesters in May you asked to see a list of the officers. I imagine you were quite surprised to see the name of Osmond Burgess. After all, he was supposed to join the Worcesters. It was an administrative hitch that sent him to the Leicesters instead. I bet you didn't have to mull over what you would do about the man who could expose you for what you did at Gallipoli. The Germans soon gave you an opportunity you couldn't have wished for.

"Picture the scene again, Lucas. The fog. The attack. Watching Burgess disappear into no man's land. You must have been thanking God for your good fortune. So you decided to follow Clarke to make sure what the Germans had started you would finish. You heard Clarke fire on the Germans and you moved in. You murdered an honourable man, a British officer and you were about to do the same to Burgess but he fought you off. You lost him in the fog but the shock of seeing what you did tipped him over the edge."

"I told you he was a basket case," sneered Lucas.

"No. What you did traumatised a young officer who was already on the edge as a result of all the horrors he'd endured. He was unable to talk about what had happened until I spoke with him and triggered the memory by chance when mentioning your name. You did all that just to ensure no-one could tell what a gutless coward you really are and all to protect your bloody reputation and your crooked scheme."

Lucas placed the cigarette between his pursed lips. He struck a match and lit it. Oscendale noticed his fingers were quivering slightly.

"Then you discovered I was on to you so you lured me to Poperinghe and ordered your men to make sure my investigation into your corrupt activities ended there. But one of them still had some semblance of humanity left and he found he couldn't kill me there and then so he took me out in no man's land."

Lucas drew heavily on the end of the cigarette. He exhaled forcefully, blue and grey smoke pouring out of mouth, before he raised his voice and said loudly, "Listen, Oscendale. You're out of your territory. I'm warning you once and for all. Keep out of my way or you'll spend the rest of the war interviewing the VD cases to see which French whore they caught the pox from!"

Oscendale knew he was winning. Lucas was plainly rattled. It was time to push a little harder.

"Lucas, you're far too gutless to do anything as decisive as that. You get other people to do your dirty work for you. But you leave a trail of broken lives in your wake. Phillips saw through your façade so you had him killed. Burgess was a ghost from the past so he had to be dealt with in a more subtle way. The same way you tried to get rid of me. Leave me half-dead and expect the Huns to finish me off. Burgess has more courage in his little finger than you'll ever have despite that row of coloured ribbons on your chest. Bravery? Courage? You don't know the meaning of the words!"

"Shut up!" Lucas spat vehemently, furiously stubbing out his cigarette in a glass ashtray on his desk. "I earned these, Oscendale, doing front line soldiering. Something you know nothing about."

"No you flaming didn't," replied Oscendale. "You're a coward who left other men to die."

"Like your pal, Jack?"

It had been the one name Oscendale could not bring himself to mention. Lucas saw it.

"Yes, your pal Jack. Jack and Jill going up that hill. The pair of you. Tinpot little heroes. Sometimes, Oscendale, it's just a matter of getting in first."

Oscendale tried one more roll of the dice. "And I don't suppose it will be too difficult to track down Roberts either."

Lucas laughed. "Come on, Oscendale, you don't think that's his real name do you? Men like him aren't that stupid. A man who can kill like he does can never be traced. He's a dangerous man, Oscendale. I should watch my back if I were you. After all, you're the only man left in my way."

Oscendale decided he now knew enough.

"I see. Well, if you'll be so good as to ask Major Avate to come in."

"What are you talking about, Oscendale?" asked Lucas, mystified.

"The door, Lucas. Didn't you see Hope left it ajar? Everything has been overheard next door. Come in, sir."

Lucas's face was contorted with dread as Avate and a pair of MPs entered.

"Just one last thing, Lucas. You had Albert Maskell killed but why his wife?" enquired Oscendale.

Lucas frowned. "What are you accusing me of now, Oscendale? Why would I want to kill his wife? Got your facts wrong again, I'd say. You're obviously not as infallible as you like to think."

CHAPTER 45

Le Havre, France – Monday, 3rd September 1917

"I'M SORRY, SIR, but your travel warrant is no longer valid." The speaker was an MFP corporal. Oscendale thought he had misheard.

"What?" he replied irritably. "What the Dickens do you mean, 'not valid'? I have a passage booked on that ship." He pointed at the troopship that towered over both of them on the dockside.

"I'm sorry, sir," said the man with what Oscendale thought was a certain amount of satisfaction in his eyes. The opportunity of belittling an officer did not come along too often and it was clear the man was determined to enjoy it. "Your warrant has been revoked. See here." He handed a piece of paper to Oscendale. It was a list of soldiers whose travel warrants had all expired. Halfway down he saw the name, *Oscendale, T. Cpt.*

It was absurd. How could a travel warrant that had only been issued earlier that day have expired already?

The corporal spoke again, growing in confidence now. "If you'll be so good as to stand aside, sir. There are other men waiting to board." Oscendale complied numbly. His name was on the list and that, it appeared, was that. He was not going to be able to board the troopship and return to Blighty as he had planned. He thought for a moment then motioned to Loram to follow him. They approached one of the single-storey wooden docks buildings that littered the waterfront and walked until they were sure they were out of sight of the checkpoint and the officious corporal.

"What's going on, sir?" asked Loram bemused.

"Looks like somebody doesn't want us to leave France. My

name has been added to a list of men who are *persona non grata* on that ship." He pointed once more at the *Brighton*, daubed in olive paint as camouflage against preying German U-boats. "And take a guess who had signed at the bottom of the list?"

"Major Avate," confirmed Loram. "He doesn't want you to travel. He knows what you're going to do, sir and he doesn't think you're up to it yet. Perhaps he's right."

"Listen," snapped Oscendale angrily. "I don't have the time to waste. I need to be on that ship before it sails. A woman's life depends on it."

Loram nodded thoughtfully and peered at something over Oscendale's shoulder, then asked, "Was my name on the list, sir?"

"Not that I saw," said Oscendale, wondering what was going through Loram's mind.

"Good," answered Loram. "In which case I have an idea. Follow me, sir."

Loram led Oscendale to a nearby building where scores of wounded men lay on stretchers, waiting to be taken on board. Loram sidled up to a counter where some of the stretcher-bearers had discarded their overcoats and tunics owing to the heat of the day and the strenuous task they were undertaking. Through an open doorway they could see a procession of soldiers in shirt sleeve order striding up a gangplank carrying men on stretchers, while a file of them returned down another one. A doctor was walking between the lines of stretchers, issuing instructions to a nurse whose cape fluttered in the breeze blowing along the quayside.

Loram quickly removed his tunic and covertly took a greatcoat and two Red Cross armbands from the counter. Oscendale took his cue from him and removed his tunic as well. Loram passed him an armband and quickly both men fastened the armbands to their left upper arms.

Loram then pointed at an unused stretcher. He threw his jacket and cap onto it, added the greatcoat and Oscendale followed suit. Loram grabbed a blanket from a pile in the corner and mocked up the clothing beneath it until it resembled a human figure. He and Oscendale lifted it up and joined the queue for the gangway.

"I'm not saying I don't trust you, Loram," whispered Oscendale, "but how do you think we're going to get through the checkpoint this time?"

"Look at the MPs," Loram replied in a similar hushed tone out of the corner of his mouth. "They're so busy they're not checking the bearers or the patients; they're just waving everyone through."

They passed swiftly through the checkpoint, Loram giving his name, the MPs taking no more than a passing interest in them. They were at the foot of the gangway when Oscendale felt a tap on his shoulder. Turning nervously around, he saw a stern-looking MP with a wallet in his hand.

"I think you just dropped this," he said. Oscendale saw it was his brown leather wallet. It must have fallen out of his tunic. He took it gratefully, muttered his thanks and began the ascent up the steep gangway.

Once on board they were swallowed up in a huge area full of patients, nurses and doctors. They put their stretcher down quickly, took their clothes and caps and beat a hasty retreat along one of the corridors. The room was so busy that nobody paid them any attention. They were just two more stretcher-bearers amongst many.

Oscendale discarded his Red Cross armband and they made their way up onto the deck. They leaned on the railing and gazed down at the hustle and bustle of the port beneath them. "Bloody well done, Loram. Just as well you're not a criminal."

"Good luck then, sir," replied Loram. "I'll be off now before

I'm listed as AWOL as well." He saluted, turned on his heel and was gone.

Oscendale lit a cigarette and watched the smoke drift, then disappear into the invisible arms of the sea breeze. A few more hours and he would be on the train to Barry to complete some unfinished business. And to see the woman with whom he was falling in love.

He glanced down at the quay and saw Loram manoeuvring his way through the crowds. He looked upwards and gave Oscendale a thumbs-up before disappearing into a throng of troops.

The voyage back across the English Channel would begin shortly and he would be making it as a Military Police officer absent without leave. The irony was not lost on him.

CHAPTER 46

Barry – Tuesday, 4th September 1917

"ARE YOU SURE, my dear?" Mrs Graham said, feigning disappointment. "You can still change your mind. We can take the later train to Cardiff…"

"Yes, I'm sure. The break will do you both good. I'll be fine. Besides which I promised to see cousin Eveline before she leaves for France." Hannah's reply was of little importance to Mrs Graham who was busy making the final adjustments to her appearance.

"But how on earth will you manage?" enquired Mrs Graham.

Hannah sighed. "Mrs Jones will be here this afternoon to prepare my dinner. I'll be fine. You go and enjoy yourselves." *Would they never go?*

When the goodbyes were eventually over, Hannah Graham stood alone in the hallway of the home that was anything but hers. The house was peaceful except for the grandfather clock that chimed the passing hours, the precious hours until the Grahams returned on Saturday. They were hours that she willed would pass slowly. She peered through the windows out over the park and further to the sea. *The future or the past. She now had to decide.*

A walnut box sat on the bedside table. A tasselled key poked out of the mother-of-pearl escutcheon. Geometric patterns wrapped around the edges of the box which bore in the centre two gold intertwined initials and a date.

He picked up the box and his fingers traced the lines of the letters. "J and H," said Oscendale curiously. "You and James?"

Hannah sighed and turned to lie on her back, eyes focused on the ceiling. "Yes," she replied. "I loved him once, Thomas, you have to understand that, although I know he never loved me. Not for an instant. He was too… distracted to show me the love I wanted, that was always here, deep inside me. And when I heard he was gone…"

Oscendale examined the box again. "And why this year, 1917, written on the lid as well?"

"It was a gift from him last Christmas when he was home on leave. He said I was to keep his letters to me safe in the box. That way they could remain close to me at night when I was alone without him. It was as if he was trying to fall in love with me at last. What false hopes we all have, Thomas Oscendale. What lies we tell ourselves."

He placed the box back on the bedside table before turning to look at her again.

"It has been different this time, though." She sensed he was hurt or confused. Turning towards him now she wrapped her warm body around him in an effort to comfort him and gently stroked his cheek.

He did not know what to say. She was his but somehow she was not. There was a part of her he did not understand, that she kept remote from him. Hidden, fenced off.

"Hannah, I don't want to talk about him. I want to talk about us. What all this means for both of us," he said.

He felt her grow tenser; she was no longer relaxed. "No, I don't want to talk about James either. He's not here and it's just us. Like this," she said, looking at him closely.

But he felt there was something hollow about her words. He looked once more at the box; its polished surface was telling him something. James Graham was not gone, just not here. He was still part of the picture. What were her real feelings for her husband? Was she deluding herself or was he, Oscendale, just part of the healing, purging process? A distraction until her husband's memory faded completely and she was strong enough to fully love again?

She looked at him longingly. He desired her more than ever and drew her smooth body closer to him, breathing in the sweet scent of her hair. Their bodies entwined, caressing each other softly, kissing lightly then with more passion, the urgency of their previous lovemaking becoming more measured. Slowly they discovered one another again as they moved instinctively together, knowing that they were now as one.

Hannah unfurled herself from Oscendale's protective arms and sat on the edge of the bed. She looked over her shoulder, bent down and kissed him before standing up and walking softly across the room. He opened his eyes and followed her naked body profiled in the shadowy light as she opened the bedroom door and left him alone with his nagging thoughts.

He was drawn again to the box. *Damn it!* There was the shadow of another man in this room and he would not leave. He opened the lid and reached inside. His fingers closed on a piece of paper and he drew it out. It was part of a letter from James. It was tender, loving and passionate. *What did you expect, Tom?* he asked himself. *She told you she loved him. Perhaps as he felt his death approaching he realised what he had once had with her.* He stopped reading and replaced the letter back inside the box, resting it once more on top of the pile of letters she had kept. *Were they all from James?*

"Thomas, come here, I miss you," Hannah called from the bathroom, teasingly.

He stood in the doorway of the bathroom. She lay in the bathtub, eyes closed and he watched as she gently sponged herself. Her hair was coiled up but some stray ringlets fell down across her flushed cheeks and he bent forward to twirl them around his fingers. She turned her head so that her warm, moist lips found his fingers and gently kissed and nibbled them. His desire for her increased as he gazed down at her naked, wet body. She guided his hands into the warm water and placed them on her perfect breasts.

"Do you want to come in here with me?"

Without waiting for his answer she made room for him to step into the bath. He squeezed in with his knees drawn up which made her giggle and playfully splashed water on his face and chest, the water running in rivulets down his muscular, bruised body.

"Turn around Thomas, let me soap your back."

Her lathered hands slid across his skin, massaging his shoulders then following his spine as he murmured his approval. She swilled off the soap and stretched out a finger, following the line of one water droplet as it made its way slowly down his shoulder blade. She noticed a pale white scar on his arm.

"What's this from?" she asked, nuzzling up to his back, her nipples brushing lightly against him as she did so.

Oscendale contemplated the scar. "Bullet wound, a lifetime ago." The memory associated with it was too painful for more detail and she sensed it. The wound scar reminded him of another time, another love, another disappointment.

She ran her hand across the scar but he reached out and took it, holding it to his lips, inhaling deeply the fragrance of her warm, perfumed skin.

CHAPTER 47

Barry – Wednesday, 5th September 1917

S ILENTLY, HE LET himself in through an unlocked downstairs window. *Tut, tut,* he thought, *how careless you are, Mrs Gough. No need to knock at the front door today.* He dropped down into the room and stood perfectly still, listening. The house was still and quiet.

The silence continued. Wherever Cerys Gough was, it was not nearby. He could detect no sound of movement at all so he checked his pockets again. Each had the required contents so began to creep slowly and silently across the carpet.

One is never really alone in a room. The ghosts of past inhabitants watch from the corners, he thought. *Well, watch this. This will be more entertainment for you all.*

He peered into the gloom of the hallway beyond, letting his eyes adjust slowly to the lack of light. When he was sure that his vision was as good as it was going to get, he walked forward again.

Still nothing. He stopped, twitched his head from side to side and thought. She must be here somewhere; he had seen her come in just a few minutes before. Just then there was a faint creak from upstairs and a door opened and closed. There was the sound of footsteps treading on the squeaking floorboards above his head. He took a sharp breath then swallowed as the adrenaline began to surge around his body.

A wall clock in the living room struck three times as he crept into the kitchen. Opening the china cabinet, he took out a dish. It was chipped, which irritated him, but it would have to do.

He moved quickly to the foot of the stairs and placed his

hand on the newel post. It was smooth, warm and round. He caressed it as the excitement began to build in him. Above him another door opened and closed so he moved stealthily, like a predator about to attack its prey, taking the stairs two at a time, bending his knees to absorb the impact and mute the sound of his approach.

He was soon at the top and stepped onto the landing. Ahead of him a bedroom door was closed. She was behind it. His heart pounded furiously in his chest. *Calm, keep calm, and enjoy the moment.* Barely able to contain his state of agitation, he drew a deep breath and knocked on the door.

There was a shuffling movement beyond and a voice he recognised said, "Who is it? Who's there? Is that you, Helen?"

He told her who he was and invented a plausible reason for why he was there. "I was walking past and noticed you had left your keys in the door."

"Oh you frightened me for a minute. How foolish of me. I'll be out in a minute."

With that he threw open the door.

"That's right. Dab it on. All over your pretty face. Like you do when you're getting ready to go to church every Sunday, you hypocritical slut." He smiled at the half-dressed, terrified woman kneeling in her undergarments before him.

Cerys Gough patted her face with the cotton wool, her hand trembling as she did so. Tears upon tears filled her eyes, not just from the smell of the noxious fluid. The man was becoming a blur. Moisture began to run along the side of her nose and down her cheeks until she could taste the saltiness in her half-open mouth.

"Don't cry! We don't want any waterworks!" he said firmly. Then soothingly and quietly, "You'll dilute it with your tears. It will take longer to burn and we wouldn't want that now would we? The pain will last longer that way, your suffering more terrible." His cruel eyes bulged as he stared at her slowly moving the piece of cotton wool from the dish he had so thoughtfully provided to her face and back again.

"Dab it on. That's it. Dab, dab. Don't forget those rosy cheeks." Fearfully she obliged. "Faster, you bitch!" he shouted impatiently and in her terror she knocked the dish over, spilling the greasy liquid onto the rug on the floor of her bedroom. He tutted irritably, muttered something blasphemous, and refilled the dish, slowly, precisely.

When he was satisfied her face was covered, he told her to stop. She placed the cotton wool into the dish, crying and begging, "Please don't! I'll do anything. Anything you want but not this! I don't want to die!" He withdrew a box of matches from his pocket, ignoring her pleas and enjoying seeing the look on her face as she realised what he was about to do.

"No! Don't! Please!" she screamed but he struck a match and held it up to his own face, watching the colours of the flame. Then he flicked it towards her. It landed on her shoulder and fell onto the floor. She looked down in horror at the match burning itself out. Then he lit another one and this time his aim was more accurate. In an instant her face was a mass of scorched and burning flesh. She screamed briefly until her mouth closed up and she tore at her face with her hands, attempting vainly to put out the fire.

He watched her dying, inhaling deeply the smell that he loved – the smell of burning fuel. *And roasting flesh.* He went to the dressing table and poured water from the pitcher into the washing bowl. He dipped a piece of cloth into it then wrapped it around her face, extinguishing the flames. She had slumped backwards onto the floor and lay still. He removed the cloth and studied her. The flames had closed her throat and melted her mouth, suffocating her.

There was just time to open the heavy black Bible on the chest of drawers. What passage to choose today though? Ah yes. The words of St Peter. '*For when they speak great swelling words of vanity, they allure through the lusts of the flesh, through much wantonness, those that were clean escaped from them who live in error.*'

Smiling with satisfaction, he wrung the cloth into the washing bowl, folded it neatly and put it away inside his jacket. He picked up the dish and went downstairs to wash it in the kitchen sink. After drying it and putting it back in a cupboard, he climbed out of the unlocked window. He then halted and peered cautiously up at the windows of the houses all around. Seeing no one, he moved quickly down the garden path and into the lane behind the house. Slowing down and whistling as he went, he pulled out his fob watch and realised he was just in time for his next appointment.

CHAPTER 48

Barry – Wednesday, 5th September 1917

WOODFIN LOOKED DOWN at the body. Cerys Gough's head was unrecognisable, featureless. Two rows of teeth grinned grotesquely up at him from the place where her mouth had been. Her eyes, ears and nose had been replaced by a blackened, wrinkled mass. Her brown skull was exposed where her burning hair had removed her scalp.

Having seen enough, he pulled the grey blanket back over what was left of the woman's head. He stood upright, watched intently, as he was well aware, by his uniformed sergeant. "Horrible mess, sir. What sort of sick mind does that to a woman?"

"To anyone, Streeter," corrected Woodfin. "A particularly nasty way to die. Did you notice that the rest of the body was not burnt? Any marks at all on it?"

"Nothing, sir," replied Streeter. "No sign of a struggle either. We found out how he came in, though. An open window in the back room downstairs. She must have left it unlocked."

"Any disturbance to her… er… undergarments?" asked Woodfin.

"No sign of any interference like that at all. Just her head."

There was the sound of voices from downstairs and a few moments later Woodfin smiled grimly at the man who entered the room. "Welcome back, Tom. Didn't expect to see you so soon. Another one, I'm afraid. Thought you might want to be involved again."

"Yes. I got back yesterday. There was a lot here that was unresolved, as you know." He shook the memory of Hannah out of his mind. "I think I might be facing a charge though, when I get back." He stared across the room at the form underneath the grey blanket. "Mind if I take a look?"

"Feel free," Woodfin replied. "But be warned. Once more it's not pretty, Tom, so steel yourself."

Oscendale knelt and drew the blanket down to the dead woman's chest as he took in the grotesque sight that lay before him. The smell of burnt skin filled his nostrils and he instinctively pinched his nose with his thumb and forefinger. It was a smell he had become familiar with over the past three years, yet it had the capacity to sicken and revolt him on each occasion, no matter how many times he smelt it.

He replaced the blanket and looked at the rug underneath the body. "Have you moved the body at all?" he asked.

Woodfin replied that this was how she had been found an hour ago. "No gag, if that's what you mean. Detached house this time. Enjoyed hearing her scream, I expect."

"Have you finished examining it?" Oscendale asked.

"Yes. Again, no sign of any interference so I don't think it can tell us anything else. Why?"

Oscendale's eyes narrowed and Woodfin knew he was on to something. "What else can you smell here, Corrick?" he asked. Woodfin crouched down alongside him. He frowned.

"Apart from that ghastly smell of burnt human flesh, nothing."

"Help me move the body," he asked Streeter. Together they lifted the corpse of Cerys Gough onto the bed.

Oscendale dropped to his knees and examined the rug. He lowered his face until it was almost touching the fibres and began sniffing like an inquisitive animal. He tapped a small section of it with his finger. "Here. Smell that, Corrick."

Woodfin knelt down. "Petrol," he said and looked into Oscendale's face.

"He's using bloody petrol to ignite their faces," said Oscendale. "But that doesn't narrow it down much. Anyone can get hold of petrol. Everyone with a motor vehicle in Barry."

Woodfin replied with a snort as he got up. "Omnibus drivers too. We're no further forward with that."

"But you've spoken to the neighbours, yes?"

"Of course, my men were out making enquires as soon as the body was discovered," replied Woodfin. "But as with the last two, no-one saw anything unusual. It's as though he's invisible or something, a ghost. Enters and leaves without anyone seeing. Nothing. We've drawn a total blank. He's very good, it seems."

Oscendale thought for a moment. "But who can enter and leave a house in broad daylight without being seen by anyone? And why is he doing this? It's not sexual so what does he get out of it?" They both fell silent for a few seconds, puzzling over the implications.

"And I've had another one of these," said Oscendale, removing a postcard from his pocket and holding it out to Woodfin.

Woodfin took it. It was a postcard of All Souls Church. He turned it over. On the back was written:

Dear Oscendale,
You've been away! I missed you. So glad you're back.
Loki

"Why do you think he's taunting you like this? What's the link between you and him?"

Oscendale was biting his lip. "I don't know, Corrick, but it's starting to get to me, making it difficult to think clearly. Perhaps my nerves haven't straightened out yet."

"Maybe, Tom. Maybe. Anyway, we can learn nothing more here," concluded Woodfin. "Streeter, you and Wilkins search the house from top to bottom. If you find anything that's out of place let me know immediately. I'm going to speak to the boys outside to see if they've been able to find out any more from the neighbours. If so, we can interview them later at the station."

"This is evil itself, Corrick," said Oscendale. "This sadistic bastard has a soul so corrupt that he's walking a fine line between reality and madness."

Woodfin nodded slowly in agreement, "God knows, we have all plummeted into that pit from time to time, especially in our line of work."

"But there is nothing of his soul remaining that is in any way good or salvageable. All that is left is a voice, a terrible voice that calls out constantly in his head and drives him on to do things like this." Oscendale paused and lifted his pint glass to his lips. His words hung in the air and Woodfin felt as if he could reach out and grasp them, so heavy was the atmosphere that lay in the space between the two policemen.

"And what do you think that voice will tell him to do next?" he asked as the silence became awkward.

Oscendale stared at the wooden floor of the public house, then he raised his head and for a moment Woodfin saw fear in his friend's face.

"This one will need trapping. Trapping like an animal. He's clever, very clever." Oscendale's gaze returned to the floor, his mind lost in thought. "I thought I knew who he was," he muttered quietly after a time. "The sycophantic Archibald Mepham. But I was wrong. When I was over there it came to me."

Woodfin was all ears. He stared intently at Oscendale.

"Mepham may have killed the first victim, Susan Maskell. The link with Edmund Lucas was just a coincidence. Another war widow alone in her house, an easy target for a lustful sod like Mepham. She rejected his advances so he murdered her."

"And Jennie Lake?"

"I thought he also murdered Jennie Lake. Maybe because she rejected him as well or maybe just because he found he enjoyed seeing women suffer. Perhaps he learnt that in India as well." He paused. "But I was wrong."

"So was there a link with Lucas?"

"Lucas's men or Mepham could have killed Susan Maskell. But there was no link between Lucas and Jennie Lake. It had to be Mepham. Yet when I leaned over him in the church he was trying to tell me something. I think it was that he wasn't responsible for the two deaths, just the first. Lucas also told me he had nothing to do with Susan Maskell's death. He was only interested in silencing her husband."

"So who is committing these vile murders?"

"I don't know yet. He enters the houses unseen, in broad daylight, kills and then leaves, totally unseen by any of the neighbours, even the ever-watchful Minnie Geddes."

"So what do we do next? Wait for another war widow? The way things are going at Ypres we won't have to wait long."

Oscendale smiled ruefully. He paused before saying, "We *are* going to catch this one. He has to be caught before he mutilates another poor woman."

Woodfin offered him a cigarette and placed one in the corner of his own mouth, flicking open his brass lighter, "So what's the trap, Tom? I know you've got some idea, some plan of what to do. Do we bait it and with what?"

The awful implications of his words hit them both at the same time. They were contemplating playing with someone's life and if they erred then that person would die.

Oscendale did not reply and Woodfin noticed he was staring intently at an ashtray of spent matches and cigarette ash.

"What is it, Tom?"

Oscendale looked up aghast. "I know why he's doing this, Corrick. This is all about one person."

"Well, tell me then," demanded Woodfin.

Oscendale said nothing, scrutinising the other drinkers in the bar while the barman placed two plates of stew on their table. It was busy with customers from all walks of life. Some labourers were rewarding themselves with a well-earned pint or two after the hard graft of a day's work. Four men dressed in blue serge from one of the military hospitals in the area laughed and joked, clearly on the mend. He and Woodfin had attracted some curious looks and Oscendale realised that they had been talking far too loudly.

"Not here," he said and began eating his food. When he had finished he downed the remnants of his beer. "Right Corrick, I'm off. I'll see you later back at the station. In the meantime, there's something I need to do."

The light was failing and a sunset was descending over the seafront. Oscendale gazed out of Woodfin's office window for some minutes, staring at the scene before him. Over the mud flats wave ripples gleamed in the wet sand and the breakwater, like some huge outstretched arm clad in stone, protectively cradled the harbour. Woodfin knew better than to interrupt him so he attended to some paperwork as Oscendale was clearly lost in thought, watching the sun, now casting a crimson, ethereal light around the room.

Like the tide suddenly turning, Oscendale span round and began pacing around the room. "There are two links that we can find between the three victims. They were all members of the same church, one of the biggest in Barry. So far three of them are dead. All three were also war widows."

Woodfin frowned. "So when do you think he'll strike again? There are hundreds of war widows in this town, dozens who attend All Souls Church. It could be any one of them."

Oscendale stopped and turned to face Woodfin. "Tomorrow afternoon."

Woodfin looked puzzled. "Tomorrow afternoon? How do you know that?"

"Because I'm the link, Corrick. Remember the postcards? He's taunting me. Why didn't he kill again while I was in France? No, it began again as soon as I returned to Barry last night. Each victim has been killed when I was here. I'm the one he really wants. He has to make his move before I go back."

Woodfin thought for a moment. "But why tomorrow?"

"Because," smiled Oscendale, "he thinks that I'm returning to France on the 10.15 a.m. train on Friday morning. I don't know who he is but he knows who I am. He's arrogant, Corrick. Those letters told me that. He knows he's going to get caught eventually so he'll speed up, take a shorter gap. Don't forget he's enjoying himself. He can't wait until after I've gone. He has to kill again while I'm still here in Barry."

"But how does he know you're leaving on Friday?"

"I've told him."

"You've told him? What the hell do you mean you've told him?" Woodfin was exasperated at the convolutions of his friend's line of thought. "You said you didn't know who he is!"

"That's right. I don't," replied Oscendale calmly. "But I know he'll read this." He tapped a piece of paper that lay on Woodfin's desk. "This is an article I've just helped a correspondent write for tomorrow's edition of the *Barry Dock News.*"

"And how do you know he'll read it?" asked Woodfin sceptically.

"This is how he finds out the names and addresses of the war widows. All Souls Church is just a blind. He used that link to throw suspicion onto Mepham but he's decided to keep the chain going, just for his own amusement."

Woodfin snatched up the sheet of paper and began to read.

"It's on page five," said Oscendale. "Beneath an account of the fighting at Ypres by 'One Who Is There' will be a short article entitled 'Barry Military Policeman Returning to Front'."

Woodfin read:

Former Barry policeman Captain Thomas Oscendale, who has been serving overseas with the Military Foot Police, has been home on leave this week assisting Inspector Woodfin in his investigation into the series of inexplicable murders which have occurred in the West End of Barry.

Unfortunately, Captain Oscendale has to return once more to the Front and will depart from Barry Station on the 10.15 a.m. train on Friday morning. We wish him well and God speed his safe return.

Woodfin finished reading, lowered the paper and looked at Oscendale.

"I looked at the list of war casualties, Corrick. Only one in this week's paper has a link with All Souls Church. She's the woman he'll select tomorrow."

CHAPTER 49

Barry – Thursday, 6th September 1917

S HE WAS THERE waiting for him, sitting on their bench in the park. His eyes never left her as he approached; she was nervous, anxious, wringing her gloves in her hands. He almost stopped in mid stride, sensing disappointment, but kept going towards her.

He had received the note that morning. *Thomas, I need to see you urgently. Meet me at Romilly Park, usual place at noon.* He had resisted the temptation to rush round to her house and had tried to take his mind off her by focussing on the case but even that complex puzzle had failed to fully engage him. Hannah's face drifted in and out of his mind. *What could it be?*

"Hannah," he said with concern as she got up from the bench and walked swiftly towards him. He bent forward to kiss her.

"Thomas, don't kiss me." Her voice was cold and clear. "Please don't. Not now."

She drew away, then stood up and looked furtively from side to side. She motioned to him to follow her.

"What's the matter, Hannah?"

"Listen, I need to tell you something important." She paused and once more twisted her gloves in her hands before continuing. "James is coming home. It changes everything."

The words felt like lead in his heart. This was unexpected and cruel. "Home? What? What do you mean home? To be buried?"

"No," she replied. "He's not dead, Thomas. He's still alive."

Oscendale was transfixed, paralysed with astonishment. His world was turning upside down. They stood in silence.

She looked at him, her face a jumble of emotions. "It was all a mix-up. He was missing, presumed dead, but it appears he was wounded last month and, I don't know, some administrative error meant that I was sent the wrong telegram. He's coming home and that's all that matters to me."

"How long is he home for?" he asked in a voice full of emotion. He thought of them in her marriage bed again and a wave of jealousy washed over him.

"For good," she replied. "He's been wounded and it looks like he's going to be discharged."

"But… how can this be? He can't just turn up like that. Somebody must have known he was still alive. Why didn't he write to…?" His words halted as he realised the significance of the letter that he had found in the wooden box by her bedside. "You knew, didn't you? You knew before today and you didn't tell me. Hannah, I can't believe you did that. I thought we were going to be together. You let me make love to you and all the time you knew your husband was still alive and you were really his, not mine?"

"How could I tell you, Thomas? I thought he had died and then out of the blue I received a letter from James telling me it was all a ghastly mistake and that he was on his way home. I didn't want to hurt you and I thought I could let you down gently if I had more time with you. Or maybe…" She stopped and looked at him for a time. He could not do the same and looked away instead.

They had reached a series of ponds that followed the contours of the slope of the hill on which the park was formed. They stood together, neither saying anything for a moment with just the sound of the water emerging from an underground spring and flowing from one pond into another. His dreams were flowing too, running away from him like the water beneath his feet.

"How could you do that?" he asked her. "How could you lie in bed with me when you knew he was coming home?"

"I don't know! I can't explain it!" she replied irritably. "I… I didn't want to let you go straightaway. It was too soon, too sudden. Thomas, my feelings for you…"

"Your feelings. Let's not start talking about feelings because they obviously don't come into it." Oscendale turned his face away.

"Of course they do! How do you think I feel? A husband who, I'm told, is dead suddenly comes back to life and I'm supposed to just pick up the pieces and carry on. And after I'd met you."

He turned back to her and saw the tears in her sad eyes.

"Oh, Thomas," she said, her voice breaking. "I can't leave James now. The ties are too strong."

"But you told me there was nothing between you."

"You don't understand. There's more to a marriage than just… You and I… Well it was the first time I've felt that way…"

"So I just filled in the time while he was away. Is that it? From the first time…"

She blushed as the memories came back to them both of their time together in the watchtower. "Thomas, that's not fair. I thought he was dead and I was free to be with someone else. That was… I have to pick up my life again with James now that he's back for good. I can't abandon him. That would be impossible."

Oscendale breathed in deeply. This was all so unexpected. Yet again he had made the mistake. She had been so right for him. He had thought she would forget her marriage to James Graham and be with him for the rest of their lives. But he knew in his heart it never worked out like that in reality. This previous man in Hannah's life would always be there, a constant reminder of her love or loyalty for another man. Here she was, telling him it was over, mentioning the word love, then saying that she was going back to a man who didn't love her or even want to touch her. He shook his head. Would he ever get this right? When would he sort out his own life?

Her face was shaded under her hat. It all seemed so long ago that he had first seen her here in this park. So much had passed between them and yet it was ending, another memory to take back to the war.

"Hannah, I don't understand any of what you're telling me, but I'm not going to embarrass myself by staying any longer. I think you're making a mistake, for what it's worth, but I accept it's over. I'll go now. I won't bother you again."

She lowered her head, the gentle summer breeze ruffling stray strands of her hair, and Oscendale experienced the urge to reach out and touch her again, to raise her up, hold her in his arms and never let her go. But the moment was too painful and he let it pass. They stood there on a bridge, staring down into the silver water of the stream. Her tears fell silently and were swept away by the bubbling waters below them. Memories filtered slowly across their minds. He waited for her to say something but there was silence between them now. There was nothing more to say. He felt empty and lost.

"Goodbye, Hannah," he said quietly and turned away. The sun was still shining, the children were playing and somewhere, far away, a different world was turning. Each step took him further away from the cause of the hurt he felt deep inside. He imagined her watching him go, regretting her words and the decision she had made, but when he turned back at the gates of the park the path was empty and she was nowhere to be seen and he knew even that last faint hope was gone.

CHAPTER 50

Barry – Thursday, 6th September 1917

T HE POSTCARD HAD been waiting for him when he returned to Mrs Owen's lodgings at lunchtime. No stamp or postmark was present this time. It had been hand delivered. He had been right about the killer's sense of urgency.

> Oscendale,
> *Next time it's an officer's wife. Be quick! 3pm today!*
> Loki

"When did this arrive, Mrs Owen?"

"It was on the doormat this morning," she replied.

"Then why didn't you give it to me at breakfast?" he asked angrily.

The woman shrugged. "I just forgot. You've been getting quite a few of these, haven't you?"

"What's that got to do with it?" he asked, his patience with the obstructive woman growing very thin.

"Well, I thought another one wouldn't matter, so I just put it on the kitchen table and forgot all about it."

Oscendale looked at Mrs Owen, something he usually tried to avoid. He saw a selfish woman with bitterness ingrained in the lines on her face. "Your lack of interest in my post, Mrs Owen, may well end up costing an innocent woman her life. That will be on your conscience. And mine," he added, his lips clenched in fury.

He went straight to the Harbour Road Police Station and asked to see the previous day's official list of reported casualties. He then compared it with the list in that morning's *Barry Dock News*. Thankfully, as he thought, there had been only one local officer who had been killed in action: *Captain John Slater, Warwickshire Regiment.*

"Do we know where he lived in Barry?" he asked Sergeant Streeter.

"Yes, sir," the dependable policeman replied. "I've already checked for you, 36 Oxford Road, opposite the church."

Woodfin appeared at his side, placed his hand inside his waistcoat pocket and withdrew his gold watch. "Tom, I think this joker is making it too easy this time. We know he'll try to do something around 3 o'clock and we know his target is a war widow." He paused then added, "One war widow. I think he's trying to lead you down the wrong path."

"No, Corrick," replied Oscendale. "He's a man fixated by his routine. These murders are not random, they're predictable. This man has a methodical, precise mind. I know he's intent on killing the widow of John Slater. The links between these murders are clear. Trust me."

Woodfin shrugged. "Look, I think you're wrong this time. You and Willis go to visit Mrs Slater, if you want to. Take a constable with you. Streeter and I will visit the home of the widow linked with All Souls Church – the one you mentioned last night. I think you should stick with your original plan. This note could just be a ruse." Oscendale looked at his old friend. It was rare for Woodfin to disagree with him and a sense of doubt began to gnaw away at him. But he was convinced he was right and would not be dissuaded. *Slater must have been a member of All Souls Church as well.*

Oscendale looked at his watch. 2.30 p.m. Plenty of time to set the trap for this maniac. Willis lifted the dull, unpolished brass door knocker and rapped it hard on the wood. There was no reply. He tried again, with even more urgency. He was just turning to tell the constable behind him to break down the door when they heard a bolt being drawn back and the door opened a fraction.

A thin face peered out. "Oh, the police," sighed a weary-faced woman. "Can I help you? Goodness, are you all policemen?"

"Yes we are, ma'am," replied Willis. "We'd like to speak with you, Mrs Slater."

"I'm not Mrs Slater," said the woman. "I'm her sister."

"Well is Mrs Slater at home?" asked Oscendale impatiently.

"Yes," she replied, opening the door fully. "She's in the sitting room. Can I answer your questions? You see my sister has just lost her husband and she's…"

"It's extremely urgent that we come in and speak to her. I'd like my constables to check the rear of the house too, if you wouldn't mind, ma'am."

The woman, suddenly flustered, raised a lace handkerchief to her mouth. "Yes. Oh dear, what's all this about? Do come in but I'll just warn my sister."

Willis spoke quietly to the constable who immediately set off along a side lane to examine the rear of the house.

A minute later the sitting room door opened and she gestured for them to enter.

Dorothy Slater sat with hunched shoulders staring at the photograph of her late husband on a table, a piece of paper cradled within the folds of her black skirt. She cut a pathetically sad figure. Red-eyed and with her lips drawn in, she motioned for them both to sit.

Oscendale tendered his sympathy to the widow. Willis added his condolences and asked if anyone from her late husband's regiment had visited and she replied that no-one had been in touch since she had received the telegram.

Choking back the tears, Mrs Slater held out her hand towards her sister who sat opposite her. "I don't know how I would have coped without the support of dear Edith." Edith took Dorothy Slater's hand and patted it comfortingly.

So as not to alarm the two women unduly, Oscendale strung out the conversation for as long as possible. It was not an easy dialogue. One woman was still suffering the agonising early pains of sudden loss and the other was devoid of any willingness to engage in conversation. They sat together, an odd foursome, and waited for the hands of the clock to reach three o'clock. The widow saw Oscendale looking at the clock and several times asked him if he had another appointment. Each time he replied no and he and Willis then struggled to keep the conversation flowing.

Willis looked at Oscendale, who was lost in thought. *If the killer was not here this afternoon, then where was he?* He was turning the options over in his mind in desperation. Dorothy Slater fitted the *modus operandi* – a member of the congregation of All Souls Church who had been made aware that her husband had been killed on active service.

Oscendale fidgeted. He and Willis could stay here and wait with the policeman he intended to leave on guard or he could check again the casualty roll in his pocket to see if there was any other officer's wife in Barry who had recently been informed that she was now a widow. *Could he possibly have missed something?*

He looked at the brass carriage clock ticking away on the mantelpiece. It was 2.50 p.m. Ten minutes to the killing hour.

"How long have you been a member of All Souls Church, Mrs Slater?" he asked, realising he had not checked this point so far during the painful conversation. It had been omitted from the newspaper report but he was sure the link would be there.

Dorothy Slater looked up from her marble-white hands and regarded him quizzically. "What made you think I attend that church? My sister and I are members of Porthceri Methodist Church, as were our parents before us, my late husband too."

Then the penny dropped. It was not Mrs Slater. How could he have allowed himself to be tricked? It was someone else and he immediately knew who it was.

"Excuse me, Mrs Slater. I've just remembered something very important I have to do. The constable will remain here. Come on, Willis!" He rose from his seat and left the two women to their grief.

Willis was bemused by his actions and hesitated. Why were they abandoning the next intended victim? But Oscendale's urgency convinced him he was right so he quickly told the policeman to stay at the house and guard the two women while he set off after Oscendale, who was now running along the road a short distance ahead.

Everything looked normal enough as Willis caught up with Oscendale who was peering through the curtains frantically praying his worst nightmare was not about to come true.

"No sign," he said to Willis. "I'll go around the back. You stay here." He set off along the lane that ran to the side of the house until he reached the back gate. It was bolted so he levered himself up onto the stone wall and dropped down into the garden.

The back door was unlocked. With his Webley drawn he crept cautiously through the kitchen and into the dark hallway that led to the front of the house. For a moment the horror of his time in the German dugout came back to him and he scratched his left hand subconsciously. *Memories he thought he had laid to rest.*

As if in replay, he stumbled over a body lying inert on the floor. He regained his balance and bent down. The dead face of Sergeant Streeter looked up at him with glassy eyes. Time had not moved on. He was here in the dark again with a body lying on the floor beneath him. Forcing the fear that rose up back into the recesses of his mind, he made his way out of the passageway and quietly up the first flight of stairs, placing his feet at the extreme edges of each step, as he had done when playing hide and seek as a child.

He reached the first landing. There were five doors leading off it but he noticed that the front bedroom door was the only one ajar. What he caught sight of through the opening shocked him to the core.

Hannah Graham was on her knees, her hands tied behind her back. A man stood over her with a box of matches in his hands. She was shaking uncontrollably and her face was wet. At first Oscendale thought it was the moisture from her tears but as he looked he could see a sheen to her skin. Her face was wet. *Petrol! James?*

Oscendale told himself to stay calm and tried to suppress every emotion but his heart was beating far too quickly for that. The figure was talking to her in a low, steady voice. It was almost like a religious chant. As Oscendale drew nearer he began to make out the words.

"Beauty is only skin deep anyway. And without your looks you are nothing. The Bible says…."

He knew the voice at once. Oscendale stepped into the room and the man turned towards him. But it wasn't James Graham who stood facing him.

"Put it down, Corrick." His Webley revolver was pointed directly at Woodfin's face.

"Ah Tom! Caught up with me at last, eh? Well, did you enjoy the little puzzle I set you? All those postcards you showed me." Woodfin laughed. "I did think I would have more time for this, though." He turned his gaze from Oscendale to Hannah.

"You heard what I said. You've got three seconds before I pull this trigger." For another moment he was again back in the

German dugout, a flame burning down a thin piece of wood towards his fingers. The end of the light approaching. The end of a life.

But Woodfin ignored the threat. "So, here we are then. You, me and your lady love. Except that she's not quite that is she? She has such a lovely face. But beautiful women always cause mischief and she tells me she's going back to her husband. Dear, dear. Poor old you."

Woodfin's words cut deep into his soul. Oscendale saw the pistol begin to tremble at the end of his outstretched arm. But he forced himself to remain focussed on what was happening in the room.

Woodfin's low, soothing voice continued. "Yes, back to James. You don't like that do you? No more lovey-dovey for you, eh? Oh yes, I saw you together that morning." He raised his voice an octave and mimicked the man they had seen on the seafront. "Morning, young lovers." He paused to look at the response on Oscendale's face. "She's going back to the man she really loves," he sneered. "You never meant anything to her. And you had the arrogance to think this was all about you. No, Tom, it's about watching them die, watching all that beauty melt away. Now drop the gun or I will light her up like a bonfire."

Hannah sobbed. "Don't listen to him! Shoot him, Thomas! Shoot him!" she screamed. Her face was contorted by terror and tears were now running freely down her face.

Woodfin saw Oscendale's gaze move from him to Hannah and he took advantage of the distraction to strike a match and flick it at the kneeling woman but she twisted herself away and it fell short. She closed her eyes and bowed her head as if praying between her sobs.

Oscendale heard movement behind him. Willis's finger pulled firmly on the trigger of his revolver and the blast and Hannah's screams rang out simultaneously in Oscendale's ears.

The first shot hit Woodfin in the chest and he fell to the floor directly onto the still-burning match, which had already ignited part of the carpet where the petrol had spilt. There was the sound of crunching glass and within seconds he was transformed from a human being to a flaming mass. A piteous shriek came from the fireball, which tried to raise itself to a standing position. Willis pushed past Oscendale, revolver held out in front of him, and fired two more shots into the burning shape. What was left of Woodfin was thrown backwards by the force of the impact and collapsed on the floor, the flames continuing to eat away at his body.

Oscendale rushed to Hannah and carried her to the bathroom, leaving Willis to put out the flames. He cut the rope that Woodfin had used to tie her wrists and quickly but tenderly he washed the petrol from her face while she sobbed in terror. He held her wet face between his hands, brushed a strand of hair away from her face and kissed her on the mouth. She did not resist and he was the first to pull away.

Willis appeared with a Bible which he had found open on her bedside table, placed on top of the wooden box. He held it up. A passage was underlined. It read: *Marriage is honourable in all, and the bed undefiled: but whoremongers and adulterers God will judge.*

CHAPTER 51

Barry – Thursday, 6th September 1917

"SO IT WAS Woodfin all along, not Mepham. Shame he's dead, I would've liked him to hang. Bloody hell. Still can't get over it. The evil bastard," said Willis.

"Yes. I realised that Mepham wasn't responsible for the murders when I was behind the German lines." *An imitation, a veneer.* "Mepham was a lecher, preying on vulnerable women. But he wasn't a murderer. Woodfin set it up perfectly and I fell for it. And all the time it was a man I thought of as a friend. God, how he must have laughed as we sat together discussing the case. And those bloody notes too. Even when I was on my way here the thought of him being the killer never struck me. A policeman? No, I was too involved this time. Too close. It clouded my judgement." He shook his head. "I didn't know whose face I was going to see when I entered that bedroom and when I saw it was Woodfin I froze. If it hadn't been for you, Willis, I'd be dead. Woodfin could have portrayed me as the killer. *Brave policeman shoots murderer dead.* I can see it now. He used his position to throw us off his trail and utilised all his skills to enter their houses and mutilate and murder those poor women." Oscendale paused. "Mepham was involved in one of them, however."

They were outside now, standing in the garden of 21 Porthceri Road, looking down at the blanket that shrouded the charred body of Corrick Woodfin. A collection of inquisitive neighbours was being held back while several policemen made ready a vehicle to take the body away.

Willis was frowning. "Mepham? So he did kill Susan Maskell?"

"Not quite," replied Oscendale. "But he *was* at the scene. When he arrived with thoughts of seducing Susan Maskell, I think he found her dead, her face burnt to a crisp. Woodfin had already paid her a visit, you see, and killed her. But he had his own, quite different purpose. Mepham panicked. After all, being found in the bedroom of a dead woman would ruin the life he was trying to rebuild after his scandal in India."

"So he wrote the note you found in Susan Maskell's mouth?"

"Yes, to be read later when Woodfin returned in his other guise as an investigating police officer," added Oscendale. "It was a warning to Woodfin. Mepham suspected him for some reason. Perhaps he had seen him enter the house earlier on. After all, Mepham didn't want to be seen going in so he probably hid nearby and watched to ensure Susan Maskell was alone. If it hadn't been for one inquisitive neighbour we might never have suspected him. He tried to tell me Woodfin would kill more as he lay dying but I misunderstood his words."

"But what was the link between Woodfin, the church and the victims?" asked Willis.

"I think his view of religion was different to ours. In his mind he saw women as the Devil's agents," said Oscendale. "The more beautiful the woman, the more corrupt she was – at least in his twisted mind."

"Befriending them through the church?" asked Willis.

"Yes, getting to know their habits and then when they became widows, planning to kill them."

"Torture them more like. How could he do that to them?"

"The deaths of their husbands left them vulnerable. But it also left them free to find another man. Or should I say tempt another man – at least in Woodfin's eyes. Women were taken in by his charm, so when he called on them they sensed no evil intent, just a policeman who cared about their grief. Someone who could offer the comfort of a shared religious belief. To Woodfin, beauty as evil was an image he had carried round in his head for who knows how long. Rejected by a beautiful woman when he was younger? Recently? I don't know. That's something that you'll have to find out. Whatever triggered it, beauty was corrupting so he destroyed it with fire. Fire and brimstone. God's wrath on the unfaithful. In his mind his actions were merely an extension of the teachings of the Bible. He was doing God's work."

Willis sniffed with distaste. "Evil, as you say. Pure bloody evil. And to think that he was right amongst us, working with us on the case every day."

"That's how he could carry out his foul work. He knew where we would be so he chose a victim from his list who lived in a different part of town."

"His list?" said Willis incredulously. "He had a list?"

Oscendale held out a piece of paper with several names and addresses on. "I found it in the overcoat he hung up in the hallway when Hannah let him in. He knocked on her door and was invited in without any hint of suspicion, as he did with some of the others. A policeman and a churchgoer? Who could be more respectable and less dangerous to a woman on her own?"

Willis sighed deeply. "What is it about this world, sir? There's enough killing going on where you are without more of it here at home. It's all so senseless. One man's warped mentality and five more people are dead. But to use God as his justification. To do things like that in the Lord's name. Attending church every Sunday just to identify the victims for his abominable deeds, to put faces to names he'd read about that week in the local paper."

Oscendale raised his eyebrows and shrugged. He looked

down at the stricken form of his old friend. A man whom, it was now apparent, he had barely known.

"It depends on your point of view, what your belief is. The churches will be full again this Sunday with people worshipping in different ways. People will go for all sorts of reasons. God is an entity to some. They visualise him, portray him and Woodfin did that as well, don't forget. His God spoke to him and told him what to do. He believed he was merely acting out God's will."

"How could he be serving God?" snapped Willis.

Oscendale spoke calmly in response. "Willis, look across the Channel. There are tens of thousands of men dying in God's name over there. We believe God is on our side and so do the Huns. Do you know what they have on their belt buckles? *Gott Mit Uns.* God is with us. Well, he can't be on both sides, can he? So whose side is he on? Shall I tell you? He's on the side that kills the most and wins. That's all. We use God for our own devices, to justify killing. Woodfin was doing the same. Demons walk among us. They always will."

Willis did not respond. Oscendale stood under the ornate Edwardian veranda of the grand house that looked down over Romilly Park and beyond. He stared past the group of people gathered outside, each wondering what had happened. He was lost in his thoughts, reminded again of when they first met. *Hannah.*

Looking back at the large picture window, he saw her face looking out. Other figures were scurrying around inside, kindly neighbours offering tea and more sympathy to her again, no doubt. She raised her hand and waved animatedly.

He was about to wave back when he heard a disturbance in the crowd that had gathered. A raised voice belonging to a man in an officer's uniform was saying, "Let me through! It's my house. I live here!" as he pushed his way through the crowd. He spoke to one of the policemen who promptly stood aside.

Without even looking at Willis and Oscendale, James Graham hurried quickly along the path and disappeared into the house. The crowd began to clap, people happy to see a returning hero.

Oscendale looked again at the window. All he could see was the reflection of his own face, haggard and drawn.

Then a lamp was lit inside as the gloom of the overcast day began to grow. He saw Hannah in her husband's arms and Graham kissing her. Oscendale watched the couple for a few seconds more, hoping her eyes would turn back towards him but they never left James Graham's face, so eventually he turned away.

Willis was looking at him. "That's it then, sir. It's over."

"Yes," replied Oscendale sadly. "Yes it is."

"I'd better go in and talk to the husband," said Willis. "Let him know what's happened." With that he disappeared in through the Grahams' front door, leaving Oscendale standing outside.

The crowd was starting to disperse now as there was nothing more to see. Oscendale saw a movement and looked back towards the house. The front door was closing but he was just in time to see James Graham look at him. Their eyes met and Oscendale felt something pass between them. The door finally closed and Oscendale knew that he was shut out of their marriage. Hannah was gone, back into her own world, and their time together had passed. There was only her memory and his future. A future that was bleak. His life felt as barren and endless as the landscape he would now return to.

EPILOGUE

Cardiff – 16th April 1927

D AWN IN APRIL is the most optimistic time. The clarity of the light brings hope for renewal and encourages expectation. Yet April can also be the cruellest month, as one poet described. *Such thoughts!* he told himself.

Unlocking the box, he slowly lifted the lid. The Webley revolver lay supine and inert in its velvet mould, an instrument of death lying in a wooden coffin.

It was time to remember again. As if he could ever forget.

For a long time the man in the grey woollen suit sat looking at the pistol. There was a time when for nearly two months he had carried this piece of metal in a brown leather holster attached to his belt. In moments of madness he had extracted it, held it out and attempted to kill people. Sometimes he had succeeded. And he had been lauded for it. The thoughts came back to him, the faces of dead men emerging from the shadows. Instinctively he looked up, as if the ghosts of the men he had killed were with him again. The blood and the horror had never really left.

But he was here. *Insurance. Still dealing in life and death. Cut-throat business.* Another day at the office, success perhaps for some of the agents he managed. A good day's hunting within their territories. The death claims, the accident claims. A day no different to any other.

He sat at his desk within the three-storey building. In the distance he could hear the trams as they travelled up and down Queen Street. But the real disturbances were in his head. He closed the lid again. No, not the Webley. It had saved his life several times and he was damned if he was going to turn it on himself now.

He held his head in his hands and thought back ten years. *Ten years.* Was it really so long ago? He had been younger then of course. Different. Stronger, for a time at least. Less inclined to flights of fancy. After the treatment anyway. He shuddered at the recollection. And less inclined to those terrible dreams in the night, when the faces and the deeds came to him again while he lay alone in his bed. But recently the dreams had returned, growing remorselessly in intensity and frequency.

Ten years. Ten years ago he had… He stopped. The thoughts had kept him awake most of the night. Most of every night now if the truth be told. *If the truth be told.* It was time to stop lying to himself. Time to stop pretending he could cope. Time to drop the happy, mad smile and be himself. Could anyone ever be themselves? Didn't everyone act out a role every day, pretending to be someone they were not? And living in constant fear of being found out?

His scared, terrified, anxious self was back again. And once he had thought it would go away. Be gone forever.

The din continued in the street below as the world started to wake up and life began to join his solitude. Time had gone so quickly. Night was over once again. The darkness was beginning to fade and the promise of a new dawn was arriving. *Time to stand to.*

He rose stiffly from behind his desk and limped to the window. The sun was golden. The sky was a burning glow. *The guns.* He turned away from the hope of the future to the pain of the past and stared again at the box.

If not that way, then how? He wandered out of the main office and into an adjoining kitchen, partially lit by light coming in through a small casement window. Shelves were lined with cups, sugar, tea and coffee. *A place for everything and everything in its place.* On the table stood a gas ring and kettle. *Gas.* He could smell the tarry odour of the carbolic soap that sat in an old saucer placed on the wooden draining board. Then his eyes fell on the galvanised metal bucket tucked underneath the sink; next to it was a bottle. He pictured the cleaning lady, happy and unaffected. Heard her voice as he had worked late into the evening yet again. *"Sorry, Mr Burgess, I didn't realise you were still here. Don't you ever go home?"* Always singing the same song, 'Roses of Picardy', as she went about her cleaning duties.

The faces from the past came back in the photograph album of his mind: Phillips and Maskell whose lives had ended so tragically. Newcombe with all his easy wit. Clarke who had come to his aid, out there when… And the military policeman. *What was his name? Oscendale? Such a strange name.* But he had drawn the sting and brought the horror to the fore, which had helped him cope for a time, but now it was all back again. His friends had moved on into the shadows. It was time to join them.

His hands grasped the bottle from beneath the sink and he looked at it for a while, oblivion lurking within. *That was it then. The decision made, the deed had to be done.* He removed the stopper and without sniffing the clear liquid, swallowed half the contents in several gulps. His throat began to burn immediately and he held his chest as his throat began to close. *Nothingness at last.*

At 8.55 a.m. the office girl found him lying face down underneath his desk where he had fallen. He was still breathing so she called for the message boy who turned him over and attempted to revive him, but by the time the doctor arrived fifteen minutes later Ossie Burgess was dead.

Time to remember…

Also by the author:

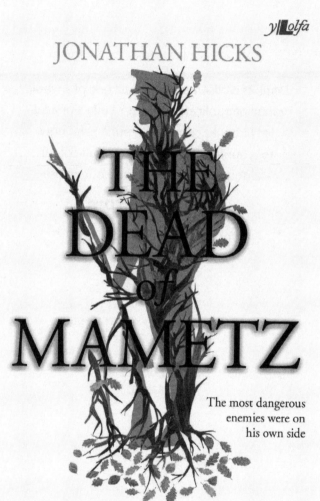

JONATHAN HICKS

y Lolfa

THE
DEAD
of
MAMETZ

The most dangerous
enemies were on
his own side

THE FIRST THOMAS OSCENDALE NOVEL

£8.95

Demons Walk Among Us is just one of a whole range of publications from Y Lolfa. For a full list of books currently in print, send now for your free copy of our new full-colour catalogue. Or simply surf into our website

www.ylolfa.com

for secure on-line ordering.

TALYBONT CEREDIGION CYMRU SY24 5HE
e-mail ylolfa@ylolfa.com
website www.ylolfa.com
phone (01970) 832 304
fax 832 782